NIGHT
VISION

ALSO BY PAUL LEVINE

To Speak for the Dead

NIGHT VISION

Paul Levine

BANTAM BOOKS
NEW YORK · TORONTO · LONDON · SYDNEY · AUCKLAND

This is a work of fiction. Names, characters, places, and incidents are either the product of the author's imagination or are used fictitiously. Any resemblance to actual persons, living or dead, events, entities or locales is entirely coincidental.

NIGHT VISION

A Bantam Book / October 1991

Grateful acknowledgment is made for permission to reprint the following:
Excerpt from *Equus* by Peter Shaffer used courtesy of the Lantz Agency.
Excerpt from *Long Day's Journey Into Night* by Eugene O'Neill used courtesy of Cadwalader, Wickersham & Taft.
Excerpt from "Try to Remember" by Tom Jones and Harvey Schmidt used with permission. Copyright © *The Fantastics*, Tom Jones and Harvey Schmidt. All other rights reserved.
Excerpt from *Pygmalion* by G.B. Shaw courtesy The Society of Authors on behalf of the Bernard Shaw Estate.
Excerpt from *Who's Afraid of Virginia Woolf* by Edward Albee reprinted by permission of William Morris Agency, Inc. on behalf of the author. Copyright © 1962 by Edward Albee.

BOOK DESIGN BY GRETCHEN ACHILLES

Library of Congress Cataloging-in-Publication Data

Levine, Paul (Paul J.)
    Night vision / by Paul Levine.
      p.   cm.
    ISBN 0-553-07796-1
    I. Title.
    PS3562.E8995N54   1991
    813'.54—dc20   91-14918
                                  CIP

Published simultaneously in the United States and Canada

Bantam Books are published by Bantam Books, a division of Bantam Doubleday Dell Publishing Group, Inc. Its trademark, consisting of the words "Bantam Books" and the portrayal of a rooster, is Registered in U.S. Patent and Trademark Office and in other countries. Marca Registrada. Bantam Books, 666 Fifth Avenue, New York, New York 10103.

PRINTED IN THE UNITED STATES OF AMERICA

BVG   0 9 8 7 6 5 4 3 2 1

For my parents,
Stanley and Sally Levine

I am losing the light of my Youth,
And the Vision that led me of old,
And I clash with an iron Truth,
When I make for an Age of gold.
And I would that my race were run,
For teeming with liars, and madmen and knaves,
And wearied of Autocrats, Anarchs, and Slaves,
And darken'd with doubts of a Faith that saves,
And crimson with battles, and hollow with graves,
To the wail of my winds, and the moan of my waves
I whirl, and follow the Sun.

—The Earth, speaking to the aging poet
in "The Dreamer" by Alfred, Lord Tennyson

Acknowledgments

I am indebted to a variety of doctors, lawyers, journalists, and police. This will acknowledge some of them. South Florida's medical examiners, Dr. Joseph Davis and Dr. Ronald Wright, and assistant medical examiner Dr. Bruce Hyma continue to provide expert assistance. Attorneys Stuart Grossman, Neal Roth, Albert Caruana, and Richard Ovelmen have been generous with their time and devoted in their friendship. Columnist-author Carl Hiaasen taught me the basics of bonefishing. I have also benefited from the expertise of Miami Police Major Mike Gonzalez.

Special thanks to my editor Kate Miciak for her support and my agent Bob Colgan for his guidance.

This book is set in Miami, where black buzzards still fly endless circles around the spire of the county courthouse. Contrary to local legend, the sinister birds are not souls of lawyers doing eternal penance. In my experience, lawyers never repent.

PROLOGUE

Live at Five

Look at those legs.

Look at those goddamn floor-to-ceiling million-dollar legs, Michelle thought, then unconsciously sneaked a peek at her own. Short. Stubby little shapeless legs. God, how she hated them.

Shit, now they're on a two-shot. Look at the monitor. Next to her I look like a double amputee.

Then there was her hair. Thick, auburn hair brushed straight back. And her skin, that patrician paleness so out of place in Miami. Just a subdued line of gloss on full lips . . . *She probably gets dressed and made up in ten minutes.*

If Michelle didn't spend half an hour covering her freckles with pancake, Max Factor Number Two, they'd ship her back to Scranton to handle neighborhood weather from Nanticoke. The legs, nothing you could do about those. But thank God for plastic surgeons and periodontists. A rhinoplasty—the Sandy Duncan model, pert but not prominent—and capped teeth called "Hollywoods." Thanks to law-

1

yers, too. Two hundred bucks to change Mabel Dombrowsky to Michelle Diamond.

"So, Dr. Metcalf, your book suggests that serial murderers share certain characteristics," Michelle said.

"Well, we can place them into distinct categories," Pamela Metcalf replied. "There are the organized murderers, who are above average in intelligence and are socially and sexually competent. They are usually the eldest sons in the family. Ordinarily they know their victims and plan the crime. The crime scene is neat and orderly—"

"Well, neatness counts," Michelle Diamond chirped. Inside the control booth, the director groaned.

"The disorganized murderer is quite the opposite," Dr. Metcalf explained, ignoring the interviewer and smiling politely at the camera. "Below average in intelligence, socially inadequate, sexually incompetent. Usually the last or next to last born. His crimes are more spontaneous. The victims are usually strangers, and rather than using conversation, he subdues with sudden outbursts of violence. Often he will perform sexual acts after the death of the victim. . . ."

Oh shit, how do you follow that one up?

"In either case," Dr. Metcalf said, "the killers have highly active fantasy lives. The fantasies often are of rape, torture, and murder. When they can no longer differentiate fantasy from reality, the two become one."

And that upper-crust voice. Like Masterpiece Theatre.

Michelle cleared her throat, and the sound man cursed, his earpiece clacking like an enraged rattlesnake. "We seem to have more mass murderers in our country—"

"Serial murderers," Pamela Metcalf corrected her. "Mass murderers kill many persons at the same time. Serial murderers kill many over time, usually at random."

Michelle felt her face heat up. "Yes, of course. Is there something uniquely American about these *serial* killers? Something about our violent society?"

"Goodness no. In Britain we had Jack the Ripper, Germany its Peter Kurten. During the time of Joan of Arc France had the infamous Gilles de Rais, who killed hundreds. There have been serial killers throughout history."

Damn. Like being lectured by Jane Seymour with a medical

degree. Michelle racked her brain for news stories. "Yes, but here we've had Ted Bundy, the Hillside Strangler, the Night Stalker"—Michelle strained to keep up the patter—"the Son of Stan . . ."

"Son of Sam," Dr. Metcalf helped out. "No doubt America has had its share. My primary interest is in understanding the reasons for these motiveless murders. We know that serial killers frequently cannot separate sex from aggression. We don't know whether this psychological deficit is caused by genetic, chemical, or hormonal reasons."

Thank God the director cut to a close-up of the British bitch.

Michelle caught a cue from the floor manager. "We'll be back with Dr. Pamela Metcalf, author of *The Murderer Within Us*, right after this. . . ."

The news director's door was open, so Michelle walked in. Jerry Abrams was devouring a bacon cheeseburger. Late thirties, bushy mustache, disheveled, overweight. He chewed noisily, occasionally burping as he kept his eyes on one of three TV screens in his glass-enclosed cubicle.

"Hey, Michelle, get a load—"

"Me-chelle."

"Okay, Meeee-chelle, get a load of this turkey."

On the screen a crew-cut blond man with a string tie was reciting baseball scores. The sound was turned low. Jerry Abrams always reviewed audition tapes this way. Watch the way they look, nobody listens anyway, he explained.

"Wanna play?" Jerry Abrams asked.

"I dunno, Jerry."

"C'mon, guess."

"El Paso?"

He shook his head.

"Albuquerque?"

Jerry fished a french fry out of a paper sack. The office smelled of grease and charred meat. "The Wyatt Earp tie's throwing you off. Smaller market, farther north."

"North Platte, Nebraska," she said.

"Good guess. Quad Cities, Iowa. Hayseed wants to come to Gomorrah-by-the-Sea."

He punched a button on the remote control and grabbed another cassette. More than a hundred were stacked around his desk.

"Jerry, I'd like you to relieve me on the five o'clock. Just for a couple weeks."

"What? During sweeps? Jesus, no!"

"But I'm working on an investigative piece. . . ."

He stopped in mid-bite. A glob of ketchup clung to his mustache. "What investigative piece? Who assigned you?"

"No one. I've been working on my own. A blockbuster I can't tell you about, yet. I've got a confidential source."

Jerry loosened his tie, which was already at half-mast. He plugged another cassette into the VCR. After the color bars and the countdown, a petite Oriental woman appeared in front of a burning building. She held a microphone and showed a dazzling smile likely used for stories of quintuplet births and plane crashes alike. Michelle noticed that her orange helmet clashed with her green flak jacket. She wondered if the teeth were real.

"Meee-chelle, baby," Jerry said, "you're not Bob Friggin' Woodward. You're a face, a very good face, and your numbers are catching up with *Gilligan's Island* reruns on Channel Four."

She tried to give him a tough look she learned from numerous Jane Fonda films. It had the effect of crinkling her collagen-injected lips.

"Now, don't pout at me," Jerry said. "Hey, that was a great interview today. What's a looker like that doing with mass murderers?"

"Serial murderers."

"Whatever," Jerry Abrams said.

The bedroom's jalousie windows were cranked open, and Michelle could hear nighttime traffic on Ocean Drive. The trendy club and barhopping crowd. Michelle smiled, relieved to be free of the feigned happiness of the South Beach full-time floating-disco-party team, junior varsity, second string. What with chlamydia, herpes, and gonorrhea creeping around, not to mention AIDS. Hadn't they just done a show on the misery of venereal warts, images of rashes and itches giving her the willies right on the set.

Having one man—even a part-time married man—was better than a bunch of sweaty one-night stands. Even though her man was, more often than not, a thirty-minute slam-bam-thank-you-ma'am stand. Which is why she didn't consider it cheating to spend an occasional night with a carefully chosen lover in a more leisurely mode.

Michelle stretched a hand across the sheets and touched a warm thigh. She heard the regular, measured breaths of peaceful sleep and smiled again. It had been wonderful for them both, better than she had dared hope for something so new, a warmth that had grown slowly, gently caressing her, building into a flame that had nearly consumed her. Better than with . . .

There was a stirring next to her and she watched her lover turn to one side. Great body, too. Silently, Michelle climbed out of bed. She had tossed her blue silk dress, specially chosen by her fashion consultant, across a chair. Her matching spike-heeled shoes, her panty hose, and discarded uplift bra formed a trail from living room to bedroom. Naked, Michelle entered the bathroom and closed the door. She removed the tinted contact lenses and scrubbed three layers of makeup from her face. There hadn't been time before, it had happened so fast. She slipped into a black silk camisole, headed for the tiny kitchen, and grabbed a low-fat vanilla yogurt from the refrigerator. Then she sat down at a desk in a corner of the living room and turned on her computer.

Michelle punched up the directory labeled "INVST-1" and started typing:

When your platoon entered the village of Dak Sut on January 9, 1968, what orders did you give?

"No," she said to herself. "Too direct." Christ, this wasn't like interviewing celebrity authors. She tried to imagine how Geraldo Rivera would do it.

For the next hour she kept typing and retyping questions.

Was there evidence of NVA or VC in the village?

He's going to say yes. Then what? How do you follow up? This is harder than it looks.

The last time you saw Lieutenant Ferguson alive, was he—

Forget it. She could try again tomorrow. She punched a button and magically transported the questions to her computer's hard memory. She exited the word-processing program, then hit the keys for the modem, which automatically dialed a local number. After a few seconds the computer tinkled a romantic ballad and the medical symbols for the male and female of the species appeared on the screen, the male's arrow piercing the female's circle. The symbols changed shape, becoming the figures of a nude man and woman, until they, too, electronically unwound and formed letters and then a word. "Compu-Mate."

DO YOU WISH TO ENTER THE MATING ROOM?
YES.
YOUR HANDLE, PLEASE.
TV GAL.

She had been meaning to change her handle after several Compu-Mate correspondents asked whether she enjoyed cross-dressing. She typed a numerical password, and after a moment the computer purred, and a new message scrolled down the monitor.

HERE'S WHO'S IN THE MATING ROOM NOW:
SUPER STUD
CANDY FEELGOOD
PASSION PRINCE
BUSH WHACKER
HELEN BED
ICE GODDESS
CHARLIE HORSE
BIGGUS DICKUS
TV GAL
ORAL ROBERT
HOT BUNS

A sound came from the bedroom. A sliver of light appeared under the door. Michelle punched into the chat mode and made some connections. Oral Robert told her he'd save her ass and to hell with her soul. Bush Whacker tried to type dirty but couldn't spell any word over four letters. Biggus Dickus, a nearly normal guy she remembered from last week, asked about her work. *Bor-ing!* She brushed them off.

HELLO, TV GAL. LIGHTS, CAMERA, ACTION—PASSION PRINCE.

A little jolt went through her, as it always did. A new name, a voice in the dark. Maybe this time. She heard the bathroom shower turning on. It wouldn't be an all-nighter after all.

HELLO, PASSION PRINCE. WHAT ARE YOU UP TO?

NO GOOD.

Just dancing around and she didn't have all night.

TELL ME ABOUT YOURSELF, PP.

EIGHT FEET TALL, GREEN SCALY SKIN, A LONG SNOUT, AND LARGE TEETH . . .

Christ, a comedian. Why not just a sincere, single, self-supporting male, thirty-five, gainfully employed, likes dining out, movies, and romantic walks on the beach?

. . . AND YOU, TV PERSON?

Might as well give him a cheap thrill.

FIVE-NINE WITH LONG, LONG LEGS. LARGE ROUND BREASTS, A FLAT, SMOOTH STOMACH, AND FULL HIPS.

She stared at the screen. Nothing. Maybe scared him off. She waited. Outside, an ocean breeze rattled the windows.

WHAT ABOUT YOUR ASSHOLE?

Oh brother. One of those.

IS IT NICE AND TIGHT?

She started to hit the escape button but stopped. In the bathroom, the water was turned off, the pipes clanking in the old apartment. The prince of passion was still typing.

DO YOU LIKE POETRY?

NOTHING DIRTY, PASSION GUY.

WHEREOF MY FAME IS LOUD AMONGST MANKIND, CURED LAMENESS, PALSIES, CANCERS. THOU, O GOD, KNOWEST ALONE WHETHER THIS WAS OR NO. HAVE MERCY, MERCY! COVER ALL MY SIN!

THAT'S POETRY? SOUNDS LIKE FATHER McCORKLE IN WILKES BARRE.

She hoped that would stop him, but the electronic blips kept coming, the words marching across her screen.

7

THEN, THAT I MIGHT BE MORE ALONE WITH THEE, THREE YEARS I LIVED UPON A PILLAR, HIGH.

I BEEN STONED, TOO, BUT THREE YEARS? THAT'S HEAVY.

NO, NO TV-GAL. DO YOU KNOW NOTHING OF THE STYLITES?

Jeez, I don't know what's worse, Michelle thought, a pervert or a bore. She looked toward the bedroom. The door was open, the light off.

A MO-TOWN GROUP, RIGHT?

AH, PERHAPS MUSIC IS MORE TO YOUR TASTE.

Ought to sign off now, Michelle thought, play hostess, offer a good-bye drink and exchange lies about next time. So quiet, the only sound the hum of the computer, the only light the luminous black-and-white display of the monitor. Now what was he typing? Rock 'n' roll lyrics. What's with this guy? Can't he think for himself? Trying to tell me I shake his nerves and rattle his brain. He was rattled long before tonight. And don't tell me what drives a man insane. But there he goes, hammering out the whole damn song. And he probably can't even carry a tune. She heard footsteps behind her.

OK, OK, PRINCE . . . I BROKE YOUR WILL AND GAVE YOU A SUPER-DUPER THRILL, BUT I REALLY GOT TO GO NOW.

A shadow crossed the screen, then stopped.

She didn't turn.

She expected a caress, a lover's hug.

"Hello, darling," Michelle said.

There was no reply.

She hit the escape button, punching out of the program, and stared into the black background of the screen. The outline of shoulders . . .

Two hands grabbed Michelle's neck from behind and yanked her out of the chair. For a moment she thought it was a joke. But it wasn't funny, and rough sex after tender loving didn't make sense. She thought of a man who wanted her to choke him just before he came. Oxygen deprivation to enhance the orgasm.

Weird. Now this.

The hands slipped from her neck, then closed again. Michelle clawed at the hands as they pressed harder. She kicked backward and tried to scream, but nothing came out. She gasped for air, fought off the nausea, and sucked in a breath as the hands relaxed again. But she was losing consciousness and her strength was gone.

She barely felt the hands this time, and her last memory would be a tiny sound, a sickening crack like a wishbone snapped in two.

The hands continued to squeeze for a full minute, then dropped her back into the chair. A moment later, they grabbed Mabel Dombrowsky by the hair and roughly jammed her head forward into the monitor, shattering the screen, shards of glass piercing her eyes. From inside the broken screen, an electronic pop and fizzle and a puff of flame.

"Great balls of fire!" sang a voice she never heard.

CHAPTER 1

A Matter of Honor

If Marvin the Maven tells me not to yell in closing argument, I don't yell. Marvin knows. He's never tried a case, but he's seen more trials than most lawyers. Drifting from courtroom to courtroom in search of the best action, he glimpses eight or nine cases a day. Five days a week for the last seventeen years since he closed up his shoe store in Brooklyn and headed south.

Some lawyers don't listen to Marvin and his friends—Saul the Tailor and Max (Just Plain) Seltzer—and they pay the price. Me, I listen. The courthouse regulars can't read the fine print on the early-bird menus, but they can spot perjury from the third row of the gallery.

Marvin, Saul, and Max already told me I botched jury selection. Not that lawyers *pick* jurors anyway. We *exclude* those we fear, at least until we run out of challenges.

"You're *meshuga*, you leave number four on," Marvin told me on the first day of trial.

10

"He's a hardworking butcher," I said defensively. "Knows the value of a dollar. Won't give the store away."

Marvin ran a liver-spotted hand over his toupee, fingering the part. "Lookit his eyes, *boychik*. Like pissholes in the snow. Plus, I betcha he lays his fat belly on the scale with the lamb chops. I wouldn't trust him as far as I could spit."

I told myself Marvin was wrong and that he hadn't intended to shower me with spittle to make his point.

Some lawyers hire psychologists to help with jury selection. They'll tell you that people who wear bright colors crave attention and feel for the underdog. Plaintiff's jurors. Dark colors are worn by introverts who don't care about people. Defendant's jurors. Hoop earrings and costume jewelry are good for the plaintiff, Rolex watches and three-karat diamonds for the defense. To me, that's a lot of malarkey. I pick jurors who smile when I smile and don't fold their bodies into tight balls when I stand close.

No second-guessing now. Closing argument. A time to sing the praises of freedom of the press, of the great newspaper that fulfills the constitutional function of blah-blah-blah. And Marvin said don't yell. No emotion. *The jury don't care about the Foist Amendment.* Besides, Nick Wolf is a great schmoozer, Marvin told me. The jurors love him. Number five, a Cuban receptionist, keeps batting her three-inch eyelashes at him.

And I thought she had trouble with her contacts.

The four men on the jury are your real problem, Marvin said. One black, two Cubans, one Anglo, all men's men. Nick's kind of guys.

So what am I, chopped liver?

He gave me that knowing look. *Ey, Lassiter, it ain't your jury; it ain't your day.* And with that, the gang took off, a kidnapping trial down the hall drawing them away.

Nick Wolf's lawyer, H. T. Patterson, yelled in closing argument. Hell, he sang, chanted, ranted, rocked, and roiled. A spellbinder and a stemwinder, H.T. worked the jurors like a Holy Roller. Which he was at the Liberty City Colored Baptist Church while attending law school at night in the days before Martin Luther King.

"They subjected Nick Wolf, a dedicated public servant, to scorn and ridicule, to calumny, and obloquy," Patterson now crooned in a seductive singsong. "They lied and distorted. They defamed and defiled. They took his honorable name and soiled it. Besmirched, tainted, and tarnished it! Debased, degraded, and disparaged it! And what should a man do when they stain, sully, and smear his good name?"

Change it, I thought.

"What should a man of honor do when those with pens sharp as daggers poison his reputation, not in whispers but in howls, five hundred three thousand, six hundred seventy-nine times?"

Five hundred three thousand, six hundred seventy-nine being the Sunday circulation of the *Miami Journal,* and Sunday being the day of choice for fifty-megaton, rock-'em-sock-'em, take-no-prisoners journalism. Which is what the *Journal* is noted for, though I thought the offending story—STATE ATTORNEY VIOLATED CAMPAIGN LAWS—lacked characteristic punch. Not sharing my opinion was Nicholas G. Wolf, bona fide local high-school football star, decorated Vietnam war hero, former policeman, and currently state attorney for the Seventeenth Judicial Circuit in and for Dade County, Florida. The article accused Wolf of various technical violations of the campaign contributions law plus one unfortunate reference to accepting money from a reputed drug dealer.

"The man should seek redress in a court of law," Patterson solemnly declared, answering his own question, as lawyers are inclined to do. "He should come before a jury of his peers, citizens of the community. So, my friends and neighbors, ladies and gentlemen of this jury, it is time to pay the piper. . . ."

I didn't think the metaphor held up to scrutiny, but the jury didn't seem to notice. The men all nodded, and number five stopped fluttering her eyelashes and now stared mournfully at poor, defamed Nick Wolf.

"It is time to assess damages; it is judgment day, it is time to levy the penalty for these knowing, reckless lies. And I ask you, ladies and gentlemen, is it too much to ask that the *Miami Journal,* that behemoth on the bay, that monster of malediction, pay ten dollars for each time it lied, yes, ten dollars for each time it sent its message of malice into our midst?"

I never did better than *C*s in math, but I know when a lawyer is asking for five million bucks from a jury. Meaning H. T. Patterson hoped for two million, and I was beginning to wonder if taking this case to trial was so damn smart after all.

"A letter of apology, a front-page retraction, and fifty grand might do it," I told the publisher six months earlier in his bayfront office.

Symington Foote bristled. "We don't pay extortion. A public official is fair game, and we had a bona fide tip that Wolf was taking dirty money."

"From a tipster who refuses to come forward and a reporter who won't even reveal his source," I reminded the publisher, trying to knock him off the soapbox.

"But we don't need to prove the story was true, do we, counselor?"

He had me there. As a public official, Nick Wolf could win his libel suit only if he proved that the newspaper knew the story was false or had recklessly disregarded the truth. A nice concept for judges. For jurors, it's the same as in most lawsuits. If they like the plaintiff's attitude and appearance more than the defendant's, the plaintiff wins. Simple as that.

The case had been cleanly tried. A few histrionics from Patterson, but his tricks were mostly subtle. When I stood to make an objection, he would move close, letting me tower above him. He was a bantam rooster in a white linen three-piece suit, and alongside was a bruiser representing the unrestrained power of a billion-dollar company.

So here I was about to deliver my closing argument in the big barn of a courtroom on the sixth floor of the Dade County Courthouse, an aging tower of gray limestone where buzzards of the winged variety soar overhead and the seersuckered birds beat their wings inside. Heavy drapes matted with dust covered the grimy windows. The walnut paneling had darkened over the decades, and an obsolete air-conditioning system rumbled noisily overhead.

Several years ago the electorate was asked to approve many millions of dollars in bonds for capital projects around the county. The voters said yea to a new zoo and nay to a new courthouse, expressing greater regard for the animals of the jungle than for the animals of Flagler Street. And who could blame them?

Now I stood and approached the jury box, all six-two, two-hundred-something pounds of me. I tried not to get too close, avoiding the jurors' horizontal space. I shot a glance at the familiar sign on the wall above the judge's bench: WE WHO LABOR HERE SEEK ONLY THE TRUTH. There ought to be a footnote: *subject to the truth being misstated by perjurious witnesses, obfuscated by sleazy lawyers, excluded by inept judges, and overlooked by lazy jurors.*

Planting myself like an oak in front of the jury, I surveyed the courtroom. Symington Foote sat at the defense table next to the chair I had just abandoned. The publisher fingered his gold cuff links and eyed me skeptically. Behind him in the row of imitation leather chairs just in front of the bar were two representatives of the newspaper's libel insurance company. Both men wore charcoal-gray three-piece suits. They flew in from Kansas City for the trial and had that corn-fed, pale-faced, short-haired, tight-assed look of insurance adjusters everywhere. I wouldn't have a drink with either one of them if stroking the client's pocketbook wasn't part of my job. In the front row of the gallery sat three senior partners of Harman and Fox, awaiting my performance with anxiety that approached hysteria. They were more nervous than I was, and I'm prone to both nausea and diarrhea just before closing argument. Neither Mr. Harman nor Mr. Fox was there, the former having died of a stroke in a Havana brothel in 1952, the latter living out his golden years in a Palm Beach estate—Château Renard—with his sixth wife, a twenty-three-year-old beautician from Barbados. We were an old-line law firm by Miami standards, our forebears having represented the railroads, phosphate manufacturers, citrus growers, and assorted other robber barons and swindlers from Florida's checkered past. These days we carried the banner of the First Amendment, a load lightened considerably by our enormous retainer and hefty hourly rates.

Much like a railroad, a newspaper is a glorious client because of the destruction it can inflict. Newspaper trucks crush pedestrians in the early-morning darkness; obsolete presses mangle workmen's limbs; and the news accounts themselves—the paper's very raison d'être, as H. T. Patterson had just put it in a lyrical moment—can poison as surely as the deadliest drug. All of it, fodder for the law firm. So the gallery was also filled with an impressive collection of downtown hired guns squirming in their seats with the fond hope that the jury would tack seven digits onto the verdict form and leave *The*

Miami Journal looking for new counsel. When I analyzed it, my only true friend inside the hall of alleged justice was Marvin the Maven, and he couldn't help me now.

I began the usual way, thanking the jurors, stopping just short of slobbering my gratitude for their rapt attention. I didn't point out that number two had slept through the second day and that number six was more interested in what he dug out of his nose than the exhibits marked into evidence. Then after the brief commercial for the flag, the judge, and our gosh-darned best-in-the-world legal system, I paused to let them know that the important stuff was coming right up. Summoning the deep voice calculated to keep them still, I began explaining constitutional niceties as six men and women stared back at me with suspicion and enmity.

"Yes, it is true that the *Journal* did not offer testimony by the main source of its story. And it is true that there can be many explanations for the receipt of cash contributions and many reasons why State Attorney Wolf chose to drop charges against three men considered major drug dealers by the DEA. But Judge Witherspoon will instruct you on the law of libel and the burden of the plaintiff in such a case. And he will tell you that the law gives the *Journal* the right to be wrong. . . ."

I caught a glimpse of Nick Wolf, giving me that tough-guy smile. He was a smart enough lawyer in his own right to know I had no ammunition and was floundering.

"And as for damages," I told the jury, "you have just heard some outrageous sums thrown about by Mr. Patterson. In this very courtroom, at that very plaintiff's table, there have sat persons horribly maimed and disfigured, there have sat others defrauded of huge sums of money, but look at the plaintiff here. . . ."

They did, and he looked back with his politician's grin. Nick Wolf filled his chair and then some. All chest and shoulders. One of those guys who worked slinging bags of cement or chopping trees as a kid, and with the good genes, the bulk stayed hard and his Brahma-bull neck would strain against shirt collars for the rest of his life. On television, with the camera focused on a head shot, all you remembered was that neck.

"Has he been physically injured? No. Has he lost a dime

because of this story? No. Has he even lost a moment's sleep? No. So even if you find the *Journal* liable . . ."

H. T. Patterson still had rebuttal, and I wondered if he would use the line from Ecclesiastes about a man's good name being more valuable than precious ointment or the one from *Othello* about reputation as the immortal part of self.

He used them both.

Then threw in one from *Richard II* I'd never heard.

"You could have advised us to settle," Symington Foote said, standing on the courthouse steps, squinting into the low, vicious late-afternoon sun.

Funny, I thought I had.

"Three hundred twenty-two thousand," I said. "Could have been worse."

"Where the hell did that number come from? Where do these jurors get their—"

"Probably a quotient verdict. Someone wanted to give him a million, someone else only a hundred thousand. They put the numbers on slips of paper, add 'em up, and divide by six. They're not supposed to do it, but it happens."

Foote sniffed the air, didn't like what he smelled, and snorted. "Maybe it's time for a hard look at the jury system. I'll talk to the editorial writers in the morning."

He stomped off without telling me how much he looked forward to using my services in the future.

CHAPTER 2

Three's a Crowd

I was late for dinner with Doc Riggs. But I hadn't expected to make it at all. With a jury out, you never know.

I spotted Charlie's unkempt hair and bushy beard, now streaked with gray. He wore a khaki bush jacket and sat at his usual table on the front porch of Tugboat Willie's, a weather-beaten joint located behind the Marine Stadium on the causeway, halfway between the mainland and Key Biscayne. Charlie had been coming to the old restaurant since his early days as county medical examiner. It was one of the few places where neither the management nor patrons seemed to mind the whiff of formaldehyde. Sometimes Charlie caught his own fish and asked the cook to make it any old way as long as it was fried. Sometimes he ordered from the menu. Willie's is a great place as long as the wind isn't out of the northeast. The restaurant sits just southwest of the city sewage plant at Virginia Key. On a tropical island filled with cypress hammocks and white herons—one of the few bayfront spots not auctioned off to rapacious developers—Miami chose to dump its bodily wastes.

The evening was warm and muggy; not a breath of air stirred the queen palms in front of the ramshackle restaurant. Toward the mainland, low feathery clouds reflected an orange glow, not from the setting sun, but from the anticrime mercury-vapor lights of Liberty City.

Charlie was already digging into his fried snapper when I climbed the steps to the porch. Next to him was a woman with long auburn hair and fine porcelain skin. She wore a tailored blue suit that meant business and, best I could tell, no makeup. She didn't need any. In the gauzy light of dusk she glowed with a look that Hollywood cinematographers crave for the starlet of the year. Her cheekbones were finely carved and high, the eyes green, wide set, and confident.

I slid into an empty chair next to the woman and tried to use my wit. "Charlie, I can't leave you alone for one evening without your smooth-talking some sweet young woman. . . ."

Then I gave her my best crinkly-eyed, pearly-toothed smile out of a face tanned from many indolent afternoons riding the small waves on a sailboard not far from where we sat. I am broad of shoulder, sandy of hair, and crooked of grin, but the lady's eyes darted to me and back to Charlie without tarrying.

"I don't mean to argue with you, Dr. Riggs," she said in a clipped British accent that sounded like royalty, "but most of these so-called killer profiles are so much rubbish. Just the modern version of detecting criminals by the shape of their noses or the size of their ears."

Charlie's fork froze in mid-bite. "But even you have identified characteristics. In your book—"

"Yes, yes. But they're of little import. What is consequential is that these men are incapable of forming normal relationships. They do not see themselves as separate human beings or recognize the separate humanity of any other being, and we don't know why. To a Hillside Strangler or a Yorkshire Ripper, a human being is no more animate than a block of wood. We'll never make any progress until we understand what made them that way."

I nodded my agreement, hoping Charlie would bring me up to date, or at least introduce me. But the old billy goat was having too good a time to notice.

"This is the classic distinction between our disciplines," Charlie said, sipping a glass of Saint-Veran white burgundy, while I sat, parched, irked, and apparently invisible. "The medical examiner searches for the clues of *who* did the crime and *how*. The forensic psychiatrist yearns for the *why*."

"And the lawyer says the devil or his mother or irresistible impulse made the rascal do it," I offered.

Charlie noticed me then. "Oh, my manners! Dr. Metcalf, this is Jacob Lassiter, a dear friend of mine. When I was the county ME, Jake was a young public defender, and how he made my life miserable. Now he's a successful civil lawyer, eh, Jake?"

"Some days. How do you do, Dr. Metcalf."

She nodded and seemed to appraise me with green eyes spiked with flint. The eyes lingered, decided I was an interesting specimen but hardly worth an afternoon tea, and returned to Charlie. I gave Doc my pleading, hang-dog look, which he recognized as acute deprivation of female companionship.

"Jake was quite creative when he was a PD," Charlie said. His eyes twinkled behind thick glasses held together with a bent fishhook where they had lost a screw. "He'd be defending a Murder One and ask me on cross in very serious tones, 'Isn't the fact that the decedent fell from a tenth-floor balcony consistent with suicide?'"

I laughed and said, "And Charlie would look at the jury, scratch his beard, and say, 'Only if we omit the fact that a second before falling, the decedent was shot in the back by a gun covered with your client's fingerprints.'"

The English lady nearly smiled, and it didn't seem to hurt.

"Pamela's on a book tour," Charlie told me, "and my old friend Warwick at Broadmoor asked her to look me up."

"Warwick at Broadmoor?" I asked, with a blank face.

"Dr. Warwick heads the forensic unit at Broadmoor. Hospital for the criminally insane," Charlie added, as if any dolt should know. "In London. Dr. Metcalf was instrumental in apprehending and then treating the Firebug Murderer."

I was silent, not willing to admit my ignorance quite so often.

The lady psychiatrist rescued me. "Just a lad, really. The fellow would find lovers parked in their cars, snogging away—"

"Snogging, were they?" I asked, eyebrows raised in mock disapproval.

"Yes, what you would call . . . oh, Dr. Riggs, help me."

Charlie coughed and said, "Necking and what have you."

I nodded, knowingly.

"In any event," Dr. Metcalf continued, "this poor wretch would seek out lovers, pour petrol over them, and set them alight."

"Indeed?" I said, in an unintended imitation of her accent.

"Quite," she replied, giving me a look that said she did not suffer fools, particularly of the American wise-guy variety.

I signaled the waiter for a beer by elegantly pointing a finger down my throat. Then I turned to the lady psychiatrist with practiced sincerity. "Tell me about your work, Dr. Metcalf. How do you treat these firebugs and murderers?"

"I *study* the psychopath," she said. "I want to know why he acts the way he does."

"Or *she* does," I added, believing in equality of the sexes in all departments.

"The subject is so complex," Pamela Metcalf said, ignoring me. "We study the childhood antecedents to murder—"

"Environment," Charlie Riggs said.

"But we also know that there are neurological, genetic, and biophysiological components, too."

"The extra Y chromosome in men." Charlie nodded.

"Yes, we know the XYY abnormality is four times more prevalent among murderers."

"So are killers made or born?" I asked.

"That's what I've been trying to determine ever since I became fascinated with the Cotswolds Killer."

I showed her my vague look. It comes naturally.

"You know the section called the Cotswolds?" she asked.

"The Catskills, I know. . . ."

"In Oxfordshire, wonderful hilly sheep country. I grew up there near Chipping Camden. I was still a student when someone began killing farm girls. One near Bourton-on-the-Water, one just outside Upper Slaughter."

"Upper Slaughter," Charlie muttered.

"Each of the girls had been strangled. Like so many of them nowadays, each had been sexually active at age fifteen or so, highly active, and their several boyfriends were initially suspected."

"Any of the boyfriends know both the girls?" Charlie asked, still trying to earn his detective's shield.

"No. And no strangers were implicated, either. The crimes were never solved, and . . . well, it just got me started."

I thought about pretty Miss Metcalf scouring the sylvan English countryside for clues of murder. The thought didn't last. The waiter brought my beer, and I ordered yellowtail snapper broiled, some fried sweet plantains, and black beans with rice. The pathologist and the psychiatrist were still carrying on, regaling each other with tales of death and derangement.

"Dr. Riggs, I still can't believe you've retired. I've so enjoyed your articles."

Charlie beamed. "Oh, I continue my research. *Vita non est vivere sed valere vita est.* 'Life is more than merely staying alive.'"

She reached out and put a hand on his shoulder. "For you, no *taedium vitae.*"

They both laughed, and I managed a weak smile. Maybe when I'm pushing sixty-five, women will fall all over me, too. They kept trading war stories and Latin phrases, and I kept popping the porcelain stoppers on sixteen-ounce Grolsches. I was on my third bottle, letting a soft buzz take the edge off, when I decided to break into the party. Having just been whacked by a jury, scolded by a client, and ignored by a beautiful woman from another continent, I figured there was very little to lose.

"Ah-chem," I said.

No one seemed to notice my brilliant opening line. Pamela Metcalf was still focused on the old coroner who, until twenty minutes before, was my mentor and best friend.

"I was fascinated by your article on the forensic aspects of strangulation," Dr. Metcalf gushed.

"It had me all choked up," I said, then took a hit on the Grolsch.

Dr. Pamela Metcalf's emerald eyes shot me a pitying look, then returned their full concentration to the bearded wizard. "Your method for determining the time of death by assessing the degree of postmortem lividity in a hanging victim was quite helpful to homicide detectives."

"Yep," I offered, "the cops were at the end of their rope."

Charlie Riggs furrowed his brow, and the air seeped further out of my ego. That peculiar macho known to all men ached to haul out the trophies and merit badges, maybe tell her about the days before I wore a blue suit and wingtip shoes. Hey, lady, I once came off the bench to sack Terry Bradshaw on an all-out blitz in a playoff game. *Now playing at outside linebacker, from Penn State, number fifty-eight, Jake Las-siter!* Maybe Charlie would ask me how the knees were doing, and I could ease right into—

"Mr. Lassiter . . . Mr. Lassiter."

The waiter was tapping me on the shoulder. Now what? In fancy places they sometimes toss me out. But tonight I was wearing socks *and* long pants, and neither was required at Tugboat Willie's.

"A policeman on the phone, Mr. Lassiter. Says it's urgent."

I followed the waiter to an open alcove near the kitchen. The air was pungent with fish and garlic. From behind the swinging metal door, I heard the singsong of Creole mixed with the clatter of dishes. A black cat with yellow eyes was pawing through a garbage can, debating between grouper and dolphin for an entrée.

"Detective Alejandro Rodriguez here," said the unfamiliar voice on the phone. "Hold for State Attorney Wolf."

Ah, the accouterments of power. Using a policeman—a detective no less—for a secretary. Probably calling to rub it in. Nick Wolf had been so busy dispensing victory statements to the press, he hadn't even needled me after the verdict. I waited, listening to the faint traffic noises that told me Wolf was calling from his state-owned Chrysler.

"Jake, you did a helluva job for that fish wrapper they call a newspaper," Nick Wolf boomed.

"Maybe you can tell that to Symington Foote. He thought I should have attacked when I played defense."

"He's an asshole. Downtown power-clique country-club asshole. You low-keyed it, kept the damages down. A savvy lawyer knows when to do that."

I didn't tell him I get my savvy from Marvin the Maven.

Wolf paused, and so did I. We were out of conversation, or so I thought.

"Jake," he said finally, "I'd like you to meet me at a homicide scene."

"Should I have my alibi ready?"

He didn't laugh. "Three seventy-five Ocean Drive, South Beach, second floor. I need independent counsel to head the investigation."

"Why me?"

From somewhere at his end a police siren wailed. "Because you're honest and not plugged into any of the political groups. I checked you out. Latin Builders, Save-Our-Guns, English Only . . . nobody's heard of you since you used to sit on the bench for the Dolphins. I don't even know if you're a Democrat or Republican."

"Audubon Society."

"Huh?"

"My only affiliation. Charlie Riggs and I like to stomp through the Glades and look at the birds. Blue herons, snowy egrets, roseate spoonbills. Makes you believe in a Creator or at least a damn fortuitous Big Bang."

"Charlie Riggs," Wolf said, almost wistfully. "Tell that old grave robber to stop in and see me sometime."

"Tell him yourself. He's about ten yards yonder, putting away some key lime pie and amusing a British lady psychiatrist with murder and mayhem."

"Her name Metcalf?"

I looked around for a hidden camera. "You're getting some pretty good intelligence these days."

"Lucky guess. I have a man waiting at her hotel. She was one of the last people to see the decedent alive."

"This decedent have a name?"

"This line's not secure. I'll see you in twenty minutes. Bring Riggs and the lady."

When I returned to the table, Charlie was halfway through the story of the widow whose first two husbands died after eating kidney pie laced with paraquat. The third husband was smart enough to refuse her cooking, but deaf enough not to move when she rode the El Toro mower over the spot where he was sunbathing.

Charlie looked up at me, a dab of whipped cream stuck to his beard.

"Saddle up," I said. "We been deputized."

CHAPTER 3

Catch Me If You Can

Retirees still sit on plastic rockers on the front porches of the art-deco hotels. Hookers, fences, dealers, TVs, pimps, chicken hawks, and runaways still stroll Ocean Drive, hustling their wares. But the Yuppies have staked claims to South Beach, spiffing up the old buildings with turquoise and salmon paint, dressing themselves in bright, baggy cottons and silks, and hovering on the perimeter of perpetual trendiness. Over the whine of the window air conditioner is heard the agreeable hum of European engineering as the young lawyers, brokers, accountants, bankers, and journalists steer their Saabs, BMWs, and Volvos into oceanfront parking lots.

Cafés and comedy clubs now occupy once-abandoned storefronts. Stylish restaurants abound, strands of pasta hanging on wooden rods like moss on forest trees. Saloons with etched-glass mirrors and polished brass rails offer exotic tropical drinks at outrageous prices. Fresh tuna is seared ever so slightly on open grills. And for reasons inexplicable, a sushi bar stands on every corner. Raw fish is fine for shipwreck victims, but with all the crud floating in our waters, I prefer my seafood well done.

The apartment building was built in the 1930s, which in Miami Beach qualified as an historic site. The building had been empty for years, before the resurgence of South Beach brought fresh money and fresher hucksters to town. The newspapers coined the term "Tropical Deco" to describe the renovated hotels and apartment buildings. This one was called Flamingo Arms and consisted of a series of curved walls, glass block, and cantilevered sunshades that looked like stucco eyebrows. The paint was the color of a ripe avocado. Two metal flamingos formed a grillwork on the front door, and the same motif was picked up in the lobby with a mural of several of the pink birds high-stepping through a fountain.

The three of us—the coroner, the shrink, and the mouthpiece—were let in by a uniformed cop who recognized Charlie Riggs. We climbed a winding staircase with a looping metal railing to the second floor. It was a corner apartment facing Ocean Drive with just a sliver of a view of the Fifth Street Beach. Nick Wolf stood in a corner of the living room, his face drawn into a tight mask. Whispering in his ear was a cop in plainclothes. Nick Wolf shook his head and didn't move. The cop came over to us.

"Alex Rodriguez," he said, shaking my hand, and nodding to Charlie Riggs and Pamela Metcalf. He looked just right for a detective, which is to say he looked like your average forty-two-year-old, middle-class man who sells power tools at Sears. His dark hair was beginning to thin at the crown. He was of average height, average weight, and average demeanor, except for his nose, which, he later told me, had been head-butted one direction by a drugged-out citizen and smashed the other way by his partner's errant nightstick while quelling a domestic dispute.

"I'm glad you're here, Dr. Metcalf," Rodriguez said. "You too, Charlie. Lassiter, give Nick a minute. Then he'll talk to you. Now . . ."

He left it hanging there, and we all turned toward a desk in a corner of the room where a young assistant medical examiner was still snapping his photos. The ME nodded toward Charlie but kept at his work. His pale hair was parted high on his head and clipped short on the sides, a style favored by the current crop of young professionals.

In rebellion, I keep mine unfashionably long and shaggy, and when in the company of callow youth, I incessantly hum Joan Baez tunes. He wore a white lab coat with a name tag. He didn't look old enough to be a doctor, but I figured, no matter what, he couldn't kill the patient. His little kit was open, and he had lined up his sketch pads, gloves, sponges, plastic bags, thermometer, trowel, chalk, and tape recorder.

Charlie walked straight to the body. She wore a black silk camisole and nothing else.

She was sprawled—legs akimbo—in her chair at a desk.

Her head was jammed through a computer monitor. The keyboard was pulled open.

Maybe Charlie Riggs was used to homicide scenes. Maybe it was just another day at the office for him. But not for me. The aftermath of violence chilled me. I didn't know this woman, didn't even know her name. I had no sense of loss for a loved one. I would not miss a laugh I had never heard. But I knew someone—a mother, a lover, a friend—would cry out her name. And somewhere, I knew, was someone who didn't cry for anyone or anything. Someone so foreign to me as to be unfathomable.

My life has been circumscribed by rules. I tried not to hit after the whistle, and I never lied to a judge, though I've been tempted to take a poke at one or two. But there are games people play without rules. The hard-eyed cops know the players, stare them down every day. Could I do that? At the moment, filled with a mixture of anger and dread, I didn't know.

I looked at Pam Metcalf, who seemed to be studying me. "Of course it's dreadful," she said, "but scientifically, Mr. Lassiter, it's quite fascinating, too."

Charlie Riggs took control. He gently pulled the body back into the chair. "Lividity of the face and lips, engorgement and petechial hemorrhages in the conjunctivae."

He examined her neck. "No sign of a ligature. Crescentic abrasions on the skin, most likely fingernail marks. Probable cause of death, hypoxia due to throttling."

Charlie Riggs turned to the assistant ME. "Manual strangulation. Any evidence of sexual battery?"

"Nothing . . . visible," he stammered. "No contusions or lacerations other than the head and neck injuries. I swabbed the genitalia. No visible semen. However, vaginal secretions are consistent with . . . uh . . . sexual activity in close proximity to death."

"You'll check the smear for spermatozoa, of course."

"Yes, sir. I thought I'd use methylene blue."

Charlie Riggs shook his head. "You'll never distinguish sperm cells from artifacts with that stain. Try hematoxylin and eosin for better differentiation."

"Yes, sir."

"What else, what other tests?"

"Well . . . I don't know."

"What if the fellow's had a vasectomy, or he's an alcoholic with cirrhosis? Won't find any wagging tails there, eh?"

"In that event," the young doctor recited, as if taking his oral exams, "acid phosphatase determination will reveal the presence of seminal fluid. If the man's a secreter, we can identify A, B, or H blood types."

"*Verus,*" Charlie said, beaming, a professor whose student had finally caught on. "Be alert to every detail. Don't believe that old saw *Mortui non mordent—*"

"I never did," I chimed in.

"'Dead men carry no tales.' Hah! They can tell us stories *horribile dictu*, horrible to relate, but essential to our understanding of their deaths."

The young doctor was nodding his head vigorously.

"Now, what about odor?" Charlie Riggs asked.

"Beg your pardon?"

"Vaginal odor? It's okay to take your sweet time with the lab tests, but you've got one chance to work up the crime scene. Just don't forget to use the old schnoz."

"Tell him about the time you opened a stomach and ID'ed the restaurant by smelling the beer in the barbecue sauce," I prompted Charlie.

"Only one ribs joint in town had sauce like that," Charlie said. "Wasn't hard to figure where he had his last supper, then a waiter identified his dining companion, a hired killer."

The assistant ME bit his lip, shot an embarrassed look toward Pam Metcalf, and sank to his knees. His head disappeared between two pale, slightly chubby thighs.

"Three-to-one the kid says he smells barbecue sauce," Detective Rodriguez whispered to me. He had been in the department twenty years and had little time for rookies in any field.

A voice without a face came from the general vicinity of the corpse's pudendum. "What smells should I be . . . uh . . . looking for?"

"Anything, son!" Charlie boomed. "The latex of a condom or a surgical glove, maybe soap, talcum, or a douche scented with lily of the valley, even a man's distinctive cologne. Some men splash it on their privates, you know. Maybe we find a guy who's crazy for Aqua Velva."

"Or Listerine," Rodriguez suggested, "depending on his proclivities."

There was the sound of a bloodhound sniffing, then the assistant ME picked himself up, looked sheepishly toward Charlie, and said, "Sorry, sir, but . . . it's just plain pussy to me."

"Oh, never mind. You'll want to do a complete autopsy, of course. Take a good look at the neck. I'd advise elevating the shoulders, eviscerate the body, and remove the brain. If you want a dry field, don't dissect the neck until the blood has stopped draining. Don't let the homicide detectives rush you. Take your time."

The kiddie coroner nodded, then piped up, "I'd say the assailant was right-handed, Dr. Riggs."

From behind me I heard a snicker. *"Fantastico,"* Detective Rodriguez said. "I'll put out a BOLO for all right-handed guys."

Doc Riggs was more diplomatic. "And how do you reach that conclusion, Doctor . . . ?"

Charlie squinted at the name tag.

"Whitson," the alleged doctor proclaimed. "Well, there's a single abrasion on the right side of the neck and four on the left. So the assailant's right thumb would have made the single abrasion, the fingers of his right hand the rest."

"Assuming she was strangled from the front," Charlie added politely.

"I thought of that, sir. You can tell from the concavity of the crescents that the strangulation occurred from the front."

Charlie made a little tsk-tsking sound. He didn't want to lecture the lad in front of spectators, but he had no choice. He examined the

28

neck. "All I can tell is that the nail on the ring finger is jagged. In a couple of days, it will grow back, so the information is of very little use. As for the crescent, the direction of the concavity can be misleading. The crescent will be reversed, as often as not. Here, I'll show you. Jake, roll up your sleeve."

"Why me?" I protested. "I haven't forgotten your electrocution experiment."

"It was only two hundredths of an amp, Jake, and I turned it off as soon as you went into muscular paralysis. Now be a good scout."

Everyone was watching, so the good scout rolled up his sleeve. Charlie looked around and spotted Pamela Metcalf, who was intently studying titles of the shelved books in the small apartment.

"Pamela, perhaps you can inflict some pain on Jake for a moment," Charlie wondered cheerfully.

"Gladly," she chimed in. She placed a cool hand on my forearm and dug five fingernails deep into my skin.

"I'll always remember the first time we touched," I told her, showing my All-Conference smile.

She dug deeper, letting up just before severing the radial artery. I held up my arm, and sure enough, the crescents went the opposite direction of each nail's shape. Charlie was explaining something about the free edge of the arch of the nail having no purchase and therefore creating the reverse crescent and how fallacious it was to infer much from fingernail marks. I just looked at the little dents in my arm and said to Pamela Metcalf, "I'll bet you leave a mark on every man you meet."

"With some," she replied, "it takes a sledgehammer."

Having exhausted my store of witty repartee, I stood silently, surveying the scene. The apartment was sparsely furnished in Yuppie Modern—white tile and green plants, a large-screen TV and CD player, a few bookshelves. There was a galley kitchen with a few pots and pans and a cupboard containing bran cereal, microwave popcorn, bottled spaghetti sauce, and spinach pasta from a gourmet market. The oven was practically sterile, indicating either an immaculate cook or no cook at all. The refrigerator had four different flavors of yogurt, none of which had expired, bottled water, an eyemask filled with what looked like antifreeze, and not much else. The bedroom and bathroom were down a hall, but I hadn't seen them yet.

Young Dr. Whitson picked up his camera and click-clicked through several roles of film, shooting the body, the furniture, and even one or two of me. Charlie puttered around the body for a while, giving more tips to the young pathologist. Pamela Metcalf walked through the little apartment, her green eyes bright, taking everything in, letting nothing out.

Nick Wolf motioned me onto the small balcony where we were alone. I looked him in the eye. I was half a foot taller, but he had impressive width. A stocky fireplug of explosive energy. "Michelle Diamond," he said. "Ever see her on *Live at Five?*"

I shook my head. Usually, I'm still working then. If not, I'm playing volleyball on the beach or fishing with Charlie. Afternoon television is for those in traction. Physical or mental.

"I want you to be a special prosecutor and lead the investigation," Nick said. "Present a case to the grand jury when you've got a suspect."

"Why can't your office handle it?"

He didn't hesitate, just shrugged those big shoulders. "Conflict of interest. I was seeing her. Not heavy-duty. But I'd slip over here in the mornings or she'd come by my place at night. It's sure to come out in the investigation.

Before I could ask, he said, "I've been separated for six months. Irretrievably broken and all that."

"So the first statement I take is from you," I said.

He showed the hint of a smile. "Should I have my alibi ready?"

I looked at him hard. His girlfriend's body was drawing flies and he makes a little joke. A used little joke.

"I don't show much emotion," Wolf said, reading my mind. "Not in public, anyway. Maybe tonight I'll get drunk by myself. Maybe I'll put my fist through a wall. But that's none of your business. Your job is to find the slime that did this, get an indictment, and try the case."

Through the glass I saw Pamela Metcalf talking to Detective Rodriguez. He was nodding and making notes on a little pad. Across the street the ocean breeze rattled the palm fronds. Traffic crept along Ocean Drive, young people cruising at a pace to see and be seen.

I came in and told Rodriguez what I wanted. A computer whiz to print out everything inside the beige box on Michelle Diamond's desk and the disks in her drawer. All her address books, appointment schedules, credit-card receipts, a list of her friends, relatives, and coworkers, and a chronology of her daily routine. I wanted statements from her gynecologist, her hairdresser, her pharmacist, her landlady, her maid, and her masseuse. I wanted to know every man she dated in the last three years and anyone she met in the last three months. Did any deliverymen bring her groceries or furniture or laundry? Where was she every minute of the last week? Within forty-eight hours, I wanted to know more about Michelle Diamond than her best friend, her mother, or her lover ever did.

It wasn't asking too much. Anyone who cares to can know everything about us. Somewhere, I am sure, there is a giant computer that stores a thousand megabytes about each of us. What we got in geography and who we took to the senior prom. Where we eat, what we buy, who we call. How much money we make and how much we give away. What airlines we use, where we sleep, how much we spend on clothes, booze, and pills. Traffic tickets, domestic disputes, diplomas, and the books we buy. Modern life is one sweeping, cradle-to-grave invasion of privacy. An encroachment on our ever-narrowing space. Behind us we leave a trail of carbon copies and floppy disks. Fodder for the snoop and the historian alike.

In the twenty-first century, they tell us, our houses will be smaller, our lawns nonexistent. We'll work at home and recycle our garbage into compost. Our bathroom scale will record our weight, pulse, and blood pressure and transmit the information to the company physician and anyone else with the right seven-digit password. The computer will link us with the office, the grocery store, and each other. The paper trail will be obsolete, but in its place, microscopic chips and laser scanners will transcribe details even the most astute biographer would overlook.

"Lassiter, come take a look back here."

It was Rodriguez, motioning me through the bedroom and toward the bathroom. I moseyed back there and stood, filling the doorway, peeking over Charlie Riggs' shoulder. It was old-fashioned but clean, a small porcelain sink, shower stall, and toilet crammed into a room without a window. There were powders and perfumes and white fluffy towels, and on the mirror above the sink was a message scrawled in bloodred lipstick: **Catch me if you can, Mr. Lusk.**

"We got ourselves a show-off," I said. "Now, who the hell is Mr. Lusk?"

"Probably some guy she was playing tag with," Rodriguez said, "and it looks like he caught her."

In the mirror I saw Charlie's jaw drop in astonishment. It was not his usual expression. He moved closer, as if the image might disappear at any moment. "Pamela, come here please!"

In a moment Pamela Metcalf joined the party. And there the four of us stood. I hoped somebody knew more than I did.

"Mr. Lusk." Pamela's voice trembled.

"Yes, Mr. Lusk," Charlie said.

"You know the hombre?" Rodriguez asked.

"George Lusk," Charlie Riggs mumbled, shaking his head in disbelief.

"I'll bring him in," Rodriguez said.

Charlie laughed but there was no pleasure in it. "Sorry, detective. Mr. Lusk is quite dead."

Rodriguez squinted at the mirror. "Then who's—"

"In the fall of 1888, in the East End of London, the Whitechapel section, there were a series of murders of young women."

"I get it," Rodriguez said. "George Lusk was the cop who cracked the case."

"Not exactly," Charlie said. "He was a private citizen who formed the Whitechapel Vigilance Committee to patrol the streets and help the police. One day Lusk received a parcel in the mail. It contained a kidney cut from the body of one of the victims and a most grisly note. I can't remember the contents exactly, but the note concluded—"

"'Catch me if you can, Mr. Lusk,'" Pamela Metcalf said.
Charlie nodded.

"Hey," Rodriguez said. "You're talking about Jack the Ripper."
Charlie nodded again and looked straight at me.

"And I guess that makes me Mr. Lusk," I said.

CHAPTER 4

Breaking the Ice

They had already zipped the body into a plastic bag when I made a final pass through the living room. The assistant ME had packed his bag and capped his camera. The cops were growing bored and filing out; there were other bodies in other apartments and the night was young. Charlie Riggs was on the staircase outside with Pamela Metcalf, reminiscing about murders most foul. I looked around and struggled to remember everything the old canoe maker had taught me.

Be alert to every detail. I tried to memorize everything in the room. The computer was an IBM clone, the desk white oak, the telephone a new Panasonic. Michelle Diamond had been sitting at the computer when she was killed. I looked closer at the phone. Two lines, a bunch of buttons. One button was for making conference calls, another put you on hold, a third activated the speaker phone.

Then the last one. "Redial."

I congratulated myself on how smart I was. Half a dozen cops and nobody thought about it—maybe the last person Michelle

33

Diamond spoke to just a dial tone away. And maybe with some luck, that last person was the guy who squeezed the life out of her. *Don't you dare come over here, Harry, we're through!*

Then again, it could be the weather number, a wrong number, or the public library. Only one way to find out. I picked up the receiver and hit the button. Seven electronic notes played do-re-mi in my ear.

A click and then the whir of a woman's recorded voice. "Welcome to Compu-Mate, where the person of your dreams awaits you. Dial ROMANCE, 766-2623, on your modem, and we'll put you in touch. Why not let Compu-Mate find your life mate?"

"Or your death mate," I answered the mechanical voice, "as the case may be."

I put the top down on my ancient Olds 442 convertible, deposited Charlie Riggs in the back and Pamela Metcalf in the passenger bucket seat. It's the Turbo 400, yellow body, black canvas top, black interior, rallye wheels, four-speed stick. An overgrown kid's toy.

"No sign of a break-in, nothing missing from the apartment," Charlie yelled over the roar of three hundred sixty-five horsepower. "No apparent motive."

It was a cloudy June night; the air was humid with a hint of salt. We were approaching the *Miami Journal,* just on the Miami side of the MacArthur Causeway. The boxy building sat there, lights twinkling against the blackness of the bay, taunting me.

"An organized crime scene," Pamela Metcalf added.

Above us, on the superstructure, yellow lights flashed and we came to a stop at the drawbridge. When the lights turned red, the traffic gate lowered into place, the tender yanked on a long steel lever, and the bridge started clanking skyward. Below us, a nighttime sailor aimed a sleek Hinckley with a towering mast through the opening.

"Based on a cursory review," she continued, "I would say you're looking for a white male in his late twenties or early thirties, probably firstborn, height and weight within norms, higher-than-average intelligence, though an underachiever in school. He probably knew the victim or at least had seen her and followed her. His socioeconomic background is at least average, and he probably had a two-parent household, but he never formed a stable relationship with his father."

"I suppose the family dog got run over by a truck when he was going through puberty," I said, with just a hint of sarcasm.

The psychiatrist stared at my profile. The sight did not weaken her knees. "Actually, he probably tortured and killed pets. Slicing open a cat's belly and pulling out the intestines would be typical."

That muzzled me for a moment. The bridge dropped back into place, the gate lifted, and we were moving again. I swung onto the I-95 connector and headed south, tires singing on the concrete thirty feet above the mean streets of Overtown. Then I said, "I'm not sure that shrinks have all the answers they think they do."

"Don't sell forensic psychiatry short," Charlie Riggs shouted from the backseat.

"I don't. But the data doesn't do any good. We can't haul in all the firstborn sons in town."

"No," Pamela Metcalf said, "but we can predict this killer's future behavior based on studies of past serial killers. He has fulfilled the fantasy of murder. He will repeat it, and will add to it his other fantasies he has so far repressed."

"You're assuming it's a motiveless crime. Not a jealous boyfriend or a bumbling robber."

"Unless you discover a pecuniary motive or an emotional one, you will find the murder quite motiveless, except in the deranged mind of the psychopath who committed it."

It's hard to argue with someone so obviously used to being right. We rode in silence as I pulled off the interstate and onto the Rickenbacker Causeway. The moon was coming up over Key Biscayne, spreading a creamy glow across the water. I pulled up in front of Tugboat Willie's. On the front porch a couple of old salts were debating the merits of rubber jigs—the Zara Spook versus the Mirr-Olure—for catching jack crevalle. Charlie got out and came around to the driver's side.

"Why would Nick Wolf appoint you to head the investigation? Why not one of his cronies, someone he could control?"

"Says he wants to do the right thing. Not even an appearance of a conflict of interest."

"You believe that?" Charlie asked.

I shrugged. "Why shouldn't I?"

"Timeo Danaos et dona ferentes."

"That's what I always say," I said.

Dr. Metcalf helped me out. "Loosely translated, 'Beware of an enemy bearing gifts.'"

Charlie nodded, then climbed into his mud-spattered pickup truck for the drive westward to the Glades. Pamela Metcalf had taken a cab from her hotel, so I graciously offered to drive her back. Her eyes shot a look toward Charlie's truck, as if to ask if I was trustworthy, but he was gone. Either she decided to risk it, or she couldn't get out of the shoulder harness, because she wordlessly stayed in her seat.

It was a short ride to the Grand Bay Hotel in Coconut Grove, but the doctor made it seem like a transatlantic flight. I mentioned the beauty of the moon and she said, "Umm." I remarked on the nighttime feeding habits of the turkey vultures, gliding above the sewage plant at Virginia Key, and she said, "Umm." When she gave me the same reply to the question of how long she'd be in town, I asked if she was practicing her mantra. That drew only silence, so I slipped a Beach Boys tape into the slot, and keeping time with palm slaps on the steering wheel, provided my own off-key praises to California girls, doubtlessly adding to the doctor's impression of me as a simpleton and rapscallion. To her credit, she never once complained about my singing or the dank evening air. When a few fat drops from a passing shower splattered our windshield, she never once asked me to put up the top. The wind blew her long hair straight back, and like a California girl without the tan—or the smile—she stared ahead into the nighttime breeze.

When I finally pulled under the canopy of the hotel, a teenage valet crept from the darkness and appraised the old yellow chariot.

"No shit, my old man used to talk about his 442," the kid announced, "but I never seen one."

I held him off and asked the doctor if she'd like a drink before retiring.

She studied me. "Whatever for?"

That one stumped me. "To . . . uh . . . wet the whistle. To talk."

"Talk? What about?"

"I don't know," I said defensively. "I don't plan that far ahead."

"I can see that. Then why invite me to share spirits?"

I thought of Jack Nicholson telling Shirley MacLaine that a stiff drink "might kill the bug you got up your ass." I thought of John Riggins, the great, wild running back of the Redskins, telling Justice Sandra Day O'Connor at a White House dinner to "loosen up, Sandy baby." But what I said was, "Because we can work together on the Diamond murder."

She paused long enough for me to toss the keys to the valet, and I escorted her to the glitzy bar on the mezzanine. The usual crowd was there, Colombian cowboys, businessmen delaying the inevitable confrontations at home, a collection of upper-middle-class snorters and pretenders driving leased Porsches, leaning close to young women in sequinned designer knockoffs.

The lady asked for Pimm's over lemonade, and the barman didn't bat an eye. He poured some red stuff into 7UP, added a slice of cucumber, and Pamela Metcalf nodded with appreciation after a dainty sip.

"Dr. Riggs is quite fond of you," the doctor said, as if she couldn't imagine why.

"And I of him."

"He said you used to play . . . rugby?"

"Football."

"Yes, we have your football on the telly now. Grown men in knickers with all that stuffing inside their clothing. Jumping onto each other with incredible aggression."

I smiled at her imaginative but entirely accurate definition of pro football.

"Freud conceived of aggression as a derivative of the death instinct," she added. "Others debate whether aggression is a primary drive itself or just a reaction to frustration."

"I just liked hitting people. It was fun."

She opened her eyes a little wider. The green shimmered in the muted lighting. She pursed her full lips and thought a private thought. I expected her to start taking notes, maybe send me a bill later.

"Fun?" she pronounced carefully, as if trying out a new word.

"Sure. The hitting, the contact. Tackling is fun, particularly a good, clean hit that knocks the wind out of the runner. The kind that jolts him, makes the crowd go *oooh*."

"The sounds of the crowd. Did it represent to you a woman's sighs, her moans of ecstasy?"

I didn't like where this was heading. "I think I can distinguish between the two."

"And this tackling people, did it make you feel bigger, more . . . manly?"

I laughed and nearly spilled my Grolsch. "Look, if you're going to tell me the NFL is full of closet queens . . ."

She ran a hand through her thick auburn hair, now tangled from the wind. "Why are you defensive about your masculinity?"

This was getting me nowhere. "Let me tell you a story," I said. "When I was a rookie, there was a big tight end on the Jets who was so tough he made Mike Ditka look like a pussycat. He liked to talk trash at the line. So I come in at outside linebacker late in the game, and my uniform is clean and white, and he's there all muddy and bloody, and yells out, 'Here comes the cherry.' Then the QB is calling signals and all I hear is the tight end saying, 'Hey, cherry, didn't they teach you how to put on your uniform in college? I can see your dick, and it's all shriveled up.' So just like somebody saying your shoes are untied, I look down, the ball is snapped, and the tight end slugs my helmet with a forearm that could ring the bell at Notre Dame."

She considered my story and stirred her red drink. "And do you attempt to compensate for this humiliation?"

I shook my head. "No, I just don't look at my dick unless absolutely necessary."

She tried to see if I was joking, and when she figured I was, gave me a full smile. "Do you really want my help or are you just hoping to charm your way into my room?" she asked.

"I think I have a significantly greater chance at the former."

"Dr. Riggs was right. You are smarter than you look."

That was as close to a compliment as I was going to get. A winsome lass on a sailboard—perhaps overcome by sunstroke—once compared my eyes to the azure waters off Bimini. Later, she tossed me over for a scuba instructor.

Pamela Metcalf declined a second drink and we looked at each other a moment, her thoughts imperceptible. She told me she was leaving for New York in the morning, a couple of network appearances, a book signing in the Doubleday store on Fifth Avenue, then back to England. I should call her if I learned anything or if there was another killing.

"Look for messages," she said.

"Besides ones in lipstick?"

"Frankly, I'm puzzled by the reference to Jack the Ripper. Jack was a disorganized murderer, a slasher who was extremely violent and quite messy. He stalked women he did not know and used force, not persuasion, to subdue them."

"So the killer's tossing a curveball?"

"A curve . . ."

"A red herring, a bum steer."

"Perhaps. But even if the killer is tossing a . . . bum steer, the message is still meaningful. Whoever wrote it is well read, perhaps an amateur historian, or someone who knows a great deal about classic criminal cases, stories of law enforcement, that sort of thing."

"Like the honorable state attorney," I mused, mostly to myself.

"If that were the case, the crime would not be motiveless, would it? If the Diamond girl was his chippy and he killed her, there would have to be a motive. But if it's a random killing, the work of a serial murderer, you'll know soon enough."

"How?"

"Because there'll be another one presently, won't there?"

I hadn't thought about that before, but now I did. Looking for a little excitement with the gun-and-badge set was one thing, hunting a serial killer was something else again. Serial killers are lifetime obsessions of guys with little offices and big file drawers. It takes forever to nab one. Isn't that what makes them serial killers, unsolved murders over several years? What had I gotten into?

"I don't know how to catch those guys," I admitted.

Dr. Metcalf smiled faintly. "Don't feel sorry for yourself, Mr. Lassiter. The police are always complaining that serial killers are so difficult to apprehend because there is no connection between victims and no apparent motives. But they do leave clues, and usually they are quite careless. Often they contact the police or stand in the crowd that gathers at the scene."

"So they want to be caught?"

"No, a common misconception. Part of the thrill is outwitting the police and reliving the crime. There was an ambulance driver who would abduct young women, kill them, call the police, then race back to the hospital so he would get the call to pick up the body."

While I thought that over she smoothed her skirt in a gesture even my nonpsychoanalytic mind could understand.

"Thank you for the ride and the drink, Mr. Lassiter," she said with British formality, and stood up to leave.

"All my friends call me Jake . . . Pamela," I said.

She rewarded me with a second smile and then extended a finely tapered white hand. "Good evening, Jake. And good luck."

The hand was cool, the shake firm. She didn't ask me to share the view from her room, so I headed out the front where my 442 was parked in a space of honor next to a Rolls. The hood was still hot, and the gas tank was a nudge lower than an hour earlier.

I looked hard at the valet.

"Your shocks are a little soft on the turns," he said sheepishly.

I gave him five bucks. "You're telling me."

CHAPTER 5

Joining the Club

It was one of those muggy June days with fifteen hours of daylight but hardly any sunshine. A tropical depression hung over the Gulf of Mexico and raised the blood pressure of Miami's frothy weather guys. Come six and eleven, they show us their color radar and satellite photos, their computerized maps and digital barometers. They blather about wind speeds and waterspouts and reveal what we already know: baby, it's hot outside.

It wasn't even eight A.M., but already my little coral-rock pillbox was stifling. The storm in the Gulf had sucked all the wind from the Florida Straits. Ten days of rain and a month of inattention had left my overgrown yard a jungle that could get me fined if the zoning inspectors weren't busy collecting cash from condo builders who pour rotten slabs.

My house sits in the shade of chinaberry and live-oak trees just off Kumquat in the old part of Coconut Grove. It was built before air-conditioning and has plenty of cross ventilation. But when the

41

wind stops blowing, and the heavy gray sky sags over the bay and the Glades, the old ceiling fans don't do the trick. One of these days I'm going to break down and put in central air. Sure, and maybe get a rooftop dish, a combination fax and photocopy machine, maybe an outdoor whirlpool and an indoor sauna.

Adiós, forty-dollar electricity bills.

Hola, the Grove trendy set.

I wore canvas shorts and nothing else and stood on my rear porch surveying the expanse of my estate—an eighth of an acre, give or take an inch or two. The neighborhood was quiet. The one-story stucco number hidden behind the poinciana trees belonged to Geoffrey Thompson, who wouldn't be up until noon. He roamed the city streets each night as a free-lance cameraman, shooting videos of drug busts, race riots, and fatal car crashes. A budding entrepreneur, Geoffrey created his own industry when he learned that none of the local TV stations employed photo teams between midnight and eight A.M. When he was drunk enough, Geoffrey would show the outtakes considered too gruesome even for Miami's bloodthirsty viewers.

Next door there was no sign of life at Phoebe's place, which was exactly what it was called in an ad in *Florida Swingers* magazine. Phoebe had bright red hair and occasionally counted on her fingers, as she did the time she appeared at my door and asked if she could borrow three—no, make it four—condoms. Robert and Robert, who lived together and owned Robert's—what else—Art Gallery, were up and around, hauling out wine bottles and trimming their hibiscus hedge. A regular slice of Americana, that's my Mia-muh.

I dropped into the crabgrass and did my morning push-ups, fifty regular, then twenty one-armed, first right, then left. I rolled onto my back, brought my knees toward my face, and worked through a hundred stomach crunches. *C'mon, Lassiter,* Coach Sandusky yelled from some faraway field. *Get in shape.* The grass tickled my bare back and the sweat rolled down my chest. Overhead, an unseen laughing gull mocked me with its raucous call.

The ringing telephone was an excuse to declare victory in my battle to resurrect semiglories of the past. It was Granny Lassiter calling to tell me a thirty-pound snook was swimming figure-eights under an Islamorada bridge, calling my name. I told her I had a murder to solve but I'd help her eat Mr. Snook if she could catch him.

She wasn't impressed by my work and allowed as how she would catch the fish without me, but wanted to be sporting and land that sucker on eight-pound test line, using live finger mullet for bait.

Granny wasn't my grandmother, but there was some relationship on my father's side, great-aunt maybe. She raised me in the very house of Dade County pine and coral rock where I now lived. When Coconut Grove became too chic, she gave me the house and headed for the Keys, where she fishes and fusses and makes a decent home brew, if you're partial to drinking liquid methane. She's the only family I have. My father was a shrimper who was killed in a barroom brawl in Marathon when I was five years old. He had handled three bikers with his bare hands before a fourth jammed a push dagger into his jugular. Today, when I think of him, I remember his thick wrists and red, rawboned hands. My earliest memory: dangling from those poleax wrists as he would lift me off the floor.

My mother I don't remember at all. All Granny told me was that she had bleached her hair almost white and, while waiting tables in Key West, ran off with a curly-haired stranger headed for the Texas oil fields. So I never called anyone Mom, but for as long as I can remember there's always been a Granny. She taught me how to fish and how to live without doing too much damage along the way.

When I was fifteen—towheaded and suntanned and already two hundred pounds—the hormones were pounding in my ears, and I would shake the little house by jolting the pine-slab walls I considered a make-believe blocking sled. Granny didn't complain; she just hauled me off to the high-school football field, where a couple of Gainesville-bound seniors whupped me up and down. The next year, I was whupping 'most everybody else, and the recruiters came calling from just about every college in the southeast. I visited a few campuses where the fraternity boys laughed at my cutoff jeans, dilapidated deck shoes, and rawhide necklace with the genuine shark's tooth. I didn't have much in common with the players either. They were generally engaged in drunken wrestling matches followed by pissing contests—distance, duration, and accuracy.

One day my senior year in high school, Granny grilled a mess of mangrove snapper with Vidalia onions for a coach with a Brooklyn accent who kept talking about books and classes. I wanted to hear about bowl games and cheerleaders, but he was yammering away in this funny voice about SAT scores and graduation rates. Granny smiled and served him an extra slab of her key lime pie, and I went off to Penn State, where I survived frostbite, aced American Theater 461, and stayed out of jail.

I was a decent enough college player, but the stopwatch doesn't lie, and the NFL scouts could take a nap while I ran the forty. Since then, I've come to figure I must have been the three hundred thirty-seventh best player in the nation my senior year. This bit of mathematical logic stems from the fact that the pros drafted three hundred thirty-six players, none of them named Lassiter. I packed my spikes and gray practice shorts in what was then a not-yet-antique convertible and drove south. I caught on with the hometown Dolphins as a free agent, barely surviving each cut, playing second string, earning my keep by wreaking havoc on kickoffs, and occasionally starting when the star weakside linebacker was in drug rehab. When I realized I wasn't bound for the Hall of Fame (or even a league pension), I started taking night law classes. I had seen Gregory Peck playing Atticus Finch and figured I knew what lawyering was all about. After finally passing the bar exam the third try—the first time coming two days after knee surgery and hefty doses of Darvon, the second after generous rations of Grolsch—I concluded there are no more Atticus Finches. Today's lawyers are slaves to computerized time sheets, and, rather than fighting for justice, spend their days punching voluminous pleadings out of word processors and sleeping through endless pretrial depositions. But they seldom stand in front of juries and plead for *justice*, which, if it is kin to the *law*, is a distant cousin, at best.

I joined the public defender's office, where I soon discovered that my clients were not necessarily saintly just because they were impoverished. Most of them went to prison, got early release because of overcrowding, and became repeat customers in the Jake Lassiter legal merry-go-round. Then I joined the downtown firm of Harman and Fox, where I became another paper-pushing civil trial lawyer, until Nick Wolf called me back to the criminal-law jungle, this time representing the state.

I showered and put on a seersucker suit, but the sweat continued to flow. I poured some orange juice and grabbed a fresh mango, green and red on the outside, sweeter than a peach inside. The neighborhood is overflowing with mangoes and lichee nuts. Peel the nuts, slice the mango, chop a tart carambola into star-shaped pieces, and you've got a fine breakfast. No preservatives, no caffeine.

Inside the ancient Oldsmobile, the cracked leather felt slick and the carpeting smelled of mildew. I put the top down and pretended that the soggy air cooled me. I headed up Miami Avenue under an umbrella of red poinciana trees. I passed the house that once belonged to a client, a doctor who killed, and I was there when he crumbled under the weight of the guilt and the shame.

Charlie Riggs had helped me then, had taught me how to speak for the dead. He had been the county medical examiner for so long, people swore he began his career digging musket balls out of bodies at Bull Run. He still reads the first forensic medicine textbook, *Questiones medico legales*, in its original Latin. He can determine the time of death by algor mortis, livor mortis, and rigor mortis—the temperature, color, and stiffness of death. When an inexperienced assistant ME found sunflower seeds in the stomach of a dead banker who died with a smile on his face, Charlie knew that death was by horribly painful strychnine poisoning. The smile was *risus sardonicus*, a sardonic grin produced by contortions of facial muscles. The sunflower seeds were the remnants of rat poison, and a sharp-eyed hardware-store clerk soon identified the grieving widow with the million-dollar insurance policy as the town's leading pesticide purchaser.

Charlie Riggs knows so much about so many things. I could never figure how a guy who spent his life hollowing out lifeless shells could understand the living so well. There must be lots of canoe makers who know everything about in-shoot wounds and lividity and blood typing. They help the cops figure the when and how of death, and sometimes, piecing together all their clues, they even find the murderer, the who. But if you don't have bullet fragments and a matching gun, or latent prints and a matching hand, you'd better know the why to figure the who. That's why I need you, Charlie Riggs. You bearded old wizard, I need you *again*.

"Jeez, get a load of that suit," Cindy said, fishing a pen out of her rust-colored, hypercurled hair. "Why's it all crinkly?"

"It's cool," I said.

She shook her head, each concrete curl staying put. "Co-ol, *el jefe*, it ain't. You look like a Rotarian."

Cindy had been my secretary in the PD's office and came with me downtown. Her shorthand was indecipherable, her typing haphazard, and her filing disorganized. But she was smart and loyal and could sweet-talk a judge's assistant into an early trial date, and she protected me from the political piranhas in the law firm. She was also a pal.

Cindy's desk was covered with unfiled pleadings and unanswered memos.

"Any messages?" I asked.

She picked up a handful of while-you-were-out memos. "The newsboys are going bonkers over the Diamond murder. All the local stations called, plus your pals at the *Journal*, a reporter from Reuters, and somebody from *Broadcasting* magazine who wants to know if there might be terrorist plots against television personalities."

I looked at the messages but didn't plan to return the calls. What could I say? We had no leads, and if we did, we wouldn't put them on the front page. I couldn't even disclose why Nick Wolf had appointed me as a special prosecutor. An overworked office, according to the party line. But Cindy was right. The news media would hound us until the case was solved. If it went on too long, they would start wondering about the competence of the ex–football player, ex–public defender, ex–a-lot-of-things appointed to handle the case.

We average a murder a day in Dade County, but few are deemed truly newsworthy. Your average Saturday-night, liquored-up stabbing over a woman or a card game gets you two paragraphs inside the local section, just above the ads for the all-nude body-shampoo parlors in Lauderdale. But this was different. This was one of their own. And judging from the hype on the local stations—a freeze-frame close-up of Michelle Diamond with Verdi's *Requiem* in the background—you'd have thought we lost Edward R. Murrow instead of a second-rate interviewer who also read commercials on a five P.M. fluff show.

The *Journal* played it straight. The Diamond death shared page one of the local section with an exposé that revealed that a sizable percentage of our taxicabs are repainted stolen cars.

"Anything else?" I asked Cindy.

"Yeah. The managing partner wants to know why you let yourself get appointed to be Nick Wolf's flunky."

"The old man have something against fulfilling my civic duty?"

"No, something against a case that pays only a third of your normal hourly rate. He wants a written response, with copies to the New Business Committee, the Senior Council, and the Allocation Committee."

"What else?"

Cindy followed me into my office. I opened the vertical blinds and stared at Biscayne Bay three hundred feet below. Plump gray thunderheads hung motionless over Miami Beach. In fifteen knots of easterly, the bay crinkles like aluminum foil. Today, not a ripple.

"I have the poop on Compu-Mate," she said with a sly smile. She handed me a folder containing some newspaper clippings and a printout from the secretary of state. "But boss, if you're that horny, I could fix you up."

"What?"

"Rather than get hooked up with some loser . . ."

"What're you talking about?"

"My girlfriend, Dottie the Disco Queen. She likes big guys who aren't quite with it."

"What about her herpes?"

"No *problema*. In remission."

"Maybe another time," I said. "Anything else?"

"Mr. Foot-in-the-Mouth called."

"Symington? He hasn't replaced me?"

"No such luck." She handed me a bunch of newspaper stories on computer paper. "A messenger delivered these a few minutes ago."

"I'm worried about Carl Hutchinson, all that invective in his column," Symington Foote said when I returned his call.

"You're just a little gun-shy right now," I told the publisher, reassurance coating my voice like honey.

"But these names he's calling Commissioner Goldberg. She's very popular with the voters. And voters are jurors."

He was right about that. Maria Teresa Gonzalez-Goldberg—born in Cuba, schooled in a convent, married to a Jewish cop with an adopted black child—was a formidable politician. She had swept into office two years earlier with eighty-six percent of the vote. She then redecorated her office in teak, chrome, leather, and glass to the tune of one hundred fifty thousand dollars of taxpayers' money. At a time the county couldn't afford to repair backed-up toilets in public housing projects.

"Marie Antoinette," Foote was saying. "He called her Marie Antoinette!"

"Fair comment," I advised.

"Said she ought to redecorate a cell at Marianna Institution for Women."

"Rhetorical hyperbole," I counseled confidently.

"Said the 'crossover candidate' became the 'carnivorous commissioner, feeding on the flesh of the poor.'"

"A bit grisly," I admitted, "but she's a public official."

"Seems I heard that before," Foote said.

I spent the rest of the morning on the newspaper's work. I advised the business manager to accept the advertisement from the airport hotel that promised "freedom fighter" discounts to smugglers aiding the Nicaraguan contras. I told the photo editor that the picture of the model wearing a bra with a built-in holster for a Beretta was not an invasion of privacy and accurately portrayed Florida's new concealed-weapons law. I told the city editor to ignore complaints that property values would be hurt by the local map showing Dade County murders by zip code. Finally, I told the food editor that the grilled alligator recipe omitted cayenne pepper, and then I had lunch.

CHAPTER 6

The Lady
and the Jockey

I wanted to get to Compu-Mate before the afternoon storms. In the summer, the rain begins at 3:17 P.M. or thereabouts, every day. For an hour or so, gully washers and palmetto pounders flood the streets. Drops form *inside* the canvas top of my old convertible, then plop one by one onto my head.

I aimed north on Okeechobee Road, storm clouds gathering, traffic crawling. Our highways have not caught up with our growth and never will. We built a high-speed rail system too late and too small. We are a great urban sprawl, Miami-Lauderdale-Palm Beach, four million people squeezed between the ocean and the Everglades. We are low on water and electricity, but high on asphalt and cement. Our public officials are beholden to predatory developers who ply them with greenbacks and concoct their own vocabulary.

Creeping overpopulation is "growth."

Building spindly condos on Indian burial grounds is "progress."

Environmentalists are "doomsayers."

So we bulldoze trees, fill swamps, drain the aquifer, and then we build on every square inch, erecting a concrete landscape of fast-food palaces, serve-yourself gas stations, and tawdry shopping centers. Their signs beckon us from the blazing pavement. Pizza parlors, video rentals, gun shops, and a thousand other fringe businesses hoping to hang on for another month's rent.

Compu-Mate was in a renovated warehouse in Hialeah, a city of ticky-tack duplexes and stucco houses with plaster statues of the Virgin Mary planted in front lawns. In the last thirty years, Hialeah has been transformed from a cracker town of Panhandle and Alabama immigrants to a new home for Cuban refugees. Not long ago, a Florida governor named Martinez was forced to suspend an indicted Hialeah mayor named Martinez and replace him with a city councilman named Martinez. None of the men was related. Hispanics now are the majority population group in the cities of Miami and Hialeah and are approaching fifty percent countywide. Within the community, there are old *exilados*, who dream of returning to a *Cuba Libre*, Cubanzo rednecks, who drive pickup trucks festooned with American and Cuban flags, and Yubans, Yuppie Cuban professionals downtown. They are, in fact, like every other ethnic group, a diverse lot that has added considerably to the community.

I parked next to an outdoor café where men with leathery skin smoked cigars and drank espresso from tiny plastic cups. Next door, three teenagers were making a mess of a transmission, pulled out of a twenty-year-old Chevy propped onto concrete blocks.

I already knew a lot about Compu-Mate. I knew it was the latest way to profit from people's fears of loneliness. Like-minded consenting adults just a whir and buzz away, courtesy of your personal computer. Talk sweet, talk dirty, titillate your partner, and tickle your fancy until you get a phone number and address. Then cross your fingers, take a deep breath, and wait for the truth. The guy who called himself "Paul Newman look-alike" has the gray hair, all right, but the blue eyes are milky, a paunch hangs over his belt, and he's three months behind on the alimony. "Buxom blonde looking for fun" means overweight and bleached, a manic-depressive.

I had some background on Max and Roberta Blinderman, president and secretary of Compu-Mate, Inc., a Florida for-profit corporation. Previously, they operated a video dating service that went belly up, and before that, a modeling studio that left a trail of unpaid bills and unfinished portfolios. As far as Cindy's research showed, Roberta had no criminal record. Max had been a fair-to-middling jockey twenty years ago, once nearly winning the Flamingo Stakes at Hialeah before getting suspended in a horse-doping scheme. Lately he had pleaded guilty to bouncing some checks, was put on probation, and made restitution. Two other penny-ante cases: a mail-fraud case was nolle-prossed, and a buying-receiving charge was dropped when the state couldn't prove the jewelry was stolen. By local standards, he was clean enough to run for mayor.

The office was no-frills, a Formica counter up front, a green metal desk in back. Next to the desk was a decent-sized, freestanding computer that was probably leased month to month. No waiting room, no sofa, no friendly green plants. A man sat at the desk staring into a video display terminal. A woman stood at the counter licking stamps and pasting them onto envelopes—monthly bills to the customers, I figured.

"I'd like to sign up," I told the woman behind the counter.

"This ain't the army," she said, putting down her envelopes and shoving a form in front of my face.

She was six feet tall and seemed to like it. Her dark eyes were spaced wide and the lashes were long, black as sin, and well tended. The complexion, which had that cocoa-butter, coppery-tanned look with a healthy dose of moisturizers, creams, powders, and blushes, was smoothly sanguine. The black hair was layered and purposely messed, a wild look. Her nose was thin and straight and so perfect it might have cost five grand at a clinic in Bal Harbour. Her body was long and lean with some muscle development in the shoulders and small breasts that were uncaged under a white cotton halter top. The top of a denim skirt was visible below her flat, browned tummy, but her legs were hidden behind the counter.

I licked the end of the pencil like Art Carney playing Ed Norton, made a whirling motion with my right arm, and began filling out the form in block letters.

"Most of our clients just punch us up on their modems and do the paperwork by filling out the form on their computer screen," she said.

"My modem's in the shop for an oil change."

If she thought I was funny, she kept it to herself. She just watched my seersuckered self as I filled in the blanks. I wrote my real name and address, chose "Stick Shift" as my handle, used my old jersey number as a secret password, and pretended to struggle with the rest. When I was done, I handed her the form. She scanned it and scowled.

"This ain't a dining club," she said.

"Or the army," I agreed.

"What's 'rare steak and cold beer' supposed to mean?"

"It asked my preferences," I said, putting some Iowa corn into my voice.

"Sheesh. Your preferences in *bed*, Gomer. Are you straight, gay, or bi?"

"Straight as an arrow, slim. Wanna see?"

"In your dreams. Hey, next blank you skipped. You go for French or Greek?"

"*No habla* nothin' but English."

"Oh brother! You got any fetishes? B and D, S and M, water sports?"

"I'm a pretty decent windsurfer," I admitted.

She rolled her eyes toward the ceiling. "Where you been, the friggin' North Pole?"

"Maui, Aruba, the Baja," I told her. "North Pole's too cold, even with a dry suit."

"Listen, Ricky Retardo, I ain't got all day. You don't fill in the blanks, the computer will spit out your application, so you gotta tell me what you like. Now, Greek, that means bum fucking, get it?"

"Even the poor got a right to get laid," I said. "It's in the Constitution."

She narrowed her dark eyes and gave me a sideways look. "You know what French is, right?"

I didn't say *oui, madame*. I just gave her my big, dumb-guy look. It isn't hard to do.

"Like in the poem," she said, "'The French, they are a funny race. They fight with their feet and fuck with their face.' Get it?"

I scrunched my face into its genius-at-thought mode. "I get part of it."

"Part of it?"

"I mean, fighting with their feet, I get. . . ."

She turned toward the back where the man was now hunched over the keyboard of the computer. "Max! C'mere."

A little guy, all wires and gristle in black pants, black knit shirt, and white patent-leather loafers. A tattoo of a snake showed green on a veined, browned forearm. A worm of a mustache wriggled under his nose. He squinted at me through suspicious eyes. All he needed was a switchblade to pick his teeth, and he could have been a small-time grifter in *Guys and Dolls*.

"Yow, Bobbie," he answered.

"Whyn't you help Mister . . ."

"Lassiter," I announced proudly.

They traded places. Her high heels clackety-clacked as she legged it toward the back. Sleek, fine legs with a comely curve of the calf undulating with each step. As she slinked by Max he said, "Foot Long's just about got Naughty Nurse's panties off."

She sat down at the desk and peered into the monitor. "Nurse's been putting out for everybody and their cousin," she called back.

Max took his time examining my application. I wondered if anyone ever failed the entrance exam. "You can listen in?" I asked.

"Huh?"

I pointed toward the computer where Bobbie sat, her long, lean body bent toward the screen.

"Someone's gotta be the sys-op," he said. "Work the panel in case there's a glitch on-line. We can tap into any talky-talk, just like Southern Bell."

"You must hear—or read—it all."

"Yow. Till after while, it puts you to sleep. Like how many ways can they describe it?"

He returned to the form, moving his lips and tracing each line with a finger. "Say, you were just kidding here, huh?"

"Yeah."

"Bobbie don't have much of a sense of humor. Comes from having a hard life as a kid. You gotta make allowances with a filly like that." He grinned and showed me two rows of shopping-center dental work. "You're a straight shooter looking for old-fashioned cooze in the missionary position, yow?"

"Yow," I answered right back at him.

He gave me a temporary membership card and a book of rules. I gave him a twenty-dollar bill.

"Ever have any trouble with your clients?" I asked.

The word "trouble" made the mustache twitch. "Whaddaya mean?"

"Like any women complain about guys putting the make on 'em, they don't like what's being offered?"

His eyes had put up a shield. "No trouble. Woman gets hassled, she can bug out of the call. She invites a guy over or goes out with him, that's her business. We don't give no guarantees."

"You keep records of the calls?"

He sneaked a peek at the wall where his occupational license was taped over a crack. Probably figured me for a city inspector and wondered when I'd show him my palm.

I pointed back to his main computer. "All the calls stored in there?"

"Hell no! I wouldn't clog up our hard memory with that shit."

"How many members you have?"

"Three hundred fifty men. Almost two hundred women. Hey, we're a member of the BBB."

"So what's stored in there?"

"It's programmed to record how many times members call in and how long they talk. After fifty hours, you gotta renew."

"So it records who they talk to. . . ."

"That'd be an invasion of privacy," he said with undue formality.

"But it could be done, if you wanted to know who a client spoke with, say, two nights ago?"

"The calls are coded numerically. It could be—"

"What the hell!" Bobbie Blinderman demanded, towering over Max the Jockey. "Just who the hell are you, buster?" In her bare feet now, she was three inches shorter, but no friendlier. She had silently prowled back to the counter from her position as gatekeeper of erotica and her ebony eyes glared at me.

I gave her a daffy grin. "Just a lonely guy—"

"Get your jollies somewhere else!" she ordered, pointing toward the door.

"With a grand-jury subpoena," I added, pulling a blue-backed paper out of my back pocket and sliding it across the counter. Max stared at it a moment, then picked it up as if afraid to leave prints. Bobbie looked straight at me with those long-lashed eyes, the sanguine complexion a tone redder.

"Flatfoot faggot," she hissed.

"*Your* preference?" I politely inquired.

CHAPTER 7

Ladyfingers

Alejandro Rodriguez sat in the upholstered chair, a Smith & Wesson .38 in one hand, a Glock nine-millimeter in the other. He put down the .38, fondled the Glock, and sniffed at its oily barrel with his squashed policeman's nose. Then he picked up the .38 and did the same thing. He shifted the gun hand to hand and repeated the ritual with the Glock.

He wore black oxfords with rubber soles, khaki pants, a blue shirt unbuttoned at the neck, and a polyester blue blazer. A paunch from too much desk riding hung over his belt. Even a nearsighted three-time loser could spot him as a cop.

Rodriguez hefted both guns, then put down the .38 again. He pushed a magazine into the plastic grip of the Glock and pulled back the spring-loaded slide, smiling at the reassuring click.

"*Caramba!* Seventeen rounds instead of six. High-velocity steel jackets. Only eight pounds of pull. When the hell's Metro gonna get us these babies?"

Nick Wolf sat at his polished mahogany desk, head down, eyes scanning a file. "Just what I need. One of your rookies pumping an innocent bystander with seventeen slugs instead of six."

I cleared my throat.

Nick Wolf kept reading.

Five minutes later he put down the file. By then I was impressed with what an important guy he was, just as I was supposed to be. "Hey, Jake, here's one for you downtown mouthpieces," he said, winking at Rodriguez. "A man asks a lawyer his fee, and the lawyer says a hundred bucks for three questions. 'Isn't that awfully steep?' the man asks. 'Sure is,' the lawyer says, 'now what's your final question?'"

I laughed and stored that away for the next partners' meeting. Rodriguez pointed the black plastic gun at the wall where a color photo showed Vice-President Quayle shaking Nick Wolf's hand. "Miami's had the Glock two years already," the detective whined.

The county cops hate it when the city boys get something first. Doesn't matter what. Sharper uniforms, faster cars, or looser women.

"Glock, schlock," Wolf said. "Stop worrying about your fire-power and solve a few crimes." He swung his chair toward me. "That's all the cops want these days, technology. Computers and helicopters and automatic weapons. I could get a dozen more prosecutors with what they spend for one armored vehicle."

I nodded agreeably, still waiting.

"Of course, you high-rise lawyers don't have those worries, eh, Jake?" Wolf asked.

I was used to this. Little darts to remind me I was no longer a player in the criminal-justice game. Two hundred pending criminal cases, a trial every morning, sometimes another in the afternoon. You meet your witnesses five minutes before they testify by shouting their names in the corridor. The pay is lousy, the office drab, but there's a camaraderie among foxhole buddies slogging through the mud. When you leave and your pals and adversaries stay behind, they stick it to you. *Hey, nice suit, life's okay downtown, huh?* Some of them never leave the grimy catacombs because they can't cut it on the outside. Others, like Nick Wolf, could write their own tickets downtown but choose to stay. They feel vaguely superior to those who escape to cushy partnerships in skyscrapers with luncheon clubs and ocean views. They have a right to.

"Right now I've got lots of worries, Nick," I said.

"Hey, Jake," Rodriguez said, "what's the difference between a porcupine and two lawyers in a Porsche?"

"Dunno," I said.

"With a porcupine, the pricks are on the outside."

Having been taught etiquette by Granny Lassiter, I smiled politely.

Rodriguez laughed so hard at his own joke he nearly dropped the gun.

I sat there, still waiting for the warm-up act to end.

Finally Wolf stuck a finger in his shirt collar, stretched his brawny neck, smiled his winning smile, and said, "Jake, I thought you'd want to fill me in on your progress."

"What?"

"On the Diamond murder. That's why I asked for you and Hot Rod."

"Forget it," I said. "I'm not reporting to you. Either it's my investigation, or get someone else."

It crossed his face then, a moment of doubt or regret. "Easy, Jake. I'm not trying to interfere—"

"Good. I'll take your statement while I'm here. But you're not getting copies of Rodriguez's reports or any part of the file. Understood?"

He grinned at me as if we shared some secret. Maybe my toughness was just an act and he knew it because he played the same game. "Understood," he said, still smiling.

"I met Michelle through Prissy," Nick Wolf told me. "Priscilla, my soon-to-be ex-wife. They belonged to some bullshit women's awareness group."

I nodded and pulled out Rodriguez's inventory of Michelle's apartment. Her bookshelves were a road map to her personal life. *Smart Cookies Don't Crumble. How to Love a Difficult Man. Men: An Owner's Manual. Men Who Hate Women and the Women Who Love Them. The Secrets Men Keep.* The rest of her library was an amalgam of get-in-shape, dress-for-success, and get-rich-quick books with a smattering of soft-core paperbacks on women's sexual fantasies.

5 8

Wolf turned toward the window. "I came home early one day and there were a bunch of them in the living room. Yackety-yacking, sipping tea and eating, whaddayacallit . . . pussy food."

"Quiche?" Rodriguez guessed.

"No, that lady-shit . . ."

"Ladyfingers," I suggested.

"Yeah, picking 'em up real dainty so not to mess up the nail polish, sitting around complaining about men, comparing orgasms, who the fuck knows . . ."

"Amazing you and Prissy don't see eye to eye on things," I offered. "You're so sensitive to women's concerns."

He hunched his massive shoulders and glared at me. "What the fuck's that supposed to mean?"

I didn't answer, so he continued: "One of the women was this cute, short number I recognized from TV."

"Michelle Diamond," I said.

He nodded. "Prissy introduced us, real sly like she was getting a kick out of it. So we started going out. Prissy knew all about it, told me Michelle was early in her development, but later she'd bust my balls. I said that was okay, I was used to it."

"Was Michelle seeing anyone else?"

"Not that I know of. All she did was work, shop, and screw, and screwing wasn't her favorite."

It had been three days since they'd been together, Wolf said. They talked by phone the night before she was killed. It wasn't serious, just a mutually enjoyable physical relationship.

"She called herself my transition woman," Wolf said.

"What did you call her?"

"Look, she wasn't that important to me, okay. She was a young one on the make who wanted to play in the majors. She was an okay-looking babe who wore too much makeup and was a halfway decent lay, and I'm real sorry she got aced. All right?"

"What did you talk about?"

"Talk?"

"Yeah. What two people do to communicate thanks to some magical connection between the brain and the mouth."

"I don't know. Her career, my career, whether she wanted a pillow under her ass."

"That's it? Did she want more out of the relationship?"

"Hey, great question, counselor," he said, lacing his voice with sarcasm. "What are you, Dear Abby, or that pygmy . . ."

"Did she want commitment?" I asked.

"Dr. Ruth," Rodriguez said.

"What do you think, that Michelle was pressuring me to divorce Prissy and marry her, so I got pissed off and killed her? What kind of asshole are you, Lassiter?"

"A duly appointed grand-jury kind," I said.

"Then get the fuck busy investigating and stop bothering me."

If he expected me to get up and leave, he had a long wait. I just sat there looking at him while he went back to work, scanning files, signing papers. Rodriguez continued playing with his guns, pretending to shoot Wolf's plaques off the wall, sixteen times without reloading.

"If you don't have time now, Mr. State Attorney, I'll issue a subpoena for you. If you refuse to waive immunity, the papers will love it."

He stopped signing, dropped his pen in disgust, and looked up. "Fire when ready, Jake. Take your best shot."

"You're missing the point, Nick. I'm just gathering data, trying to figure out who Michelle Diamond was."

"Then let me save you some time. She was a ballsy broad who wanted to get ahead in TV land. She wanted to meet the politicos. She wanted tips about corruption probes. She wanted her bottom rubbed by the state attorney. Hey, I knew she was blowing smoke up my ass, but it didn't feel half bad."

"Anything else about the two of you?"

"Nothing much. She said she wanted to spend a weekend with me 'cause we'd never done that, learn all about me."

"You ever do it?"

"It would have been this weekend," he said, lowering his eyes. I watched him a moment and tried to see beyond the press stories, the macho shield he had erected. There was a part of him, I thought, that was touched and angered by her death. Homicide detectives say they can feel it, that there's a difference between a witness who bears guilt and one who feels loss at a death. Though he tried to hide his emotions, Nick Wolf, it seemed to me, felt loss all the way.

I sat there a while longer and thumbed through Rodriguez's report. The building manager said Michelle was a quiet tenant. Few visitors. A husky man fitting Wolf's description would come over late, leave early the next morning, his Chrysler illegally parked on Ocean Drive. None of her friends reported anything strange in her behavior. She had not complained of threats. Nothing out of the ordinary her last days on earth.

I told Rodriguez I wanted to talk to him alone. Wolf suggested his conference room, a place with more bugs than a Fourth of July picnic. Instead, we took the elevator down to the courtroom level of the Justice Building. A bailiff unlocked a door and we sat in a holding cell, our words drowned out by the cacophony of inmates yelling for their lawyers, mothers, girlfriends, all protesting their innocence at majestic decibel levels.

"Got Whitson's autopsy and lab reports yesterday," Rodriguez said. "Death by manual strangulation, just like Doc Riggs said. No evidence of sperm or seminal fluid in the vagina, plus her diaphragm was found in the bathroom drawer, dry as toast."

"So, no rape and no consensual intercourse, either."

"Right, only thing out of sync is that substantial vaginal secretions indicate sexual activity in close proximity to death."

"Find a vibrator, that sort of thing?"

He shrugged. "No. Maybe just thinking of Nick's dick was enough to wet her panties."

"What else you have?"

"Still working on the computer stuff," Rodriguez said, leaning close to block out the noise. He handed me a printout of the directories from the computer's hard memory.

COMPU-MATE	*06/26/90*	*00:03*
RECIPES	*02/12/90*	*10:35*
X-MAS LIST	*12/17/89*	*23:18*
TO-DO LIST	*06/22/90*	*06:24*
LETTERS	*05/02/90*	*21:35*
INVST-1	*06/25/90*	*23:56*
CUES	*08/29/89*	*20:12*

MAKEUP	11/02/89	08:20
VOICE	10/20/89	21:45
GOALS	05/03/90	22:49

"Not much there," he said. "The first five categories are all personal stuff. We read the letters. Family mostly. The last four are all work-related. Tips on getting ahead, that kind of thing."

A huge, bald black man in the next cell banged his hand on the bars. Our cell shook. "Ain't no mugger. Been framed by the *Man*," he yelled, looking at Rodriguez.

"Get yourself a good lawyer," I suggested.

"They never seen me do it, got no ID," the man wailed.

"That's a good defense," I said, hoping to quiet him down.

"It was way too dark in that alley," he proclaimed.

"Clients always say too much," I told Rodriguez.

I looked at the document again. "Have you printed out the files in each directory?"

"You want 'em all? They're mostly crap."

"I want Compu-Mate as soon as you can get it. What's INVST-1?"

"Don't know exactly. Thought maybe it was some investment software, you know, keep track of your stocks. But the only file in the directory is a list of questions, like some quiz or something."

He handed me another printout.

1. WHO GAVE THE ORDERS TO WALK ALONG THE DIKE PRIOR TO ENTERING THE VILLAGE OF DAK SUT?
2. AFTER THE MEDIC AND RADIOMAN WERE KILLED, WHAT WAS THE STATE OF DISCIPLINE OF YOUR MEN?
3. WHEN YOUR PLATOON ENTERED THE VILLAGE OF DAK SUT ON JANUARY 9, 1968, WHAT ORDERS DID YOU GIVE?
4. WAS THERE EVIDENCE OF NVA OR VC IN THE VILLAGE?
5. WERE THE VILLAGERS ARMED, AND IF SO, DID THEY THREATEN YOUR PLATOON?

*6. WERE ANY VILLAGERS WOUNDED OR KILLED BY
   YOUR MEN?*
7. WHAT HAPPENED TO YOUR TRANSLATOR?
*8. THE LAST TIME YOU SAW LIEUTENANT FERGUSON
   ALIVE, WAS HE*

"She didn't finish the last question," Rodriguez said.

I looked back at the printout of directories. "What time did the ME say she was killed?"

"Around midnight on the twenty-fifth. Give or take two hours either way."

"Had to be after midnight," I said, examining the first document. "She finished working on the INVST-1 file at four minutes till midnight and logged out of COMPU-MATE at three minutes past. Her last conscious thoughts might have been about Lieutenant Ferguson, whoever he is, or some playmate on the computer."

"How you gonna find the lieutenant?"

"By figuring out what she was investigating."

"Huh?"

"It's not an investment file. INVST-1. Her first *investigation.* Something about Vietnam."

A jailer came in and emptied the cell next to ours. Twelve men, chained together at the ankles in twos, filed into a courtroom for arraignment.

"Why would a bimbo on local TV give a shit about Vietnam?" Rodriguez asked.

"Wolf served in 'Nam, right?"

"Sure. A first looey with a chestful of medals. Uses it in all his campaigns."

I chewed that over a moment.

"Hey," Rodriguez said, watching me. "A million guys did their time there."

"Sure they did," I said. "But best I can tell, she was only screwing one of them."

CHAPTER 8

The Lesser
Man

Arnold Tannenbaum toddled toward the bench, his three hundred twenty pounds occupying center stage. He wiped the sweat from his forehead, snapped his fire-engine-red galluses for effect, and began: "A classic invasion of privacy, Your Honor. Prohibited by the penumbra of rights of the United States Constitution and Article One, Section Twenty-three of the Florida Constitution. Ever since *Griswold* versus *Connecticut*, Your Honor, we have held sacred the right of privacy in the home. When the bedroom door closes and the lights are dimmed, the government—here personified by Mr. Lassiter—may not intrude within. No, Your Honor, government may not poke, pry, or peep beneath our sheets."

In a matter of seconds Tannenbaum had taken us inside the home, into the bedroom, and under the sheets. I wondered how far he would go. So did Judge Dixie Lee Boulton. She peered down at Two-Ton Tannenbaum through pink glasses with fins like a '59 Plymouth. She listened for a moment, then slid the glasses off her tiny nose and let them dangle around her neck on a chain of imitation pearls. Even without her bifocals, Dixie Lee could see all she wanted of Arnie Tannenbaum, former amateur magician, failed operatic baritone, and perennial summer-stock actor. Currently, he sported a half-grown beard as he prepared to play Ephraim Cabot in *Desire Under the Elms*. Perched in the front row of the gallery was his client, Roberta Blinderman, long legs demurely crossed at the ankles, black mini hiked halfway to heaven.

"A man sits at a computer in the privacy of his own home," Tannenbaum droned on, "composing words in the darkness. And Your Honor, a man's home—or a woman's home for that matter—is his . . . that is . . . his or her castle."

It was clear Tannenbaum was winging it now, and Judge Boulton's face was wrinkled in confusion.

"By the miracle of modern technology, those electronic words are transported to the home of a willing woman who awaits his entreaties. He may have the eloquence of a Byron or the crudeness of a pornographer. But either way, it is the modern equivalent of a Romeo, nay, a Cyrano, or . . . or . . . whats'isname?"

The judge extracted a pencil from her silver beehive. "Whats-'isname?"

"Damn. In *The Fantasticks*. The horny kid at the wall . . ."

" 'Try to re-mem-ber,' " I cooed at him, putting a little tune to it.

" 'The kind of Sep-tem-ber,' " he sang out in a rumbling baritone, " 'when life was slow and oh so mellow.' "

" 'Try to re-mem-ber,' " I whispered again.

" 'The kind of Sep-tem-ber when grass was green and grain was yellow. Try to re-mem-ber the kind of Sep-tem-ber when you were a tender and callow fellow. . . .' "

The bailiff snickered, the court clerk nearly dropped her romance paperback, and the judge seemed more baffled than ever. "Mr. Tattle-beyer," she piped up, loud enough to quiet the singing lawyer.

"I'm sorry, Your Honor. Now, where was I?"

"Something about a man's castle." The judge sighed.

Two-Ton strived to rescue the moment. "Indeed. Was it not William Pitt, the Earl of Chatham, who said as much?" Then, assuming the limp of a sovereign with the gout, Two-Ton hobbled toward the bench and, feigning the accent of the House of Lords, proclaimed, "The poorest man may in his cottage bid defiance to all the forces of the Crown. His cottage may be frail; its roof may shake; the wind may blow through it; the storm may enter; the rain may enter. But the King of England cannot enter. All his forces dare not cross the threshold of the ruined tenement!"

I felt like applauding. Lord Olivier might be gone, but we still had Arnie Two-Ton Tannenbaum.

"Meaning what, Mr. Taggleborn?" the judge demanded.

Two-Ton thought about it and licked a sweaty upper lip. He was better when he didn't have to ad-lib.

"Just as the king is powerless to invade the home, so too is Mr. Lassiter, wearing the color of state authority, forbidden from demanding entry and possession of items therein. The subpoena must be smitten, must be quashed under the righteous weight of judicial power. It must be torn into shreds and cast upon the wings of a zephyr. Let it be swept away on the breeze, on the . . . the . . ."

" 'The wind they call Ma-ri-ah,' " I singsonged, but this time, he didn't take the bait.

"Very well," the judge concluded, then looked for me, hidden behind Two-Ton's bulk.

I elbowed my way around Tannenbaum to get into the judge's line of vision. "This is a murder investigation," I told her, "and the state has a compelling need for the information. We do not seek to invade anyone's home, but rather to gain access to certain business records of Compu-Mate, Inc., a Florida corporation that enjoys none of the personal rights so eloquently defended by Mr. Tannenbaum. Those business records may show the identity of the last person to communicate with a murder victim. In short, the corporation has no right to withhold the records. As for the authors of the messages, there is no precedent to suggest that there is a constitutional right of anonymity where a person blindly transmits electronic missives into the night, oblivious to the identity of the recipient."

"I see," the judge said, replacing the glasses on the bridge of her nose. Dixie Lee Boulton had worked for three Democratic governors, and when the last had been put out to pasture, she was rewarded with a judicial appointment. She hadn't read a law book since graduating from night school in 1949, but I wasn't worried. She had a fifty-fifty chance of being right.

"Motion to quash denied," she said. "Mr. Tottlebum, your client has forty-eight hours to produce the records."

Two-Ton exhaled a sigh like a foghorn and gave me a congenial slug on the shoulder. "I shouldn't have sung," he whimpered. "'Music is the brandy of the damned.'"

"William Pitt?" I inquired.

"George Bernard Shaw," he said, then waddled toward the door.

As the courtroom emptied Roberta Blinderman slinked out of the gallery and approached me. Her feelings about me must have changed. "Mr. Lassiter," she breathed. "You were so very good just now. I almost wish you were on my team."

"Well, Arnie gets a little carried away."

She smiled and moved close, enough to give me a whiff of a sweet, heavy perfume. "You're telling me. He's one of my clients. Goes by the handle 'Big Ham.'"

"I'm looking forward to learning more about your customers," I told her.

"I can tell you about the clients," she said, gesturing with a small briefcase. "Periodically, I sample them to find out if they're getting what they want."

"Which is?"

"Satisfaction, of course. That's what we all want, isn't it, Mr. Lassiter?"

She opened the briefcase. Inside were a stack of computer printouts and two hardcover books. I thumbed through the papers. A bunch of questionnaires. *On a scale of one to ten, rate the sensuous quality of your Compu-Mate calls.*

"Our peter meter," Bobbie explained.

"Doesn't help me," I said. "No names."

"We try both ways. Some surveys I do myself. You get unusual feedback face-to-face. But for statistics, you get more truthful answers if it's anonymous. Have you ever made love to a woman without knowing her name and without her knowing yours?"

"The women I know usually demand a résumé, a blood test, and three bank references."

"Try it sometime. The less you know about someone, the more honest you can be."

"I see," I said, not knowing what else to say.

"For instance, you really don't know me at all."

"What should I know about you, Mrs. Blinderman?"

"The less the better," she said, "and call me Bobbie."

We weren't good enough friends to be standing this close. She wore a black mini with fishnet stockings and stiletto heels. Our noses nearly touched. Her dark eyes flashed with black lightning, and in the fluorescence of the courtroom, a fine line of peach fuzz showed across her upper lip.

"Where's Max?" I asked. "Minding the store?"

She smiled and half turned so that her thigh pressed into my crotch. I didn't move. Why should I? It didn't hurt.

"Away," she said, drawing a long, painted fingernail across my chest, "and when Max is away . . ."

"Bobbie takes surveys," I said.

"You're a big man, Lassiter. I like a big man."

So why did she marry Max? "Uh-huh," I said.

"Max said you used to play some ball."

"Uh-huh," I repeated.

She smiled, licked her lips and recited:

> "'There once was an athletic young jock
> Who could shatter large rocks with his cock,
> But a coed said, "Dear,
> Please insert the thing here."
> And he fainted away with the shock.'"

Maybe she was mocking me or teasing me, but then again, my feeble male mind thought, maybe the sight of a shaggy-haired ex-linebacker carrying a briefcase turned her on.

"Are *you* going to faint on me, Lassiter?"

"Mrs. Blinderman, considering the fact that you're married and I'm investigating—"

"When I lock my legs around a man," she murmured right there in front of the American flag, the Bible, and portraits of judges with fine chin whiskers, "I don't let him go."

"You've been reading too much of your customers' prose."

She smiled salaciously. "Really, counselor. Do you always carry a brief in your pants, or are you just glad to see me?"

Mocking me, I decided, and tried to think of a brilliant rejoinder.

"Jake! There you are!" Charlie Riggs was beside me, pulling me away. He wore his blue courthouse suit and seemed to have combed out his tangled beard. His dark eyes twinkled with excitement. Coming out of retirement apparently agreed with him. "There's another one."

"Another what?"

"Corpus delicti, of course. Same modus operandi."

Bobbie Blinderman strode toward the courtroom door on those long, allegedly locking legs and gave a little shrug. *Another time*, she seemed to say. I was looking at Charlie, but I was hearing the clack-clack of Bobbie's high heels, fading like the clangor of a distant train.

The house was on a leafy street in Coral Gables. In-law quarters, the real-estate ads call them. The main house was a big stucco Spanish number from the 1920s with a barrel-tile roof, lots of arches, balconies, and black iron railings. In back sat a squat one-story box for guests or a Honduran maid without a green card.

The cops were still stringing yellow tape around the building. The glass jalousie windows were being dusted for prints. Crime-scene technicians crawled around the building, looking for footprints, weapons, any evidence the killer might have dropped. A business card would do nicely.

Bloodred leaves from the poinciana trees covered the stone path to the little house. Inside, the stench of death hung in the humid air.

"Can't anybody get that AC to work?" Detective Alejandro Rodriguez pleaded.

The place was one room. A bed against a wall, a kitchenette at the far end, and a desk in the middle. Mostly empty bookshelves lined a wall, a small TV and VCR taking up some of the space. The body was facedown near the front door. A young woman in a short cotton chemise with a floral motif. On the desk, the computer monitor still glowed, black background, white fluttery letters. Taped to the computer was a plastic card the size of a driver's license. Name, handle, and secret password: her Compu-Mate membership card.

"Rosemary Newcomb," Rodriguez said. His face was lathered with sweat, his blue short-sleeve shirt blotched under both arms. "Twenty-seven. Flight attendant for Pan Am. Part-time student at FIU. Rents the place from a doctor. Looks after the main house while he's gone. He's in New England for the summer, like any sensible person."

Charlie Riggs knelt and gently lifted the woman's head, brushing back short, frosted blond hair. He gently touched the neck where bruises were visible. He opened the mouth and peered down the throat with a pocket light. "Apparently fractured larynx and hyoid cartilage. No signs of ligature. Pinpoint hemorrhages on the face. Death from manual strangulation."

I tiptoed around the body to the computer monitor. "Rodriguez," I said. "I think you better dust this keyboard for prints."

The detective moved close to the screen. "Huh? Oh, we saw that. What's the big deal? The decedent wrote it before she bought the farm."

"A woman didn't write that," I said.

"No, who did?"

"I don't know. Poetry isn't my strong suit."

Charlie joined me in front of the monitor. He read silently a moment, clucking his tongue. "Alfred Tennyson," he said.

"I'll bring him in," Rodriguez said.

"I am beginning to mourn," Charlie Riggs said, "for the death of the classical education." Then he read it aloud:

"'WEAKNESS TO BE WROTH WITH WEAKNESS! WOMAN'S
*   PLEASURE, WOMAN'S PAIN—*
NATURE MADE THEM BLINDER MOTIONS BOUNDED IN
*   A SHALLOWER BRAIN:*
WOMAN IS THE LESSER MAN, AND ALL THY
*   PASSIONS, MATCHED WITH MINE,*
ARE AS MOONLIGHT UNTO SUNLIGHT, AND AS WATER
*   UNTO WINE.'*

"Quite a chauvinistic little ditty," Charlie Riggs concluded.

"Wouldn't get a great review in *Ms.*, if that's what you mean," I said. "What's it from?"

"'Locksley Hall,'" said Charlie Riggs, master of the esoteric. "A jilted lover's lament. I wonder if there's such a thing as a forensic poet. Maybe I should send this to Pamela Metcalf."

"Do it," I said, staring at the screen, trying to picture the wacko who stole the poet's words and now taunted us.

Look for messages, Pam Metcalf had said. Okay, here was one, loud and clear. A man who boasts of his unrestrained passions and belittles women. *The lesser man? Shallower brain?* I wished old Tennyson could bump heads with the current generation of the female of the species. They'd stomp him to death with their running shoes, then dash off to perform brain surgery or discover a new planet through mathematical magic. But no use getting angry at the poet. His words, another's actions. I turned back to the body. Charlie had examined the eyelids for hemorrhage, and now one ghastly eye remained open, staring at me in blind accusation. A fury grew within me, burned in my gut. I never knew Michelle Diamond or Rosemary Newcomb, but I knew they didn't deserve to die young, die hard. I wanted the maniac who did it.

A police artist in my mind sketched him. Overweight with a bad haircut and no friends. Lives alone in a room with a hot plate and a bunch of poetry collections he underlines and misunderstands. Clothes that don't match, a diet of donuts and greasy fries from a corner diner. A guy who hears voices and talks to himself on the bus while others try not to stare. A wrathful, rejected, deranged guy who strangles a woman. Or maybe two. And lets us know why.

Now I would find out who. It wouldn't be that hard, I thought. I had the brainpower of Pam Metcalf and Charlie Riggs on my side. So my mind composed a little lyric for the freak locked in his windowless room.

All thy wits, matched with mine,
Are as tinplate unto gold dust,
And as tears unto brine.

CHAPTER 9

Gone Fishing

Charlie Riggs dipped a hand into an old coffee can and came up with a half-dozen night crawlers. Juicy ones, brown and black, round and squirmy.

"If you were a bass, would you chomp one of these?" he asked.

"If I were a bass, I'd want to be a tarpon," I said.

Charlie grumbled something unintelligible and speared a fat worm with his hook. He swung his cane pole—no graphite rods and championship tackle for him—into the canal and waited. On the marshy bank, a great white heron peg-legged along, a full five feet tall on those matchstick legs.

Charlie's line drifted with the almost imperceptible current, the moon tugging the endless waters from the ocean to the straits to the bay to the great slough of the Everglades. "Can't eat the bass anymore," Charlie said. "Mercury poisoning."

I had seen the *Journal* headline: CHEMICAL THREATENS GLADES. Two inches of type, tops. A Florida panther dead, its liver laced with mercury. Nearby, a mess of bass floating belly up. I imagined an innocuous headline dated December 1, 1941: JAPANESE FLOTILLA STEAMS SOUTHEAST.

In the whirl and buzz of today's world, the men and women stuck in traffic jams cannot see the fouled streams, the poisoned pastures, the sea creatures strangled in plastic nets. Between punching in and punching out, getting ahead and stashing away their IRA, they have no time to consider the invisible menace. Meanwhile, in well-lighted conference rooms, finely groomed men in charcoal suits coolly discuss their budgets for R&D, SG&A, and the profit ratio of malignant poisons that coat the vegetables and artificial hormones that lace the beef.

Their computer models tell them how many tankers will cruise the Gulf before one strikes a reef and the appropriate tonnage that will ooze into the precious estuaries. Mathematically, they can figure when the waters of the Everglades will become as deadly as a toxic dump, when the song of a million birds will be stilled. No problem. The boys in insurance gotcha covered. Five million primary for the basic risk, fifty million excess reinsured with Lloyd's to protect the company's net worth and their own pensions. The public-relations folks—experts at damage control—are ready to fax prepackaged news releases that explain the company's profound concern at this unanticipated and unfortunate incident.

Just that morning Charlie and I heard thunder roll in the distance to the west. Not from the sky, but from underground explosions set by an oil company searching for a fortune beneath the river of grass. At dawn we watched their trucks, obscenely white, roll along the old levee, seismic sensors protruding like the antennae of steel-jacketed insects. Exploratory only, the company says, for it has no drilling permit. Just wait. After lobbyists pay their nighttime visits, it will only be a matter of time. The drilling will start, and some dark lonely night, through human error or computer breakdown or metal fatigue, the black gunk will belch into the marshy hammocks and over the sawgrass and through the canals. The crude will pour into the aquifer that supplies our fresh water. A bad enough spill and Palm Beach, Fort Lauderdale, and Miami will go bone dry. The roaches will inherit the concrete shells of forsaken condos, which in the end, might be what was intended all along.

"Itemize it for me," Charlie Riggs ordered, as if I were a fuzzy-cheeked intern.

We were sitting on the wooden dock behind his cabin on an Everglades canal. Charlie wore hiking boots and khaki shorts that were stained with fish guts or worse. I wore gray practice shorts and an old tear-away jersey, number fifty-eight, which the Dolphins somehow managed not to retire. In the glare of the late-afternoon sun, I tried to talk and pull the porcelain stopper on a sixteen-ounce Grolsch at the same time.

"Two young women who live alone are strangled a week apart. They have no known enemies, no common friends. Neither was robbed. The first may have had sex shortly before death, though it could have been a solo flight. The second victim clearly had sex in close proximity to death. Seminal fluid revealed an assailant or lover with blood type A, according to young Dr. Whitson."

"Assailant *or* lover?"

"No sign of a struggle," I said. "Other than the injury to the neck, no contusions. Also no skin under the fingernails and no torn clothing. It appears consensual."

"Unless it was postmortem."

"I hadn't thought of that."

"Well do, and please continue."

Charlie gets ornery if you overlook anything.

I said, "A message at the first scene echoed Jack the Ripper and taunted us. A message at the second scene reflected animosity toward women. Other than that, there is no apparent connection between the two murders, except . . ."

Charlie yanked on the cane pole and came up with a palm frond.

"Except," I continued, "both victims belonged to a sex-talk club. Both were frequent fliers on the computer wooing circuit, including the night each was killed."

"Anything else?" he asked, keeping his eyes on the rippling canal.

"Victim one was having a fling with the politically ambitious state attorney. Didn't seem too serious on either side. What the kids call a sport fuck."

Charlie scowled and flipped his sunglasses down from the bill of his cap like a shortstop under a pop-up. "Our language," he moaned. "*In partibus infidelium.* 'In the hands of infidels.'"

"She may have been poking into Wolf's war record."

"I assume you haven't queried Wolf whether she asked him about Vietnam."

I took a hit on the cold Grolsch. "Right. Too early. I try not to cross-examine a witness until I know at least as much as he does."

Charlie smiled. He had burned me from the witness stand more than once when my eagerness exceeded my experience.

"No one knows what Michelle was up to," I said. "The news director says she was working some investigation on her own, doesn't know what. She wouldn't tell him anything about it except she had a confidential source. He didn't take it too seriously. Didn't take Michelle too seriously, for that matter."

"Uh-huh," Charlie said. I thought the old wizard had come up with some revelation, but he was just pulling in a small blue-striped fish.

"Looks like a bream," I said.

"No. A damn tilapia. Belongs in somebody's den in an aquarium. Folks started dumping their exotic fish out here, now they've taken over the bedding areas. No wonder you can't find bluegill."

Charlie tossed the fish back, chose another night crawler, and baited his hook. "Maybe Nick Wolf didn't take her seriously either. Maybe she was just a sport—I can't say it—to him until he found out she was onto something."

"But then there's Rosemary Newcomb," I said.

"Yes, and unless you're willing to believe that Wolf killed a second time to cover up the motive for the first . . ."

"Hold on, Charlie. We have no proof Wolf had anything to do with the first. You can't take this kind of speculation to a grand jury."

Charlie smiled and scratched his beard. "Easy, Jake. We're just postulating. Covering all the possibilities. Stop thinking about probable cause and proof beyond a reasonable doubt. Be a scientist for a moment. Consider every happenstance, no matter how remote. When a person is killed, always ask, *cui bono*? 'Who stands to gain?'"

I drained the beer. It didn't help my powers of concentration. "That assumes a rational motive and not a crazed psychopath."

"And you assume we're dealing with a psychopath."

"Guys who leave nutty notes at murder scenes don't usually have rational motives, right?"

Charlie watched his line as little water bugs skittered across the surface. "Unless the messages are purposeful distractions . . ."

"That's what Pam Metcalf said about the Ripper note."

"Or they could be the product of an irresistible urge to scorn, to goad the authorities."

I nodded. "Pamela Metcalf said serial killers sometimes do that. They need thrills or something."

"Excitement," Charlie said. "Some psychopaths seek a whirlwind of excitement. Rather than seeking security, they crave risk."

I opened another beer. Before I could take a drink, Charlie chuckled and said, "You've been quoting Dr. Metcalf a lot lately. What should I read into that?"

"My admiration for her . . . credentials."

"No doubt."

I allowed myself a long, cool swallow. I started drinking two a day when I learned the brew might be good for fighting cholesterol. At the same time I cut back to only an occasional bacon cheeseburger and chocolate shake. Now I only eat red meat when doubling the ration of beer. Somehow I've convinced myself the arterial arithmetic works out.

I tried thinking it through, but my head was spinning and not from the beer. "Charlie, best I can figure, we may have a crazed killer or a sane one, or two crazed killers or two sane ones, or one of each. And the Compu-Mate connection either ties the two killings together or not, depending on whether we're dealing with one nut or two, or two non-nuts, or one of each."

"*Verus,*" Charlie agreed. "Anything is possible, but since the computer club is the only apparent connection, I suggest you pursue the computer business."

"Rodriguez is checking out each woman's calls," I said.

"You got the list?"

"From A to Z, or Android to Zorro, as the case may be. You wouldn't believe some of their handles."

I pulled out two lists that had been personally delivered to my office by Bobbie Blinderman the day before.

She had stopped traffic along the law-office corridors. Ushering the tall, sleek one into my office, Cindy had raised her eyebrows and said, "Love your shoes, honey."

It's hard to notice shoes when the red leather skirt stops a foot above the knees, but once you do, it's just as hard not to stare. The plastic see-through heels were filled with water and a goldfish swam in each one.

"The SPCA know about this?" I asked.

"It's a performing art," Bobbie Blinderman said. "The fish only last a little while. Then they go limp and die." She paused long enough to smirk. "Just like most men."

"So you keep casting for bigger fish."

"Maybe I found one," she said, laughing, and running a hand through her dark, layered hair. She tossed an envelope onto my desk. "Here's the printout of callers to Miss Diamond." Then she flipped a second one at me. "And here's one for Miss Newcomb."

I must have looked like a mule kicked me. "I read about it in the paper," she said quickly. "Some fucking maniac, huh?"

"There was no mention of either one belonging to Compu-Mate. That's under wraps."

"I recognized Newcomb's name. One of our regulars. Went by the handle 'Flying Bird.'"

"You're under no obligation to produce her calls," I said, sounding very much like the uptight lawyer who lurked deep inside.

She laughed again. "I know, but I was afraid you'd hit me with your big, bad subpoena."

Now I spread the lists on the wooden dock between the old man and the canal. On the night she was killed, Michelle Diamond computer-talked with four men.

BIGGUS DICKUS
BUSH WHACKER
ORAL ROBERT
PASSION PRINCE

Nine names turned up on Rosemary Newcomb's list.

BIGGUS DICKUS
HARRY HARDWICK
HORNY TOAD
MUFF DIVER

PASSION PRINCE
ROCK HARD
SLAVE BOY
STUDLY DO-RIGHT
TOM CAT

Charlie tsk-tsked, as was his habit when witnessing the decline of civilization. "Those names. So . . ."

"Sophomoric," I suggested.

"Crude," he said. "What on earth do the men say to the women after introductions like that?"

"Apparently, everything they wouldn't say in person. The impression I get is that your Caspar Milquetoast who wouldn't dream of speaking to a strange woman in a bar loses all inhibitions when he's tapping out messages in the night."

"Did Mrs. Blinderman tell you that?"

"Sort of. She's a little warped herself."

"You've got two matches there, you know."

"Yeah. Biggus Dickus and Passion Prince. They're first on Rodriguez's invitation list for a little chat."

"Good. I've been doing some research for you, too. Lord Tennyson was acutely aware of madness. His father, Dr. George Clayton Tennyson, was clearly manic-depressive."

I gave Charlie my how-do-you-know-that look.

"Relax," he said. "I've been to the library. You should try it sometime. Now, the poet himself was subject to great depression. He would check himself into the 1840s equivalent of a health spa. Unfortunately, these were establishments of intense quackery. He'd subject himself to hydropathy, which is a fancy word for ice-water baths and massages. All day long, freezing baths and rubdowns with wet, cold sheets, followed by meals of bread and cold water."

"Not exactly a weekend at the Fontainebleau."

"The idea was to flush out the poisons, the demons of the mind."

"Okay, what's that have to do with us?"

"Maybe nothing, but best to remember we don't have messages written by the killer. We're dealing with words written by someone who apparently influenced the killer."

"So we should learn as much as we can about that someone."

"Exactly. For what it's worth, Tennyson wrote 'Locksley Hall' after being jilted by a lover."

"Hell hath no fury like the poet scorned. What about the first message—Jack the Ripper?"

"Here, I brought something for you to read."

He motioned toward his knapsack. Inside, next to a sandwich of smoked amberjack on sourdough, was an old book. A musty old book with pages that stuck together and a title by someone who never saw a movie marquee. *A Detailed History and Critical Analysis of Police Investigatory Techniques During the Whitechapel Murders, August 31 to November 9, 1888.*

I thumbed through the book, peeling yellow pages apart. "Somehow, I thought Jack the Ripper had a longer rampage."

"Five killings over seventy days," Charlie said. "All middle-aged prostitutes, all alcoholic, all killed within a one-quarter-square-mile area. He disemboweled them, you know. Removed the uterus from one with some medical skill. With a couple, the police missed him only by a matter of seconds."

"Mary Ann Nicholls," I said, reading from the book. "The first one. 'Warm as a toasted crumpet' when found, it says here. What about the note?"

"There were at least three, actually. Turn to where I've marked it. The first letter was written in red ink and sent to a newspaper after the second murder."

I found the page and read aloud:

"Dear Boss,

I am down on whores and I shan't quit ripping them till I do get buckled. Grand work, the last job was. I gave the lady no time to squeal. How can they catch me now? I love my work and want to start again. You will soon hear of me and my funny little games.

Yours Truly,
Jack the Ripper"

"Three days later," Charlie said, "a postcard was mailed from the East End. Same handwriting."

I found the page and again read aloud:

"I was not codding, dear Boss, when I gave you the tip. You'll hear about Saucy Jack's work tomorrow. Double even this time. Number One squealed a bit; couldn't finish straight off. Had no time to get ears for police. —Jack the Ripper"

I read silently to learn what Charlie already knew. The next morning two bodies were found. Elizabeth Stride's throat had been slashed. The other victim, Catherine Eddowes, was quite a mess. Her abdomen was slashed open, the intestines pulled out and draped over her shoulder. And her left kidney was missing.

"Two weeks after the double homicide," Charlie said, "George Lusk received a cardboard box in the mail. It contained part of a human kidney and a note."

I thumbed a few pages further:

From hell, Mr. Lusk, sir, I send you half the kidney I took from one woman, preserved it for you, tother piece I fried and ate it; was very nice. I may send you the bloody knife that took it out if you only wait a while longer. Catch me if you can, Mr. Lusk.

"Cocky bastard," I said. "Showed no fear at all."

"No reason to," Charlie said, giving up at last and swinging his pole onto the dock.

"Why not?"

"They never caught the bloke, did they?" Charlie said, wiping off his hands and picking up his meerschaum pipe.

CHAPTER 10

Day in Court

"Señor Castillo," Nick Wolf said in his silky politician's voice, "do you know any reason why you couldn't sit as a juror in this case?"

The small, dark man in his stiff Sunday suit shook his head from side to side.

"Sir, can you understand English?"

"*Sí*," the man said proudly.

I waited until the jury was sworn and approached Nick Wolf at the prosecution table. "Tennyson, anyone?" I whispered.

"Huh?"

"We gotta talk."

"You bet we do, slick. What the hell you doing with the Newcomb homicide? You got no jurisdiction there."

"I have to cross the county line, like a cop in hot pursuit."

The judge was clearing his throat. "Mr. Wolf, is the state ready to proceed?"

Nick Wolf rose from his chair and bowed—"Ready, Your

Honor"—then turned back to me. "Look, I got a double Murder One to try here. We'll talk at the lunch recess."

I nodded and started to move away.

"What's on your mind?" he called after me.

"Jack the Ripper," I said.

Judge Dixie Lee Boulton was just finishing her morning motion calendar when I strolled into the courtroom, a bulky black briefcase in one hand, a leash attached to a shaggy Angora goat in the other.

Arnie Two-Ton Tannenbaum was planted in front of the bench, thrusting a copy of *Webster's Unabridged Dictionary*, Second Edition, in the general direction of the bench. "Your Honor, the indictment charges my client with entering Cozzoli's Pizzeria 'unlawfully, feloniously, and burglariously.' Now, you can look high and you can look low, but there is no such word as 'burglariously.' The indictment must be quashed."

"On what ground?" the judge asked, scowling.

"Unconstitutional grammar."

"Is there any precedent for that?"

"No, and just as well," Two-Ton answered. "It would be a pity for Your Honor to be deprived the distinction of being the first to establish the rule."

I had taken a seat in the front row of the gallery, just between Marvin the Maven and Saul the Tailor. Marvin nodded hello and ignored the goat, having seen far stranger sights in Miami courtrooms. Saul petted the animal, then pulled away before he lost a chunk of the straw hat he kept in his lap.

"Seven-to-one Two-Ton loses the motion, then cops a plea," Marvin the Maven predicted.

The defendant, a skinny nineteen-year-old with bad skin, dirty hair, and bad posture, slumped in front of the judge, vacant and hopeless. No one took the Maven's bet, and five minutes later, the judge recited the Gospel of the Guilty Plea: "The court finds the defendant intelligent, of sound mind and body, and represented by competent counsel. . . ."

It isn't easy to tell four lies in one sentence, I thought.

"He understands the nature of the charges against him and has made the plea freely and voluntarily. Three years in the state prison."

"Out in nine months," said Marvin the Maven.

"Next case," Dixie Lee Boulton announced. "South Coast Properties versus Babalu Aye Church of Santeria. Is the plaintiff ready?"

"South Coast Properties." Marvin tut-tutted, clucking his tongue. "What happened to representing honest murderers, Jake? Even a lying newspaper's better than a slumlord."

"Ready," I said, getting up and approaching the bench, leash in hand.

"*Br-aah-aay*," said the goat.

"Is the defendant ready?" the judge asked.

A dapper man of about fifty in a custom-made double-breasted powder-blue suit rose from the first row. He wore gold-rimmed glasses, had skin the purple-black of a polished eggplant, and strode to the bench with an air of authority. "I am Phillipe Jean Claude Phillipe, and I will represent my church."

"Are you an attorney, Phillipe . . . uh . . . Phillipe?" the judge asked.

"I am a *santero*, a priest of Santeria," he said, an Afro-Caribbean lilt to his voice.

"*Br-aah-aay*," said the goat.

The judge raised her eyeglasses from their string of imitation pearls and peered down from the bench. "Mr. Lassiter, is that an animal?"

From behind me, Marvin the Maven whispered, "It ain't the Queen of England."

"Your Honor, this is exhibit one in our eviction proceeding. When the church leased my client's property, Mr. Phillipe here misrepresented—"

"The Right Reverend Phillipe Phillipe," he corrected me.

"Right . . . Phil. This gentleman misrepresented his intentions. He said the house would be used for pastor's living quarters. Now we find they're slaughtering animals there. Hundreds of people show up to watch."

"To pray," Phillipe Phillipe corrected me. "It is our ceremony to

83

initiate new priests. We have thirteen gods, and to each we must sacrifice two roosters, a pigeon, a guinea hen, and . . . a goat."

"Your Honor, it's cruel and—"

"Is painless," said the Reverend.

"*Br-aah-aay,*" said the goat, unless it was Marvin the Maven.

"The place is covered with blood," I said. "It attracts flies and rodents."

The judge looked a mite pale, so I toned it down. "This is a residential neighborhood, not a stockyard. They have no license to slaughter—"

"Under your First Amendment, we have freedom of religion," Phillipe Phillipe interrupted. "Our license comes from God."

"Which one?" I asked, but the Right Reverend just looked through me.

"Mr. Lassiter," the judge said, "are you representing the rights of the landlord or of the goat?"

Behind me, I heard Saul the Tailor: "Whichever one pays."

I spoke up. "Your Honor, the church has breached its lease with the landlord, and its ceremonies violate the state's animal cruelty laws."

"He represents both beasts," Marvin the Maven said.

"The evil of two lessors," Saul the Tailor chimed in.

"To sacrifice animals is inhumane," I said.

"Is painless," the Right Reverend protested.

"The animals are conscious when butchered, they're—"

I heard the whoosh but never saw the blade. The shiny steel machete effortlessly sliced through the goat's neck. Blood spurted onto Phillipe Phillipe's powder-blue suit, onto my right shoe, and onto the clerk's lap, splattering her *Today's Woman* magazine. But the goat never made a sound. It just dropped dead in its tracks, little hooves quivering.

"Is painless," Phillipe Phillipe said.

"What's this shit about Jack the Ripper?" Nick Wolf demanded. He was attacking a rare cheeseburger, interrogating me, and howdying every judge, bailiff, and bureaucrat who passed our table in the courthouse cafeteria.

"You saw the lipstick message at the Diamond murder scene?"

"Yeah."

"It mimicked Jack the Ripper."

"So? Let the head cases at Metro Homicide worry about it. Better yet, call Sherlock Holmes."

"There's a link to Rosemary Newcomb's murder."

Nick looked up from the cheeseburger, waved to a bondsman who contributed shoe boxes of cash to his campaigns, and slid his chair toward me. "What link?"

"A message there, too. A woman-bashing poem."

"That's it?"

"Plus they both belonged to a computer dating club and both were using its services the night they were killed."

He leaned back in his chair and smiled. It was the election victory smile. "Maybe they both belonged to Triple-A, or maybe both were Girl Scouts. That doesn't mean the same guy aced them."

"No, but it's all we've got."

"You got squat, Lassiter. I'm beginning to doubt my judgment in appointing you."

"So fire me."

"Not a chance. That fish wrapper you represent would nail me. 'Slipshod Administrator' or some other bullshit editorial."

He looked toward the floor. "Hey, Jake, you know one of your shoes is all wet? What the hell is that, looks like—"

"Truth is, Nick, you're more of a trial lawyer than an administrator."

"Damn right, and that's why the public loves me. I don't sit up in the office finagling budgets or figuring crime statistics. I do battle in the courtroom, where it's all on the line."

"And the television crews have permanent spots in the front row."

He laughed. "Today I wish they weren't there. Friggin' city cops got a confession the old-fashioned way."

"Forget to Mirandize?"

"Worse. They bring in this yahoo for a double homicide, charged with killing a couple on lovers' lane out on the causeway. Except they got no weapon, no prints, no witnesses that are still breathing. So they put a colander upside down on the yahoo's head—"

"A colander?"

"Yeah, like to wash lettuce. Then they put Walkman earphones on him and tape the jack to the photocopy machine. One of them writes on a piece of paper, 'He Lies,' and slips it under the lid of the machine. Then they ask the guy if he did the deed. He says no. One cop pushes the button, the light flashes, and out pops a piece of paper. . . ."

"Which says, 'He Lies.'"

"You got it. Finally they tell him to admit the crime just to see what happens, like an experiment. One cop slips in another piece of paper. . . ."

"'He Tells the Truth.'"

"Right. Plus they turn on a tape recorder."

"Judge throw out the confession?"

He picked up his Coke. "Faster'n you could say Earl Warren."

I laughed, but he didn't. He was thinking. I tried to pick up the shadow of the thought behind those dark eyes, but it stayed inside. Finally he said, "This club called Compu-Mate?"

"Yeah. You know it?"

"My wife joined when we got separated. I'd call at night, she'd be talking dirty on the computer."

"She tell you anything else, like who she connected with?"

"Nope. Didn't interest me."

"What about Michelle?"

"I never knew she joined. What's the big deal? Probably something else Prissy got her into."

"Like women's awareness?"

"Yeah."

"And seeing you."

"Yeah."

"What else?"

"How should I know? I didn't see them together, and I didn't talk a hell of a lot to either one."

He was getting irritated. It had been at least twenty minutes since anyone told him what a great guy he was. "Did Michelle ask you many personal questions?"

"Some."

"What'd you tell her?"

"Just the usual life-story bullshit you gotta toss at them to get in their pants. I told her what it was like growing up poor. The high school-athlete stuff, going into the service. Told her all my cop stories from when I was a patrolman."

"What about war stories?"

Maybe it was my imagination, but he seemed to lose a little of the color in his cheeks. "If you mean 'Nam, I don't talk about it. Not to her, not to Prissy, and sure as hell not to you."

"But you won the Silver Star, right?"

"Yeah, right."

"It's on your campaign brochures. You talked to the *Journal* about it as part of a profile before your first election."

"So?"

"Talk to me."

He looked at his watch. "All I'm gonna say is what's in the public record. We had a translator, a Vietnamese girl, maybe nineteen or twenty, educated in one of the French convents. We got pinned down in a firefight in a village. We lost two men in the first five minutes. It was getting dark. Raining, like always. The girl was supposed to stay with the RTO, the radio operator, but she got separated and Mister Charles grabbed her."

"Mister Charles?"

"Charley, Chuck . . ."

"VC."

"Right."

"Charley backed out of the village and scattered east across some mud dikes through the rice paddies. I led one platoon in a chase. A second platoon was two clicks—two kilometers—north of us. We moved parallel to each other to the east. We caught Charley in the open on the dikes. That's all."

"You rescued her?"

He paused and scanned the room. "We recovered her body."

"And the VC?"

"Killed seven, wounded twelve."

"And your men?"

"No casualties once we got out of the village."

There was more to it, I knew. But I didn't know what. "The other platoon?"

8 7

He straightened in the chair as if it were time to leave.

"Casualties?" I asked.

"Three dogwood six."

"Three dead . . ."

"Ferguson. It was his platoon."

"Ferguson."

"Yeah. And Epstein, the witch doctor, the medic. Plus the RTO, I don't remember his name. That's all I'm going to say."

I wanted to ask more about that day, about Ferguson, whose name popped out of Michelle Diamond's computer, but I wanted to know more first. I shook my head and tried to shift gears. "You know anything about Compu-Mate?"

"Like what?"

"Any men who belong?"

"Hell no!"

"What about you? Ever join, ever use your wife's password, get on-line?"

Nick Wolf stared hard at me. "Whaddaya think, I'm some kind of weirdo? If I want a woman, I don't beat around the bush, no pun intended. I just walk right up and say, 'I'm Nick Wolf, and you've got the greatest legs I've ever seen, and I've seen them from here to Hong Kong.' Gets them every time."

"Thanks for the lesson."

"Always the legs, Jake. Never say tits or ass. Always legs."

I considered taking notes but figured I could remember the basics. "Nick, I think I have someone for you. Her name's Bobbie."

"She hot to trot?" Nick Wolf asked, deeply earnest.

"Like a Thoroughbred," I said, winking.

I stood up to leave. He stayed in his chair, "Hey, Jake, one piece of advice . . ."

"Yeah?"

"Like we used to say in-country, keep your ass down."

I looked at him and the politician's smile was gone. "Is that an order, sir?"

He summoned up a patronizing smile to take the edge off. "Just friendly advice, like yelling 'incoming' to your buddies. You stick your ass out in the wind, Jake, maybe it gets greased."

"Or maybe somebody else trips over it, takes a big fall."

I turned smartly on my heel and walked out, ramrod straight, feeling but never seeing his officer's glare.

I stood on the courthouse steps, blinking into the late-afternoon sun. To the west, thunderheads formed over the Everglades. The showers would be late, but just in time for rush hour. Overhead, a dozen black buzzards circled the wedding-cake upper tiers of the courthouse, gliding in the updrafts. The lawyers and the buzzards, birds of a feather, source of a thousand jokes.

They're really turkey vultures, Charlie Riggs informed me one day. *Cathartes aura.*

I told him not to spoil the fun.

With one eye on the birds overhead, I reached into my suitcoat pocket and pulled out the clipping Cindy had turned up when preparing to defend Nick Wolf's libel suit. The article was seven years old, published a week before Wolf's first election. I turned to the paragraphs I had circled near the end.

> *The candidate rarely speaks of his Vietnam service, and then only in modest terms, even when describing the incident for which he was awarded the Silver Star.*
>
> *"We had a translator, a Vietnamese girl, maybe nineteen or twenty, educated in one of the French convents. We got pinned down in a firefight in a village, lost two men in the first five minutes. It was getting dark. Raining, like always. The girl was supposed to stay with the RTO, the radio operator, but she got separated and the VC grabbed her. I led one platoon in a chase across some dikes through rice paddies. A second platoon was two clicks—two kilometers— north of us. We moved parallel to each other to the east. We caught Charley in the open on the dikes. It was too late to save the girl, but we inflicted heavy casualties."*

Okay, so once he flicked on the magnetic tape, out it came, same way every time. Rewind the tape, play it again, Nick. Nothing wrong with that, or was there? I thought of Laurence Harvey in *The Manchurian Candidate*, brainwashed into his story of Korean War heroics. Maybe Nick Wolf brainwashed himself, a tidy story of a rainy day in the rice paddies.

I was still thinking about it when one of the big birds suddenly swooped down and landed on the sidewalk next to an overturned garbage can. Spreading its wings a full six feet to ward off competition, it uncovered the remains of a chili dog. I approached to within a dozen feet, and when the bird turned to face me, ugly as death, I backpedaled with a scaredy-cat step of a Francis Macomber. In a moment another bird landed and picked through the rest of the garbage, keeping some distance from the wise guy who thought up the idea.

The black birds ignored me, so I tiptoed toward them. Two sets of wary eyes appraised me. Then I heard myself say in deep senatorial tones, "May it please my fine-feathered foraging friends. My fellow brethren at the bar. Nibblers of equity, scavengers of justice. Are we here to seek truth, or merely to gorge ourselves on the facts? If the truth is that the wolf is loose amongst the chickens . . . what then?"

"They got a place upstate for guys who talk to birds."

I whirled to see Cindy at the bottom of the steps, head cocked, chewing her gum happily. "Nice place," she said, "clean white sheets and rubber walls."

"I'm glad you're here," I said.

"I'll bet."

"Call Priscilla Wolf for me. Mrs. Nicholas Wolf. I want to see her as soon as possible."

"Tomorrow morning, the office?"

"No. Tonight. Her place. I need to see the lair of the wolf."

"Sure. But you oughta change first."

"What's wrong with a blue suit?"

"Fine, matches your eyes," she said. "But your loafers. One's black and one's cordovan."

CHAPTER 11

A Woman Without a Man

There must be uglier stretches of suburbia than Miami's Bird Road—maybe the outskirts of Calcutta. From Dixie Highway westward toward the Glades, Bird Road is six lanes of potted asphalt flanked by strip shopping centers, miles of wall-to-wall, plug-ugly, flat-roofed stacks of concrete blocks. Plastic pennants and helium balloons proclaim each new project, and with it, yet another gun shop, XXX video, and rental-furniture store. No matter how many vacant storefronts next door, no matter the foreclosures up the street, local bankers awash in doper cash fall all over each other to make lousy loans to shaky speculators. And downtown, the county zoning guys never met a builder they didn't like.

Sign ordinance a problem? Hire the mayor's lawyer. No *problema.*

Can't meet the parking-space requirement? Paint the lines to a Yugo's dimensions and let 'em park on the median strip. Who's counting anyway?

Concrete, asphalt, noxious fumes, and blaring horns. Bird Road has it all. Everything, it seems, but birds.

The concrete-block-and-stucco house had been turquoise with yellow-trimmed shutters. Now the colors blended into the same off-white. It was two blocks north of Bird, and you could still hear the bleat of traffic, the occasional police siren. Nick Wolf bought the place when he was a cop, and after several lean years in night law school and a civil servant's salary in the state attorney's office, he never had the bucks to move east into the Gables. There was something reassuring about the house, a testament to the fact that Nick Wolf might be the last honest public official in the county.

I parked the old convertible in the driveway next to a child's red bicycle. It was growing dark, the humidity hanging heavy in the air. A miniature backboard and basketball rim was propped in the yard, a child-size soccer ball lay against the trunk of a bottle-brush tree. The compressor of the central air conditioner whined from a concrete pit at the side of the house, and a rusty water stain streaked the stucco wall. The garage door was open. Inside sat an eight-year-old Toyota, pleading for a wax job.

There are a hundred thousand houses just like this one in our town. The domestic suburban middle-class cliché. From the outside, familial bliss, folks who can handle a VA mortgage and pay off the credit cards over time, but no frills. Inside, a thousand secrets—fractured marriages, wandering husbands, boozing wives.

The doorbell didn't work, but my fist did. She answered on the third knock. Priscilla Wolf was a tidy package in leotard, tights, and leg warmers, a wide belt that didn't hold anything up but accentuated the flat waist. The leotard was low cut in front with a tiger motif that matched her eyes, nut brown with a touch of gold. The hair was cinnamon, and she hadn't been born that way. The smile was wide and inviting.

"Come in, Mr. Lassiter," she said, leading me through a tiny foyer. In pink sneakers, she moved like a cat. All in all, one of those women who looks better at forty-two than at twenty-one. "You'll have to forgive me. High-impact aerobics after two hours of racquetball. I must look a fright."

"I'm not scared a bit."

She turned and winked at me over her shoulder, then showed me into the living room. I eased into a beige sofa that was worn in the seat. I declined coffee but said okay to something cold. She excused herself and came back a moment later with bottled water from Maine and a bowl of grapes. Ten years ago it would have been potato chips with sour-cream dip, something alcoholic to wash it down. I popped a few green grapes into my mouth, took a swig of the bubbling water, and felt gloriously healthy but in need of something salty and greasy.

Priscilla Wolf reached down and peeled the Velcro straps from her sneakers. Maybe it's old-fashioned, but I'm opposed to sneakers without laces. Digital watches and pocket calculators, too. Gizmos that make life easier and dull our minds. Besides being unable to read or write, today's kids have trouble telling time, multiplying nine times seven, and tying their shoes.

Freshly unsneakered, Priscilla Wolf gracefully lowered herself into a wing chair and tucked her legs beneath her. She studied me a moment, and I returned the look. Beads of perspiration formed between her breasts, and she shivered in the air-conditioning. She excused herself again and returned this time in red nylon shorts and a tight T-shirt with a drawing I didn't understand until I read the caption: "A woman without a man is like a fish without a bicycle."

She opened the conversation. "Nick told me about you, but he neglected to mention how damned attractive you were."

"Funny, he seemed to forget the same thing about you."

"Has he ever! Oh well, I don't sit around waiting for him to come back. I've seen too many of my friends do that. A woman turns forty, her husband trades her in for two twenties. Let the prick go and get on with your life. That's my philosophy."

"There are other fish in the sea," I agreed, gesturing at her T-shirt, where a salmon tried to ride a Schwinn.

"You got that right. A woman has to be independent these days. You can't depend on a man, because a man's not dependable."

"Expendable," I said, "but not dependable."

"You got that right," she repeated. "Now, I enjoy a man's company as much as the next woman. More than most. A bottle of wine, a hot tub. That's all fine. But in the morning, get the hell out, I've got things to do."

"A modern woman," I said.

She smiled, straightened her legs, and pointed her sweat-socked toes toward the ceiling in what seemed to be a tummy-tightening exercise. "How much you weigh, anyhow?"

"What?"

Now she was twisting her torso, attacking the love-handle zone. "Your weight, honey. What do you tip the scales at? Two hundred, two-oh-five?"

"Two-twenty-five, give or take."

"Oooh. You carry it real well. All that height helps. Nick goes about two-ten, but he's a lot shorter than you. Built like a bull and hung like a stallion. Strongest man I ever knew. We could make it standing up, he'd just grab me under the butt, lift me up, I'd wrap my legs around his hips. Never showed any strain, and could hump from here to Sunday. Takes a strong man to do that."

I didn't disagree. I just sat there, and she cocked her head, as if waiting for me to flex my biceps or otherwise challenge the Nicholas G. Wolf Olympic Stand-Up-Humping Record. I thought about it and felt a twinge between the L3 and L4 vertebrae where I once took a knee from a pulling guard.

"Not that I miss him," she volunteered. "Except . . . except the wimps I've met lately. Sheesh. Noodle necks and pencil wrists. Half the time they can't get it up, other half, you wish they hadn't."

"You meet these guys on the computer?"

"Oh, that's why you're here, right? What some monster did to Michelle. I hope you nail the bastard."

I nodded gravely and let her think about Michelle. Priscilla Wolf's smile disappeared, and for a moment the pretty face sagged and nearly showed its age.

"The computer club," I reminded her.

She seemed to shake herself awake. "Forty Something."

"What?"

"That's my handle. Forty Something. You'd think it'd scare a lot of guys off, you know, looking for young stuff. But you'd be surprised."

"You spend a lot of time on-line?"

"Too much. The computer helps pass the hours when you can't sleep and the batteries are dead in the vibrator."

"What about the men? Anyone ever threaten you? Anyone talk about killing a woman?"

She thought about it. "I don't remember that. One guy wanted to tie me up and spank me. Leather Lizard, I think. Unless it was Bondage Bill."

She smiled sweetly and pulled off her sweat socks and leg warmers, then wiggled her toes at me. "My feet are killing me," she said, kneading the palm of her foot with one hand. Then she got up, walked over, and plopped onto the sofa next to me, swinging her feet into my lap. "There's nothing like a foot rub from a man with strong hands."

Before I could figure which little piggy went to market, we were interrupted by a squeal. "Mommy! Mommy, you didn't tuck me in."

The boy wore Fred Flintstone pajamas and had a good set of shoulders for a five-year-old. There's no substitute for genes.

"Nicky," Priscilla Wolf said, swinging her legs smoothly to the floor. "Say hello to Mr. Lassiter."

He gave me a wordless sideways look that other men on the same sofa had doubtless seen. "Hello, Nicky," I said. "You look like a little fullback. You play football?"

He wrinkled his nose. "Football sucks. Soccer's rad."

Priscilla got to her feet and marched Nicky off to bed. I used the time to wander around. Just off the living room was a small study. A metal desk, shelves with law books. On the wall, plaques from every civic group in town. The room had been Nick's, but a feminine hand was creeping in. A lacy blanket covered the love seat in the corner. A flower vase with plastic tulips sat on the desk next to the computer.

She found me as I was studying an old black-and-white photo in a plastic frame. Nick was bare-chested, dog tags around his neck, the left hand holding an M-16, the right draped around another soldier's shoulder. Both wore grins and were clean-shaven and muscular, and something in their eyes said they hadn't yet seen combat.

"Wasn't he something?" Priscilla asked, the tone just this side of wistful. "Look at those pecs."

"Great pecs," I agreed.

"He and Evan were best friends. They met at OCS. Served together in Vietnam. In all Nick's letters, Evan did this . . . Evan did that. Nick looked up to him."

"Evan?"

"Lieutenant Evan Ferguson."

"They still keep in touch?" I asked, knowing the answer.

A cloud crossed her face. "Evan never came back. He was killed in an ambush or something. They were trying to save a Vietnamese girl. Nick and Evan were leading their battalions—"

"Platoons."

"Whatever. A bunch of American boys with rifles playing soldier. Something happened. Evan got killed and Nick got a medal. He doesn't like to talk about the details."

There was no way to avoid wading right into it. "Would he have talked about it with Michelle?"

She looked at me with those nut-brown eyes and seemed to consider the question.

"Doubt it. Like most men, he doesn't say boo about himself. About what he's feeling, I mean. Michelle would ask me about the war, and what Nick was like when he came back. She and I got to be close. She'd come over, we'd drink white wine and have a little pajama party, gabbing all night."

"About Nick?"

"Yeah, and other things." She thought about it. "But about Nick, a lot, sure."

"What did he tell you about the war?"

She looked away, mulled something over, and didn't let me see it. "Not much. Oh, he'd talk about liberty in Japan. But what happened on patrol, the fighting, not much at all."

"Did Michelle ever tell you she was investigating Nick?"

That stopped her a moment. "Investigating? No. Why would she do that?"

"For television. Like Mike Wallace, put him under the lights and grill him."

"Just the opposite. She wanted to do a profile, a puff piece to make him look good."

"Nick didn't tell me."

"He didn't know. At least he wasn't supposed to. She asked to see his mementos. You know, uniforms, photos, that kind of thing. There isn't that much. But she was sort of mystical about it. She'd stare at a picture or just lay her hands on his moldy old duffel bag."

"Why? Did she tell you?"

"She wanted to surprise him. Nick would come on live for an interview about some boring case in the office, and Michelle would have a profile all prepared about his childhood, the war, the crime-fighter stuff, his political life. . . ."

"This Is Your Life," I said.

Priscilla laughed. "That's what I told Michelle, but she didn't know the show. Too young."

As she talked she straightened up a bookshelf, then dusted the desk with the palm of her hand. Even the modern woman can't fight a millennium of tradition.

"Maybe you could show me Nick's war memorabilia."

She hesitated and looked at me sideways. "Not without asking him first."

"Don't bother. I'll mention it to him myself. By the way, he told me you introduced him to Michelle."

There was a touch of sadness in her smile. "I knew she would never get serious with him. She wanted to use Nick, meet all the judges and lawyers and cops you need to know in her business. She wanted to get out of the mold they created for her at the station. Get onto hard news, then move to a bigger television market, like L.A. or New York. To her Nick was just a power fuck. And to Nick, she was just . . ."

"A sport fuck."

"You got that right."

"So there was a better chance of Nick coming back than if he found some divorcée looking for commitment."

She seemed to sigh. Her look spoke of lonely nights, of the anguish Nick caused her, of the love she still had for him. The brave front was crumbling. "It was almost as if I still had him. I liked Michelle. She'd tell me what they did, what he said about me. Usually he complained. I was always pushing him, he'd say, which was right. I pushed him to go to law school, to run for office. I pushed him to become the man he is."

"And then he left."

She nodded and turned her head away.

"Life never goes the way you plan it," I said.

I got that right, too.

CHAPTER 12

Alibis

I hit every red light for fifty blocks heading east toward Coconut Grove. They're timed that way by our traffic planners, who are either sadists or extortionists who get kickbacks from the oil and tire companies.

My little coral-rock house was dark, quiet, and hot. I turned on the lights, pulled the cord on every ceiling fan, and opened the windows. The soggy air inside was soon joined by soggy air outside. I turned on the eleven o'clock news just to have some background noise.

It had been a slow news day by local standards. No gangland executions, no cockfight raids, no riots in the streets. No DC-3s dropping bales of marijuana through the roofs of convents. Just the usual assortment of *mondo bizarro* Miami news.

Lead story, a woman nine months pregnant and just off the plane from Barranquilla, sitting in a wheelchair at the airport. She told the customs agent her stomach hurt. Any other city, they would have thought the woman was going into labor. Here, they asked what she had swallowed before leaving Colombia.

Condoms filled with *cocaina*, she reluctantly admitted.

How many, the agent asked.

Ciento diez, she said, beginning to cry.

The agent didn't believe her, but sure enough, after a handful of laxatives, agents recovered a hundred and ten condoms filled with nearly two pounds of cocaine. "The woman's a real swallower," the anchorman solemnly concluded.

Then there was the Green Thumb Gang, ripping up expensive plants from residential yards. Nick Wolf's face appeared on the screen. "I'm declaring war on the black market for flowers and plants," he announced. "We'll have men working undercover at the flea markets, and we advise all citizens not to buy lilies or liriopes from anyone you do not know."

And rounding out the news, two highway attacks, only one a homicide. A woman tailgating in her Honda was shocked when the driver in front stopped his Nissan, walked back to her car, and wordlessly poured his coffee through the window and into her lap. Then a man in a Hyundai apparently turned left too slowly to suit the man in the Corvette behind him. After being hung up at a traffic light, the Corvette driver took chase and peppered the slowpoke with a burst of nine-millimeter shells from an Uzi.

"Stay cool on our hot highways," a police major was saying. "Don't blow your horn except for safety reasons. Never get out of your car unless absolutely necessary."

Welcome to Belfast. Or maybe Beirut.

I was glad there were no new stories about the Michelle Diamond case. Rosemary Newcomb hadn't even made television and was awarded only four paragraphs in the *Journal* under the headline FLIGHT ATTENDANT SLAIN. As long as we didn't release the Compu-Mate connection, the news media probably wouldn't link the two killings. Not that they weren't still pestering me. That very afternoon, a reporter, a photographer, and a grip from Channel 8 ambushed me outside the courthouse with camera rolling.

"Any new developments in the anchor-lady murder?" Rick Gomez yelled over the traffic.

I picked up my pace and cut toward the street, hoping to tangle Gomez's mike cord on a parking meter. "Your fly's open, Rick."

He looked down, cursed at his own gullibility, and tried again. "Is it fair to say the investigation is stalled?"

"We'll have an indictment about the time your paternity case comes to trial."

"C'mon, Jake! Gimme something I can use."

"Have you tried condoms?"

"Jake, please."

"See if they come in petite."

The grip was getting a charge out of this, even if Rick Gomez wasn't. If nothing else, they could show it on the blooper reel at the station's Christmas party.

I jaywalked across Miami Avenue, cut close to a city cop on horseback, using him as a pick. Gomez, a veteran street reporter, stayed on my heels. "Critics have questioned your qualifications to head the investigation."

"So has my granny."

"How many homicides have you prosecuted?"

"Same number of Emmys you've won."

I was within sight of my office building, but Gomez wouldn't give up. "There's a rumor that the state attorney couldn't handle the Diamond case because of his personal involvement with the victim. Care to comment?"

"I heard a rumor that you got run out of the Atlanta market after an incident with a fifteen-year-old cheerleader."

"Jake!"

I hit the revolving door and left Gomez and his crew in the heat of Flagler Street. I was halfway to the elevator when I heard his plaintive cry: "She was *seventeen*, you second-string son of a bitch!"

With the TV still jabbering in the background, I prepared dinner in a kitchen so small the roaches walk in single file. I opened a can of tomato soup and a can of tuna. The Grolsch comes in a bottle, so I didn't open any more cans.

I heard the weather guy explain how it would be ninety-two with an eighty percent chance of afternoon thunderstorms. He could have mailed it in.

The anchorman was inviting me to stay up late and watch a comedian tell semidirty jokes when the glare of headlights swung through the front window, a set of brakes squealed, and rear tires kicked up gravel where my lawn is supposed to be. Cops like to make entrances.

Alejandro Rodriguez walked in, helped himself to a beer, and nearly said thank you. He ran a hand through his short black hair and removed his made-for-Hollywood reflecting sunglasses, which was a good idea, since it was close to midnight. He tossed his wrinkled sport coat over a chair and removed his rubber-soled oxfords. Then he turned off his portable two-way radio, crackling with police jargon, threw down a crumpled old briefcase, and dropped into the sofa to watch TV. At the first commercial he said, "What's black and brown and looks good on a lawyer?"

"Dunno."

"A Doberman."

He had another beer, and at the second commercial he asked, "What's the difference between a rooster and a lawyer?"

"Dunno."

"The rooster clucks defiance."

I was running out of beer, so I was happy when he stood up, turned off the tube, and simply said, "Passion Prince is an English professor with a potbelly."

Then he opened the briefcase, removed a file, and slid it across my sailboard, which, when propped between cinder blocks, makes a fine coffee table. I lifted the porcelain top on my last sixteen-ounce Grolsch, sat down, and started reading. Rodriguez had handled the old-fashioned gumshoe work himself, checking out the nighttime callers. Four to Michelle Diamond, nine to Rosemary Newcomb the night each was killed. Two men chatted with both. Biggus Dickus never left his house either night, Rodriguez said. His wife corroborated the alibi.

Wife?

They played the game together. Biggus bedded down the women, conversationally at least. They talked it, right down to panting, penetration, and popping. The missus did the men. Made them both so hot, they'd get off together. For real.

Oh.

Of the other ten men, seven had alibis that also checked out. That left Passion Prince, Harry Hardwick, and Tom Cat. Passion Prince was Gerald Prince, fifty-one, an English professor at Miami-Dade Community College. Other than Biggus Dickus, the only man to talk to both women the night they died. Divorced, lives alone. No criminal record. Expressed shock at the deaths, Rodriguez said, but seemed to enjoy the attention. Was home alone at time of both killings. Or, in the words of Rodriguez's report, "Subject allegedly asleep between 2300 hours and 0600 on dates of homicides, no corroborating witnesses."

"Does Prince teach poetry, by any chance?" I asked.

"Nope. I checked. Specializes in theater."

I turned to the next file. Harry Hardwick was Henry Travers, forty-six, retired postal worker on full disability. Ordinarily found at the horses, dogs, or jai alai, depending on the season. Never married, no criminal record. Willing interview subject. Admits computer connection with Rosemary Newcomb early on evening she was killed. Claims to have been at jai alai, maybe on way home at time of homicide.

Tom Cat was Tom Carruthers, thirty-five, wilderness guide. Never married, one arrest for assault in a tavern brawl, case dismissed. Refused to be interviewed, or as Rodriguez wrote, "Subject provided minimal assistance and informed undersigned officer to 'fuck off, asshole.'"

"What do you think?" I asked Rodriguez.

He sighed and stretched out on the sofa, one tired cop. "I don't know. Travers and Carruthers spoke only to Newcomb, so you gotta start with the professor because of the double match. The retired guy walks with a limp and would have a hell of a time attacking anybody. The outdoorsman is a hardass, one of those survivalist freaks with about thirty guns, but . . ."

"Nobody got shot here."

"Right." Rodriguez grazed his chin with the back of his hand, scratching his five o'clock shadow plus seven hours. "And another thing. You deal with enough homicides, you get a feeling. Like you can talk to a guy and you just know he's a killer. I don't get that feeling here, not with any of them."

"I'm told that psychopaths can be very charming."

"None of them's exactly a charmer either." He paused, then said, "One's a weirdo, though."

"Which one?"

"Don't know, but look at this."

Rodriguez shoved a sheet of computer paper in front of me. "The crime-scene guys got this to print out of Rosemary Newcomb's computer. According to the directory, it was her last Compu-Mate conversation. She saved it into hard memory about two hours before she was aced."

HELLO, FLYING BIRD, CARE TO CHAT?
SURE. HAVEN'T SEEN YOU AROUND THE CLUB BEFORE,
    HAVE I?
NO. WHAT DO YOU DO FOR FUN, OH SWEET BIRD OF
    YOUTH?
JOG, WORK OUT, RIDE.
RIDE?
YOU KNOW, HORSES.
AH, FLYING BIRD. EQUUS THE KIND . . . THE
    MERCIFUL!
WHAT ARE YOU TALKING ABOUT?
EYES LIKE FLAMES. GOD SEEST!
ARE YOU ONE OF THOSE BORN-AGAIN GUYS? 'CAUSE I
    GOTTA TELL YOU THAT SHIT DOESN'T
EQUUS . . . NOBLE EQUUS. GOD-SLAVE . . . THOU
    GOD SEEST NOTHING!!!!
OH FORGET IT. NICE CHATTING. SIGNING OFF
    NOW . . . FLYING BIRD

"A real sicko, huh," Rodriguez said. "Wish she had mentioned his handle. Which one you think—"

"Rod, that English prof, what's his name?"

"Prince, just like his handle."

"You say he teaches theater?"

Rodriguez flipped open his file and read aloud. "'American and British Drama, 1930 to 1980.'"

"Thought so."

"That shit's from a play?"

I nodded. "He's playing the disturbed boy. Trying to get Rosemary Newcomb to be the psychiatrist, but she doesn't know the lines, has no idea what he's talking about."

"*I* got no idea what *you're* talking about," Rodriguez said.

"Galloping horses. Passion. Seeing in the dark."

"Huh?"

"Welts cut into a boy's mind by flying manes."

"Sounds like you're the one needs the psychiatrist," he said.

"In due time," I said. "In due time."

CHAPTER 13

Truth and Illusion

I slid into an empty seat in the back row of the classroom and got my first look at the prince of passion. Gerald Prince had a fine thatch of silver hair swept over his ears, a florid complexion, and a face that had clearly been handsome in his youth. His shoulders were rounded and the brown sweater was threadbare at one elbow. A paunch hung over his belt, and the pants were baggy in the seat.

He was pacing in front of the class on an elevated stage, wagging a finger at a skinny young man near the front. About thirty students were scattered throughout the classroom in various stages of semi-somnolence. "And what does the playwright tell us about truth versus illusion?" The voice surprised me. Strong, resonant, a hint of a British accent. An aging actor, a tired Jason Robards maybe.

The young man shook his head. "*No se*, man."

"Now, Mr. Dominguez," Prince sang in soothing tones, "did you read the play?"

"*Sí*, sort of."

"And its theme? Its meaning? What did it say to you?"

"That bitch, man. Liz Taylor. What a ballbuster."

A few laughs from around Dominguez. I saw him only from behind. Dark hair short on the sides, a tail in back.

The professor strutted across the bare stage, coming closer to his student. "You're talking about Martha?"

"*Sí*, Martha. I rented the video, man. I thought something was wrong with my Sony till I figured it was in black-and-white."

Prince's theatrical sigh carried to the back row. He spread his arms, threw back his head, and wailed, "'Blinking your nights away in the nonstop drench of cathode-ray over your shrivelling heads.'"

"Huh?"

"Never mind. I suppose it's better to have seen a few fleeting images than not to have encountered the playwright's words at all."

"I liked it okay."

"Good. Edward Albee will be pleased. And its theme, Mr. Dominguez? Its message?"

Dominguez scratched his head with a pencil. "*No se, pero, si fuera mi esposa*, I'd have popped her one, the way that bitch talked."

The class mumbled its agreement. Prince shook his head and turned to another student, a young black man in the front row.

"Mr. Perry, your review of the play?"

"What it is," Perry said, "talking trash like that, putting him down. My old lady do that, she'd be seeing stars. That George character, no balls."

"*No cajones*," Dominguez agreed, and his classmates—at least those who were conscious—mumbled their agreement.

"Has it occurred to any of you," Prince asked, quite certain that it had not, "that the conflict between George and Martha, the humiliation Martha heaps on him, is essential to their relationship. That they relieve the tedium with it? That it is part of their game?"

The classroom was bathed in silence.

Prince went on; "What does Martha say about her abuse of George in Act Two?"

A thin black woman next to me called out, "That he can stand it, that he married her for it."

"Yes!" Prince boomed.

For a moment his eyes seemed to catch the light, and his

shoulders straightened. "Thank you, dear girl. Then, in Act Three, 'George who is good to me, and whom I revile, who understands me, and whom I push off, who can make me laugh, and I choke it back in my throat, who can hold me at night, so that it's warm, and whom I will bite so there's blood.'"

Prince paused, then asked, "What does it all mean? What is the play about?"

"Conflict," the woman suggested tentatively.

"Yes, yes, and more." Prince moved from center stage and descended three steps toward his students, never looking down. He had been on stages before, I thought, had vaulted landings on rickety sets, and now had settled for a final run in front of a polyglot of nineteen-year-olds for whom high culture was MTV.

"Conflict is the purifying flame," he nearly shouted, heading toward the young woman next to me. "Conflict separates truth from illusion, fact from fantasy. Now, what are their illusions?"

"They pretended to have a child," the woman said. "And George had fantasies about all sorts of things. That he killed his parents, that he sailed the Mediterranean."

"Yes, and when Martha says, 'Truth and illusion, George, you don't know the difference,' what does George respond?"

The class was silent, so I piped up, "'We must carry on as though we did.'"

Prince whirled, scanned his audience, found me, wrinkled his forehead, and asked, "Do they?"

"Yes, but only for a while," I answered. "Eventually they must confront the illusions, strip them away from their relationship. They have no son. George will never be a great writer or even a decent professor. Martha's early dreams are lost in fogs of booze. They must face life the way it is."

The young woman next to me chimed in, "No matter how painful, they must face the truth. In the end all is truth."

Prince raised his arms in triumph. Two or three students nodded their heads vigorously. They understood. The rest had that empty stare of the young. It had been, after all, forty-five minutes without physical movement, roughly nine times the attention span of most adolescents.

Prince strutted back toward the stage, and Dominguez called out.

"I get it, man. But who the hell's this Virginia Woolf?"

Gerald Prince ordered Plymouth gin on the rocks and not for the first time. Up close, the florid complexion was crisscrossed with tiny, engorged veins. The eyes—if they had any color at all—were gray. The brown sweater smelled of tobacco, the fingernails were long and stained. He had snapped at the luncheon invitation, and I brought him to a bayfront restaurant downtown. Near us, bankers and lawyers feasted on expense-account lunches of rack of lamb with mint jelly.

"Even from the stage, I spotted you—the stranger—in back of the class," he said with a sly grin. "In my day, I could see right through the floodlights. One summer in Maine, in a barn—literally a barn—I saw a woman with glorious red hair, fifth row center. Three nights in a row she came. We were doing *Long Day's Journey into Night*."

"I can picture you as James Tyrone."

He laughed, a low rich chuckle. "Thirty years ago. I was Edmund, the younger son."

"The sickly one."

"Yes, and quite a challenging role for a young stag. I was robust, brimming with vitality. And virility, if I might say so. I had never tasted a drop of whiskey and had to play some scenes as if drunk."

"And the red-haired woman?"

"She thought I was smashing. The first of many such women in many such towns. I remember the scent of the pine trees around her cottage. Isn't that strange? Chilly nights, a fireplace, and the smell of the woods."

He drained the gin and smoothly signaled the waiter for another. The steaks hadn't yet arrived.

"Edmund Tyrone," he said wistfully, "walks from the beach to the house through the late-night fog. He's been drinking, and his father sits, quite drunk himself, playing solitaire."

Prince let his eyes glaze over and rocked a bit in his chair. "'It was like walking on the bottom of the sea,'" he recited, his voice carrying across the noisy restaurant. "'As if I had drowned long ago.

As if I was a ghost belonging to the fog, and the fog was the ghost of the sea.' "

He paused and seemed to await the applause. "You have some memory for lines," I complimented him.

"I was an *actor*! I was good. Not brilliant, perhaps, but with potential. I played the Old Vic when I was twenty-one. I could have—"

"Been a contender."

He smiled. "Brando was always a tad animalistic for my tastes."

"Today, in class, you said something about the 'drench of cathode-ray.' I don't remember that from *Who's Afraid*—"

" 'I'll give him the good normal world where we're tethered beside them, blinking our nights away in a nonstop drench of cathode-ray over our shrivelling heads.' "

"Now I know," I said, and I did. The tethered gave it away. "The psychiatrist in *Equus*."

"Very good. Exceptionally fine for a lawyer. Most are so . . . so . . . untutored except in their torts and contracts."

"I had a crib sheet," I confessed, and slid Rosemary Newcomb's computer printout next to the glass of disappearing gin.

Prince put on rimless glasses and examined it. "It's from *Equus*, but of course you know that." He took off his glasses and looked at me through the pale gray eyes. "So very bleak there in print, don't you think? How pathetic, a man so bereft of emotions he conjures up the words of others."

"So you admit sending this message to Rosemary Newcomb, Flying Bird?"

"As you lawyers might say, I have no present recollection of that event. But who else could it have been?"

"Why the talk of death?"

"Ask Peter Shaffer. He wrote—"

"I know. I don't care about the play. I want to know why somebody types death notes to a woman two hours before she's murdered."

"And I want to know who wrote Shakespeare's sonnets."

I narrowed my eyes. "We're going to watch you, Prince."

He laughed. They never do that to Clint Eastwood, but I couldn't rattle a half-potted professor. He ordered another drink on my tab and gleefully asked, "Aren't you supposed to say, 'Make it easy on yourself, buddy, and tell us what happened.' And I say, 'Okay, officer, I been wanting to get it off my chest.'"

"Maybe it's funny to you, but some boys downtown think you're the number-one suspect in a double homicide."

"Tell the boys downtown I plead guilty to plagiarism and innocent to murder."

It was a good line, and best I could tell, it was his own. I had nothing to lose, so I tried again. "Okay, then help me out. Two women are dead, and you may be the last person to talk to each of them."

He seemed to think about it. "My lectures might be deathly dull, but don't be ridiculous. I assure you I have neither gouged out the eyes of horses nor strangled young women. . . ."

"Who said they were strangled?"

He paused a moment, took a sip of the clear cold gin. "Your friend, Roderigo."

I studied him. "Where were you between eleven and midnight on the night of June twenty-five?"

"In a drunken stupor, no doubt."

"And July two?"

"That night it could well have been a stunken drupor. I try to alternate, you know."

"And who can corroborate that?"

"As I told your policeman chum . . ."

"No one."

"Except my old polluted liver."

"Tell me about Michelle Diamond. TV Gal?"

"We chatted."

"On the night she was killed?"

"I suppose so, if your records so reveal. But we never met. In fact, I never met any of the women. They were all so . . ."

"Normal?"

"Vacant."

"Vacant?"

He smiled an actor's smile. He was enjoying this a little too much for my taste. "As well as vapid, vacuous, and void. And several other 'V' words I cannot quite wrap my tongue around at the present

time. Vampish. Vain. Vexatious, but need I add, neither virtuous nor
virginal?"

"So why do it? Why waste your precious time?"

"You are being sarcastic, aren't you? Saying my time isn't
precious at all. That I've neither parts to play nor plays to write. That
I'm an old gasbag run out of gas. And you sit there, sturdy and
handsome like some leading man, your contempt for me written across
your unlined face."

"My contempt for you, as you put it, stems only from your
treating this as a game."

"Life is a game, my friend. Or is it a cabaret?"

"Prince. You're getting on my nerves. Why did you waste your
time with the computer game?"

"Oral sex."

"What?"

"Talking about it. Safer than a Second Avenue hooker, don't you
think?"

"So you never intended to get together with TV Gal or Flying
Bird?"

"I didn't say that. I'm sure that somewhere, deep in the bowels
of my mind . . . Gracious, what a metaphor."

"Sort of makes you a shithead, doesn't it?"

He grimaced. "You're really no good at this, Mister . . ."

"Lassiter."

"Now, where was I? Yes, somewhere, deep in the recesses of my
psyche, I must have believed that a beautiful, literate young woman
would take me into her arms and crush me with her ample bosoms. 'I
always think there's a band, kid.'"

"A band?"

"Professor Harold Hill in *The Music Man*. To the little boy,
explaining his illusions of greatness. Do not underestimate the
musical theater. Its homilies and visions of bucolic Americana are
often quite revealing, but that, I'm afraid, is another course."

He downed his drink, his eyes a little hazier. "Are we done with
the interrogation, counselor?"

"For now."

"Good. But let's do it again, shall we? You may sit in on my class
anytime you wish. We're doing *Death of a Salesman* next week."

"I've already done Biff."

"No. An actor?"

"In college. When I wasn't tearing up my knee on the practice field, I studied drama. I was Big Jule in *Guys and Dolls*."

"Yes, yes. You've got the size for that. As well as a certain pleasant vagueness of demeanor. But Biff? Biff's a serious role, a difficult role. Willy Loman has to play off his reactions."

I thought about giving Gerald Prince some of his own medicine, hauling out Biff's big scene rejecting Willy, but I couldn't remember the lines. I wondered what it would be like to discover that your father, your hero, is a fake. "Maybe I'll drop by your class again."

"Yes, you simply must come back!"

I nodded and took one last stab at him. "'Catch me if you can, Mr. Lusk.'"

He seemed startled. "Mr. *Lust*?"

"Mr. *Lusk*."

"Oh, dear me. For a moment I thought you were making a pass at me. The theater's so full of—"

"You've never heard of Mr. Lusk?"

"A character from Dickens, perhaps?"

If he was a liar, he was a good one. Still, he was the only known link between the two women. "We'll talk again," I said.

"Of course we shall. We'll do a reading. I'll be Willy; you'll be Biff. We'll analyze it for them. The play as social commentary, Willy as the modern tragic character. You do remember the theme of the play?"

"As I recall," I said, "something about illusion versus reality."

CHAPTER 14

A Meeting of Hyenas

I heard the clackety-clack of stiletto heels on courthouse tile before I saw her face. Or legs.

She wore a red leather mini with silver tights underneath. The legs were long and sleek and flashed like blades of giant scissors. The suntanned face was set in a screw-you mode. As she clacked closer along the corridor the waves of attorneys, clerks, and witnesses parted in front of her.

"Mr. Lassiter!"

It sounded like an indictment.

I turned to face her. "Mrs. Blinderman."

She stood close enough to give me a cold, but this time there was no friction of body parts. She cocked a hip and jabbed a finger at me. "How would you like to be sued for slander? Or would you prefer I just report you to the bar association?"

"Is there a third choice?" I asked. "Maybe a week in Philadelphia?"

She jammed the local section of the morning paper under my nose. "You read this bullshit?"

I allowed as how the *Journal* was part of my morning ritual, right along with fresh mangoes and one-arm push-ups. Out of the corner of my eye, I saw Doc Riggs emerge from a courtroom. I had been waiting for him. Charlie was wearing his expert-witness suit and stopped a discreet distance away, tamping cherry-flavored tobacco into his briarwood pipe. The old geezer could barely suppress a grin as he studied the tall couple standing toe to toe.

Her voice was low and icy. "And I suppose you deny being the 'source close to the investigation'?"

"That's right. Wasn't me."

"Really. Well, isn't it a coincidence that when my lawyer called the paper to raise holy hell, they said to contact their lawyer. And who do you suppose that is?"

"A fellow of great charm and wit."

She didn't agree. "You think I'm just a dumb broad, don't you? Well, appearances are deceiving. I vamp because it's fun. I'm playing a game, but I'm not stupid. I've been to college, wise guy."

"Okay, okay, you're the homecoming queen."

"You wouldn't banter with me if I was a man, you macho pig."

"If you were a man, you wouldn't grind your thigh into my crotch, which, as I recall, was your greeting last time, Mrs. Blinderman. Now, make up your mind. Do you want to be treated like a piece of meat or the sweetheart of Sigma Chi?"

"You don't know me at all. I've walked up dark staircases in parts of town you wouldn't show your face. I know the streets, and I know a conspiracy when I see one. Compu-Mate has crippled the *Journal's* personal classifieds. We're doing a free bulletin board of dating personals, and your friends at the paper are pissed. You're their lawyer, and you get brownie points for leaking the story. This is a plot to put us out of business."

It's always that way. People on the wrong side of hard-edged news stories think the editors sit around all day devising ways to bust their balls. Maybe some do, but in my experience, editors are so burdened by budgets and deadlines and cantankerous reporters that they conspire only against their own publishers. The pressure of putting out a new product three hundred sixty-five days a year leads to lots of mistakes, but few with malice aforethought. Shoddy reporting and haphazard editing, not willful character assassination, do most of the damage. And then, of course, there are the occasions— the majority, in fact—when the journalistic mugging is well deserved.

"That's crazy," I said. "The *Journal* couldn't care less about your business. No offense, but frankly, Compu-Mate is strictly penny-ante."

"That's your opinion. My lawyer's talking business defamation, injury to reputation, punitive damages."

"Yeah. Well, my lawyer can beat your lawyer. Wait a second, I'm my lawyer."

"You're not funny, Lassiter. And another thing. We're not a 'sex club.' Why the hell did it say that in the headline?"

People were starting to stare. "The same reason most headlines miss the point. Not enough time or room or ingenuity to get it right. Look, I'm as unhappy about the story as—"

She stomped her feet, *clip-clop*, like a flamenco dancer and tossed the newspaper at me. "You'll be even unhappier when I nail your pecker to the courthouse door."

It was hard to argue with that, so I didn't, and she stormed down the corridor, high heels echoing like rifle shots.

"Such language." Charlie Riggs sighed, lighting up in violation of county ordinance 87-1643A and moving next to me. "What was that all about?"

I picked up the crumpled paper and showed it to him:

SLAYING VICTIMS LINKED TO SEX CLUB

Two young women slain in their apartments within the last month both belonged to a computer dating club, a source close to the investigation revealed yesterday.

Michelle Diamond, 29, a local television personality, and Rosemary Newcomb, 27, a Pan Am flight attendant, were killed in separate incidents. Both belonged to Compu-Mate, a Hialeah sex-talk club where members are linked by computer modems. Police are investigating the possibility that the killer is a club member who wooed victims by computer chitchat, then obtained home addresses on the pretense of setting up dates.

115

"Divulging personal information by computer to a stranger is just as dangerous as picking up a hitchhiker," a source close to the investigation told the Journal. *"Any odd behavior by club members should be reported to Metro Homicide at once."*

Max Blinderman, president of Compu-Mate, declined comment. His wife, Roberta Blinderman, told the Journal *that the club is a "respectable business."*

Charlie took off his patched eyeglasses and gave a little harrumph. "Frankly, I think all behavior of Compu-Mate members is 'odd.' Now, in my day, you might ask a young woman to take a ride in your flivver, and if there was a full moon—"

"There's something about her, Charlie, I can't quite get a handle on."

"Who?"

"Bobbie Blinderman. The day I met her at Compu-Mate, she was pissed off even before I served her with a subpoena. Something about me rubbed her raw, nearly at first glance. Next time, she came on to me like a cat in heat. Today she wanted to nail my most precious and underused part—"

"Don't read too much into it. Who's the source, anyway?"

"Must be Rodriguez. Wanted a little publicity to smoke out any unreported threats, weird talk, that sort of thing."

"And you don't approve?"

"I think the benefit is outweighed by the risk that we scare the guy away. He doesn't stop killing, just finds another method of choosing victims. At least here, we had a group of identifiable suspects, a known method of communication, and a way of monitoring the calls."

"You tell Rodriguez this?"

"Sure. But the lines of authority are a little fuzzy. Technically, Metro Homicide reports to me. In reality, cops always run an investigation until there's an arrest and the prosecutor takes over. It's the classic struggle of allies, the prosecutor in his office versus the cops in the field. The general gives the orders and the troops do what the hell they want. Here it's even worse because the cops consider me a deep-carpet, downtown lawyer stepping on their toes."

"Can you get Nick Wolf to straighten them out?"

"Rodriguez wouldn't have talked unless Wolf approved the story."

"So he's meddling?"

It was lunchtime and lawyers scurried like rats from the central courtroom, where Judge Dixie Lee Boulton was holding her calendar call, trying to balance her trial schedule against the summer-vacation demands of fifty downtown mouthpieces. I nodded hello to half a dozen guys who pretended to be friends until I needed a continuance.

"Rodriguez has to work with him long after I'm gone. I'm sure Wolf knows every step I've taken. He can control the cops, plant stories in the paper, alienate potential witnesses like Bobbie Blinderman."

Charlie thought that over for a moment. Court stenographers, law clerks, and jurors with official badges jammed the corridor. "So you think he wants to torpedo the investigation?"

"Who knows?"

"I can see why Roberta Blinderman is upset with the story. Women will be terrified to join the club. Men will be inhibited for fear of being reported to the police if they come on too strong. The whole fantasy game will be stifled."

"So the killer will answer the personals column in the *Journal*, and we start from scratch."

"In which case you lose the chance to see Mrs. Blinderman, at least on official business?"

That one stopped me. "Say what?"

Charlie exhaled and enveloped me in a cherry-flavored cloud. Years ago, I had asked him to stop smoking for his health, but he refused, insisting that *Nicotiana tabacum* was his only remaining vice. Now he was grinning like a bearded leprechaun. "You are intrigued by her, are you not?"

"Charlie. It's business. I've been cultivating her because she can be useful to—"

"Yes, of course. And she has helped despite her schizophrenic behavior?"

"Schizophrenic is a little strong, don't you think? Sure, she helped by not appealing the subpoena order and by voluntarily turning over the record of Rosemary Newcomb's calls. But after today, I think the tall lady has concluded she doesn't care for me."

Charlie jabbed at me with the briarwood bowl of his pipe. "Oh, to the contrary, I'd say she doesn't like the fact that she likes you."

"How's that?"

"Did you realize the two of you were circling each other as you talked, creating your own little universe?"

"No, but what of it? Knife fighters do the same thing."

We jockeyed for position in front of the one elevator that was still working. A horde of hungry lawyers elbowed each other, their competitive juices stirred by the thought of saving ninety seconds on the way to the lobby. When we squeezed aboard, Charlie said, "It reminded me a bit—you'll forgive me, Jake—of a male and female hyena in the mating ceremony. They approach each other quite warily, then after a while lift a leg to the other, exposing their private parts. Then they sniff each other to see if they like the scent. Finally they lick each other and get on with it."

"I don't see how you can compare—"

"I think the two of you are sniffing around."

"Charlie, she's a married—"

"Now, she is attractive in a modern way, I suppose, though that androgynous look doesn't appeal to me. I like women a little rounder, a little softer. Not all angles and planes."

"Are you quite finished, you chauvinistic old lech?"

"Quite, unless you want to hear about the widow-lady toxicologist who seduced me during a spectrophotometry procedure late one night at the morgue."

"Already heard it, Charlie."

"Dear me. *Senex bis puer.* 'An old man is twice a boy.' I shall have to watch myself."

In the lobby we walked under a mural of the early Spaniards making nice with the Caloosa Indians, trading food for clothing and other blatant historical lies. On the wall were portraits of distinguished judges, some of whom had never been indicted. I started telling Charlie about the professor. He started telling me about his testimony for the defense in a malpractice case where the doctor failed to save the life of a man who shot himself in the head, trying to commit suicide. Then he interrupted himself.

"You know the female hyena is often larger than the male, and her private parts resemble those of the male. Early naturalists thought the hyena was a hermaphrodite because of the female's false scrotum and a pronounced clitoris that was mistaken for a penis."

"Charlie, is there a point to this?"

"Well, it makes you wonder about the evolutionary process. Eons ago, female hyenas with pronounced malelike features fared better than more feminine hyenas. So today every female hyena appears male at first glance."

"Or first sniff."

"Exactly. Perhaps it was easier for the male hyena if the structure appeared familiar. Perhaps androgyny is mankind's future as well. Women in pants and short hair, some looking like motorcycle hoodlums or—what is that style called—pest?"

"Punk. I don't think it ever caught on."

"*Deo Gratias!* 'Thank God.'"

We headed out the front door and down the steps onto Flagler Street. An overloaded bus belched a cloud of black smoke at us as we crossed the street to Flanigan's Quarterdeck Lounge.

"I'll buy you a Reuben on rye if you promise not to mention hyenas or bodily functions," I offered.

"A deal." Then, after a moment's deliberation, Charlie said, "I think it was Pliny the Elder who wrote that hyenas were *ab uno animali sepulchra erui inquisitione corporum.*"

"Come again."

"'The only animals that dig up graves searching for corpses.'"

"Old Pliny never met a coroner," I said.

CHAPTER 15

Flint and Steel

"Howdy," said the man in the canvas hat.

"Howdy," I said right back.

The canvas hat had little brass eyelets and a drawstring tied around his neck. Long pale hair stuck out below the hat and over the ears. The face was tanned to a tree-bark finish from the middle of the nose down. The chin was strong and the mouth firm, and if he ever smiled, he didn't let it linger. The shirt was khaki with lots of buttons and flaps, and the pants matched, with loops here and there and enough pockets to boost all the T-bones from the A&P. He reminded me of someone, but I couldn't curl my mind around a name.

I had parked next to a line of juniper bushes. I got out, contorted myself into a couple of spinal twists and dropped into half a dozen knee bends. My back had stiffened into little knots and coils on the drive up the turnpike. The ancient but amiable convertible can still hum along at ninety without tossing a piston, but there is little to relieve the tedium of a narcotizing drive through the middle of the state.

I had headed the old convertible north from Miami, past Lauderdale, the Palm Beaches, and Fort Pierce, then northwest away from the coast, through Okeechobee County north of the lake. I shot past Orlando, where ten million tourists queue endlessly under a broiling sun for a two-minute ride twenty thousand fathoms under an irrigation ditch, where every motel is walking distance to a wax museum, a water slide, a dolphin show, or a jousting tournament, where "attractions" substitute for mountains, rivers, and open spaces, where our joy is computerized and packaged and spic-and-spanned, a place where every developer, syndicator, and huckster would sell time-share parking spaces if only there were a place to park.

I made a pit stop at Fort Drum. The turnpike rest areas have been remodeled into a trendy architect's idea of Florida. It is a vision never shared by the Caloosas, Seminoles, or Miccosukees. Pink and pale blue stucco with gables and tile trim. Wooden trusses overhead like a SoHo loft or a Beverly Hills Tex-Mex eatery. On the walls, pink neon palm trees say it all.

In the gift shop, not much has changed. The orange juice is still fresh, the coconut patties still stale. Next to the alligator postcards and cretinous bumper stickers is a rack of miniature orange trees guaranteed to last twenty-four hours anywhere north of the Mason-Dixon. There is a collection of key chains, ashtrays, and doodads shaped like the Florida peninsula. Does anybody buy this junk or are those the same knickknacks I saw when I drove the old buggy down here in '74?

The restaurant has changed but the food would still make an astronaut nauseous. Premade hamburgers indistinguishable from the Styrofoam container, gritty metallic coffee from a giant urn.

Welcome to the Sunshine State. Having wonderful time. Wish you were here. Come on down, the weather's fine. Six thousand folks a week follow the postcard's advice. They leave the acid rain and radon soil and descend on a land of drained swamps, where the phone number for mosquito control is second in popularity to 911. They did a survey a couple of years back on the best place to live. Not a popularity poll, but a statistical study of crime, alcoholism, divorce, and traffic congestion. Every Florida city flunked. By objective standards, the place is a humid hellhole, a place that attracts drifters and grifters, where the streets are crowded and the streams will soon run dry.

Work crews were busy patching one of the turnpike bridges near Orlando. That's going on all over the state. Especially the newer spans. At the beginning of the century, they built concrete bridges to connect the Florida Keys with the mainland. The cement was thickened with tough granite rock and was allowed to harden for more than a week. The bridges have lasted eighty years.

In the 1980s, the smart guys in Tallahassee built new bridges of watery cement, added a dash of soft Florida limerock and a splash of chemicals to make it dry faster. The cement began cracking as soon as the saltwater hit it. No matter, though, if the new bridges don't last fourscore years. By then, global warming will likely melt the ice caps. Key West will be a suburb of Atlantis, and they'll sell beachfront lots in Orlando.

I had pulled up at the log cabin outside of Silver Springs just after nine. The parking lot was a dirt field covered with wood chips. He appeared out of the darkness, quiet as the night.

After the howdy, he asked, "You Lassiter?"

"Guilty as charged."

Tom Carruthers studied me with a drill instructor's look. "You going into the woods like that?"

"I thought the tie would be useful in an emergency. An unexpected dinner invitation, maybe."

"What the hell do you call those shoes?"

"Actually, except for right and left, I haven't named them."

He didn't crack a grin.

"But they always come when I call them," I said, looking down at my black wingtips and then at his shin-high thick-soled brown boots.

"You're a real city slicker, aincha?"

It didn't sound like a compliment, so I didn't thank him. Now, who did he look like? It still didn't compute.

"I came straight from court, drove six hours," I told him.

"You a lawyer?"

"Guilty to count two."

"I hate lawyers."

"Well, I'm not a very good one."

He pointed toward my shoes. "You can't go into the woods like that."

"I've got basketball high-tops in the car."

He spat into a bush. "Sneakers?"

Overhead, unseen birds sang little jeering songs. A stiff breeze rattled the juniper leaves and filled the air with their tangy fragrance, the violet berries glistening in the fading light. Somebody once told me that juniper was used to flavor gin. I fought off the urge to disclose this treasure of woodsy knowledge.

I had missed dinner, and Tom Carruthers didn't offer me any. Now he stood behind me and stared into the 442's trunk like a cop without a warrant. My trunk is a lot like me. Big and messy. There's enough rust on the floor to let wet windsurfing equipment drain onto the asphalt. There's a gym bag and miscellaneous beach gear crusted with sand. I tossed aside two or three universal joints, a battered sail, and a couple of booms. I found a bruised briefcase full of half-baked pleadings and a lawyer magazine with articles about your Keogh plans, your 401-Ks, and how to double-bill your clients and not get disbarred. Finally I uncovered an old pair of black high-tops with decent enough tread for pickup games on the asphalt.

Carruthers was still looking into the trunk. "No tents allowed," he said, pointing at the pile of junk.

"That's a six-meter sail, not a tent."

"Thought it was one of your new Miami fashions, a purple-and-orange tent for the fancy-pants drug dealers."

"Why would I want a tent for a hike?"

He laughed and spat perilously close to my chariot's fender. "Forty-eight hours in the woods, some folks want to use a tent. But you can't get your survival rating if you sleep in a tent. You gotta—"

"What forty-eight hours?"

"—sleep under the stars or build yourself a hut, a lean-to, a wickiup."

"A wake-me-up?"

"Wickiup. Indian hut made from tree poles covered with brush, bark, what have you."

"I thought this was just a two-hour hike."

123

He spat again. "Not with me, no candy-ass stroll to watch the birds. I put you in with a bunch from the Pensacola Survival League. A few mercenaries, ex-marines, Klansmen."

"Sounds like the juries I've been getting. If it's all right with you—"

"They're already in the forest. You're late."

"So just give me the mini-version. We walk in, talk, have a beer, walk out."

"You want a little hike in the woods, one of the park rangers can arrange that tomorrow. You want Tom Cat, you go forty-eight hours, minimum. No food, no water, no matches, no compass, no sleeping bags, no tent."

"Tom Cat?"

Finally the hint of a smile. Weathered creases showed at the edge of his mouth. "They've called me that for years. In the woods, I'm a cat. I can walk over a branch of pine needles two feet from your ear, you'd never hear me."

He bent over, put a hand on a knee, and started a slow crouching walk, bringing each foot up high, then coming down gently on the outside ball of the foot, rolling to the inside, and finally, silently bringing down the heel.

"A Seminole taught me how. I added my own refinements. Up here, they call it the Tom Cat Stalk."

"What do you stalk?"

"Everything from squirrel to deer. You ever kill a deer with just your bare hands and a knife?"

"Not that I recall."

He almost laughed. "You'd remember if you had. Stalking a deer's almost impossible, even for me. You gotta have 'em trapped, nowhere to run. Or you can jump out of a tree, get 'em by the neck. Slice and choke. They'll buck and try to throw you off. You gotta hang on, blood spurting like water from a garden hose, all hot and sticky, covering you, splashing your face, filling your mouth. Squeeze the life out of them, but love them all the while."

I just let that hang there. I didn't have a comparable story to swap. Once I had shooed a land crab out of a lady friend's kitchen, and she had taken me to her bed in gratitude. Still, it didn't have the same flair.

"Never kill an animal for sport," he went on. His voice was flat and unemotional, his eyes hooded under the brim of the canvas hat. "Only for food. The Indians used every last part of the deer. Ate the venison, tanned the hides, boiled the hooves into glue, strung fishing line from tendons, and carved bones into utensils."

"Complete recycling," I said.

He nodded gravely. "I don't expect you to kill a deer. . . ."

"Lucky for Bambi."

"You don't need that much food."

"A bacon cheeseburger would do fine right now."

"Too late for that."

"Even a turkey on rye, if we're watching the cholesterol."

He motioned me toward a path behind the cabin. Behind it lay the blackness of the Ocala National Forest. "There's lots to eat in the woods. Nearly all your furry mammals are edible. Weasels, foxes, bobcats . . ."

I must have been shaking my head because he kept running down the late-night snack menu. "Rodents too. Voles, mice, lemmings, rats. In a pinch, I've made a stew out of maggots and earthworms. Loaded with protein."

"Come to think of it, I should cut down on the meats."

"No problem. Grasses, cattails, pine needles. You ever drink acorn tea?"

"Does it come in instant?"

He grimaced. "I'll bet you don't even know how to make a fire out of a spindle and bow."

We were wending down a rocky trail in the moonlight when I got around to asking him about it. "They got any women up here?"

He snorted. "Scarcer than hen's teeth."

"Not like in Miami. Boy, we got all kinds."

He didn't bite.

"So what do you do for excitement?" I asked.

He hopped over a fallen log, graceful as a jaguar. "You either make friends with the palm of your hand, or you get the hell out of here. Gainesville's got the coeds, a horny bunch if ever there was.

Orlando's filled with divorcées from the north, all coming down for a fresh start."

"A guy like you must wow them with this buckskin bullshit."

He stopped in his tracks and I nearly bowled him over from behind. I thought I had offended him, and maybe he'd pop me one, but he just put a finger to his lips and cocked an ear toward the darkness.

"Black bear," he whispered. "Season doesn't open till November."

I didn't hear anything and didn't have a license, anyway. A moment later we were moving again, Carruthers doing a brisk version of the Tom Cat Stalk and Lassiter bringing up the rear with a city-slicker shuffle, tripping and cursing over every branch and rock in the darkness.

I got my mind back on track, thinking of the role I had to play. A college drama professor once told me to visualize the character to become him. My mind's eye saw a sweaty-palmed guy in a bar, shirt unbuttoned to the waist, gold chains dangling on his chest. I laid on the sleaze. "Yeah, in Miami, we got your basic panorama of flesh. Every color and shape. We got your waitress types, your business and professional types. We're loaded with stewardesses."

My line drifted with the current. Not a nibble.

After a pause I asked, "You get down to wicked Miami at all?"

"Once in a while."

"Really?"

"Yeah."

"When?"

"What?"

"I mean, when you get to the city, call me. We'll go stalk the wild stewardesses."

"Too many hang-ups."

"How's that?"

"City women. Too many hang-ups. Too much talk."

"I know what you mean."

He clammed up again and we walked some more. It was growing darker under the canopy of slash pine and red maple trees. We emerged from one thicket into a clearing only to enter the woods again a few hundred yards away. Branches kept swatting me across the kisser, and my feet were still stumbling on the rocky ground. The air was moist with the sour perfume of fermenting flora, and little animals could be heard scurrying in the undergrowth. The brush grew thicker until we reached a stream. He led me across a trail of rocks to the other side. I only got one foot wet with a slip on the moss. Lousy sneakers.

"So how long since you been there?" I asked.

"Where?"

"Miami. My home sweet home."

"Couple of weeks. I give an outdoors class at the YMCA every month."

The timing could have been right for Rosemary Newcomb. I thought of her sprawled on the floor of her tiny house. Serving coffee, tea, and smiles at thirty thousand feet, hungering over the keyboard in the eternal search for Fantasy Man, a kind, sensitive, knowing gent who can fix a leaky faucet and share his innermost thoughts. Searching for love and intimacy and commitment and all the other words that have been *Cosmo*'ed into them. And maybe she found the deerslayer, a fantasy with a nightmare ending.

We stopped in a clearing and sat down, cross-legged, like Indians in a western. It was a cloudless night, and I could see his tanned face clearly in the moonlight.

"Okay," he said, "what's your best choice for shelter?"

"The Holiday Inn on Route 200—"

"This land's sloped. Figure the angles, so if it rains, you don't have a stream through your bed."

"—preferably with room service."

"Start by finding some good, strong branches for your ridgepoles. There's plenty of brush, tree boughs, and bark for the roof. Get some leaves to make a bed."

I hadn't seen him remove the knife from a sheath on his leg, but now there it was, gleaming in the moonlight. A row of sawteeth on one edge, a smooth bevel on the other, it looked big as a machete.

"You don't seem to be into this, Mr. Lassiter."

"It just takes me a while."

He scraped the blade of the knife against a rock. Some people are afraid of snakes. With some, it's guns. With me, it's a foot-long blade of stainless steel. I hate a knife.

"That's some blade," I said, forcing a smile.

"Combination Bowie and Rambo. Can chop down a tree or field-dress a deer. You wouldn't believe how it can open a rib cage."

I believed it. I took a breath and said, "Bet you could slice out a kidney with that."

"What?"

"A guy who guts animals probably has a pretty good idea about anatomy."

"I know the intestines from the liver, if that's what you mean."

"Catch me if you can, Mr. Lusk."

"Huh?"

His face was blank, showing neither malice nor curiosity.

"Tom, would you agree that 'woman is the lesser man'?"

"The fuck you talking . . . ?"

"Never mind," I said.

He brought the blade of the knife across a rock, harder this time, and the metallic grating sent a shiver up my spine. "Flint and steel," he said. "All you need for a fire. Bring me some dried leaves, little twigs for tinder."

I unwound my stiff legs and, like a good scout, gathered a pile of forest flotsam, which I dropped at his feet. He didn't look up. "We get all types up here," he said. "Doctors, company presidents, retired folks. Even had a couple fairies from Lauderdale a few weeks back."

"Imagine that."

"Not too many lawyers."

"Be thankful for small blessings."

Little sparks shot from the blade into the kindling. He leaned close to the ground and gently blew into the pile. I could see his face, half-shadowed, half-lighted in the orange glow of the small fire.

"Most guys," he said, "when they come up here, they want to know about the trees and the animals and the dewpoint. You want to talk about women in Miami."

"Just a red-blooded all-American guy, what can I tell you?"

"There was somebody up here a few days ago, a Miami cop. I told him to fuck off."

"Well put."

"I hate cops."

"And lawyers," I agreed.

"Cop wanted to know the last time I was in Miami. And if I saw women down there. Then a guy in shiny shoes drives two hundred fifty miles to take a walk in the woods, asks the same questions. What would you think?"

"Life is full of coincidences. Sixty-five million years ago, when the dinosaurs bought the farm, all the plankton in the ocean died, too. What do you think of that?"

He stood up without using his hands or breaking a twig. "I think you're a cop-lawyer or a lawyer-cop, and I think you'd better find your way home by yourself, mate."

In his silent half crouch, it took only a few seconds for Tom Cat to creep into the darkness of the forest.

Then it hit me. *Mate.* Crocodile Dundee, but without the charm.

CHAPTER 16

Duck Soup

The Prosecutors. Earnest young men and women clip-clopping along the corridors of the Justice Building, barging from courtroom to courtroom, slinging a cargo of files. Always hustling. Always grim. An atmosphere of perpetual motion, of jobs undone, of calendars clogged. Nolle prosequi, refile, plead 'em out, nolo contendere. Bring in new batch. Waive the jury, face the judge, try 'em, minimum mandatory. Carrying concealed firearm, probation violation, back again sucker, revoke probation, bus 'em to Raiford. Jury trial, six honest baffled souls, reasonable doubt, let 'em go, catch you later. Stack 'em up and move 'em through.

The Accused. In the corridors, accompanied by uniformed county-jail guards, filing in from the holding cells. The funnel of law enforcement pours out its refuse here. Some bewildered first-timers, shackled at the feet, shuffling into court, eyes darting toward the gallery for a friendly face. Then the hard guys, still swaggering despite the chains, putting on that street-wise cool as a shell against the world.

The Civil Servants. Drab halls jammed with the faceless players in the game of crime and punishment. An army of workers from a dozen state agencies scooting through the building, feeding the monster. Social workers, probation officers, drug counselors, victim advocates, all committed to the impossible task of imposing order on the bedlam of the American city. In cramped offices overhead, an invisible legion of administrators, secretaries, and file clerks push the paper, stuff the files, and record every twist and turn of the swirling universe called the criminal justice system. Your Tax Dollars at Work.

I squished along the corridor, my wet high-tops leaving a perfect trail of tread on tile. Nick Wolf's receptionist gave me a look reserved for unshaven men in soggy clothes who interrupt the boss's breakfast before the nine A.M. staff meeting. I didn't wait for an invitation to join the great man in his inner office.

He had company.

"You know Commissioner Caycedo's new Lincoln?" Wolf asked. He sat at his desk, a linen napkin jammed into his already tight collar, protecting his white-on-white shirt and burgundy power tie. In front of him was a serving tray with a plate of eggs Benedict, a glass of orange juice, and a pitcher of steaming coffee.

Alex Rodriguez sprawled in an upholstered client's chair, reading the sports section of the *Journal*. "Yeah. That blue-black number about a block long with tinted windows like he's *el presidente*."

Wolf poured coffee for himself and did his best to ignore me. He was good at it. "See, he's got the car, maybe two weeks, doesn't even have pecker tracks on the velour. Every antitheft device known to Detroit, the kill switch, the remote alarm, the fuel-line switch, the cane hook, the portable motion sensor, the telephone-activated alarm, the window beeper."

"I think I see this coming," Rodriguez said, still reading the box scores.

Wolf sliced into a poached egg and a dollop of yolk squirted out. "But all that electronic shit doesn't do any good if you just double-park in front of Manny Diaz's restaurant—"

"El Pollo Loco."

"—and leave the car running, door open."

"Uh-oh. I picture it now," Rodriguez said, cracking a grin.

"So the commissioner waddles into the kitchen to collect the week's bolita receipts. He still would have been okay, but then he stops for a *media noche* on the way out with a side of *frijoles negros* and a little flan for dessert."

"Bad for his heart, if he had any."

"So he's wiping the grease off his chin just in time to see some jackrabbit hop into the Lincoln and tear down Calle Ocho." Wolf paused, sipped the coffee, and continued, "Now the fat fuck's busting *my* chops."

Rodriguez nodded solicitously. "What's he expect you to do, call out the National Guard?"

"A major crusade against grand theft auto. It'll be his theme for the next election. He's got the figures. Thirty-six thousand stolen cars a year in Dade alone, a hundred a day. In the course of a year, one out of every fifty cars in the county is snatched. He figures every voter either is a victim or knows someone who is."

Rodriguez smiled with appreciation. "Caycedo might be fat, ugly, and crooked, *pero el no es estupido.*"

"Plus he wants his car back."

"Lots of luck." Rodriguez laughed. "It's probably on a boat to the Dominican Republic."

Wolf took a swallow of his orange juice. "Nah, we found it last night. Fished a local doper out of a canal and the divers came across the Lincoln by accident. Radio and tape player ripped off, nothing else missing, car in twelve feet of muck."

Rodriguez shook his head. "Your crack addicts got no respect for value."

Wolf looked up, well fed and delighted with himself. "Yo, Jakie. You look like shit. What's that, mistletoe in your hair?"

Rodriguez put down the newspaper and laughed. "Jake's a happy camper, aincha, Jake? Been earning his merit badge from some a-hole in the woods. I'll bet Jake spent the night with him. Separate sleeping bags, I hope."

I squeaked over to the window and caught a fine view of morning rush hour above the trestles of the interstate. "Is this what you guys do all day? Wait for me to make a fool of myself?"

"Doesn't take all day," Nick Wolf answered.

Rodriguez giggled. "Hey, Jake, what's the difference between a porcupine and two lawyers in a Porsche?"

I didn't say a word.

"On a porcupine the pricks are on the outside."

"Ole Jakie doesn't have a Porsche," Wolf said. "Drives a rusted relic of his youth that—"

"Has six hundred miles more on the odometer today than yesterday," I said. "Alex, your pal Tom Carruthers doesn't believe in sleeping bags. Likes to sleep in trees and hump white-tailed deer."

"Told you he was a hard case," Rodriguez said.

"He's a bit off center, but I don't think he's a serial killer. The professor is a boozer with a vivid imagination, but I don't see him strangling young women, either."

Nick Wolf's laugh was laced with derision. "Christ, is that how you investigate? Talk to the suspects, decide if they seem like murderers."

"Thanks for the critique, but you were supposed to stay out of the Michelle Diamond case," I said.

"And the Newcomb case is out of your jurisdiction."

"But if they're related, we gotta work together, Nick."

Wolf shook his head. "Jakie, you're jumping to conclusions. You've lost your feel for this side of the tracks, been downtown too long with the fancy divorces—"

"Hey," Rodriguez interrupted, "I was downtown getting a warrant from Judge Simons the other day—this is the truth—and I'm waiting for this divorce case to finish. The judge turns to the husband and says, 'I'm giving your wife eight hundred dollars a month in alimony.' So the guy looks up at the judge and says, 'Great, Your Honor, I'll chip in a hundred bucks myself.'"

"Shut up, Rod," Wolf commanded. "Listen, Lassiter, the grand jury doesn't give a shit how you feel about these assholes. How about collecting some evidence?"

"What do you suggest, Nick, planting one of your men in the woods disguised as a tree? We don't have enough to get a search warrant or a wiretap. So far as I can tell, it's no crime to talk sexy to a willing woman. That's all we've got on Daniel Boone and the professor."

Rodriguez was fondling his .38, lovingly loading and unloading it. "What about Harry Hardwick?" he asked.

"Aka Henry Travers. I'm going to see him tonight, after I find out if I still have a job downtown."

Wolf drained his coffee cup, tore his napkin loose, and tossed it on the desk. "I don't like your approach. You oughta let Rodriguez's boys do the spadework. A couple of experienced cops to Mutt-and-Jeff these guys. If one's a loony, maybe he'll crack. Some of the nut cases love to confess. You don't believe me, hire one of those psychiatric experts to consult with. Shit, the state's got lots of money for shrink time. I can recommend someone who'll—"

"That's okay," I said. "I've got someone in mind."

I used Wolf's executive bathroom to shave and wash my face. When I came out, Rodriguez was gone, headed to the firing range, and Wolf was dictating the agenda for his staff meeting. I decided the hell with it, just blurt it out. "Michelle ever ask you about Vietnam?"

"What?"

"Vietnam. Your experiences. The Silver Star, all of that."

He dropped the dictaphone and studied me. "What's that got to do . . . ?" He stopped, not liking where he was going. "I already told you about 'Nam. That's all I'm going to—"

"But she asked, didn't she? About you and Evan Ferguson."

He turned in his chair and looked toward the plaques on the wall. But he didn't see them, his eyes blank with the thousand-yard stare of a thousand wars.

"Sure, she asked me some things."

"Why do you suppose . . . ?"

"You know reporters. A million questions."

"But why Ferguson?"

"Prissy probably mentioned him. They always talked about me, comparing notes, I suppose. There's a picture of us—Ferguson and me—in the house. Michelle must have asked about it. What's the big deal?"

"I saw the picture."

He swiveled toward me, glaring. "You were in my house?"

"Yeah."

"What the hell for?"

"It's my job. Interview persons who might have evidence."

"You talked to Prissy?"

"Sure."

"You think I killed Michelle, you crazy bastard?"

"No. As far as I can tell, you had no motive."

He nodded. His face softened just a bit.

"Of course Priscilla might have," I added judiciously.

A fist crashed on the desk, and a file slid to the floor. "Fuck you! And the horse you rode in on! There's a couple of nuts running around out there and you think my wife killed the babe she fixed me up with."

"Just raising possibilities," I countered. "Charlie Riggs taught me the method."

"Then you're both getting senile!"

"Two women—your wife and your girlfriend—were fascinated by you," I said calmly. "And from what I know, Michelle was preoccupied with Vietnam and Lieutenant Ferguson."

"How do you know that?"

"Privileged information. Work product. Top secret and for my eyes only. But if you'd open up a little, maybe you could convince me it's a dead end."

Nick Wolf was quiet a moment and then blurted it out. "He was the best friend I ever had, the finest man I ever knew. He died in my arms."

I stayed quiet. In the corridor I heard the faint sound of laughter. Nick Wolf didn't hear it. He was on another continent in another time.

"It was January 1968, a month before Tet. Like I told you before, my platoon got pinned down in a village, Dak Sut. Evan called it Duck Soup. No air support, so Evan's platoon hauled ass to bail us out. Two men, Gallardi and Boyer, dogwood six, killed in the firefight. Four more dogwood eight, wounded. Evan brought his men in like the U.S. Cavalry and Charley beat it. But they grabbed our translator, a Vietnamese girl named Phuong. We licked our wounds, evacuated the dead and wounded by slick—helicopter—and took off after Chuck and the girl.

"We'd been in the field four days. The men were tired. At least three looked like they had malaria. Two others were popping some pills that had 'em wired. We're tromping through rice paddies, staying on top of the dikes, trying to keep dry and keep moving at a decent pace. Evan's platoon on one dike, ours on another about two thousand meters away, moving parallel to each other, watching the horizon. No sign of Chuck.

"Except for a couple of water buffalo, we're the only things moving. A bunch of boys from the south and midwest, carrying M-16s, playing soldiers, feet bleeding into their boots, diarrhea staining their pants. Just sticking out against the sky."

He stopped, his face drained of color. He gave no sign of continuing.

"Sniper?" I asked.

"Creature from the Black Lagoon. Came up out of the mud alongside Evan's platoon. Covered with glop, he goes for the officer first. Suicide mission. Evan takes I don't know how many rounds. He's all chopped up. The medic's right next to him. He gets it in the throat before Evan's men get off a round. The RTO's dead, too. I slide down the dike and wade through the water. It's like slow motion. Running through the muck. I fall flat on my face a couple times. Evan's still alive, still conscious when I get there, but I knew he wouldn't make it. Half a dozen sucking chest wounds. He died in my arms."

Wolf turned back to me. His look said the history lesson was over.

"Did you tell Michelle?" I asked.

"I never even told my wife, not the details. Prissy had asked me a few times, tried to convince me it would be good to talk about it. But I'm not one of those guys to go crying to the VA, sit in a circle and spill my guts to a counselor."

"No survivor guilt?"

"Fuck no! Survivor *joy*. I did my job and got back. Evan wasn't as lucky. It could have been me but it wasn't." He stared at the wall, his eyes unfocused. "But you're right about one thing. . . ."

Good, that filled my quota for the month.

"Michelle kept bugging me about 'Nam. 'Talk to me,' she'd say. 'Talk so I can understand you, get close.' All that feminine bullshit."

"But you never responded."

"Negative. I told her I would talk. Tell her the whole story. But before I could, she . . ."

"So you never mentioned Dak Sut to her?"

"No Dak Sut, no Duck Soup."

"Or the sniper?"

"No."

"Evan was killed after the firefight in the village, right?"

"Of course, right. I just told you—"

"Evan was still alive when you left the village."

"Jake, what's wrong with you? Of course he was still alive or he couldn't have been shot by the gook sniper on the dike."

I don't have a polygraph machine in my head, but he looked like a man telling the truth. Of course, I believed Gerald Prince and Tom Carruthers, too. Maybe Nick Wolf was right about me. Maybe I'd lost that cynical edge that comes with the territory. Maybe I'd gone soft downtown advising husbands how to avoid alimony and companies how to breach contracts. Maybe billing by the hour fattened the wallet and dulled the instincts. But I could still recognize two stories that didn't match. There was Nick Wolf's story and there was Michelle Diamond's printout:

1. *WHO GAVE THE ORDERS TO WALK ALONG THE DIKE PRIOR TO ENTERING THE VILLAGE OF DAK SUT?*

2. *AFTER THE MEDIC AND RADIOMAN WERE KILLED, WHAT WAS THE STATE OF DISCIPLINE OF YOUR MEN?*

3. *WHEN YOUR PLATOON ENTERED THE VILLAGE OF DAK SUT ON JANUARY 8, 1968, WHAT ORDERS DID YOU GIVE?*

4. *WAS THERE EVIDENCE OF NVA OR VC IN THE VILLAGE?*

5. *WERE THE VILLAGERS ARMED, AND IF SO, DID THEY THREATEN YOUR PLATOON?*

6. *WERE ANY VILLAGERS WOUNDED OR KILLED BY YOUR MEN?*

7. *WHAT HAPPENED TO YOUR TRANSLATOR?*

8. *THE LAST TIME YOU SAW LIEUTENANT FERGUSON ALIVE, WAS HE*

The chronology didn't match. Nothing added up. And if Wolf hadn't told Michelle about the incident, how did she know enough to ask the questions?

Nick Wolf picked up a file and began reading or pretending to.

"Tell me more about what happened in Dak Sut," I said.

"Look, other than formal reports to command and my personal log, I simply have never . . ."

His eyes glazed over, but only for a moment. Then he turned to me, the old Nick Wolf, a glint of anger just beneath the surface. "I don't know what you're getting at, Lassiter, but you're barking up the wrong tree. How about interviewing Harry Hard Dick, or whatever he calls himself, and get the hell out of here."

"I intend to do just that."

"And don't let him bullshit you. Shake him up if you have to. Tell him you've got his prints at the scene—"

"That's not the way I play the game."

"The game," he said derisively. "I used to watch you play ball, Jake. And you know what I remember? One Sunday against the Cowboys, you were blitzing from the weak side. Staubach rolled your way and tripped. Just stumbled over his own feet and went down. Nobody had touched him, so it was a live ball in the days before quarterbacks wore skirts and the zebras blew the whistle every time a money player got a hangnail. He was down, ribs exposed. Fresh meat, and you had a clean shot. You could have speared him, taken him out. Worth fifteen yards, right? Even a good shoulder might have done it. But you just played tag and hopscotched over him."

"I never played to hurt anybody."

"You never played to *win*!" he thundered.

"I stuck my head in there like everybody else."

"Sure, you were physically tough. You threw your body around like it was somebody else's. But that's not the point. You played to have *fun*. I watched you. You'd help the runner up. You laughed out there, always chattering, clapping your hands like a schoolboy. You never knew it was war."

"It wasn't. It was just a game."

His laugh was scornful. "You don't fucking understand, Jake. I'm not talking about football. I'm talking about life. You coast along, just doing your job, making your little jokes. You weren't committed to winning on the field and you haven't changed. You're not serious because you don't see what's going on. Well, I've seen life up close. In the jungle, on the streets, in the eyes of the scumbags and the faces of their victims. Being a cop is war. Being a prosecutor is war. You think the assholes out there play by the rules? You think the guy who killed Michelle gives a shit what's in our fancy books? It's just like in-country. We own the day, Charley owns the night. Only it's worse now. It's pitch-black twenty-four hours a day. Damn it, Jake, you got to have night vision. You got to see in the dark."

CHAPTER 17

Quiniela

The explosive crack of a rifle shot.

The squeaking of sneakered feet on concrete. Murmurs in Spanish, a low whistle, then applause mixed with groans.

A haze of cigarette fog hung over the jai alai fronton. Wednesday night and the place half-empty. Some of the regulars slouched in their cushioned seats studying the program, trying to build two bucks into a hundred with a lucky trifecta.

Henry Travers, aka Harry Hardwick, leaned over the rail at the end of the court near the front wall. He held a stubby pencil and was scribbling in the margins of his program. His stomach ballooned from under a bright aloha shirt. His pants were low slung and drooped over brown loafers with worn heels. His face was creased, his dishwater hair uncombed, and he looked at life through thick, rimless glasses. He appeared to be a man who spent much of his time alone.

Two new players took the court as I sidled next to Travers at the rail. I studied him close up. He hadn't shaved this morning, and if he had showered, he should return his deodorant soap for a refund. His taproom pallor was beyond pale; I had seen better suntans on death row.

At the first crack of pelota against the wall, Travers looked up from his program and toward the court. The player in the red jersey cleanly handled the rebound and, in that peculiar whipping motion, hurled the pelota high against the front wall. The second crack was louder, and there was nothing but a white blur as the player in blue climbed the sidewall, reached high with his cesta, and made the catch. In one motion he pivoted and whirled, rocketing a low screamer toward the front wall. The man in blue tried to short-hop the bounce like Ozzie Smith on a double-play ball, but there's only one Ozzie Smith, and the pelota dribbled off his cesta into the protective screen.

"Goddamn Guernica," Henry Travers muttered.

"It's only one point," I advised.

He turned toward me. It was just another bettor in a Dolphins jersey. Except mine was real. Travers said, "His confidence goes to shit after he loses the first point. Here, look."

He shoved his crumpled program at me. There were handwritten numbers on it. They didn't mean anything to me.

"Guernica finishes in the money forty-six percent of the time when he wins the first point, twenty-one percent when he doesn't."

"Like getting on the board first in football," I said.

"Same principle. I took Guernica, Maya, and Chucho in the trifecta, then wheeled Guernica in both the quiniela and perfecta."

"Good luck."

He snorted. "Should just burn my money, be faster."

Guernica had already lost the second and third points when I asked Travers if he cared for a beer. He said no thanks and then I opened my wallet and showed him my official, laminated, gold-starred, special-assistant-state-attorney badge signed by the Honorable Nicholas G. Wolf. A beer would be just fine, Henry Travers allowed.

We sat at a dirty plastic table sipping watery American beer from Styrofoam cups. At the next table a couple of retirees in baseball caps nodded to Travers.

"I couldn't help noticing you have a slight limp," I said. "Your right foot drags a bit."

"Disc problem. Total disability from the postal service."

"Funny how the heels on your shoes are worn evenly. You'd think the left one would deteriorate faster from carrying more weight."

Behind the thick glasses, his eyes narrowed. "What're you trying to prove?"

"Earlier tonight, when you came out of the head, you were practically skipping so you wouldn't miss a point. You could have been the drum major for the A-and-M marching band. After I said hello, you were hobbling like a cornerback with a pulled hamstring."

He took a long pull on the beer. "Just started acting up. Sometimes it hurts more than others."

"I'll bet. When anybody who smells like government begins asking questions, it must hurt like hell."

He got loud. "You trying to fuck with my pension? Look, I walked these streets for twenty-three years. Pavement so hot your shoes stick to the asphalt. Wearing those goddamn knee socks and striped shorts. Little Havana, Overtown, Gables Estates—you name it, I worked there. Don't know what's worse, the jungle bunnies in Overtown or the rich bitches in the Gables in their two-hundred-dollar bathrobes, asking me to carry their trash to the curb. Do I look like the sanitation department?"

"No, you look like a two-bit grifter who plays the angles and loses three out of four."

He had the expression of a mutt who'd just been kicked. Sometimes you charm a witness into talking. Other times you hit him over the head with a two-by-four. I went for the whole tree.

"Travers, you look like a guy who used to have a buddy clock in when you wanted to goof off, if you had a buddy at all. You look like a guy who can't wait to get rear-ended so you can soak the insurance company for a new paint job and take a month off at full pay 'cause your neck hurts. You look like a guy who'll pick up the silverware from the diner and jiggle the pay phone till a quarter comes out. In short, Travers, you look like a small-time sack of shit."

He licked his lips and his watery eyes darted back and forth. Other bettors were starting to stare. Maybe I was embarrassing him in front of his cronies.

"I don't have to take this," he said. "I put my time in. Now I got sciatic neuralgia."

"You don't say."

He leaned close and let me get a whiff of his sour breath. "Yeah, and I got affidavits from two chiropractors and an osteopath to prove it."

"I don't give a shit about your pension. I want to know where you were on the night of July two."

He took off his glasses and wiped them on his shirt. When he put them back on, they were no cleaner. "Like I told the detective, I was right here. Ten o'clock, maybe a little after, I headed home."

"What about proof? Who saw you?"

"Everybody. Sal the beer guy, Dave the Deuce who works the two-dollar window, but they don't know one day from the next."

"You have any tickets from that night?"

He laughed. "I don't keep 'em as souvenirs. I cash 'em if I win, toss 'em if I lose."

"And when you got home, you went on-line with Flying Bird, right?"

"What if I did? I live alone, okay? I bought this computer. I play some games on it. I got a program that handicaps the horses, another that balances my checkbook. I see an ad for this Compu-Mate. Meet your life mate, right? I never been married."

I nodded, and he quickly added, "Hey, don't think I'm one of those. When I was in the army, I got my share when you could still get it for five bucks and a carton of Luckies. And a guy doesn't deliver the mail all those years without getting invitations for a cold drink or two, if you catch my drift."

I nodded again to let him know we were both a couple of regular guys.

"I mean, times have changed," he said. "Ten years ago, who'd have thought Henry Travers would be richer than John Connally, holier than Jim Bakker, and get more pussy than Rock Hudson?"

"Or be more full of shit than Virginia Key."

"Hey, what gives? I talked to a few women on the machine. I went out with four or five. Older ones, you know. Divorcées, widows, hungry for a man. A lot of lonely women out there."

"And Flying Bird."

"We chatted on-line. Just a kid. She wanted one of those young lawyers or bankers."

"Did you resent that?"

"What?"

"That she thought you were too old for her. Not upscale enough."

"You think I killed the girl because she wouldn't go out with me?"

Behind us, the crowd applauded a winning point. "So that's what happened," I said. "Old Harry Hardwick got shot down. A bitter guy on disability, a guy who lives in one room with a leaky window air conditioner—"

"I got central air!"

"—a guy who gets pissed off. Who does she think she is? Like those rich bitches in the Gables who think you're the garbage man. Maybe get even with them, too."

"You're out of your mind!" He started to get up, but I grabbed his forearm and yanked him back into his seat.

"Maybe she shot you down real good that night, huh? Maybe old Hardwick shoulda changed his name to Droopy. And maybe she'd already given out her address after the invisible man described himself as looking like Tom Selleck, but she found out otherwise. Is that what happened, Travers? You slip over there to teach the bitch a lesson?"

"Friggin' crazy! I'm a taxpayer and I'm gonna complain to my congressman. If Claude Pepper was still alive—"

"She really made you angry, didn't she?"

"She wasn't even my type."

That stopped me cold. "How do you know? You'd never seen her. Did you fantasize about her, follow her around? Beats watching TV, staring at the computer all day."

"Hey, I don't even know where she lived."

"Right, *lived*. Most people, they'd say, *lives*."

"What's the big deal? Your cop friend told me she was dead. I'm sorry for the girl, but I had nothing to do with it."

With that, Henry Travers hoisted himself up and looked toward the scoreboard. Valdez won, Alonso placed, and Ecenarro showed. I watched Travers's hands as he tore a thick batch of quiniela, perfecta, and trifecta tickets down the middle. Strong hands. He showered me with the confetti, then hustled back to his post at the rail. His sciatic neuralgia must not have been acting up.

•   •   •

I had a second watery beer, then headed for the exit when I heard the voice boom behind me.

"Repent! Make peace with the children."

I turned, expecting one of the Jesus freaks, pamphlets in one hand, tin cup in the other. But I found Gerald Prince, tie at half-mast, gray cardigan unbuttoned. Hardwick and Prince, what a quiniela.

"Do you remember the scene in the restaurant?" he asked.

"What are you talking—"

"*Death of a Salesman.* Willy in the restaurant with his sons in the second act, remember?"

"Vaguely," I said.

"Willie tells his boys he's been fired, and he's looking for some good news to tell the missus."

"If that was my cue, I missed it. I can't remember Biff's lines."

"Don't worry, we'll rehearse."

"Are you telling me the college fired you?"

"Of course not, I've got tenure. They can only discharge me for committing bestiality in the quadrangle at high noon, and then only after arbitration. It's in our contracts."

He was holding a bag of nachos covered with melted cheese and salsa. He gestured with the gooey mess, offering to share the bounty, but I declined. "So what are you doing?"

"It's called acting," he said.

"I mean doing here. I didn't know you followed jai alai."

"Moronic game. Never been here before in my life. I called your office. I was informed of your whereabouts by your delightful secretary."

"Cindy must have been replaced."

"Jai alai, she told me. And I always thought that was some form of Japanese poetry."

We walked together toward the parking lot. He was saying something, but a 747 taking off from Miami International drowned him out. When we reached my old convertible, he put a hand on my shoulder. "And that's all there is to it. Flying Bird, yes, TV Gal, no."

"Are you confessing?"

"To being a fool, Mr. Lassiter. When you suggested I spoke to both of those unfortunate young women on the nights they were killed, well, naturally, I assumed you were right. You are an authority figure.

In a play I'd cast you as a man of character with strength, but with doubts nonetheless, a man's man who appeals to women, but is—"

"Could you get on with it?"

"Of course. Well, after our meeting, I belatedly realized where I was the night of June twenty-five."

"Talking on the computer with TV Gal. I've got the printout."

"So you said before. But that was the night I passed out in the library, and not the only time. I never would have remembered, but I have the books stamped on that day. An anthology of British drama plus several studies of erotica, including a most provocative one with selected writings by women authors."

"I'm not following you."

"Sometime that evening, in the college library, I sat down with the books and Jack Daniel's."

"Who is not, I assume, the dean."

Prince patted the pocket of his cardigan and produced a silver flask. "Only a pint, really. As I say, I settled down to do some reading. The chairs are really far too comfortable. I must have nodded off around ten-thirty or so. They lock the place up at eleven, and I was stuck there until six A.M. when the cleaning crew arrived."

"So there'd be witnesses. Whoever let you out."

"Goodness no. I sneaked out, headed home and showered, and made my eight o'clock class, remedial English, if you can imagine. Do you think the Philistines appreciated my efforts?"

In an effortless motion Prince opened the flask, took a swig, and slid it back into his pocket. I unlocked the trunk of the 442, tossed aside a catcher's mask, a tennis racket with popped strings, a snorkel and fins. Finally I uncovered my briefcase. I extracted a computer printout and handed it to the professor.

He squinted to read under the mercury vapor lights of the parking lot. "What's this, 'eight feet tall, green scaly skin . . .'?"

"That's you, Prince, the night of June twenty-five."

"The hell you say!"

He read aloud. "'What about your asshole? Is it nice and tight?' Surely, you don't think . . ."

"It's got your handle on it."

"But does it sound like me? With my command of the language, would I grovel in such sordid feculence?"

"I don't know, but you don't mind borrowing a line now and then, do you?"

I pointed at the bottom of the page. He continued reading silently, then shook his head. "You think I stole this . . . this pelvic-thrusting doggerel about too much love. Really now."

"Peter Shaffer or Jerry Lee Lewis, what difference does it make?"

He arched his eyebrows so high the gesture would be visible from the balcony. "What difference! You compare the finest of contemporary theater with . . . with rock and roll!"

"Which do you find more insulting, being accused of murder or of stealing lyrics?"

"The latter, of course. With the world's great literature at my fingertips, I never would have stooped to that monosyllabic drivel. As for the stylites poem, I suppose you know it's by Tennyson."

"So I've been told. That's what links Michelle Diamond's green scaly monster to the Newcomb murder scene."

Somewhere across the parking lot, a car alarm bleated. It held no interest for the security guards at the gate. Prince reached into his other pocket and pulled out a worn paperback. "A gift for you, my thespianic barrister."

While I riffled through a book of poetry, Prince started professoring. "Tennyson was having a bit of fun with religious fanatics, ridiculing the ancient ascetics who mortified the flesh by living atop pillars. I doubt, however, that the poor soul who communicated with Miss Diamond understands the poet's sarcasm."

A muffled roar came from inside the fronton.

"But *you* do."

He raised his fine chin and did his best to look offended. "Meaning what?"

I tossed the book into the trunk of my car and looked him dead in the eye. "Meaning you know a lot about Tennyson, and for all I know, you collect rock 'n' roll classics, too."

"Let me see if I follow you. I have a passing acquaintance with the work of an illustrious poet. A killer quotes the same poet. Therefore, I am the killer. Gracious, lad, did you ever take a course in logic?"

"The evidence—"

"The evidence is what you fellows call circumstantial, is it not?"

"I believe it was Henry David Thoreau," I said, trying to lecture

147

the lecturer, "who said that circumstantial evidence can be very strong, as when you find a trout in the milk."

Maybe it was the mention of milk that made Prince blanch, or maybe he didn't expect the literary reference from a guy in a faded football jersey, or maybe it was a look of guilt. Whichever, he recovered quickly enough. "Oh, come now! As you simply refuse to hear, I spent the entire night in the library. . . ."

"Where's the proof?"

"I have the books stamped on the twenty-fifth."

"You could have checked them out at noon. You have *no* proof."

He seemed to straighten and his voice rumbled from deep within. "There is my honor!"

I didn't laugh. I didn't even sneer. He might have been serious. Or he might have been playing some long-forgotten role.

He looked toward the airport, showing me his sagging profile. *"Tout est perdu fors l'honneur."*

"And when honor is lost, you'll have nothing."

"Precisely."

"According to the computer, Passion Prince talked to TV Gal around eleven P.M. on the night of June twenty-five. Two hours later, TV Gal was dead."

"The computer is wrong."

"You admit being Passion Prince?"

"With all that melancholy sobriquet implies."

"And *prior* to that night, you chatted with TV Gal?"

"But of course."

"And you admit talking with Flying Bird, Rosemary Newcomb, on the night of July two shortly before she—"

"Yes, yes. We've been over all that. You have my flagrant plagiarism from *Equus.*"

"So why do you deny what the computer says is true?"

He smiled a sad smile. "Come now, Mr. Lassiter. Does a computer know truth from illusion? How can it, when those who feed it are just as blind? What is a computer anyway but the mechanical mind of a man, a man stripped of emotion? Can a computer feel passion? Does it have a soul? Does it know the freedom of the human spirit?"

"You lost me somewhere between illusion and passion."

"My dear boy, welcome to my class. You played football, didn't you, just like Biff. Your darling secretary told me you were a professional gladiator."

"Not very well and not very long."

"Surely you recollect Willy's speech at the end of Act One, the wistful remembrance of Biff's last football game, the celebration of lost youth and promise."

"Vaguely, something about a star never fading away."

"Yes, yes. But what does it mean?"

Give them tenure and two courses a semester, and they wallow in their little world, playing their little games. He looked at me, the demanding teacher, awaiting a response.

"Okay," I said. "Willy was lost in his illusions. His son once played a game, but there was no substance to it. Not when the rest of his life was built on lies."

"Precisely."

"Precisely what?"

"Shall I put it in terms you can understand?"

"If it's not too much trouble."

"In Act Two, Willy's out in the garden at night and Biff tells him he's going to leave home and not come back."

"Yeah."

"Remember Willy's lines?"

It was there somewhere, buried in the attic trunk of memories. "Willie was planting carrots, putting some seeds down."

"Yes, very good. And what did he say about Biff's leaving, about his son's failure as a man?"

I was still rooting around for it. "Something about not taking the rap for him?"

"Right. We each bear responsibility for our own actions, but that's all."

I stared blankly at him. He reached into his pocket for the silver flask and, with the same hand, unscrewed the cap, letting it dangle on a chain. He took a healthy slug, and in an instant the flask was back in the pocket, two ounces lighter. Practice, the coach always said, makes perfect.

Professor Gerald Prince smiled and looked at me through watery eyes. "What I'm telling you, my dear Biff, is quite simple. I was framed."

CHAPTER 18

Passwords

The plaintiff leaned back, crossing his arms in front of his chest as if to ward off blows. He was a short, slender Oriental man in his fifties, and he fidgeted in a squeaky chair. He wore a short-sleeve white shirt and baggy trousers and kept shooting glances from the stenographer to me and back again.

H. T. Patterson crammed all of us into his miniature conference room—Chong Gong Wong, his client; Rosalina Bustamente, the stenographer; Symington Foote, publisher and noted critic of the legal system; and little old me, courageous battler for the rights of Fortune-500 companies. Patterson sat next to his client, trying to calm him with occasional smiles and soothing pats on the arm. The room had no windows, one table and six chairs, and was overflowing with the detritus of the plaintiff's personal-injury practice—models of the spine and circulatory system, printed posters totaling damages for nearsighted jurors, blowups of various rear-end collisions at local intersections, and a tire that suffered a blowout with ominous results.

Either the air-conditioning was broken or my crafty adversary was employing the oldest trick in the book for shortening his client's deposition. It didn't matter to me. I just took off my suit coat, rolled up my sleeves, and plunged ahead.

"In fact, Mr. Wong, shortly after the *Journal's* review appeared, you changed the recipe for the duck à l'orange, did you not?"

Wong didn't say a word but his chair squealed.

"Ob-jec-tion!" H. T. Patterson sang out.

"On what ground?" I demanded.

"Remedial measures are inadmissible," Patterson proclaimed with a heavy dose of self-righteousness.

I corrected him. "This is not a case where a defendant has remedied a safety problem after an accident. A city would never fix a pothole after an accident if the remedial actions were admissible. But your client is the plaintiff, and the doctrine simply does not apply."

"Thank you for a most cogent lecture on the rules of evidence, Mr. Lassiter, but my objection stands, and I instruct my client not to answer your insulting and harassing question. If you disagree, I suggest you take it up with the judge after the deposition."

I disagreed, but I didn't have time to run to the courthouse. I also was getting nowhere with Chong Gong Wong, owner-chef of the Chez Saigon, Miami's only French-Vietnamese restaurant.

"Can he get away with this?" Symington Foote whispered.

I leaned close to Foote's ear. "As long as we're in his office and deposing his client, he's the boss. We'll file a motion to compel after the depo."

Sweat dripping from his patrician nose, Foote sneered his disapproval and made a note in his pocket calendar. Tomorrow, I suspected, the *Journal* would condemn lawyers who prolong litigation and cause untold expense to our last bastion of freedom, billion-dollar media conglomerates.

"Now, Mr. Wong, what *is* your recipe for duck à l'orange?"

Again, Wong clammed up and the chair creaked. Patterson said, "At what point in time?"

A lawyer will never use one word when five will do.

"Before the newspaper published the review," I told him.

"Objection! Irrelevant."

"What about the current recipe, Mr. Wong?"

151

Before Wong had a chance not to answer, Patterson sang out, "Objection! Trade secret."

Patterson sat there smiling at me, resplendent in a three-piece white linen suit, unfazed by the heat and humidity. I wanted to strangle him with his Italian silk tie, and he knew it.

"Tell me, H.T., is there any question I can ask this transmitter of ptomaine, this bearer of botulism, that won't draw an objection?"

"What he say?" Chong Gong Wong demanded. The chair was silent.

Patterson slapped the conference table in mock horror. "Slander! Defamation! Obloquy piled upon libel! Is it not enough that your illiterate restaurant critic referred to the acclaimed Wong entrée as 'duck à la slime'?"

"Fair comment," I retorted.

"Is it not enough that he called the rice soup 'cream of phlegm'?"

"Hyperbole, nothing more."

"That he denigrated the foie gras as 'toxic scum.'"

"A timely reference to environmental concerns."

"That the rabbit cassoulet tasted like 'road-kill muskrat.'"

"Intended humorously, no doubt."

Patterson bounded from his chair, put a hand on his client's shoulder, and thrust his chin toward the heavens. "Lies! Prevarications! I have never witnessed such calumny—"

"Save it for the jury, H.T. Look, we're wasting a lot of time. You've got a waiting room full of clients, and from the looks of them, most are lucky to be out on bond. Let's conclude discovery, ask for an early trial date, and finish this."

"—a string of malicious canards impugning my client's cuisine, damaging his reputation, assaulting his honor. The jackals of the *Journal* shall pay the ultimate price; their ledgers will flow with red ink in this, the Mother of all Lawsuits. And may I enlighten you as to how Shakespeare described the importance of a man's reputation in *Richard II*?"

I'd already heard it, something about the purest treasure mortal times afford. By now I figured Patterson was getting paid by the word or maybe the syllable. He would go on for a while, making the stenographer earn her keep. I checked my watch. Three-thirty. Barely time to beat rush hour on the drive to Hialeah.

"A man loses everything in his war-ravaged country . . ."
Odd, since Wong was a Viet Cong sympathizer.
"Then in our land of opportunity, he employs dozens of unfortunate souls from the Caribbean, South America, and the Orient. . . ."
Not one green card in the bunch.
"Our city leaders dine at his famous establishment . . ."
Freebies for the commissioners, no kitchen inspections for Wong.
"Until that savage reporter unleashes his venom. . . ."
Actually he was drunk and the copy editor asleep.

Max Blinderman looked me up and down and didn't like anything high or low. "She ain't here," he announced, leaning on the counter in the Compu-Mate office.

I gawked over his shoulder, which isn't hard to do when you're nearly a foot taller. True enough, Bobbie was nowhere to be seen. Max wore a black T-shirt with a pack of cigarettes rolled up in the sleeve. I hadn't seen anything like it in years.

"Actually, I came to see you," I said, and waited for my nose to grow.

He looked at me skeptically. On his forearm, the tattooed snake seemed to hiss. Looking down, I noticed a bald spot expertly camouflaged by some vigorous back-to-front combing and a healthy dose of hairspray.

"I wanted to apologize for that story in the *Journal*," I continued, making it up as I went along. "Bobbie threatened a lawsuit because of what it would do to your business. I just wanted you to know that I had nothing—"

"Fergit it. Hey, business never been better. Babes are calling in, wanting to join, talk to the murderer. Some kind of turn-on, can you believe it? And guys, too, one wants the handle 'Sexy Strangler,' I won't give it to him." He paused a moment to pat himself on the back. "This is a classy operation."

I nodded in agreement, and my nose was still normal except for a curve where an elbow once came through my face mask. "It's a strange world out there, eh, Max?"

"Yow."

"One more thing. When Bobbie responded to the subpoena, she

gave me a printout of the calls to both women on the nights they were killed."

"Yow."

"Could the list be wrong?"

"Whaddaya mean?"

"Is it possible for someone's name to be listed by mistake? Can the computer be wrong?"

He loosened up a bit, probably figuring I'd have served him with a warrant by now if that was my mission. "Don't see how. The computer records the handle automatically when the customer gets on-line. No human error possible."

"What about an impostor? My handle's Stick Shift, but what's to keep me from logging in as Passion Prince?"

"Won't work. Customer's handle can only be used when matched with his password. And that's something known only to the customer."

"Not quite," I said.

"How's that?"

"*You* know all the passwords, don't you, Max?"

A smile flashed like a blade beneath his mustache. "Yow. What of it?"

CHAPTER 19

Tourist
Season

"But I can't go to England."

Charlie Riggs continued packing his battered leather suitcase.

"I've got a partners' meeting next week. If I miss another one . . ."

Charlie neatly folded a heavy mackinaw and placed it in the case. Next came a woolen scarf and a pair of gloves.

"I've got a libel trial with H. T. Patterson. If I can prove that Chong Gong Wong pisses in his soup . . ."

With his hand Charlie dusted off an old fedora that Harry Truman would have loved. He placed it lovingly on top of the clothes and gently closed the case.

"To say nothing of the Diamond murder investigation. I'm stuck with a suspicious state attorney and a horny professor, and I don't think either one is Jack the Ripper. Plus the reporters are driving me crazy. Rick Gomez was hiding in a mango tree this morning when I went outside to water the crabgrass."

"Precisely why you should accompany me to London. While I'm lecturing, you can follow up on the Ripper connection. Tour the East End if you wish. Call New Scotland Yard. Anything."

"I don't know, Charlie. I think the Mr. Lusk stuff is a curveball."

Charlie was stuffing his favorite pipe with cherry-blend tobacco. He would have to go eight hours without a puff and was going to miss it. "I'm sure Nick Wolf would approve your travel expenses as part of the investigation."

"No doubt. He probably wants me out of town."

"It could be useful, getting away, thinking about the case. *Tempus omnia revelat.* 'Time reveals all things.'"

"It doesn't feel right, leaving just now."

Charlie shrugged. "It's up to you. And maybe just as well. You didn't seem to get along that well with Pamela Metcalf."

"What's she—"

"As the hostess for the lecture tour, she'll be around quite a bit. I can understand your reluctance to go if the two of you don't—"

"What time's our flight?"

The Miami airport in July. An air-conditioned icebox stocked with frozen tourists. Shorts and thongs and legs broiled lobster red. Europeans on charters to art-deco South Beach. South Americans booking off-season rooms and escaping winter back home. Miamians heading for Asheville, Bar Harbor, and Aspen.

Intentional tourists. Tourists from the islands hauling boxed Sonys and Panasonics, tourists from the midwest loaded with tax-free liquor from the islands. Tired children screaming, caged dogs yowling, monotone messages in three languages on the PA.

And the businessmen. Another day, another city. Gray suits, blue shirts, rep ties, a thousand weary faces. Briefcases stuffed with forms, dictaphones, and calculators. Guys from sales or marketing peddling software or mainframes or this season's widget, sitting at the gate, figuring last week's commissions, fudging the expense accounts, making lists, taking inventory.

The modern drummer, poised for his daily dose of cardboard food and stale air. No more Willy Lomans in the Studebaker getting just past Yonkers. These days a guy from Richmond or Memphis can make the Atlanta hub for the morning flight to Pensacola or Biloxi, hop the bus to the rental lot, slip into the still-wet Taurus, and have lunch with the purchasing agent he's been sweet-talking all year. If he makes the sale, great, and it's bourbon on the rocks at the Holiday Inn before dinner alone and a pay movie in the room. No sale, there's always tomorrow and a hot new prospect in Mobile.

Charlie spent the interminable flight reading the *Select Coroners' Roles, A.D. 1265–1413* while I went over what I knew. As usual, it was less than I didn't know. I knew Michelle Diamond was curious about Nick Wolf's war record, but I didn't know why. She wanted a story, of course, but what story and why wouldn't Nick open up? Maybe I should talk to Priscilla Wolf again. Maybe there's something she left out, something she knew from years ago. What happened in Dak Sut and on the dike outside the village and which happened first? Michelle thought the shooting on the dike happened before the troops entered the village. If it did, when was Evan Ferguson killed? And what about the translator? How did she die? What did Michelle know, anyway? And if Nick thought she had something on him, would he have killed to silence her?

So many questions.

What about Gerald Prince? He denied chatting with Michelle even though the computer recorded his password and handle attached to the crude dialogue. Then there were the frenzied lyrics from "Great Balls of Fire." It isn't too much love that drives a man insane, I thought. But what is it? Maybe Dr. Pamela Metcalf knows.

Thinking about the professor inspired me to grab two little bottles of Jack Daniel's when the flight attendant rolled by. I listened to the drone of the engines, my eyes growing heavy, my mind drifting over the clouds.

Tom Carruthers. Now there's a character. Homophobic, chauvinistic tough guy in rawhide and boots. Who knows what evil lurks in his heart?

Henry Travers. A sad, middle-aged faker, scrounging for two-dollar winners and lusting for the friction of body parts. A lifetime of resentment against women by a guy who never did anything but lease them.

And how about Max Blinderman? He could have been an electronic imposter, plugging into Michelle's line by signing on as the Passion Prince. But a guy with a record of misdemeanors doesn't usually leap to a Murder One. Unless he's done it before and has never been caught.

Back to Nick Wolf. Maybe he liked beating me in court and wanted me to play the fool twice. If Nick Wolf killed Michelle Diamond, unthinkable as that is, who killed Rosemary Newcomb? Someone did, after apparently consensual sex, but why? And what does it have to do with Michelle?

Keep thinking, Lassiter.

No thank you, miss, not another of the little brown bottles, rich cool liquid twirling down the throat. On the other hand, it's my duty to lighten the load you have to push down the aisle.

Who knew both women? Biggus Dickus and Passion Prince. The first one has alibis, Alex Rodriguez said. The second one has his own frustrations, but a killer? I would ask Pamela Metcalf about that, too.

Ah, Dr. Metcalf. Sexy and sagacious. Tall, brainy, beautiful Dr. Metcalf who stiff-armed me like Larry Csonka jolting a linebacker. I pushed the rewind button in my mind and played it back. I saw her in my old convertible, hair flying, as we crossed the drawbridge on the night we met, lights of the city shimmering in the bay. But the scene was out of kilter. She had been unsmiling and unresponsive, unimpressed by an ex-jock mouthpiece with a crooked grin and an ancient chariot. I hadn't made a dent in her armor.

Okay, admit it, Lassiter, it's not the first time. There've been others, wise to your aw-shucks counterfeit charm, to the sports-pub patter, the barbed sarcasm that passes for humor. Maybe the English lady sees through the veneer to the guy inside, the guy who despises renting himself out by the hour to the client with the largest checkbook. Which is almost always the client with the blackest hat.

No, Your Honor, Asbestos-R-Us shouldn't have to remove its exemplary product from the Sunnyvale Elementary School. No problem if microscopic spores pierce the lungs of little Jack and Jill. Toughen 'em up.

So after a while the guy inside didn't care anymore, and maybe it started to show on the guy outside. But now, with two women dead, something to care about. I didn't ask for it, but someone pinned a badge on me. Maybe someone who wanted me to boot it, someone who saw me lose and liked what he saw. Damn it, Lassiter! So full of doubts under all that swagger. Just buckle on the chin strap and dive into the pile. Make something happen. Hit somebody!

I chased away the gremlins, closed my eyes, and thought of Pam Metcalf for a while, maybe a long while, as the 747's giant engines droned on, and the warmth of Tennessee sour mash spread through me, and when I opened my eyes, the plane's tires were screeching against the tarmac and I was still thinking of the psychiatrist lady, and I was happy and sad at the same time and didn't even know why.

CHAPTER 20

The Huddle

A gray rain fell against a gray sky, and a gray chill hung in the air.

The only thing gray about Pam Metcalf was her silk blouse. The skirt was a rich black wool, the pumps black leather and sensibly low-heeled, but the scarf was an exclamation point of fiery scarlet. I pictured her in front of the mirror that morning, brushing back the thick auburn hair, slathering an extra daub of gloss on the lips, maybe starting for the door, then doubling back to tie that flirtatious scarf around her neck.

Great fantasy, Lassiter. Man is never so foolish as when he fools himself.

I tossed our bags into the back of Pam Metcalf's silver Range Rover and let Charlie join her in the front seat. Pam expertly ran through the gears and got us out of the maze of Heathrow and onto the highway to the city.

"I like the Rover," I told her from the backseat. "Great to have four-wheel drive in case we run into quicksand in Piccadilly."

As usual, she thought I was hilarious. She showed this by ignoring me, doubtless out of fear she'd bust a gut laughing.

Charlie was packing his pipe after eight hours of quarantine on the flight. Pam Metcalf said, "The staff is anxiously awaiting your lecture."

"Me too," I admitted, "and so is the customs inspector, judging from the look on his face when he opened Charlie's bag of tissue samples and internal organs."

"Some people have never seen a hand floating in a jar of formaldehyde," Charlie said, as if he couldn't understand why.

"Or a skull with an ax blade embedded in it," I agreed.

Pam Metcalf turned toward the backseat. "Mr. Lassiter . . ."

"Jake," I reminded her.

"Jake. If you wish, I could arrange some meetings for you during Dr. Riggs's first talk. It could be useful to your investigation. Of course, you may not want to miss—"

"No problem. I've heard Charlie lecture so many times, I've stopped throwing up during the slide show."

"Very well," she said, "you might find my therapy group very stimulating."

We drove without speaking for a while, listening to the clack of the windshield wipers and the hiss of the tires. As we neared the city Charlie nodded sleepily, and I stifled a yawn with the back of my fist.

"If the two of you are weary, perhaps a short nap would be in order," she suggested. "I could wait in the lobby, then knock you up in an hour."

I was intrigued by the possibilities but figured she was only offering a wake-up call.

"No need," Charlie said. "A cold shower, and I'll be good as new. It's best our bodies get adjusted to the time change."

I stretched my legs across the backseat and caught a glimpse of Pam Metcalf in the rearview mirror. Our eyes met and hers flicked back to the road. "Perhaps the two of you would be interested in a weekend in the country," she said. "It's particularly nice this time of year in the Cotswolds."

"Not to be confused with the Catskills," I piped up, remembering our first conversation of promiscuous farm girls and uncaught murderers.

"Sounds delightful," Charlie said.

"My family's summer home is in the Cotswolds," she said to the windshield.

Family. It finally occurred to my dense brain matter that maybe the English lady was married. I pictured a dry Cambridge professor or a balding vicar, a stooped guy in a tattered tweed coat puttering around a drafty house, stirring the fire with an ancient poker.

"My mother's home, really. It's been in the family for two hundred years."

Mother, blessed mother.

"I keep a flat in London, of course. But every fortnight or so, it's ever so nice to go home. So peaceful. It's sheep country and some roads are rather primitive. The Range Rover is quite useful there."

Aha. The crack about the Range Rover had drawn a response after all. So she wasn't ignoring me. And the enchantment of that crisp voice: *rather primitive . . . quite useful.* How do they learn that unhurried enunciation?

In the city she negotiated the traffic circles they call round-abouts, smoothly shifting and accelerating, rarely yielding the right of way. The rain-polished streets were jammed with spacious black taxis and double-decker buses. On the sidewalks, tidy, well-dressed businessmen and women poured from banks and shops, walking briskly, umbrellas poised against the chilly rain.

"Not much of a day for sight-seeing," Pam Metcalf said, "but that's Trafalgar Square off to the right."

I looked over my shoulder and caught sight of the National Gallery on one side and Buckingham Palace on the other and figured I had filled my culture quota for the trip.

Pam Metcalf dropped us at our hotel for a quick shower before Charlie's first lecture at the Covent Hospital for the Criminally Insane. I was quicker than Charlie and in fifteen minutes found Pam sitting in a leather chair in the lobby, legs crossed, staring through large-rimmed eyeglasses at a bundle of papers in her lap.

She looked up, tossed the papers onto a side table, and slid the glasses on top of her head, brushing her hair back. "Medical students write such rubbish," she announced.

I nodded and sat down on a sofa facing her.

"So easy to condemn something they don't understand. So very avant-garde to denounce radical psychiatry."

"Haven't heard of that," I admitted.

"An unfortunate name for an innovative way of viewing psychiatric conditions. A radical psychiatrist would say that mental illness is a myth, that those we call mentally ill are just as rational as anyone else from their own perspective."

"You mean they're not crazy because they don't know they're crazy?"

"They're not crazy, as you say, because their actions are just as goal-directed and motivated as yours or mine. They are perfectly reasonable from their point of view."

"That's nuts! I'm sorry . . . I mean it's just semantics. They're crazy or ill or whatever you call it because they can't conform to society's standards of normal behavior."

She gave me the tolerant look an extraordinarily patient trainer might show to a particularly inept chimpanzee. "You may be surprised to learn that some schizophrenics actually choose careers as mental patients. They appraise their alternatives in the outside world, then make a rational choice as to their actions."

It didn't make sense to me, but then abstract concepts are not my strong point. "If their actions are violent or bizarre, does it matter if we call them rational or not?" I asked.

"Perhaps not, but it affects the very roots of psychiatry. Radical psychiatrists argue that the unconscious is a myth, that all wishes, emotions, and feelings are conscious thoughts, and if not conscious, they don't exist at all."

"Hold on. I thought the whole game you shrinks play is that the unconscious affects behavior."

"Historically accurate, but our science is changing."

"Are you saying it isn't the subconscious that causes someone to kill and kill again, are you chucking out the old plea of not guilty by reason of insanity?"

"The fantasies acted out by serial murderers are clearly conscious. Your FBI has conducted lengthy interviews with imprisoned killers that demonstrate the extent of conscious fantasizing from the planning of the crime to the crime itself to disposal of the body."

"But the fantasies are the product of the unconscious, aren't they?"

"Prove it," she demanded.

Then it dawned on me. "You're a radical psychiatrist."

"Let's just say I have an open mind."

I mulled that over a moment and she continued: "Dr. Riggs rang me up about the second murder last week. The messages are quite interesting. *Equus* is a British work, you know."

I knew.

"The protagonist is a psychiatrist, you know."

I knew that, too.

"How do you interpret the *Equus* message?" she asked.

"I don't know. It was written to Rosemary Newcomb by a professor who teaches drama when he isn't drunk. I was hoping you had some thoughts."

"Well, one thing is quite obvious. Judging from the differences between the messages, I would say it is unlikely that the professor wrote both the *Equus* excerpt to Miss Newcomb and the 'green, scaly monster' rejoinder to Miss Diamond." I stayed quiet and she slid the glasses back down and looked directly at me. "Additionally, you have the other messages to deal with. The Jack the Ripper taunt at the Diamond murder scene and the Tennyson poem at the Newcomb scene. They are all so different, it is difficult to know where to begin."

Now we were getting somewhere. I knew the lady shrink would be helpful. I was concentrating on every word, something made more difficult by the fact that her black wool skirt was starting to ride up her thighs. Her legs, as any objective eyewitness with moderate powers of observation could testify, were long and slender and carved from ivory. I forced myself to look at a spot in the middle of her forehead. "I'm not sure I follow you," I said.

"If you're trying to build a profile of the killer, you must be certain that the factors you build into it are derived from the killer. With these messages, some obviously are and some are not. But which? *Equus* is fiction, lyrical, and metaphorical. It's not about murder."

"The boy blinds six horses with a spike. He is deranged, as the killer must be."

"But the play is not about mutilating the horses, is it?"

As I thought it over, well-dressed London matrons carrying umbrellas began filling the lobby. The hotel apparently served an afternoon tea. Behind us, an elevator opened and some distinctively American voices—loud, complaining—filled the air. A family in warm-up suits and sneakers tromped out, festooned with video gear, the husband griping at a majestic decibel level about the price of fish and chips in Soho.

"No," I said finally. "It's about materialism and the blandness of modern life, about our losing the capacity for passion."

"Whereas the Jack the Ripper message is starkly literal, harshly real. A madman killing women and jeering at the authorities."

"And you don't think the same person, the same killer, can be both literal and metaphorical?"

"It's unlikely, but the person who wrote the *Equus* note—"

"Professor Prince, by name."

"—may well have written the Tennyson poetry at the second murder scene."

"Whoa! Whoever wrote the poetry killed Rosemary Newcomb. He left it for us just as the Ripper note was left at the Diamond scene."

"Is the professor not the obvious suspect, a man who knows literature and drama?"

"Yes, but he doesn't seem capable—"

"Read me the poem, just the last two lines."

I tried it with some feeling:

"*'Woman is the lesser man, and all thy passions,*
matched with mine,
Are as moonlight unto sunlight, and as water unto wine.'"

She raised her eyebrows and smiled an enigmatic smile. "Now read this." She reached into a folder and handed me the last page of the last scene of *Equus*. "The psychiatrist's speech to the boy," she said.

I read aloud, "'He may even come to find sex funny. Smirky funny. Bit of grunt funny. Trampled and furtive and entirely in control. Hopefully, he'll feel nothing at his fork but approved flesh. I doubt, however, with much passion! Passion, you see, can be destroyed by a doctor. It cannot be created.'"

She smiled again. "You read quite well. Both the poem and the play are laments to lost passion, are they not?"

"In a way, but—"

"The professor admits sending the *Equus* message the same night Miss Newcomb is killed," she continued. "The murder scene was organized, no blood or entrails dripping from the walls. An organized murderer is usually intelligent and able to converse with his victims. Rather than using violence to subdue, he controls with conversation. He assumes a position of authority, not unlike a teacher with a class. He can be quite winning. He frequently has problems with alcohol. Your professor fits the profile quite nicely, don't you think?"

In the movies, this is when the detective takes a long pull on his cigarette, exhales, and says, "A little too nicely, eh, babe?" But I don't smoke, and it all seemed to fit, just like the lady said.

Somewhere in my head, a memory was stirring. "After we left Michelle Diamond's apartment, you said something about an organized crime scene."

"And you made a rather pathetic joke demeaning psychiatry."

"I just thought it was a little much, your profiling the killer as somebody who got *B*s in math and wasn't close to his father."

She shrugged.

The rest of the memory filled itself in. "And that's when we got off on the wrong foot," I said.

She seemed to think about it. It took a moment of self-analysis. "*Before* that. About two seconds after you joined Dr. Riggs and me at the restaurant. You came on as some sort of American—what do they call it?—hulk?"

"Hunk?"

"Yes. A big, Yank hunk. A cocky, grinning male predator."

"Me?"

"You."

"And how long have you had these feelings of insecurity in the presence of the male animal?"

She smiled but didn't say a word.

"I think you got me wrong," I said. "When I met you, I'd just been drop-kicked out of the courthouse. My ego was dragging. If anything, I needed feminine companionship to buoy my spirits. I was trying to impress you and it didn't work. I regret it."

She thought it over. "You sought validation that your product was still good."

I nodded.

"So perhaps you overcompensated."

I nodded again, eagerly anticipating her compassion.

"And I misinterpreted your pitiful yearning."

She seemed to be convincing herself that I wasn't half-bad, and who was I to argue?

"My goodness! I've been so frosty to you, haven't I?"

"Like Green Bay in January," I agreed.

"Then I apologize."

"Accepted."

Again, she slid the glasses back to the top of her head. She let her hand push the hair back and it tumbled over her shoulders. Then she looked at me the way a woman looks when she wants to be looked at right back. "Now, what were we saying?" she asked quietly.

"Something about the organized murderer."

She appraised me with those wide-set intelligent eyes, the flinty specks lost in the green. She didn't seem to have murder on the mind when she said, "Actually, I was thinking about *you* a few days ago."

"Really?"

"Yes, I was watching one of those American football shows on the telly."

"And the mindlessness of it reminded you of me."

"Well, I thought there must be more to it than meets the eye. I mean, just jumping onto each other and all. I thought you could explain it to me."

"Gladly. Where should we begin? First downs? Touchdowns? The I-formation or full-house backfield?"

"Actually, I was wondering about all the committee meetings?"

"The what?"

"Every few moments the lads stop, gather 'round a circle, pop their asses into the air, and have a meeting."

I could see we would have to start at the beginning. I remember my high-school coach the first day of practice. "Girls," he would say, "this is a football."

Pam continued: "You were quite proficient at the game, weren't you?"

"Not really."

"But Dr. Riggs said you won an award. At university, you were an Early American."

"*All*-American, honorable mention, my senior year. It's not that great."

We were interrupted by a shout. *"Deus Misereatur!* I'm so late."

Charlie was trundling across the lobby, his coattail flying, a wad of index cards in his hand. "I was going over my notes and now look at it. *Tempus fugit!"*

Pam Metcalf assured him that his audience would wait, and we headed out of the hotel and back into the Range Rover. "I hope you two found some common ground," Charlie said, somewhat hesitantly.

"Your friend is actually quite nice," Pamela Metcalf responded.

Charlie didn't have a coronary. He didn't even snicker.

"We were talking about radical psychiatry, the myth of the unconscious, that sort of thing," I told him, trying not to boast.

"Dr. Metcalf must have been doing the talking," Charlie said, "because you don't know diddly—"

"Now, now, Dr. Riggs," she clucked, angelically rising to my defense, "Jake is quite knowledgeable about the law. I'm sure he knows many esoteric procedures that are quite foreign to you and me."

"Like how to spin webs of gold from piles of manure," Charlie harrumphed.

"Now, now, Dr. Riggs," I chided, pinching the back of his neck. He harrumphed again and shut up. I think the old goat was jealous in an avuncular kind of way.

Pam deftly guided the Rover out of the Mayfair section past St. James Park and across Westminster Bridge over the Thames. The rain had stopped, and the sun was peeking out of the clouds. She gunned the engine, and as we barely avoided a major pileup at a roundabout, Charlie turned to me and whispered, "What were you talking about, really?"

"Royalty," I said.

"The queen, the Duke of Windsor?" Charlie asked.

"The prince of passion," I said.

CHAPTER 21

The Group

"Fantasies?" mused Clarence the Chemist. "I've had fantasies since I was eleven years old."

"About killing women?" asked Dr. Pamela Metcalf in a neutral tone.

"If you could call my mother a woman."

"What do you call her?"

"Dead," Clarence said, suppressing a grin.

"Braggart," chided the Fireman, from his seat across from Clarence.

"It got easier," Clarence continued. "First, the fantasies were about the victim, then about the killing, then perfecting the killing."

The Fireman scowled, then in a derisive singsong voice said, "The fantasy becomes reality, and then the fantasy develops structure. Blah, blah, blah. It's all so boring, Dr. Metcalf."

"And Clarence's fantasies are so drab," complained Stephanie, fiddling with her nails. "Poisoning is so impersonal. So tacky."

Clarence the Chemist stuck out his tongue at Stephanie. It was a small pointed tongue and it flicked out and back again, snakelike, as he bobbed his head.

"Oh, you'd like to, wouldn't you?" Stephanie taunted, hiking up her pink hot pants and flashing a smooth expanse of thigh.

Clarence holstered his tongue. "If you were a woman, I'd . . ."

Stephanie bristled. "You'd what, you insignificant worm?"

Clarence the Chemist shrank back into the metal chair and jammed his hands into his pockets. On the far side of forty, he was short and stout, a bland face topped by wispy, blond-gray hair, a brother-in-law look you'd never remember. He wore a brown wool cardigan buttoned up. Next to him was Ken the Doll. Ken was in his twenties, handsome in a nondescript way, brown hair short and neatly parted, his pale face without lines, his thin lips without expression. He wore a blue blazer jacket worn at the elbows.

Next to Ken the Doll was Stephen aka Stephanie. All giggles and flirtatious movements, she smoothed her short, bleached-blond hair with exaggerated motions. Her halter top was tight and bright, and she kept squeezing her small breasts together with her arms. She spoke breathlessly in a poor imitation of Marilyn Monroe.

"There isn't a real man in the room," she complained, batting her eyes, "unless it's him." She dangled a handful of black lacquered fingernails in my direction.

"Bitchy, bitchy, bitchy," responded the Fireman. He was tall and lanky with prominent cheekbones, and his jaw muscles worked as he chewed a thick wad of gum. He could have been thirty or forty, and as he talked, his eyes danced to a tune all their own. "Stephanie, darling, if you hate your penis so much, why not let me dip it in kerosene and set it alight?"

That started a buzz. Clarence the Chemist smacked his lips in a boorish smooching sound and nodded his head vigorously, welcoming an ally. Ken the Doll cracked his knuckles, and the Fireman grinned maniacally at his inestimable wit. Stephanie hissed at all of them.

I just sat there and tried to act nonchalant in the presence of three men and a whoozit who collectively had killed fourteen women. The room was drafty and dark, the floor dirty linoleum. The windows were crosshatched with metal screens secured by heavy padlocks. The door was steel and opened electronically when an attendant turned a key and pushed the right button. Two floors above, Charlie Riggs was preparing to speak to an assembly of British coroners, homicide detectives, medical students, forensic psychiatrists, and, I supposed, assorted other ghouls.

I surveyed The Group. Clarence the Chemist was a pharmacist who had poisoned his victims. As a child, the Fireman had dissected live cats, then torched them. More recently, he raped women and killed them, though not in that order. He always burned their bodies. Ken the Doll wasn't named Ken at all. But as a child, he would rip the head off his sister's Barbie doll, then masturbate into the open neck. He once knifed a woman in the abdomen, then attempted sex through the wound. Stephanie was a transsexual in her late twenties, a woman trapped in a man's body. Hormone treatments had given her breasts and removed her facial hair, and in a dim bar, she would be considered attractive in a slatternly way. Judged unstable even before she killed anyone, she had been turned down for the surgery that would remove the male equipment and construct an artificial vagina.

Clad in a white lab coat, different-colored pens sticking out of a pocket, Dr. Pamela Metcalf sat on the edge of the group, her legs demurely crossed, a clipboard on her lap. "Stephanie, what was your earliest fantasy?" she asked.

"Being just like Mother."

"Mother, mother, mother," Clarence the Chemist chanted.

"Fucker, fucker, fucker," the Fireman chimed in.

"Did you fantasize about wearing women's clothes?" Pam asked.

Stephanie bristled. "If you mean, did I have a fetish about cross-dressing, don't be ridiculous. I was never a transvestite, those wretched faggots jerking off into their wives' underwear. I was born a woman. I will die a woman."

"Any day now," muttered the Fireman.

"Oh, Stephanie," cooed Clarence the Chemist. "Is it still two pounds sterling for you to suck off the guards in the WC, or has the price gone up?"

"It has," the Fireman said, furiously working his chewing gum. "Now Stephanie will pay five pounds."

Even Ken the Doll laughed at that one.

"Ignore them," Pamela told Stephanie.

But boys will be boys, even homicidal-maniac boys, and they were getting pretty worked up.

"Stephanie," the Fireman said, "do you know how to make a hormone?"

Stephanie looked straight ahead and said nothing.

"Don't pay her!" Clarence answered triumphantly.

These two were going to make everybody forget Abbott and Costello. When the clapping and foot-stomping stopped, Pamela looked Clarence in the eye. "Perhaps I should call Clive and order up a double dose of Thorazine. We could end group now, and everyone could return to the ward for a nice long nap."

That got their attention. The noise stopped, and Pamela continued. "Stephanie, your mother dressed you in girls' clothes, didn't she?"

"Ever since I could remember. Bows and frills. Just like Mother." Stephanie's voice had taken on an eerie little-girl quality.

"And Father, what did he say?"

"He was too potted to say anything, and after a while he wasn't there at all."

"And why did you kill the shop assistant?"

The question was jarring, as it was meant to be. Stephanie didn't bat a false eyelash. "The tart was throwing herself at a man."

"A man?"

"My man . . . the man I wanted."

"So you killed her?"

Stephanie shrugged. It was rational, I thought, remembering my earlier conversation with Pam. She killed the woman out of jealousy. The woman was after the man Stephanie wanted. And probably more important, the woman possessed the body parts Stephanie coveted, was lucky enough to be born with them.

"Kill, kill, kill," chanted Clarence the Chemist, quieter this time.

"Burn, burn, burn," answered the Fireman.

"Let's talk about the new boy," Stephanie said.

Suddenly they were looking at me.

"He's big," said the fireman.

"Handsome in a loutish way," said Stephanie.

"Do you kill them first or fuck them first?" Clarence asked.

Talk about leading questions. "Usually I make a joke and they just go away," I said.

Pam Metcalf began passing out photocopies like a teacher to her class.

"Ooh, show-and-tell," Stephanie breathed.

Clarence drew a pair of spectacles from his shirt pocket and studied the papers. The Fireman industriously folded his copies, making three paper airplanes, licking the seams along the wings. Ken the Doll simply stared toward the screened windows.

"Clarence, you liked to leave little missives, didn't you?" Pam Metcalf asked.

"Poetry. I wrote poetry. 'Ode to White Arsenic.' 'On Turning Blue.' 'Sighing with Cyanide.' You've read them all, Dr. Metcalf." He examined the papers. "But this . . . this ranting about horses' eyes. This is sick."

"What about the others?"

Clarence read aloud. "'Catch me if you can, Mr. Lusk.' Not much to it unless old Lusky is a pedophile."

Clarence flipped to the next page. The Fireman sailed a paper airplane across the room, where it did a nosedive into a steel-screened window.

Stephanie said, "If he's cute, Mr. Lusk can catch me if he wants."

Again, Clarence read aloud. "'Weakness to be wroth with weakness, woman's pleasure, woman's pain . . .' A little dated, wouldn't you say, doctor?"

Pam Metcalf turned to me and shrugged. I looked at Clarence. "Keep reading," I told him, wondering if Tennyson had ever been heard in these surroundings.

He continued silently, then said, "I can't relate to this, if that's your question." He screwed his face into a look of disapproval and read aloud again. "'Woman is the lesser man, and all thy passions matched with mine, are as moonlight unto sunlight, and as water unto wine.'"

"What a pansy," the Fireman said.

Clarence said, "I never loved a woman and would surely not mourn over her loss."

The Fireman nodded in agreement.

"The poem was left at a murder scene," I said. "Does it mean anything to any of you?"

"A bit showy for my tastes," Clarence said. "Maybe something

Ken would do. He likes the grand gesture. You dumped a body in front of Plymouth Church, didn't you, Ken?"

Ken wasn't talking, and the Fireman was licking the seams of another imaginary bomber.

"Strangled them," Clarence said. "Actually placed his hands on their filthy bodies. How unsanitary. Now, take cyanide. . . ."

"Oh, yes, do!" shouted Stephanie.

Clarence ignored her. "The respiratory enzymes are poisoned, the body is paralyzed, and death occurs in seconds. And afterward, the body turns such a bright red. So delicious, like a big, plump cherry."

"What about it, Ken?" I asked. "Would you leave a note for your local constable?"

He glared at me. I didn't think he would say a word. Finally he turned back toward the window and softly said, "Actions speak louder than words."

From the corner of my eye, I saw Stephanie squirming in her chair. Pam Metcalf acknowledged her with a wave of the hand.

"I hate to admit it, but the poem is right," Stephanie said, cocking her head to one side coquettishly. "I mean, it sounds strange for me to say it, since I'm a woman and all, but with the men I've known, the ones who've lusted after me, you have no idea, their passion. It's exhausting. And there are times when I have it, you know, the male sexuality. As you taught me, Dr. Metcalf, all of us are bisexual to some degree, and I guess, me more than most. When I get it, that flow of hot male blood, it's different. So powerful and overwhelming, so intense, so lush. Lord knows, I love a man. I love to do nice things for him. But when I need a woman, it's difficult to describe, but it comes over me in waves, my passion inflamed a thousandfold."

"What happens then?" I asked.

"I fuck her, of course. Good and proper."

I nodded and waited, and then it came.

"And hate her for it." Stephanie's voice was a whisper. "For making me the male beast. So who can blame me for killing her? I mean, really? Who can blame me?"

Pam Metcalf apologized to me before leaving to join Charlie's lecture. The group had twenty minutes left, so I stuck around. We could play poker or swap tales of homicide. There didn't seem to be any poker players in the bunch.

Clarence was the most willing to talk; Stephanie stared at me and occasionally engaged in heavy breathing; the Fireman kept folding and unfolding his paper airplanes; and Ken couldn't care less.

Clarence leaned forward in his chair, elbows on his knees, and whispered conspiratorially, "Dr. Metcalf is teaching you all the mumbo jumbo, eh?"

Stephanie smiled. "Sweet bitch. Are you in her pants yet?"

"He's not her type," the Fireman said. "Only he doesn't know it yet."

I just looked at them.

"We're a cottage industry, you know," Clarence said. "We need each other, the psychiatrist and the crazed killer. Without us, how would they get their government grants or appear on the tube?"

"You like playing the role?" I asked.

He shrugged. "It's expected. Your FBI behavioral-science lads came up with the childhood profile, bed wetters who slice up animals and start fires—"

"Burn, baby, burn," the Fireman interrupted.

"—and we can read as well as the next chap."

"So it's all a game," I ventured, again remembering Pam's talk about intentional schizophrenics.

"And a self-fulfilling prophecy." He smiled and leaned even closer. "We tell the psychiatrists our hallucinations. Voices ordering us to kill."

I nodded. "Right. In New York, a young man hears a dog telling him women are evil. So he used a .44-caliber pistol to kill a few."

"Yes, and the tabloids call him the Son of Sam and he goes to a mental hospital instead of prison. Better food, a higher class of tenants."

"You think it was phony?"

"What difference does it make?" Clarence said. "Evil or crazy, the victims are just as dead." He fixed me with a cunning smile.

"You never heard voices, Clarence?"

He sat back and beamed. "Only my own."

The group was growing restless. In a few moments the attendants would take them back to their high-security ward. Ken the Doll allowed as how he needed to use the facilities and stood up and walked toward the lavatory. He came behind me and fingered my sport coat, draped on the back of my chair. It sent a chill up my spine. "Nice," he said, walking away.

Stephanie giggled and yelled after him. "Stay away from the new boy, Kenneth. He's mine!"

A moment later, the door buzzed and two white-uniformed attendants came in. Stephanie, Clarence, and the Fireman stood up without being told.

"All of you back to Ward D and no lollygagging," one attendant demanded in what I took for an Irish accent. He was tall and heavy, big-boned, but no fat. Brawny wrists stuck out of the white uniform shirt. He had roughly cut dark hair and a pale complexion with blue eyes. He might have been handsome if he smiled. He didn't smile.

"I'm a visitor," I said pleasantly. "Lassiter. Guest of Dr. Metcalf."

His eyes never moved from mine. The other one, a thick-necked youth with a shock of unruly red hair, circled to my left. These guys had some training. If I went for one of them, the other would nail me.

"Identification?" the tall one asked, the tone formal without being nasty.

I reached for my sport coat. Pam Metcalf had pinned the badge on the lapel.

Damn! Now where was it?

"It must have fallen off," I said, sounding guilty even to myself.

Now the redhead was directly behind me.

"Sure it did," the tall one said. "There are supposed to be four lunatics in this group, and unless my Gaelic eyes deceive me, there's four of you here. So how about falling in with your friends?"

I smiled and tried to look sane but felt myself a grinning madman. "The fourth . . . uh . . . lunatic went to the head. I'm sure if you—"

"My patience is wearing thin, laddie."

"Careful," Stephanie warned. "Francis likes to hit more than he likes to fuck."

"Ken went to the head," I said. "He must have taken my visitor's badge. Maybe he's escaped. Perhaps you should sound an alarm. I'm Lassiter."

He looked at me skeptically.

"I'm a lawyer," I went on, "a barrister."

"Hear that, Clive, he's a bloomin' pettifogger," Francis told his buddy.

"I'm a specially appointed prosecutor from America. I'm looking for a murderer and I came here asking these . . . these murderers for help."

Even I didn't believe me.

"Classic schizophrenia," Clarence the Chemist said, "with guilt-induced denial."

"Clarence!" I pleaded. "Tell them. Tell them I'm not crazy."

Francis looked toward Clarence, who shrugged and said, "He's no crazier than the rest of us."

Stephanie gave me an adoring look. "Now, Kenneth. Don't you want to come back to the ward and continue where we left off?"

Clive put a meaty hand on my left shoulder. I swatted it away, and both men took a step backward and began circling me, keeping out of range, just like they were taught.

"I don't like being touched," I said.

"'E donna like bein' touched," Francis mocked me, laughing.

They continued circling. It was supposed to make me dizzy. But I was focused on a stationary spot on the wall. I was getting ready. The fog of the transatlantic flight was lifting. My nerves were coming alive, little lights blinking away, alarm bells sounding red alert. Some spigot deep inside opened wide and the adrenaline flowed. The heat started in the pit of my stomach and spread to my chest, through my shoulders, and into my arms and hands. Unused muscle fibers began twitching, and the heart picked up the pace. My fingers tingled. I flexed my knees and let my arms hang loosely at my sides. Somewhere far away, the crowd was getting to its feet, a rumble growing. Thirty seconds to kickoff. I wanted to hit somebody.

I didn't know how they would signal each other, so it would have been smarter to take the first shot. But I was the victim, after all, and while I was thinking about it Clive winked at Francis, who was behind me. I never saw Francis move toward me, but I felt him there, poised to grab me. He never saw my elbow shoot down, but he felt it. In karate, they call it the *ushiro hiji-ate*, the back elbow strike.

I heard Francis's *ooomph*, my elbow sinking into his gut. In a second, Clive snatched my right forearm with two strong hands and was twisting my arm behind my back. He was quicker than he looked. But he must have been thinking that my left arm was in his pal's grasp the way they planned it, and it wasn't, so I reached around, grabbed him by the hair, and pulled him off me and spun him around.

I was starting to enjoy this. Isn't that what I told Pam Metcalf that first night: hitting people was fun? Before I had a chance to submit myself for analysis, Francis had recovered and landed a short punch in my kidneys from behind. Would this guy ever face me head-on? I must have left my flak jacket in the locker room, because the punch hurt. So did the second one, and some of the starch oozed out of me. But the adrenaline was still flowing, and I whirled, and while he was trying to tag me with a hook to the body I brought a forearm up under his chin. A solid chin but a pretty solid forearm, too, and it sent Francis to the hard floor. I didn't know whether to expect the fans' cheers or fifteen yards for unsportsmanlike conduct. I got neither. Clive tackled me from behind, a good hit for a guy who probably never went one-on-one with a blocking sled. He got me around the waist with those big arms and drove me to the floor. He hammered a shoulder into the small of my back and used his weight to keep me down. My face was crushed against the cold tile floor, my ear squashed beneath my head.

From above me I heard Stephanie's voice. "Don't hurt him, you brutes."

Francis got up cursing and holding his jaw. He must have missed soccer practice because he decided to take a few penalty kicks. He bounced a hard-toed shoe off my temple and three into my ribs before getting tired. Then he slipped something out of his back pocket. Clive was still holding me down, my arms pinned over my head, when they put the plastic handcuffs on me.

"Get the needle, Clive," Francis said.

I hate a needle almost as much as I hate a knife.

My head was a spinning satellite, and through the glare of a thousand suns I saw Clive unlock a drawer and withdraw a syringe and small vial.

"A day without Thorazine is like a day without a funeral," Clarence intoned from across the room.

"Oooh. When he's out, I'll give him a good licking," Stephanie cooed.

My hands were cuffed together, but in front of me, not behind my back. These guys had clearly never seen *Miami Vice*. Francis was hauling me up by the elbow while Clive approached gingerly with the needle. Clive was still a half-dozen steps away, and I was hunched over, breathing through my mouth, moaning. Playing possum.

Francis relaxed his grip on my elbow. I brought both arms down hard to shake him off, and then, fists together, I swung the arms up and smashed him on the point of his nose with both fists. There was a *pop* of breaking cartilage, and I was showered with blood, sticky and warm on my face. The punch stood Francis up, wobbled his knees, and he fell over backward.

Clive was impressed. He circled me, brandishing the needle like a switchblade. He feinted and I ducked. He stabbed and I slipped to the side. He aimed high and I dropped to the floor, throwing my shoulder at his knees in a chop block. I rolled into him, my body pinning his left foot to the floor while my shoulder turned his leg sideways. I heard the crack and knew his anterior cruciate ligament was blown into shreds of spaghetti. He hollered and clutched the knee, rolling from side to side. I heard Stephanie screaming.

I struggled to my feet and saw a shadow over my shoulder. I swung at it and it disappeared. I swung again and missed again. Twisting my neck, I saw it once more. It seemed to be attached to me. I turned the other way, and the shadow became the plunger of a syringe. The business end was stuck into my shoulder just behind the blade. Clive must have taken a shot at me as I went for his knees. I hadn't felt it. My hands were still cuffed in front, and I couldn't reach it.

Francis was still on the floor. If he was conscious, he wasn't solving ten-digit logarithms. I tested him with a foot. He groaned but didn't move. I knelt down, fumbled with his belt, and removed a key ring. After seven keys, I still hadn't found the right one, so I said to hell with it. I managed to push a couple of buttons on the wall, and the door opened with a buzz and a clang.

I bolted into the corridor, possessed of no particularly brilliant ideas. I was handcuffed, panting, covered with blood, and had a needle sticking out of my shoulder. Two men in white coats were walking thirty yards down the corridor. I waved to them with my cuffed hands. One waved back, did a double take, then they started for me. I used the good shoulder to push through some swinging doors and headed up a set of steep metal stairs. I was dizzy and nauseous. I thought I heard shouts behind me as I took the stairs two at a time, my footsteps resounding like distant echoes.

Three flights up, I heard the roar of amplified words that seemed to envelop me. I stopped, my heart pounding in my ears, my vision hazy.

A dignified voice proclaimed: "There are four manners of death. . . ." For a moment, in my wooziness, I envisioned the PA announcer at the Pearly Gates. *Have your admission tickets ready. Lassiter, Jacob Lassiter? We have no record of your reservation.* I took a deep breath and let an invisible force lead me up the stairs to a peaceful hereafter. I was vaguely aware of a secret pleasure that I hadn't headed toward the basement.

The electronic voice recited: "Accident, suicide, homicide, and natural. Distinguishing them is the first task of the medical examiner."

Wait. I had heard the voice before. The words too. Authoritative, though hardly heavenly.

"If the body has a black eye, is it from a punch, or from a fall after a heart attack?"

I was so sleepy. So ready for rest.

"An autopsy can only tell you so much. You must take as much care at the scene of the crime as in the morgue. Take precise photographs. Measure and diagram the scene. Preserve the evidence, including hair and fibers at the scene. We all remember the Wayne Williams murder trial in Atlanta. Fiber evidence from Williams's car was crucial to the conviction. And, of course, bullets. You have no idea how many times I've seen bullets crushed by a physician's instruments. We even had one assistant ME who would etch his initials onto bullets he removed. That's one way to lose friends in ballistics."

Good old Charlie Riggs, his voice booming over a loudspeaker. He would take care of me. Put me to sleep. Whoops, all his patients were sleeping the big sleep. On stainless steel tables with wooden pillows in a room that could give you—but not them—a cold.

I stumbled through a door, up three more steps onto the skirt of a wooden stage. Heavy purple drapes separated me from my old friend. I peeked through an opening and saw him, a blaze of lights at his feet, an unseen audience beyond.

"A medical examiner must never be surprised. Neither by physical evidence nor human behavior. The medical examiner remains objective, cool, dispassionate, unfazed in the face of horror and . . ."

I burst through the curtain with my last reserve of strength and collapsed at Charlie's feet. I heard a gasp from beyond the footlights. For some reason, I pictured Gerald Prince playing Julius Caesar.

I looked up at my old friend. *"Et tu,* Charles?" I asked.

Charlie Riggs looked down at the bloody, sweaty, needle-stuck body at his feet. *"Mea culpa,"* he whispered. "I never should have left you alone here."

I brought myself to my knees, looked up at him, and smiled a peaceful smile. Then I promptly vomited on his genuine L.L. Bean hiking boots.

"Perhaps," I heard him say into the microphone as I rolled free of the mess and rested my face on the cool floorboards, "we should take a five-minute break before the slide show."

CHAPTER 22

Dream a Little Dream

"Do you really feel up to driving?" Pamela Metcalf asked.

I gave her my steely-eyed confident look.

"You're not groggy at all?"

I shook my head.

"Why should he be groggy?" Charlie Riggs scoffed. "He slept fourteen hours, then called room service at six A.M. and ordered french fries and a chocolate shake."

"Chips for breakfast." Pam clucked with disapproval.

"With vinegar," Charlie tattled.

We were standing in front of the hotel, waiting for the Land Rover to emerge from the car park. It was a fine summer day in London, which is to say it was dark, wet, and cold.

"I'm fine," I said. "A little headache, that's all."

"Better than those poor lads at the hospital," Pam scolded. "Knee surgery for Clive, a broken nose for Francis. I must say, your conduct required some creative explanations to the administrator."

"Those two knuckleheads wouldn't listen to me."

"So you created an affray?"

"They were going to lock me up."

"They would have put you in the ward. How long do you think it would have taken to straighten it all out? An hour, two?"

"I wasn't thinking that far ahead."

"At the first provocation, at the first excuse to act out your hostility, you battered those working-class lads who haven't had the benefits you've enjoyed."

I felt my bruised face redden. "Those working-class lads are a couple of thugs."

"Did you enjoy hurting them?"

"Look, lady—"

Charlie stepped between us just as the valet swung the Land Rover under the portico. "Now, now. I see the truce lasted all of one day. Jake, why not let Dr. Metcalf drive? She knows the route and . . ."

I ran a Z-pattern that Jerry Rice would admire and grabbed the keys from the valet. The doorman, a tall fellow in a red tunic and a fur hat two feet high, tried to stow our bags, but I grabbed those, too, and tossed them unceremoniously in back. Then I boldly opened the door, slid behind the steering wheel, and slammed the door behind me like a spoiled brat who's fled to his room.

Only I wasn't behind the steering wheel at all. Because the wheel was on the right, and I had gotten in on the left. This wasn't my ancient convertible in the good old U.S. of A. This was a lady psychiatrist's thirty-grand-plus glorified jeep in a country where they talk funny and drive on the wrong side of the road. I remembered all the movies where the guy walks into the closet, thinking it's the front door. No wonder they stay inside. There's no graceful way out.

Finally Pam Metcalf came around to my side, opened the door, and showed the barest hint of a smile. Not a supercilious or condescending smile. More of a tolerant one. I got out without pouting and she got in without any help from me. I headed to the other side while Charlie climbed into the back. The doorman watched with as much amusement as they allow and gave me a "very good, sir" when I palmed him a two-quid tip.

I didn't have any trouble the first hundred yards. But hitting second gear brought the clang of metal on metal. "Whoops," I apologized, "not used to shifting with my left hand."

I felt spastic. Kensington Road was no problem until I ran over the curb. Cars coming at me on the right made me pull harder left. The bumper is made to bounce off elephants, so the Rover was fine, and so was the guy whose newspaper kiosk I had flattened, once I gave him a wad of bills.

"Why not let Pamela drive until we're out of the city?" Charlie suggested.

It was two against one, so we switched places again. The rain let up, and the sun peeked out of some low-hanging gray clouds. Pam Metcalf said, "There's someplace I want you to see." She wound off the main streets and through a series of turns and kept driving until we pulled into a narrow alley in a part of the city they don't show in the tourist brochures. Abandoned warehouses, empty windows gaping like missing teeth, lined each side. A few delivery trucks drove by, but there was no foot traffic.

"On these very cobblestones," Pam Metcalf said, "Jack the Ripper stalked and killed."

"Of course, Whitechapel!" Charlie Riggs was as delighted as a country priest whisked to the Vatican.

Pam stopped, put on the parking brake, and we got out. It was mid-morning, but my mind conjured pictures of foggy nights and gaslit streets. "August thirty-first, 1888," Pam said. "Mary Ann Nicholls. Throat slashed, nearly severing her head. Nine days later, Annie Chapman, stomach slashed, intestines draped round her neck. September thirty, Elizabeth Stride, throat slashed and on the same night, Catherine Eddowes, throat slashed, body mutilated. Finally on November nine, Mary Jane Kelly, throat slashed and body severely mutilated."

"All prostitutes, all slain within a stone's throw of each other," Charlie whispered in reverent tones.

"Then the killings stopped," I said. "Why?"

"There are all sorts of theories, mostly rubbish," Pam said. "The murders have been blamed on everyone from Queen Victoria's grandson Prince Eddy to Freemasons. Some believe that Montague John Druitt, a failed barrister, was the killer. He ended up floating in the Thames not long after the last killing. Others believe he was a scapegoat, used to cover a scandal involving the royal family."

"In any event," Charlie said, "the killer was never caught and his motives never known."

"But we've come such a long way since then," I said, "with all our psychological profiles and investigative techniques."

"One would think so," Pam said, "but it took five years and thirteen killings before the Yorkshire Ripper was captured."

"A baker's dozen," Charlie said, shaking his head.

We stood, peering into the shell of what Pam said had been a slaughterhouse, the wooden floor stained black from dripping carcasses. "He hired prostitutes, smashed them on the head with a hammer, then stabbed them with a screwdriver. The psychological profile built a picture of a socially incompetent, unattractive loner living in a furnished room. Turned out he was a happily married lorry driver, a decent-looking fellow with a trimmed beard, who lived with his pretty wife in a two-story house with two cars in the garage."

"Go figure," I said.

"The investigation cost four million pounds, the police interviewed three hundred thousand persons, and the man was captured only when he was found with a prostitute in a car with stolen license plates."

"It's often that way," Charlie said. "All the computers and all the files go for naught, but then a tiny slip, and the bugger's caught."

We all smiled at Charlie's unintentional rhyme and headed back for the Rover. Pam opened the passenger door for herself and tossed me the keys. "Drive," she said.

Somewhere near Oxford on M-40 I finally got the hang of it, easing into a speed lane and letting the Rover purr. That seemed to relax everybody. Charlie fell asleep in the back and Pam stirred a little. "Did you learn anything from my group?" she asked.

"Only to follow the backward elbow strike with a left jab if there's a guy in front of me."

"Other than the fisticuffs."

"I'm not sure. Clarence was highly manipulative. The Fireman seemed dangerous, or at least wanted to appear that way. Ken was inscrutable, and Stephanie was—as the kids used to say—a trip."

"It may be," Pam said, watching the roadside fly by, "that you don't have enough information yet about your killer."

"I've got everything the cops have put together."

"But they have only two victims. You may need . . ."

She stopped, both of us realizing the horror when bodies become data, mere input for the computerized profile, grist for the thesis and the government grant.

"There will be more deaths, won't there?" I asked.

"Yes, if the first two, or either of them, was a motiveless murder. If a psychopath is about."

I heard Charlie snoring in the backseat. I turned and saw him curled contentedly in the fetal position, his mackinaw under his head for a pillow. Probably dreaming of an historic autopsy where he found a rare poison in the pancreas.

I opened a window and let the crisp air fill the Rover. I had sore ribs and an angry red knot was blossoming on my temple, but it was turning into a fine day in the English countryside. I turned and looked at the beautiful woman sitting next to me. I wondered why I misfired with her at every opportunity. She seemed genuinely peeved about my conduct at the hospital.

I decided to confess. "I was scared."

She looked at me skeptically.

"In the hospital with four lunatic killers and your two minimum-wage goons."

"There was no reason to be frightened of the group. They only kill women, you know."

"And their reasons for killing women?"

"Answering that question is my life's work. But we're talking about you. What frightened you?"

"Confinement, I guess. Claustrophobia, maybe. Not being able to come and go. Having hands laid on me. Plus the fear of getting knocked around by a couple of guys who know how to inflict pain without leaving scars."

"I see." She bit her lower lip and seemed to ponder my case. She was staring straight out the windshield, or windscreen, as she called it when we stopped for petrol, but she was thinking about me. I liked the attention. But I didn't know if she was interested in the big lummox as a person or merely an interesting case study. Freud had his Rat Man; maybe Metcalf wanted her Macho Man. "I wonder," she said delicately, "if you are using claustrophobia in a colloquial sense or if you have a true phobia, an anxiety far out of proportion to its danger."

"I don't know," I admitted.

"As for Clive and Francis, with your background as a footballer, you can certainly handle yourself, as you proved."

I passed a double trailer in fifth gear and looked straight ahead. "But I was afraid, even then."

"Afraid, playing your game?"

I nodded.

"Afraid of what? Losing?"

"The pain, both physical and emotional. Getting hurt, getting embarrassed. I was always one step from getting cut."

"Cut?"

"Fired, canned, let out to pasture."

I politely allowed a Jaguar to take me on the right side. Pam seemed to be mulling over the contradictions of the ex-linebacker admitting his weaknesses. She inched closer in the seat. Maybe she liked me better this way, two hundred twenty-five pounds of neuroses. "What caused these fears?" she asked.

I shrugged.

"We could find out, you know."

"You mean analysis."

She nodded happily. "Let's call it a preliminary inquiry concerning your mental health."

"Fire when ready."

"Did you like playing your game?"

"The game . . . the game is stupid!" I stopped short. I'd never said that before, never even thought it, not consciously at least. Then I wondered if there is a subconscious. Or was I becoming a radical psychojock?

"What makes it stupid?" she asked.

I kept my eyes on the road. "Let's start with the uniform."

"Those knickers and plastic hats."

I nodded. "And the game itself, smashing into each other at full speed, pushing an odd-shaped ball a hundred yards, back and forth, according to a set of arbitrary rules. Only one forward pass per down, can't touch a receiver when the ball's in the air, offensive line can't hold but they all do. Viewed objectively, it's a pretty stupid game and a pretty stupid way to make a living."

Her eyes brightened. "But the smashing was a release of hostility like steam from a kettle. Or is there another reason you chose a profession certain to cause you anxiety and conflict? That's a classic counterphobic attitude, you know, taking pleasure in precisely the activity that arouses anxiety. And when you derive satisfaction from triumphing over the anxiety, it's just a manifestation of a manic defense."

"Something like a pass prevent?"

"More like an all-out blitz."

My foot slipped off the gas pedal and I gaped at her, astounded.

She shrugged. "I've done a little research on your game, that's all."

"Why?"

"To better understand you. Why do you suppose you derived pleasure from the smashing and hitting?"

"Isn't my fifty minutes up, doctor?"

"Please. Don't joke your way out of this. We're making progress concerning the omnipotence you felt from mastering your fear of pain and failure."

"I never felt omnipotent getting blind-sided by the tight end."

She settled back into her seat, annoyed. "Perhaps that's all we can accomplish for today."

We sat in silence for a few moments, and then she pointed to the left to keep me from missing the turn toward Chipping Camden, ancestral home of the Metcalf clan. If I'd stayed on the highway, we'd have headed straight for Stratford-on-Avon, and my mind wandered to Professor Prince and whether he ever played Hamlet in his meanderings.

After a while Pam Metcalf asked, "You don't *want* to explore what's under the surface, do you?"

That started something buzzing in the back of my mind. What was it?

"On the flight over here," I said, stirring up a fuzzy memory, "I dreamed about you."

"Oh!" She straightened, tugging at the harness restraint. She was genuinely excited, whether from professional or personal curiosity I still didn't know.

"Yes, but it's hard to remember. I fell asleep thinking about you and woke up the same way, and in between . . ."

"Yes, yes. Think about it."

"You were in Miami. You must have been, because it was very warm. And we were on the beach."

She raised an eyebrow. "We?"

"You and me. I was rigging a sailboard."

She gave me a quizzical look.

"A Windsurfer," I said. "It was one of those spring days, a strong warm wind from the east, whitecaps on the water, sand blowing down the beach. I was tying the boom to the mast, and you were next to me. Yes, I see it now, in a bikini!"

"Indeed?"

"A red bikini, and your hair was blowing downwind. And you were saying something. What the hell was it?"

She didn't know and I didn't either, but I dredged it up, or was I making it up? Dreams are so fuzzy, who can tell? I thought of George in *Virginia Woolf*, unable, or unwilling, to distinguish truth from illusion. The thought was there, so I spit it out. "You said, 'Jake, I can't hold on.'"

She leaned closer. "Hold on to what, or to whom?"

I wrinkled my forehead and thought some more. "I don't know. That's all I can remember. But you were frightened, and so was I."

"The sensation of falling is a common dream experience, but you seem to have transferred the anxiety to me. Quite interesting."

She thought about it awhile, so I concentrated on the road, which by now had shrunken to two undersized lanes. On either side were rolling farmlands, alternate patches of brown and green, an occasional herd of sheep grazing on grassy slopes. Tractors hauling plows chugged along the road, hogging both sides and crowding me toward the ditch on the left.

After a few moments Pam Metcalf said, "Freud wrote that dreams often express a repressed, unconscious wish from childhood."

"Makes sense. Ever since puberty, I wanted to spend time with girls in bikinis."

Her emerald glance chided me. "You're being too literal. The unconscious wish is repressed, so it cannot be given direct expression even in a dream. The dream must distort the wish, so the dreamer need not face the cost of recognizing the true wish, which has been disguised."

"You're saying I don't really have a repressed desire to see you in a bikini on a windswept beach?"

"No, but it represents something. The bikini may signify that you wish to see me stripped bare—"

"I can buy that."

"—stripped of the barriers each of us erects to protect ourselves. The color red can signify violence or bloodshed. As for what you heard, perhaps you have a desire to see me fall, a metaphor for fail."

"Why would I?"

She considered it. "I don't know, are you somehow threatened by me?"

"Intrigued, yes. Threatened, no. I'd like to get to know you. And not just in my dreams."

She smiled and sat back, alone in her thoughts.

It was slow going as I followed her directions up a winding road. The asphalt turned to gravel, and as the road narrowed and overgrown shrubs clawed at each side of the Rover, the surface became brown dirt, pocked by holes. After bouncing through a few of the axle breakers, I heard a stirring in the backseat. Charlie Riggs was stretching like a bearded cat.

"There it is," Pam said, pointing up a hill.

"Now, that didn't take long at all," Charlie mumbled, leaning over the front seat to take a peek.

I pulled into a gravel driveway that led to a large limestone house topped by a thatched roof. Pam caught me staring at the shaggy top of her home. "Our insulation," she said. "The reeds are stacked a foot thick and nailed down by thousands of wooden stakes. Keeps us warm in the winter and cool in the summer. Only needs to be replaced every sixty years or so, but the fire insurance is quite exorbitant."

"Splendid, just splendid," Charlie was saying.

"Shall we?" Pam asked, gesturing toward the house. "I've told Mum all about you."

"You, singular or plural?" I ventured.

"Plural," she answered with the biggest smile to date. Then she darted close and kissed me. It wasn't a kiss that would lose a PG-rating in Hollywood. It was more of a whisk of lip across cheek, but my spirits soared to the top of the thatched roof where a weather vane pointed west. "Gracious," Pam said. "It's nearly tea time. Let's see if Mum still remembers how to make a Bakewell tart."

We headed up a flagstone path to a huge front door. It came to me then, a nagging question from earlier in the day. "Why would the royal family be killing prostitutes?" I asked her.

"It had to do with Prince Albert, called Eddy in the Court. He was the son of King Edward VII and Alexandra. He was in line to be king. But he was known to be bisexual, and there were scandals involving relationships with boys. Those were fairly easy to hush up. Not so easy was the rumor that he had surreptitiously married a young Catholic shop girl, who gave birth to a baby girl. The royal family is said to have spirited the shop girl off to an insane asylum, kidnapped the child, and forcibly returned Eddy to the Court. All was accomplished very efficiently, except there was a witness. A friend of the shop girl: Mary Jane Kelly."

"The last Ripper victim," Charlie said.

"Yes. She was an East End harlot."

"But five women were killed," I said.

"The others were the smoke screen, necessary to create the myth of a Ripper indiscriminately killing prostitutes."

"The royal family had *five* women killed to protect the prince's reputation?" I asked, incredulous.

"It's one theory," Pamela said.

"Bizarre," Charlie Riggs concluded.

"Farfetched," I agreed, mulling it over. "As ridiculous as a state attorney killing a woman to protect his reputation as a war hero, then killing another to cover up the first."

CHAPTER 23

Tea Time

An ancient clock above the marble fireplace bonged four times and a uniformed kitchen girl rolled a silver cart of scones, muffins, and crumpets into the drawing room. The walls were hung with gold silk damask and matched the festooned curtains. The floor was dark wood covered with a carpet of burgundy and gold. On the walls were grim portraits of Victorian folk, stout men with long tangled hair and pale women with swan necks.

We sat on chairs with carved knees and ball-and-claw feet. Overhead was a cut-glass chandelier. Mrs. Penelope Metcalf personally poured steaming tea from a china pot decorated with roses. She never took her eyes from mine as she handed me the cup and saucer with a steady hand. She was a trifle too large for the long, fitted silk chiffon dress the color of a sapphire. White beads formed leaflike shapes over the shoulder and down each sleeve. Red beads swirled like a cloud of dust over an ample hip. The dress was cut daringly low, and Mrs. Metcalf threatened to spill over with the tea.

She had a fine head of gray hair piled high, a long patrician nose, and green eyes she had graciously passed on to her daughter. "Lemon?" she asked, barely suppressing a smile. "They tell me you Yanks use lemon, though I haven't the foggiest idea why."

Pamela smiled. "Some of them even drink their tea over ice."

"No!" protested Mrs. Metcalf, a twinkle in her eye. "Whatever for, to quell a fever?"

"Philistines," I agreed, realizing they were putting me on. I declined the lemon and accepted a dash of milk.

We made tea talk. Mrs. Metcalf was too polite to ask why someone used my face for a soccerball. Instead, she discussed the relative qualities of West Bengal Darjeeling compared with Russian. Charlie Riggs allowed as how he favored the smoky aroma of Lapsang souchong from the Fujian province because Darjeeling always reminded him of muscatel.

I know more about Dutch beer than Chinese tea, so I kept quiet and watched Pamela, who sat regally on a stiff chair, her legs crossed demurely at the ankles, cup and saucer balanced daintily on her lap. She had changed into a summer sweater of white cotton and a long denim skirt. A tad casual for the formal room, perhaps, but it didn't bother me. I just admired the lady's ankles, as Victorian men must have done in similar rooms a century before. Mrs. Metcalf seemed entranced by Charlie, who was waxing enthusiastic about the furniture, which, to me, looked like Early Flea Market.

When he finally stopped talking, Charlie Riggs slathered clotted cream and strawberry jam onto a warm scone and inhaled the aroma of the sweet cakes and steaming tea. I hadn't seen him this happy since he had snookered a young public defender in a pretrial deposition in a homicide case.

"And what was the cause of death?" the PD had asked.

"Acute lead poisoning," Doc Riggs said with a straight face.

The young lawyer could barely contain his joy. "Really?"

"Yes, indeed. Of course it was caused by two .38 slugs in the heart from your client's gun."

I forgave him later.

Charlie bit into the scone and decorated his beard with a glob of the cream. Then he looked around the room, furrowed his bushy eyebrows, and said, "If I'm not mistaken, Mrs. Metcalf, that sofa is Early Hepplewhite."

"Quite right," she said, smiling. "About 1765, best we can tell."

"And those too," Charlie said, gesturing toward gilt-wood armchairs, "perhaps a bit later."

Mrs. Metcalf nodded. "We've established them at 1790."

This went on for a while. The cabinets on either side of the fireplace dated from 1795, the mahogany table with satinwood inlay about 1775, and the pianoforte—just like Beethoven's—was made in 1798 by Rolfe of Cheapside. I decided neither to comment on Rolfe's marketing strategy nor to bang out my risqué rendition of "Louie, Louie."

"Would you care for a brandy snap?" Mrs. Metcalf asked me.

I scooped up a confection of ginger and whipping cream and washed it down with—who knows?—some Indian, Russian, or Chinese tea.

"Pamela tells me you're a barrister," Mrs. Metcalf said.

I nodded, tipping my cup.

"I've always adored the law," she said. "When Pamela was at Cheltenham Ladies' College, I so hoped she would pursue that noble profession."

My smile was sincere. Where I come from, lawyers are called shysters, mouthpieces, or ambulance chasers.

"Mother never approved of my life, nor I of hers," Pam said tartly.

"Pamela!" Mrs. Metcalf's smile dropped at the edges, giving her an odd, frozen look.

"Mother can scarcely say 'psychiatry' without breaking out in hives."

"It's not *psychiatry* I object to," Mrs. Metcalf protested. "But in your practice, the *people* . . ."

Pamela shrugged.

"When I think back," her mother said a bit gloomily. "Mr. Metcalf had just passed on, and Pamela was quite distraught, naturally. Then those poor girls were killed, right here in the Cotswolds, and Pamela was at such an impressionable age. Perhaps that explains how she chose such a . . . gruesome profession."

"When I was studying psycholinguistics at Cambridge, Mother practically disowned me."

"Kidnappers! Her specialty was *kidnappers*."

"Ransom notes contain marvelous clues," Pam said. "I developed a computer program that analyzed every word of the note. The computer then compared how the words in the note are used compared to the same words in ordinary speech. Properly done, this yields signature words that reveal the kidnapper's background."

Mrs. Metcalf shook her head. "I thought it was just a phase, that when she decided on medicine, it would be for a traditional career. Pediatrics perhaps. But she was a house woman, what you call, what is it, Pamela . . . ?"

"An intern."

"Yes, at St. Thomas Hospital in London, do you know it, Dr. Riggs?"

"I believe Florence Nightingale worked there."

"Yes." Mrs. Metcalf nodded. "Then to Maudsley Hospital for psychiatry and Broadmoor for the criminally insane. One place worse than the next. Dealing with policemen and the deranged. Oh my, don't get me started. Perhaps if I'd raised her differently . . ."

"I don't think she turned out half bad," I said, in a semichivalrous way.

"Well, Mr. Lassiter, I ask you, should a young lady like this be spending her time in those horrible prisons?"

"*Hospitals*, Mother!"

"Hospitals, with cages over the windows and those awful squeaky floors . . ."

"Linoleum," Pam said. "Mum hates linoleum."

"Working the worst imaginable hours, how can a young woman even find a suitable husband? I mean when a man comes home from the office, he wants a good roast beef, not a repulsive story, isn't that right, Mr. Lassiter?"

"Actually, I'm cutting back on red meat."

"If a woman has no time to form relationships with men—"

"But then, " Pam interrupted, "you've made up for both of us, haven't you, Mother?"

I heard the tinkle of china in Mrs. Metcalf's hands. The afternoon sun slanted through the heavy windows, but the room had turned frosty. So this is what the English do at their genteel teas. Haul out the dirty linen.

Mrs. Metcalf straightened in her chair. Her face betrayed nothing, the perfect example of the stiff upper lip. "Pamela, no argie-bargie, not today."

"As you wish, Mother."

Mrs. Metcalf managed a formal smile that reminded me of Nancy Reagan. "I won't say another word about it, but I'll never understand why a proper lady would want to soil her hands with that sort of work. Don't you agree, Mr. Lassiter?"

"Well . . . I don't know," I sputtered. "Pam's work is very important. The day may come when she can re-create the personality, the emotional and mental makeup, the domestic situation, even the appearance of the psychopath."

Pam gently placed her cup in its saucer on the side table. "How unexpectedly gallant. Rising to my defense when all this time you scoffed at my work."

"Not so," I protested. "I always respected it, even if I didn't understand it."

"Rapists!" Mrs. Metcalf exclaimed, ignoring our byplay. "My daughter spent a year interviewing rapists in their cells. Can you imagine?"

"I categorized them by their behavior," Pam explained impassively. "The angry, the socially inept, the sadomasochistic."

"Sadists. So very sick," Mrs. Metcalf chided.

"All of us have the capacity to inflict pain," Pam said quietly.

"Closet sadists?" I asked.

"We are all born psychopaths, born without repressions," she said. "Society teaches us the restraints of proper behavior and helps us develop a conscience."

I allowed Mrs. Metcalf to pour me another cup of tea. "Some learn and some don't," I said.

Pam said sternly, "And if the restraints come off, if society encourages antisocial behavior, we are only too willing to comply."

Charlie Riggs sliced himself a piece of fig loaf and said, "The Nazis are proof enough of that, burghers manning the ovens."

"And on a lesser scale," Pam said, "the average man will inflict pain when it is acceptable to do so. In a college study thirty years ago, students were encouraged to give ever-increasing electric shocks to volunteers."

Charlie nodded. "The Milgram study."

"The shocks were bogus," Pam continued, "but the students didn't know that, and they were only too happy to comply, even as the voltage increased and the volunteers writhed in apparent pain."

"*Homo homini lupus,*" Charlie said sadly. "'Man is a wolf to man.'"

We thought about that a moment, the shadows lengthening outside the gold-curtained windows. The mood of the afternoon tea had turned melancholy.

"Well, I don't know how we got off on that ghastly subject," Mrs. Metcalf said after a moment. "Perverts and monsters. How I resent all of them, including their psychiatrists, for blaming women for their evil. With the Yorkshire Ripper, they blamed his wife. With the Hungerford killer, his mother. Your profession, Pamela, is so . . . so . . ."

"Misogynistic," Charlie offered.

"Exactly!"

"But then," Pam said, looking straight at dear old Mum, "it's difficult to overestimate the damage a mother can do."

Mrs. Metcalf sighed and carefully replaced her cup and saucer on the silver tray. They must have been down this road before. She smoothed an imaginary crumb from the shimmering blue dress and shifted in her chair as if the tea were coming to a close. "Dr. Riggs, may I offer you a last slice of mincemeat cake with the brandy-butter sauce?"

Charlie patted his stomach and demurred, and Mrs. Metcalf dispatched the pastry cart with a wave of the hand to her kitchen girl and told us we'd be having roast quail for dinner. I figured a five-mile run would be the prerequisite for that feast and would have made it, too, if a nap hadn't sounded so good. Mrs. Metcalf showed me a room at the end of the second-floor corridor, and the four-poster practically invited me to drop in. The bed was high enough to store a steamer trunk underneath. Topside, it had a thick mattress, cool pink sheets, and high fluffy pillows.

I stripped down and drew the heavy curtains, blackening the room. The combination of jet lag, Thorazine, and two thousand calories of sweets took its toll. I was already asleep and dreaming of clear skies and steady winds when a sixth sense told me of a presence in the room. Unless I was dreaming.

I opened my eyes and, in the light of a candle, saw Pamela Metcalf. She wore white panties and a white bra, and my waking sensation was that an erotic nurse was about to minister to her patient. She was fuller of hip and larger of breast than she appeared fully clothed, an enchanting swirl of womanly curves. She slid out of the panties and unfastened the bra. She shook her long auburn hair free over a bare shoulder and put the candle on the nightstand.

"I really don't own a bikini," she whispered, crawling into the cool bed and burying her head against my chest. "Red or otherwise."

There was the initial excitement of fresh silken skin and sweet womanly scents. There was the slight awkwardness of exploring new but familiar terrain. There was the customary kissing and touching and sighing and nuzzling, and there was finally the joining of bodies. Which, no matter the depth of feeling, the mutual care, comes down to the mutual thrusting of loins, the roar of engines in sync, the pure physical explosion of chemical energy. But even as my motor revved I thought the same was somehow out of kilter. There was, after all, *no* depth of feeling or mutual care. My pursuit of her had been halting and unsure, her response caustic and defensive. Then, the sudden change of moods; she became interested. In me or my neuroses, I didn't know which. But she was asking all the questions. She was filling in the blanks about me. That was fine. But who was this woman? I didn't know her at all. I didn't know the meaning of what we were doing, or why suddenly I needed to know, or why my spirits had plunged. It never used to be that way. Not in the days of the AFC Traveling All-Star Party Team. But damn, we change without knowing when or why.

So, after we unlatched, as my heartbeat slowed to its normal snail's pace, I had a short argument with the friend who sits on my shoulder, a smarter guy than me.

Lonely. That's what I feel. My arms wrapped around a beautiful woman who came to me, and I feel lonely. . . .

What are you complaining about, Lassiter? You got yours, didn't you, fella?

Yes, but . . .

But what?

I want some caring with the caresses.

You're breaking my heart, big guy.

There's even some new words out there. Commitment. Love.

I'm gonna bring out the violins any minute now.

This didn't feel right. So meaningless.

Postcoital depression. Discuss it with your therapist. Hey, isn't that her . . . ?

Somewhere, under the blanket of sleep, I heard a tapping against the windows and felt a chill in the room. There was the sense of movement, of clouds clearing, that perception below consciousness. Then invisible fingers flipped the switches and turned on the juice, warming up the brain.

I stretched an arm across the cool sheet and found myself alone.

"Looking for someone?"

"Found her," I said.

She stood at the foot of the bed, draped in a black velvet robe with gold piping. A candle flickered on the mantel. Outside, a summer storm pelted the windows with rain.

"I must be dreaming," I said.

"And not of me on a beach, I'll wager."

"Why do you say that?"

She sat on the bed.

"Now that you've had me, the repressed wish has been fulfilled. Time to move on to other wishes, other dreams."

She said it analytically, coldly, and I didn't like the way it sounded. "Is that a general comment on the male gender or should I take it personally?"

She was silent, so I said, "Or do you have some fear of abandonment?"

"You treated me as a transitional object," she said, "as a child would a teddy bear. To you, I'm something halfway between yourself and another person. Just a comforter for your infantile narcissism."

Oh. So that's what it was. It's so convenient to have a doctor in the house. Still, like most men, I prefer not to have my ego bashed just after sex. "Hold on, now. If I'm not mistaken, there was an appreciable amount of cooing and sighing coming from your side of the bed. Unless you were acting, things were pretty equal in the heat department."

"Is that it!" she demanded. "Were you measuring my galvanic skin response, the square inches of the blush on my chest? Is that all it is to you, the thermodynamics?"

"Time out! I was lying here peacefully. You're the one who came in, slithered out of her pants, and—"

"Bastard! Rotten bastard! It's what you wanted, the old slap and tickle."

"Wrong. I wanted *more*."

She stood and turned away. With the candlelight behind her, her profile appeared in silhouette. "And I didn't want to be treated as a need-satisfying object as you would your mother."

"My *mother*? I never knew my mother."

"It shows. Your suckling my breasts was the manifestation of an obsessional need."

"Where I come from, it's considered appropriate, even appreciated by many females of your generation."

"Really? Boasting now of your prowess, adding another notch to your belt."

"No, damn it! I think we made a mistake here. We weren't ready for this. You shouldn't—"

"Blast and damn! It's my fault, is it? Why didn't you send me away?"

"Because I wanted you. I just don't know what you expected."

"Not a bloody thing! You're all alike."

"I'm glad it isn't personal."

"It is, you blockhead. Have you ever tried talking, comforting? Afterward, you didn't say a word unless your silent melancholia followed by snoring is considered suitable communication among females of my generation."

Suddenly I wasn't lonely anymore. I *wanted* to be alone. I was tired of having my head analyzed and my lovemaking criticized. I went on the offensive. "As long as we're talking about mothers, you were downright rude to *your* mother today."

"Now you're an expert on etiquette as well as orgasms, is that it?"

"My granny taught me to be kind to stray cats, to wipe my shoes before coming in the house, and to pee before I got in the shower. I figured out on my own it isn't nice to call your mother a tramp in front of company."

"You think you know everything, don't you?"

"I know you're a grown-up lady and so is your mother, and the two of you ought to just let each other live the way each one wants."

She sighed and her shoulders sagged. When she spoke, it was softer. "It's best if you stay out of what doesn't concern you and what you know nothing about."

"I'm willing to listen, to learn."

She thought it over before speaking, then said, "My father didn't die. That's been her story for twenty years, but the truth . . ."

Somewhere down the corridor, a telephone rang.

"The truth is he simply left when he learned he'd been cuckolded."

"I'm sorry," I said, then realized I just expressed sorrow at learning her father was likely still alive.

She sat in silence a moment. "Is that all you have to say?" she asked. "You really don't know anything about me and you give no indication of wanting to know."

From somewhere I heard a muffled voice, answering the phone.

"I'm sorry, Pamela. But after getting roughed up yesterday, being driven halfway across Britain today, and rolling with you between the sheets, I am not up to par in the conversation department. Next time I'll have my devastatingly witty repartee ready."

"Next time! How utterly presumptuous. And keep your wit to yourself, thank you. I'm talking about communication, sharing feelings, not wisecracking."

Boom! Another mood shift. I propped myself up on an elbow and studied her in the darkness. I couldn't make out her face, just the chiseled outline of that perfect profile against the flickering light. "Pam, whatever I did or didn't do, I'm sorry. Now, why don't we get dressed? It must be about dinnertime."

She laughed. "Dinner was hours ago."

"Oh."

"Don't worry. Mum will understand."

"Good. Some mothers would be—"

"That would be the pot calling the kettle black. But who am I to talk? God, I hate myself when I'm so easy."

I heard footsteps outside the door, then a sharp rapping.

"Jake, wake up!"

"C'mon in, Charlie," I said.

Charlie Riggs swung the door open and bustled in. At least it looked like Charlie, bushy beard and all. I just had never seen him in a crimson kimono and pink satin bedroom slippers. The sight of Pamela Metcalf standing by the bed froze him.

"Oh my," he said. "Dr. Metcalf, so sorry to intrude." He looked down at himself. "It's most irregular, I know. But my pants are in your mother's bedroom. That is . . . she wanted to show me the workmanship on the four-poster with its painted cornice. It dates from 1785, you know. Of course you know. It's your house, after all. But I had never seen such workmanship . . . and well, oh, dear me . . ."

"I understand," Pam said evenly.

Charlie seemed to sigh. "There's a phone call. For Jake . . . from Miami . . . Detective Rodriguez."

I grabbed my shorts and started for the door without asking, so Charlie just blurted it out.

"Priscilla Wolf is dead," said the man in the crimson kimono.

CHAPTER 24

They

"I get you out of bed, amigo?" Rodriguez asked.

"Forget it. What happened?"

"Nick had the kid for the weekend. The missus was home all alone, talking whoopee on the computer till about eleven. We got the printout. Around midnight, best we can figure, she has a visitor. Must have known the guy, no sign of a break-in. Anyway, she ends up strangled."

"Sexual assault?"

"Well, the ME says she had sex within an hour of death. Seminal fluid reveals type-A blood. But the place is neat as a pin. There's no evidence of violence other than the bruises on the neck. Nothing missing from the house. A neighbor found her today when she didn't show for a ladies' lunch."

"An organized murder scene," I said.

"Ey, you're learning the jargon, counselor. Anyway, to my

practiced eye, it looks like consensual sex followed by manual strangulation."

"Just like Rosemary Newcomb."

"*Verdad,* five'll get you ten, same guy did all three. The way I figure, he was fooling around with Michelle but couldn't talk her out of her pants, so he just offed her. The Newcomb girl and Priscilla were easier, that's all."

So the killer wasn't a drooling maniac or one of those social outcasts collecting bottle caps in a rented room. More like a demented Don Juan.

I thought about Priscilla Wolf. Pretty and tough. Cynical and smart. Lonely and dead.

I remembered her in leotards and sneakers. Stretching and aerobicizing, dieting and fretting. Fighting middle age and winning. So long, Nick, hello, world. Picking up the pieces without missing a step. At least that was the side she showed. But at night, in the lonely hours, huddled over the passionless box with its microchips and electronic blips, she reached into the darkness, blindly groping for warmth and rapture. Surely there must be someone out there just as appealing, just as hungry, just as deserving of love.

No. No, Priscilla, I wanted to shout through time and space. Bolt that door against the night. The creepy crawlies aren't all on the late show. They drive Chevys and mow their lawns and order home-delivery pizzas. They spank on after-shave and make chitchat and smile through lying lips. They kiss and then they kill.

"How's Nick taking it?" I asked.

"Pretty hard, though he tries not to show it. Most guys I know would just be happy, no more alimony."

"Most guys you know are cops, coroners, and criminals. Gives you a jaundiced outlook, Rod."

"Maybe, but Nick's tops in my book. And so is . . . was Prissy."

"Didn't know you were acquainted," I said.

"For years. Nick and Prissy would double-date with Maria and me before we got divorced. After Nick moved out, I'd see Prissy for dinner once in a while."

He paused and I listened to some overseas buzzing and hissing.

If he wanted me to ask about their relationship, he had a long wait. Sometimes the best questioning technique is total silence.

"It wasn't romantic or anything," Rodriguez continued. "Just friends. Nick knew all about it, didn't give a shit."

I filed that away and asked, "You said you had a printout?"

"More poetry signed by the asshole that did the deed. You want to talk to him?"

"What? You got him! Why didn't you say so?"

"Slow down. I'm telling you. In fact, he'll tell you."

"Whoa! You Mirandize him?"

"Twice, but he needs detox more than legal advice. Fifty bucks says his blood tests for bourbon at eighty proof. The rest will be type A."

"Yeah, so's mine and forty percent of the U.S. Congress."

"I'd arrest those fuckers, too, if I could."

"Rod, if the guy's drunk, the confession is no good."

"Never said he confessed. Just said we had him."

There was a pause, and in the background, Rodriguez said, "*Cojé esto,* asshole. Talk away."

The voice was slurred but there was no mistaking those deep tones, trained so long ago on so many stages. "My dear Biff, where have you been? Are you holding out for top billing?"

"Prince, not you."

"'Tis I."

"They tell me you killed Priscilla Wolf."

"They?"

"Look, Prince—"

"Please, call me—"

"Okay, Gerald."

"—Ishmael."

He was growing tiresome, but I tried again. "Prince. They want to charge you with Murder One."

"*They?* Always, *they*. Third-person plural, a way of distancing yourself from the bureaucratic horror, eh, Biff? *They* need someone don't *they*? Three women dead, *they* need a fall guy to take the rap, that's how *they* speak, isn't it? *They,* dear God how I adore that word, it's so . . . so Kafkaesque. Tell me, Biff, in *The Trial,* do you think K. represents innocent mankind forced to vindicate himself in a totally alienated world without really knowing why, or is he guilty of something? Is he a part of the faulty world, deserving of his death? I prefer the former view, one of total desperation, rather than the hope for salvation through a higher law."

"No more, Prince. Save it for your students or the guys in the psycho ward. If you want, call a lawyer. They get paid by the hour to listen to bullshit."

Then there was silence, and finally, barely above a whisper, he said, "I want to tell you something very important that's been weighing heavily on my mind."

"You want to confess?"

"I want to do *Long Day's Journey into Night*. I want to play Edmund again. I thought you would understand."

I gave him no sympathy. "You're too old for the part."

"Of course the critics would say so, but what feeling I could bring to it now. Poor sickly Edmund, racked by consumption, drinking whiskey with his miserly father over the game of cards, telling him of his travels as a seaman. Do you remember?"

"No."

Suddenly his voice became youthful, thickened slightly by drink but perfect for the part. "'It was a great mistake, my being born a man. I would have been much more successful as a sea gull or a fish. As it is, I will always be a stranger who never feels at home, who does not really want and is not really wanted, who can never belong, who must always be a little in love with death!'"

"Is that it, Prince, are you in love with death?"

I heard his labored breathing along with the static. "That is for me to know and you to find out."

"But Edmund was speaking of his own death. He wasn't a killer."

"Nor am I," he said softly.

"Did you talk on the computer with Priscilla Wolf the night she was killed?"

"I spoke with Fortyish—"

"Forty Something."

"—who, I must say, was both amusing and intelligent. Your friend Roderick tells me she's been slain and that her name is Petula—"

"Priscilla!"

"Precisely."

"Priscilla Wolf! She's dead. Did you—"

"*Absolve, Domini,*" he chanted, "*aminas omnium fidelium defunctorum ab omni vinculo delictorum.*"

"Prince!"

"*Et gratia tua illis succurrente. . . .*"

"Prince, stop it!"

"I was born a Catholic, you know."

"Prince, you're confusing illusion and reality. That isn't you. It's George chanting the Requiem Mass for his dead son in *Virginia Woolf.*"

"Is it, now?"

"Yes, but there was no son! He was imaginary, invented by George and Martha. Priscilla Wolf was real."

"Not to me."

Then he put a tune to it, a nursery-rhyme tune, and six thousand miles away, ice water dripped into my veins. "Who's afraid of Pris-cilla Wolf, Pris-cilla Wolf, Pris-cilla Wolf?"

There was no reaching him. He had sailed into a foggy sea and didn't want to make port. Filled with self-knowledge and self-loathing. He knew he'd never again play the Old Vic or romance women under the Maine pines. Maybe he had a death wish, too. But was he a killer?

"Who's afraid of Pris-cilla Wolf, early in the morning . . . ?" The singsong voice grew weaker, and I heard the phone clank as if it had fallen from his hand. Rodriguez came on and told me Prince was asleep in his chair and that he'd be placed in a special cell and put under a suicide watch. I told him that was fine and I'd see him as soon as I could get home.

"Sure thing, Jake, but Nick's got Metro Homicide, the forensics boys, and the ME's office all working overtime. They'll nail this fruitcake to all three homicides faster than shit through a goose."

They, I thought, then realizing . . . I was one of Them.

CHAPTER 25

Woman Is His Game

Charlie Riggs was eating Hershey's Kisses and reading the latest report on figuring time of death by calculating the age of maggot larvae in body cavities. Forensic entomology, he called it, thumbing pages, sucking his chocolate, smacking his lips, occasionally hum-humming and making notes in the margin.

Alex Rodriguez was reading the *Miami Journal*, shaking his head. He looked up at me. "Your lousy paper got suckered on the so-called Cocaine Baby case. Everybody knows that's an old hoax perpetrated by bored customs agents. Never been a dead baby stuffed with cocaine come through the airport. Been stuffed turkeys, been stuffed yams, even been statues of the Virgin Mary stuffed with the white lady. But never been a dead baby."

Nick Wolf wasn't reading anything. He paced in front of his desk, his face growing red, his right hand slicing the air as he cut off Rodriguez and made a point. "Jakie, Jakie, you got a classic case of the hind-tit syndrome. The guy who doesn't crack the case always thinks the guy who did got the wrong man. Am I right, Rod?"

"*Verdad*," Rodriguez responded, on cue.

"See." Wolf gloated. They were beating me up like tag-team wrestlers. Nick Wolf turned to Dr. Pamela Metcalf, who sat quiet and saintly in a chair by the window. "There's probably even a fancy psychological term for it, right, Dr. Metcalf?"

"The denial defense mechanism," Pam Metcalf said.

Rodriguez chimed in, "It's like this, Jake. It hurts your pride to be wrong. Like getting kicked in your machismo."

Pamela Metcalf smiled coyly. "Castration anxiety," she said.

I stared stupidly at her. "You're on their side, too?"

"With a dash of persecutory complex," she added for good measure.

Nick Wolf stopped pacing and looked down at me, a bully asking if I'd had enough.

I hadn't. I get paid to argue. "Look, Prince knew you were tapping the Compu-Mate calls. I'd already shown him his *Equus* rantings. He's not stupid. Why would he kill someone he's just chatted with? He'd have to be crazy to—"

Sometimes I say too much. Nick Wolf smiled his cat-to-the-canary smile. It shut me up. "Jakie, face it. Your nutty professor is the guy. I'll bet even Doc Riggs agrees."

I turned to Charlie. He was muttering to himself. "Never paid much attention to blowfly larvae. They lay their eggs in the mouth or the nostrils, you get live maggots in a few hours. How useful is that if you don't find the body for days?"

"Charlie!"

He looked up, a brown smear of chocolate across his mustache. "So many misconceptions about death. Jake, do fingernails grow after death?"

"Yeah. I've heard that."

"*Sí*," Rodriguez said. "I found a stiff dead two weeks, you could tell the nails had grown an inch."

"*Deceptio visus*," Charlie said. "The tips of the fingers and toes shrink, so the nails appear longer. Nothing more."

"You mean appearances are deceiving, don't you, Charlie?" I asked hopefully. With Doc Riggs, you have to read between the lines.

He smiled back at me.

I kept going. "You're saying Prince didn't do it."

Charlie shrugged. "What do we have so far? Circumstantial evidence. Prince appears to have chatted with three women shortly before each was killed. He admits speaking to two of them, denies the first, which is curious but not conclusive of anything. We have no matching latent prints at any of the scenes. The autopsy of Miss Diamond reveals rather modest bruising over the thyroid and a partially fractured hyoid bone, which is consistent with strangulation by moderate force."

"A limp-wristed English professor," Wolf said, making his point with a dainty wave of the arm, "a wacko drunk pervert. What more you want, Jake?"

"On the other hand," Charlie said, "Ms. Newcomb and Mrs. Wolf suffered somewhat greater damage. Larynx snapped in two. Fractured hyoid, thyroid, and cricoid, the whole shebang."

Wolf shrugged. "He got better at it, maybe sobered up. Doc, don't forget the blood typing."

"Prince tests for blood type A, as do the semen specimens from Miss Newcomb and Mrs. Wolf. Have you done the DNA testing?"

"It's at the lab," Rodriguez said. He put down the newspaper, glommed a chocolate Kiss from Charlie, unwrapped the foil, and popped it into his mouth.

"Well," Charlie said. "No use speculating now. When they line up the alleles for each polymorphic locus, there'll be no mistaking it. Either it's Prince's semen or not."

"So what if it matches," I jumped in. "That doesn't exclude the possibility that he had sex with each woman, then after he left, the killer arrived."

Wolf laughed. "Oh, gimme a break, Jake! What is this guy to you, some Mr. Chips character?"

I didn't answer, but Charlie did. "If there's a DNA match, it means Prince is lying. He says he never met any of the women, much less . . ."

"And if he's lying," Nick said, scooping up the ball and heading for the end zone, "he's the killer. Admit it, Jake."

"It'd be enough to sustain an indictment," I conceded glumly.

"Enough to pull the switch at Raiford," Nick Wolf concluded.

I looked at Pam Metcalf. She placidly watched them take shots at me. Maybe she liked it. I'd been surprised when she told me to book *three* seats to Miami. Wanted to fulfill some speaking engagements, she said, help with my investigation, too. Surprised me again when she accepted my invitation for room, board, and affection at the little coral-rock house between Kumquat and Poinciana, rather than a fancy, oceanfront, phone-in-the-bathroom, twenty-four-hour-room-service hotel. We had shared my bed under the paddle fan on the second floor, the pungent aroma of neighborhood mango trees wafting through the open windows on the sticky nighttime breeze. We had listened to distant police sirens and each other's heartbeats. We had curled around each other, and I said sweet things into her neck, all of which I meant at the time.

I always think there's a band, kid. Professor Gerald Prince, master plagiarist, said that. So did Professor Harold Hill, knavish music man. And Jacob Lassiter, bloomin' pettifogger. Fakers all.

Rodriguez had given me the manila folder with the printout from Priscilla Wolf's computer. I looked at it for the third time.

DO YOU LIKE TO PAMPER A WOMAN, PASSION KING?
PRINCE. JUST A PRINCE, LIKE YOUNG HAMLET.
PAMPERING? IS THAT WHAT YOU NEED?
DON'T KNOW. NEVER HAD IT. MIGHT BE NICE FOR A
    CHANGE.
IF YOU CAN'T STAND THE COLDNESS OF MY SORT OF
    LIFE, GO BACK TO THE GUTTER.
THE GUTTER! LISTEN HERE, PASSION PRICK. I'VE BEEN
    A WIFE AND A MOTHER AND HAD DINNER WITH THE
    GOVERNOR AND DROVE CAR POOL, AND I'M A LADY
    ALL DAY, AND AT NIGHT, I DO WHAT THE HELL I
    WANT.
NO. NO. NO. TRY THIS. "I'M A GOOD GIRL, I AM."
WHAT?
TRY IT. "I'M A GOOD GIRL, I AM. AND I KNOW THE LIKE
    OF YOU, I DO."
WAIT!!! THAT'S FROM A PLAY.
BY JOVE, SHE'S GOT IT. I THINK SHE'S GOT IT.
SURE. MY FAIR LADY. YOU WERE DOING THE REX
    HARRISON PART, RIGHT?

I PREFER TO THINK OF THE PLAY AS PYGMALION, *AND
I WAS DOING HENRY HIGGINS AS WRITTEN BY SHAW. I
THOUGHT YOU MIGHT TRY A FEW OF ELIZA'S LINES.
OH PRINCE. YOU'RE VERY LITERARY. I LIKE THAT. MY
HUSBAND NEVER HAD ANY TIME FOR PLAYS.
FOOTBALL, BUT NOT PLAYS. AND TRY TO GET HIM TO
THE BALLET. HE CALLED IT FAIRIES' BASEBALL.
WELL THEN, PERHAPS WE COULD GET TOGETHER.
LOVE TO. CALL ME AGAIN. BUT GOT TO GET CLEANED
UP, CHANGE CLOTHES NOW. HEY. I MEAN IT. CALL
ME TOMORROW.*

I put the file down and thought about it. Charlie went back to his maggots, Rod to his paper, and Nick Wolf sat down at his desk beneath the wall of commendations and merit badges. Pam Metcalf studied me from across the office. It was the professor, all right, sliding in and out of an old role. According to the printout, they signed off at 10:05 P.M. Priscilla said she had to get cleaned up, change clothes. *Not* get cleaned up, go to bed. She was going out. Or someone was coming over. Late. And not the Passion Prince. Someone she already knew. But who?

Nick Wolf, maybe.

Or Alex Rodriguez, her pal.

Now, those were thoughts best kept to yourself. I opened the file again. When they found Priscilla Wolf, wearing a silk negligee, strangled in the foyer near the front door, there was a faint light from the corner of what had been Nick's study. A steady hum came from the IBM compatible on the desk. On the screen, white on black, a message from hell.

*MAN IS THE HUNTER; WOMAN IS HIS GAME;
THE SLEEK AND SHINING CREATURES OF THE CHASE,
WE HUNT THEM FOR THE BEAUTY OF THEIR SKINS.*

Tennyson again, they told me. I didn't know the poem, but I can read English. Regardless of the poet's meaning, there was no mistaking the intent here. Someone was collecting the sleek, shiny pelts of the female of the species and bragging about it.

Got to get cleaned up, change clothes now. Who was it? Some sick creature out of the swamps who looks just like you or me. Or Nick Wolf or Alex Rodriguez. There it was again, the thought hanging on like a summer cold.

I told everybody I was going to put the top down and take a little ride just to clear my head. No one seemed to care. As I stood up, Nick Wolf said, "Jake, let me give you some advice. You've got to look out for your reputation. This case could make you look like a bozo."

"Meaning what?"

"Don't get defensive. I'm trying to help you out. Look, I know stories about you when you just started practicing. A lot of people thought you played ball too long without a helmet."

"I made some mistakes," I admitted.

Nick turned toward Rodriguez, his one-man fan club. "One day when Jake was just out of the PD's office, he went to federal court. Remember, Jakie, the story was all over town. The judge had assigned the motion to a magistrate. Jakie had never appeared before a magistrate before and didn't know how to address him. So when he's asked whether the plaintiff is ready, Jakie here says—"

"Yes, Your Majesty."

Rodriguez snickered. Pam smiled politely. Charlie kept reading.

"It seemed right at the time," I said.

"I checked up on you, Jakie," Wolf said. "At Harman and Fox, your first deposition in a big civil case, one of the senior partners tells you it's a formal proceeding. So you show up—"

"In a tuxedo," I said.

Even Charlie laughed at that, and he's my best friend.

"So the point is, Jakie, like I told you before, keep your ass down, it won't get shot off."

I took the expressway west past the Orange Bowl, pale and faded now that the Dolphins had moved uptown to a new amphitheater with massive replay screens and skyboxes for the heavy hitters. I turned south on the Palmetto, past Flagler Street and Calle Ocho, past Coral Way, and exited at Bird Road. I was sandwiched between two semis, and I inhaled equal portions of carbon monoxide and diesel fuel. I headed west again, past the same car dealers and gas stations, gun shops and XXX videos, beauty parlors and rental furniture stores. Plastic signs proclaimed the lowest prices, the largest selections, the newest models, and the biggest, bestest, beautifulest products money can buy.

The afternoon sun still hung above the horizon, the day soggy and sweltering, the shadows long. My white shirt stuck to my back, my striped tie was at half-mast. The house was buttoned up tight and wrapped in yellow tape courtesy of Metro police. I rooted around in the trunk of the 442 until I found an old pair of windsurfing gloves. They were nylon and fastened at the wrist with Velcro straps. I looked like a burglar who didn't want to leave prints. Appearances are not always deceiving, Charlie old buddy.

The garage door handle was rusty. I hoped it would hold. I bent at the knees and, keeping my back straight, grasped the handle with two hands. I slowly straightened my legs, pulling up. Everybody has different talents. Some can hit high C, others can paint landscapes on bleached bones. I can lift deadweight. Lots of it.

The handle bit into the meat of my palms, even through the gloves. Cords and strings in my back snapped and screeched curses at me and the lactic acid pooled in my triceps until they nearly cramped. I kept pulling. Hey, if Atlas could hold up the world, a guy with decent lats and traps ought to be able to . . .

Crack. An old pin snapped in two and the door rumbled up under my chin. I ducked inside, pulled the door down, and found the way to the kitchen. Inside, the air-conditioning was pumping away, all those kilowatts keeping the emptiness cool.

I walked into the living room where Priscilla Wolf had fed me bland and healthy tidbits and asked me to rub her feet. I went to the study that had been Nick's, where Priscilla spent her evenings, gabbing the boredom away. The computer was still there, turned off now, the message from the screen preserved on hard copy.

Whoever wrote it, I thought, knew a little something about computers. You can't just turn them on. You have to get into the word-processing directory. You have to type. And you have to know some poetry by heart, I figured, unless the killer totes his Tennyson with him. I saw the dust layered among the keys, the lab boys scouring the keyboard for prints. But the killer had either worn gloves or wiped the place clean.

What else? He had to be calm. He'd just strangled a woman and he sits to type his little message, and does it with no typos, no sweat. Freaky.

I looked around the study, opening drawers, alert for notes or letters, hoping to find it laid out for me: *See you Sunday night at 10:30, your place. Signed, Joe Jones, the hunter.* With an address and phone number attached. But there was nothing. If there had been, Metro would have found it.

So what was I doing here? Trying to prove Nick Wolf wrong. He had put me down good. Right in front of the crusty ex-coroner and the beautiful lady who were my little team. Why? And what are you going to do about it, *Jakie?* Run home crying to Granny Lassiter? Hey, you're a big boy. You can bench-press large buildings in a single bound. Or something like that.

I tossed a few ideas around and dropped a couple on my toes. If Nick Wolf thinks you're such a loser, why does he appoint you to head a murder investigation? Because he thinks you're such a loser, that's why, dummy! Which means what? That Nick Wolf is afraid a smart guy would find things out that are not good for the health and welfare of Nicholas G. Wolf.

Okay. So time to get smart.

I walked into the foyer, the chalk outline of Priscilla's body still on the floor. I wandered back to the master bedroom and looked through a closet, then walked into little Nicky's room and finally the guest room.

The guest room.

Michelle Diamond had stayed there overnight. Pajama party. It was barely ten by ten, an oak floor, grass-cloth wallpaper. On the wall was a still-life watercolor—a bowl of fruit and a bottle of wine. Jalousie windows overlooked a small backyard. A dresser was stuffed with women's clothes that hadn't been worn in some time. There was a double bed with a fluffy beige comforter. I looked under the bed for nothing in particular and found just that. I lay down in the bed and stared straight up. No bright ideas were written on the ceiling.

I stood and opened the folding door to the closet. Old clothes, a couple of suitcases. With a hand, I pulled out some women's dresses and looked into the darkness. On the floor something green. Army green. I reached down and pulled it out by a canvas strap. An old duffel bag stuffed to the drawstrings.

I loosened the strings and yanked out some fatigues, a pair of boots, a vicious sawtooth knife, and a Colt .45 pistol. There was more. There were socks and shirts and a little velvet case lined with medals and ribbons. There was the smell of age and mustiness. I turned the bag upside down and shook it. A pair of dog tags clattered to the floor. Nothing else. I fondled the old duffel bag and tried to feel the vibrations. No magic. I tossed it aside and it landed with a slap. Not a canvas-on-wood sound. I picked up the bag and turned it over. Under a flap, a zippered pouch. *Zip.* I reached inside and pulled at something. It slipped from my hand and hit the floor. I had a case of fumble-itis. It lay there on the floor next to the dog tags and boots and green undershirts.

A small book just staring at me. Underneath a plastic cover, neatly printed so long ago, so far away: *Officer's Log, Lt. Nicholas G. Wolf.*

I picked it up and turned to page one. "Now, Nick," I said. "Talk to me now."

CHAPTER 26

Habeas Corpus

"The writ is an ancient one, Your Honor, as holy as the Scriptures, mightier than any sword. The crown may imprison, but the court, Your Honor, the court may always set free."

Arnold Two-Ton Tannenbaum slipped his right hand inside his bulging vest and held his heart. Either he was pledging allegiance or imitating a blimp-sized Napoleon. He wore a freshly pressed suit of friendly brown and a look of sincere concern.

"Habeas corpus ad subiciendum," Tannenbaum intoned. Charlie Riggs would have been proud. Judge Dixie Lee Boulton peered down from the bench through her bifocals, wrinkled her forehead, and waited.

"Ha-be-as cor-pus," the corpulent mouthpiece proclaimed, as if the words would cast a spell. "Bring the body to the court. How can the state justify holding such a man without a formal charge? A man with no prior arrests of any kind. A man renowned on the stages of two continents. A man who devotes his time to imparting wisdom to the young. An actor, yea, but also, Your Honor, this is a *man*."

Two-Ton extended a massive arm toward Gerald Prince, who sat proudly at the defense table. Prince wore a green jailhouse smock and had swept his silver hair straight back. He jutted his fine chin forward and appeared to be looking somewhere over Dixie Lee Boulton's head.

I moseyed over behind the defense table and bent down toward Prince.

"Are we going to hear one of your soliloquies today?" I asked.

He put a finger to his lips. "Silence," he whispered, "is often the greatest achievement of an actor. Make them watch your face. Only the face. Like the Indian in *Cuckoo's Nest*."

"Or Harpo Marx in *Animal Crackers*," I agreed.

"In sum, Your Honor, it is indefensible, unconstitutional, and utterly intolerable to detain this famed thespian without a formal charge," Tannenbaum concluded.

"Thank you, Mr. Tattlebum," the judge said. "Who speaks for the people of the state of Florida?"

Just little ole me, I thought.

"Under the statute," I began without pleasantries, "the state has twenty-one days to indict Mr. Prince. He can be held until then unless the defense demonstrates that the proof is not evident and the presumption of guilt is not great. Now, Mr. Prince has been incarcerated only four days, and the state submits there is sufficient evidence to detain him."

I ran through the evidence for the judge, the computer messages, the blood type, the lack of alibis, and reminded her of the seriousness of the crimes.

"Additionally," I said, "we had hoped to have the DNA results ready for today's hearing. Unfortunately, they've been delayed. When they are received, we expect the grand jury to return indictments for three homicides. *Three* first-degree murders, Your Honor."

I was a reluctant warrior. It had gotten too complicated. Three women were dead, the state attorney was married to one and sleeping with another. The chief homicide detective was a pal of the wife. The third woman didn't belong to the happy little Wolf clan, but all three played nighttime chitchat on their computer's sex channel. The state attorney had expanded my duties to prosecute all three. Pretty soon you would need a scorecard. How did I get into this? And what was going on?

The judge looked at me, perplexed. "I don't like to hold defendants without the issuance of indictments or criminal information," she said. "Is there any formal charge you can file today?"

Nothing I could think of, unless overacting was a misdemeanor, in which case Two-Ton would be jailed along with his client. Before I could reply, the courtroom door swung open and a young man in a white lab coat came hustling in. He said something to the bailiff, who pointed at me. Just like on TV, the missing witness bursting in to save the day.

"Your Honor, may we present some brief testimony in support of the state's position?" I asked with grateful charm.

"I suggest you do," the judge said.

I tossed an arm around the young man and hustled him to the witness stand. He looked like an earnest graduate student, bushy mustache and unkempt hair. He held a manila folder and glanced nervously at the judge.

"Ever testify before?" I whispered.

"No . . . and maybe we should talk—"

"No time, the judge is about to grant the writ."

He placed his left hand on the Bible and raised his right hand with a jerky motion that tossed his folder across the courtroom like a Frisbee. I retrieved it. He sat down and told us his name, Dr. Sanford Katzen, his profession, mathematician and geneticist, and yes, he performed various tests on semen samples from two of the decedents and the blood of the defendant.

"What do you call these tests?" I asked.

"Restriction fragment length polymorphism analysis."

Don't you just love doctors? "Is there any other name . . . ?"

"Oh, you probably know it by its colloquial term. Genetic fingerprinting."

"And how do you perform these tests?"

"Oh my, that would take several hours to explain."

Judge Boulton cleared her throat. "Young man, I have nine more hearings before lunch, so perhaps you could just cut to the chase."

"Well, simply stated, and grossly oversimplifying, so you must forgive me, we compare the deoxyribonucleic acid from two different samples. If the size of the genes match, the acid came from the same person. It would be a mathematical impossibility for two random samples to match up."

He opened the folder and pulled out several X rays. I mounted them on the viewer usually used in auto-accident cases. Dr. Katzen came down from the witness stand without tripping and stood humbly at my side.

"Please describe what the X rays show," I said.

"These are the autoradiograms. First we chop the DNA into small fragments using enzymes. Then they're placed on a gelatin slab, shot with an electrical current, transferred to a membrane that's exposed to a radioactive probe, and pressed against the X-ray film which you see—"

"Dr. Cashman," the judge interrupted. "Could you please get to the point!" Dixie Lee was ready to deny the request for the writ, if only the witness would say the magic words.

"Sorry. Well, as you can see, there are three parallel tracks representing DNA from each sample. The distance between these bands is measured down to one hundredth of a kilobase. That's about one thousand rungs on the DNA ladder, which has some three billion lines. So, as you can see, the measurement is quite precise."

The judge was fidgeting. "Doctor! The results, please."

"Well, if the length of the polymorphic loci match, there's no chance that the samples came from different people. Oh, I shouldn't say no chance, should I? There is perhaps one in one-point-five quintillion, but for statistical purposes—"

"Dr. Katzen," I said, "the results. What does your autoradiogram show?"

"Oh, quite clearly, the kilobases from each decedent match exactly."

"Exactly," I said.

"So that the semen taken from Ms. Newcomb and Mrs. Wolf obviously came from the same man."

"Obviously," I agreed.

"Of course, as you can see with the naked eye, there is no match with the blood from Mr. Prince."

"Of course," I said.

Wait a second.

What did he say?

"No match at all," he continued. "Not the slightest chance that the semen from either of the bodies came from Mr. Prince, though, as I said, they did come from the same man, whoever he might be."

A thousand blowflies could have laid their eggs in my mouth and still had room for an apple. I was nailed to the floor. Out of the corner of my eye, I saw Gerald Prince get to his feet at the defense table and nod toward the judge. The nod became a bow. He did it again. Waiting for the curtain call. Someone was saying something. What was it?

"Mr. Lassiter, does that conclude your presentation?"

"Yes, Your Majesty," I said.

The sky darkened at precisely three o'clock, huge thunderheads gathering over downtown, hanging low, bashing each other, lightning crackling. At ten past the hour, the rain came, swirling with the winds, sweeping across Okeechobee Road. An old Pontiac had flooded out and sat, hood up, blocking traffic for five miles. The rain pounded on my canvas top, cold drops sliding inside the window and splatting my left leg.

"I can't imagine why you're so upset," Pamela Metcalf said. "You thought he was innocent the whole time. You should be happy."

"Happy to play the fool?"

"Is that it? You're embarrassed that justice was done. Would you rather convict an innocent man?"

"No. I'd rather have stayed out of this. I was set up. To win, lose, I don't know. But I'm going to find out."

I turned down a side street in Hialeah, the Olds splashing through a series of foot-deep puddles. I pulled up in front of a renovated warehouse.

"C'mon," I said to Pam. "I want you to meet Ozzie and Harriet."

Max the Jockey was slouched at the counter, playing solitaire. Cheating. He wore a black muscle T-shirt and the snake tattoo on his forearm coiled as he dealt the cards. "Howdy, shyster," he said. "Your pants are wet."

Pam smiled and said, "Hello, Ozzie."

Max gave her a puzzled look and turned over the deck, trying to find a red queen. In the back, Bobbie's long body was hunched over a silent computer at the sys-op desk.

"How's business?" I asked.

"Slower'n a whorehouse on Sunday morn," Max said.

"What's the matter? Thought every time there was a murder, you two were off to the bank."

His jaw muscles were working up a storm. Either he was sucking his teeth, or he had swallowed his tongue. "Not this time. I figure, after the Newcomb girl got it, the babes thought it was exciting to fool around, that it wouldn't really happen again. Just like those assholes who throw hurricane parties when the red-and-black flag goes up. They never think it'll hit until their condo gets blown away. So now another babe gets killed, it ain't so much fun."

Bobbie was stirring in the back. She wore black nylon running shorts and rubber thongs. Her midriff was bare; an elastic halter covered her breasts. Barely. She started long-legging it toward the counter, chewing a wad of pink bubble gum, her eyes glued to Pam Metcalf. "What's a classy dame like you doing with a dork like him?" she asked.

"Treating him," she said.

"Royally," I added with an inane grin.

Bobbie shrugged and blew a bubble in my face. "Lemme show you something, Lassiter."

She shoved her clipboard under my face, a stack of papers attached. At the top, a male symbol was jabbing the female symbol with his arrow. "Our latest client survey," she said. "Ninety-one percent of the men and eighty-three percent of the women rate our service as very good or exceptional."

I riffled through a bunch of completed questionnaires. "Only a couple written in crayon," I said with admiration.

"Always the smartass. We're a solid business. Satisfaction guaranteed. Just look at these."

She was right. There were numerical listings and eloquent testimonials to Compu-Mate. "Hot and wet," wrote Muff Diver. "Lotsa, lotsa men," gushed Helen Bed. "Need more fetishists," complained Cruel Mistress. Another one caught my eye. "Bitches wouldn't know a real man if they blew one." Signed, Tom Cat. Pithy, you had to give him that.

"So what can I do you for?" Bobbie asked, still looking at Pam.

I drew a subpoena out of my suit coat. "I want to see copies of everything you turned over to Detective Rodriguez. Printouts, membership lists. Everything."

"I thought he worked for you."

"Yeah, I thought so, too."

She shrugged again and waved us back. Her thongs flip-flopped along the tile as she escorted us to a file cabinet next to the computer. She looked at my pants and said, "Is it raining outside, Lassiter, or you get excited on the way over here?"

I ignored her, and after a moment she found the right file and handed me a batch of papers. I didn't know what I was looking for, but it didn't take long to find.

On the left-hand side of the page was the handle. On the right was the real name and address.

"Those are in chronological order by date of membership," Bobbie said. "The computer can alphabetize them, if you want."

"No need." I thumbed through half a dozen pages and found the right one:

DAWN DELIGHT	*DARCY NOLAN*	*2340 SW 103 ST.*
LOUNGE LIZARD	*P. FREIDIN*	*1865 BRICKELL AVE.*
HONEY POT	*LOUISE MAROUN*	*14000 SW 70 AVE.*
ORAL ROBERT	*BOB MARKO*	*635 MICHIGAN AVE.*
ROCK HARD	*S. GROSSMAN*	*120 SAPODILLA DR.*
BANANA MAN	*D. RUSSO*	*3540 SALEM BLVD.*
FORTY-TWO DEE	*DEE ANN REYNOLDS*	*2318 NE 168 TER.*
HORNY TOAD	*P. FLANIGAN*	*1683 TAGUS AVE.*
BIGGUS DICKUS	*A. RODRIGUEZ*	*7560 SW 26 ST.*

Boom! Just like that. The little jolt of adrenaline. Then the moment of doubt. There are fifteen pages of Rodriguezes in the Miami phone directory. Nineteen listings just for "A. Rodriguez." Not that Alejandro Rodriguez would be any of those. Detectives don't stick their home addresses in the book. Too many guys short on humanity and long on memory for that. And I didn't know his home address. But easy enough to find out. Just drive by the Twenty-sixth Street address tonight, look for the county-owned Plymouth out front.

It would be there, I knew. All the many pieces fit together. I found the first printout I had spread in front of Charlie Riggs on the dock. On the night she was killed, Michelle Diamond computer-talked with four men.

BIGGUS DICKUS
BUSH WHACKER
ORAL ROBERT
PASSION PRINCE

Nine names turned up on Rosemary Newcomb's list.

BIGGUS DICKUS
HARRY HARDWICK
HORNY TOAD
MUFF DIVER
PASSION PRINCE
ROCK HARD
SLAVE BOY
STUDLY DO-RIGHT
TOM CAT

"Who talked to Priscilla Wolf on the night she was killed?" I asked Bobbie.

"Passion Prince. I told the detective that."

"Yeah, I know. Who else?"

She shrugged again, popped a pink bubble, and slinked to the computer terminal. She punched a few buttons and waited for a blip and a bleep and then called out, "Banana Man, Tom Cat, and Biggus Dickus."

"Bingo!"

"What is it?" Pam asked.

"Only two men talked to all three women on the nights they were killed. Prince and Dickus. And we know Prince is innocent."

"So you think it's Mr. Dickus," Pamela Metcalf said.

"Unless you have a better idea," I said.

CHAPTER 27

Chumming

I was poling the skiff across the Key Largo flats half a mile off the marshy hammocks on a sweltering day that held no hint of a breeze. The surface glistened in the harsh light, and in the shallow water tiny crabs scurried across the bottom, searching for specks of food. Sweat poured down my bare back and stained my canvas shorts. Somewhere under a hat of green palm fronds sat Charlie Riggs, cool as a six-pack in white cotton clam diggers and an aloha shirt festooned with lavender orchids.

"Great day to be alive." Charlie chortled, nearly squirming with joy. "And thanks for the new rod. My goodness, it's a beauty!"

"Just figured it was time you looked like a fisherman."

"Now, if you'll point me in the direction of some *Albula vulpes*, we can get to work."

Charlie lovingly fondled his new seven-foot, five-ounce graphite rod. It was equipped with an open-face spinning reel, wrapped with two hundred fifty yards of eight-pound test line. He was going to drop some unweighted shrimp in front of Mister Bonefish, if I could find him. At your service, Jake Lassiter, old salt-fishing guide. I'd been poling and watching for an hour and had nothing to show for it except five pounds of lost water weight. Where were those little monsters with the recessed chins?

Charlie practiced a few casts, easily handling the light rod, holding the tip above his head at one o'clock, then flicking the wrist and releasing the line at eleven o'clock, adjusting the length of the cast by thumb pressure on the reel spool. After a few tries he could drop the bait on a lily pad at forty yards.

"So, Jake, you bring me out here to fish or talk?"

"Both, of course."

"Well, the fish ain't biting half as much as the skeeters, so let's get to it."

On the way down to Key Largo on Useless 1, I had told Charlie about Biggus Dickus and Lieutenant Wolf. I showed him the officer's log I had purloined from the closet. He read it silently, committing the important parts to memory. Mostly there were the mundane accountings of infantry in the field. Weather reports, platoon rosters, notes from Command, coordinates of objectives, summaries of missions, arcane military slang and abbreviations, casualty rolls, to-do lists. Occasionally a personal item suffused with unstated meaning: *Write Barker's mother.*

I turned first to the entry labeled *09 JAN '68.* The ink had run and faded. I imagined Wolf huddled in the elephant grass in a monsoon, trying to write under the shield of his poncho. Or was it sweat dripping from his forehead as he sought the words? Or tears?

> *0700—Men tired, stoned. C-rations low.*
> *1100—Rain, rain, go away, Charley back another day.*
> *Open paddies. Men slow, surly.*
> *1330—VC ambush on dike. Gallardi, Boyer, dogwood 6.*
> *Rosen, Williams, Colgan, Miciak, dogwood 8.*
> *1800—Dak Sut. Firefight. 3 VC greased. Zippo approx.*
> *20 hooches. Phuong MIA. Lt. E. Ferguson. Rest in peace.*
> *May the Lord have mercy.*

That was it. Ass-backward from the way he tells the story now, when he tells it at all. The incident on the dike happened *before* they got to Dak Sut. Evan Ferguson was killed in the village, not on the dike. Nick penned a small prayer over his loss. So why the deception? I thumbed through the log. An entry from January 12, three days later. *Filed report re Dak Sut. No queries from Command.* What should they have asked? I wondered. Maybe Michelle Diamond's questions. She couldn't ask them. But I could.

I drove the pole into the soft sand and tied us fast. I sat on the platform covering the ninety-horsepower Mercury and grabbed a Grolsch from the cooler.

"So what do you think, Charlie?"

He laid the rod across his lap and scanned the water. The skiff drew about nine inches; the water was two feet deep, tops. It's part hunting and part fishing when you're after Mister Bonefish. "What are the possibilities?"

He loves the Socratic method of teaching.

"At least two. First, a conspiracy. Wolf has his pal Rodriguez kill a couple of ladies who know too much."

Charlie removed his palm-frond hat and wiped his forehead with a red bandana. "What could have happened in a Vietnamese village that would lead him to commit murder more than twenty years later?"

So many questions, so few answers.

"Don't know, I'm working on it."

"And if he wanted to silence Michelle and his wife, why kill the Newcomb girl?"

"A distraction," I said. "Makes it look like motiveless crimes tied together by the Compu-Mate membership. Then frame a drunk who can't remember half of what he says or does."

A spotted eagle ray flashed off the bow and beat its winglike pectoral fins, scurrying through the warm, shallow water. Charlie watched it and scowled. *"Aetobatus narinari."* He dug out a fresh shrimp. "So brutal."

"A ray? Unless it whips you with a poison spine, it's—"

"Not the ray. Your scenario. So brutal and risky, allowing the time lapse between Michelle's murder and Priscilla's. What if Priscilla became suspicious, started thinking her husband had killed Michelle?"

"But she wouldn't, Charlie. That's the point. There was nothing to tie Nick in, and once Rosemary Newcomb was killed, everyone would think it was just some lunatic with a computer. Just like the royal family slaughtering four other women to cover up the killing of Mary Jane Kelly."

"Then why kill Priscilla at all? Michelle was silenced, and if Priscilla wasn't suspicious . . ."

"That's what I couldn't figure out. Whatever Priscilla knew, she's known for a long time, and she's been the good wife, silent and true. So I asked myself what's changed, and of course, it's so obvious."

Charlie picked up his rod and thought about it. "Nick left her. No reason to be loyal once he dumped her."

"Exactly. Priscilla put up a good front. Even fixed Nick up with Michelle, hoped it would be a quick fling. She had Michelle over for tea and slumber parties. One night Michelle finds the log. Probably she already looked up the clippings about Wolf's war record, so she notices the discrepancy. She starts asking Wolf about the war, but very casually. She's a little smarter than she seems. He doesn't figure it out at first, gives her the standard bit about the firefight in the village and the chase along the dike. Now she knows there's a story there. Maybe a very big story, bring down the state attorney, win a prize. Maybe she contacts survivors from the platoon, and one of them tips off Nick. And she may have told Priscilla, or Nick thought she did. He had a divorce in the works, plus a bright political future on the line. He couldn't afford to have somebody saying the medals are made of tin."

Charlie was quiet a moment. Then he spotted something, raised the rod, and cast. The excitement must have pumped up his backswing and I felt the rod buzz by my ear. The shrimp plopped thirty feet from where he wanted it, and the fish swam lazily the other way.

"Too big for a bonefish, anyway," Charlie said without regret. "Might be a cobia."

"Theory number two," I said. "Nick's got nothing to do with it. Alex Rodriguez is some kind of freak. Seduces 'em and strangles 'em."

"But you have no proof to support either theory."

"Give me a chance. Now, how about some fishing?"

Charlie was eyeing a sandy spot near a wad of sea grass. The first problem with bonefishing is spotting the little devils. I stood on the platform, watching for their tails. On the flats you sometimes see them waving like flags above the waterline, the fish digging in the sand for shrimp or crabs. Other times you see the mud churned up as they root around. More often you see nothing.

"You might try some chum," Charlie said.

Real purists may disagree, but I see nothing wrong with salting the water. We didn't have all day.

I unlimbered myself, untied the skiff, and poled toward the sandy spot. I opened a bag of live shrimp and started chopping them into shrimpettes. When I had a mess of bite-sized morsels, I tossed them over the side, leaving a trail of hors d'oeuvres for Mister Bonefish. Squinting into the late-morning sun, I poled back a comfortable distance, stuck us into the bottom, and sat back down on the hard platform.

Are we having fun yet? Charlie was watching the water, and I was thinking about the kinks in my back when he said, "Hullo."

I opened my eyes and saw one of those spooky little devils, maybe eight pounds and all muscle and fight. It was skittish, scoping the territory, wondering why somebody dumped dinner in its living room. The second problem with bonefish is getting them to bite. They're high-strung as thoroughbreds. Drop the bait too far away, they won't notice it. Too close, they'll leave town.

Charlie let fly and landed his shrimp six feet in front of its snout. The fish didn't care. It was feeding on the chum or some microscopic flecks of fish food. Then it waggled over, sniffed around, and bit. And *zip!* It ran—hell, it flew—the reel singing a metallic song. The fish broke the Olympic record for the hundred meters, then decided to do it again. Charlie let it run out. He didn't have a choice. If your drag isn't perfect, the bonefish will snap your line and be in Mexico before you get your engine started.

When the fish stopped its run, Charlie decided to see what it was made of.

Dynamite.

Charlie started pumping, pulling the rod back, letting up, and reeling in. The fish took about ten seconds of this, said the hell with it, bent the rod double, and ran again. They fought for a while, the fish running, Charlie giving ground, reeling in, letting out. Then the line snagged on something—it could have been a chunk of coral or an old tire—and it broke cleanly, the fish bolting free.

"A fine specimen," Charlie said. He considered something for a moment, then added, "You might try some chum."

"I just did."

"Not here, Jake. For Wolf and Rodriguez. See if they bite."

Oh.

"If Rodriguez is a psychotic killer," Charlie said, "he'll kill again. If Wolf thinks someone else knows enough to ruin him, he'll silence that person. So, Jake, start chumming."

The rains came in the afternoon, but we were dry inside Charlie's old Ford pickup, fighting the endless traffic up the highway from the Keys. He wouldn't let me drive, something about third gear not being up and to the right. The skiff was lashed to a rickety trailer behind us, and we bounced and splashed over the Card Sound Bridge on the way to Miami.

"You should have kept that ten-pounder," I said. "Could have mounted it."

Charlie snorted. "I never mounted a corpse in the morgue. Why would I do it to a poor fish?"

"That poor fish damn near broke your pole in two. Never saw so much fight in something so small."

"*Deceptio visus*," Charlie said, and not for the first time.

"I've been thinking about the bait," I said.

Charlie kept his eyes on the road and his mouth shut. He liked me to figure out things for myself.

"I need to know more about Biggus Dickus."

"His modus operandi?"

"Right. How he relates to the Compu-Mate women, what he looks for."

Charlie hit the defroster. Our body heat had steamed up the windows. Outside, a storm from the east slashed torrents of rain across the pavement. Lightning had knocked out the traffic lights and darkened the neon sign at the Green Turtle Inn. "You're casting for Rodriguez first."

"If he goes after another woman, it would clear Wolf, wouldn't it? Rodriguez would be just another crazed killer, except he wears a badge. If he doesn't bite, then I let Wolf know the Vietnam War isn't over yet."

"And if neither leaps at the bait? If your theories prove to be a floccinaucinihilipilification."

"A flossy . . . what?"

"Sorry. Such an ostentatious, academic word. If your theories prove to be valueless, where are you then?"

"You tell me, Charlie. Where am I if I falsely accuse the state attorney and the chief homicide detective of murder?"

"Poling for bonefish, Jake. Now and forever."

CHAPTER 28

The Hacker

Richie Bergman kept twitching his nose, and the sergeant kept staring. "And just who is he?" the sergeant asked.

"My paralegal," I said.

The sergeant turned the volume down on his black-and-white five-inch set. "And what's his problem?"

"Sinuses," Richie Bergman said.

The only thing wrong with Richie Bergman's sinuses was what he stuffed into them. He sniffled and looked away. Richie was in his late twenties, skinny as a one-iron, jug-eared, and hawk-beaked. He wore thick, rimless glasses and had a scraggly mustache that looked like a squashed caterpillar.

If Richie hadn't acquired an unquenchable appetite for the White Lady and a missionary's desire to share his good fortune, he'd be a doctor by now, and a damn fine one. In his last year of med school, Richie had a Saturday-night ritual. He would squirt chicken's blood up his nose and rush into the ER yelling nosebleed. His buddy, a resident in the trauma program, would give him a ten-percent cocaine solution used to contract the capillaries, and Richie would retreat to the lab to evaporate the liquid, leaving pure crystallized coke.

Richie was too generous for his own good. He told his roommate of the scam and the next weekend, half the med school showed up with nosebleeds. Even that might not have tipped the dean, had the lab floor not been covered with chicken feathers.

Would you believe a pillow fight? Richie asked the dean.

The dean would not.

Now Richie lived alone and worked as a computer consultant, which is a fancy name for hacker, though he preferred calling himself a cyberpunk. He could change your grades at any of four state universities or add your worst enemy's name to the county health department's list of venereal-disease carriers. For a monthly fee of twenty bucks, he could get you free, unlimited long-distance calls, and for an extra ten, you could charge them to the person of your choice. All of Richie's personal calls were billed to the Reverend Jimmy Swaggert, including a live porno hot line headquartered in Vegas.

Richie owed me a favor because I got him probation after he broke into an airline computer system and arranged a million frequent-flier miles for himself and every member of the county commission. The commissioners hadn't asked him to, but everybody who knew them thought they had, and a couple decided it was a pretty good idea in any event.

So Richie Bergman stood at my side while a potbellied, retirement-age sergeant sat on his stool at the property-room window and looked us over. "Got your name here, Lassiter, but not this young fellow. Say, son, you just do some time?"

Richie shook his head and stifled a sneeze.

"'Cause you're so pale, you look like you just did eighteen months at Dade Correctional."

"I spend a lot of time in my room," Richie said honestly.

"And what the hell you doing with that?" the sergeant demanded, gesturing toward Richie's right hand.

"TV. Like to watch it while we work," Richie said, holding a computer monitor for the old sergeant to see.

After letting us know what a favor he was doing, and how if the lieutenant would find out, his ass was grass, and don't forget him at Christmas, the sergeant let us in, and we laid the contents of the locker, *M. Diamond Case No. 91-1376-A*, on a scarred walnut table in the back of the room. The sergeant returned to the window, and I heard the volume crank up on his TV. Local news. Rick Gomez had the latest on the computer sex murders, as Channel 8 had dubbed them. The latest was that the state's case against a local English professor had collapsed due to the incompetence of one Jacob Lassiter, Esquire. "No new leads," Gomez told his audience, his voice filled with concern, "and no comment from the special prosecutor." Then I heard Nick Wolf's voice, tinny and distant, following me like a vengeful ghost. But he wasn't talking about the murders. No, it was his monthly crime-prevention tip, filler for the station and free publicity for an ambitious politician.

"Plant some fear in burglars," Nick Wolf was saying. "Under your windows plant thorny bushes that bite. Try cactus or crown of thorns. Use the Spanish bayonet, the limeberry, or the carissa, all burglar biters. In law enforcement we think of them as antipersonnel plants."

Horticulture, Miami style.

Richie moved quickly, plugging in the cables, finding an outlet for Michelle's computer, hooking up the monitor he brought along. He punched some keys, scanned the directories, found what he wanted, and went to work. I opened my briefcase, pulled out a folder containing the photos taken at the scene by Dr. Whitson, the young assistant medical examiner. There was the body, head jammed into the monitor, eight-by-tens from every angle. There were close-ups of the neck, the bruises and fingernail marks clearly visible. If Whitson couldn't hack it as a canoe maker, he could always make a living shooting pictures at weddings and bar mitzvahs.

There were several shots of the room, a couple catching Nick Wolf in the background. I studied them. His forehead was wrinkled in thought. Grief? I wondered. Or concern for his own hide? Then there was a photo of Pam Metcalf happily digging her nails into my arm and a close-up of the marks themselves, Charlie's lesson that nail marks often appear reversed on human skin.

Finally Richie motioned me over and I looked at the screen.

HELLO, TV GAL. LIGHTS, CAMERA, ACTION—PASSION
PRINCE.

I scanned the page. "Already have that. She talked with other men the same night. Earlier."

He punched some more buttons and tickled the machine's memory banks.

I CAN HEAL YOU!! I CAN HEAL YOUR WOUNDS AND
SAVE YOU, LITTLE LADY.
OH BOB, LIGHTEN UP.
NOT BOB! NEVER BOB! ORAL ROBERT. I CAN LICK YOU
INTO HEAVEN. BUT YOU GOTTA BELIEVE. I CAN LIFT
A BRICK WITH MY TONGUE.
GO SHIT A BRICK, BOB.

She had cut him off, checked who else was in the mating room, skillfully avoided a misspelled pornographic entreaty from Bush Whacker, then fielded another call.

IS YOUR ELECTRICITY ON, TV GAL?
HELLO, BIGGUS, BEEN A WHILE.
ARE YOU CABLE READY, TV GAL?
'CAUSE YOU WANNA PLUG ME IN, RIGHT? C'MON,
BIGGUS, NOT YOU TOO.
OK. WHAT'S NEW?
SAME OLD THING. BOSS DOESN'T TRUST ME TO DO BIG-
TIME REPORTING. I COULD BLOW THIS TOWN OPEN
IF THEY GAVE ME HALF A CHANCE.
REALLY, TELL ME ABOUT IT.
ANOTHER TIME. WHAT'S NEW WITH YOU?
STILL CHASING BAD GUYS.
OH, THAT'S WHAT YOU DO. YOU'RE A COP?
YEP.
HEY, I MEET A LOT OF COPS IN MY WORK. FUNNY, WE
MIGHT EVEN KNOW EACH OTHER.
WE COULD GET TO. A DRINK SOMETIME? YOU COULD
COOK ME DINNER.

I DON'T EVEN COOK ME DINNER, BIGGUS.
SO HOW ABOUT I COME OVER NOW, BRING A BOTTLE
  OF SCOTCH?
NOT NOW, B.D. IT'S INCONVENIENT.
OH, GOT SOMEBODY OVER?
SORRY.
SO WHY ARE YOU WASTING MY TIME?
'NIGHT, BIGGUS.

"That what you're after?" Richie asked. He was in a hurry to get home and perfect a system for trading citrus-futures contracts in somebody else's account.

"That's it."

But it wasn't what I expected. Sure, Rodriguez was putting the make on her. But he sounded halfway reasonable. Even cloaked with anonymity, he was just a guy looking for a date, a little miffed not to get one. Not a drooling psychopath. But there was something new here, a man in her apartment when Rodriguez called. Not Nick, his alibi was ironclad. He was attending a prosecutors' conference in Orlando, returned the next morning. Who was it, some computer chatterbug who beat Biggus to the punch? And Nick thought she was only seeing him. I smiled at that, a pinprick in his ego when I would tell him.

"Hey, Richie, you know much about women?"

"Less than most, I suspect."

"Say it's around midnight, a woman's got one guy in the bedroom, why would she be calling around, trying to meet somebody else, somebody new?"

"Dunno, maybe the guy in the bedroom couldn't cut the mustard."

Maybe, but we still didn't have a suspect, and the question was nagging at me. Who was Michelle's lover that night, and why was she still on the make?

Richie pulled all the cables, and we replaced everything in the right locker. I repacked my file and declined Richie's kind suggestion that he break into the county traffic computer and fix all the lights green for our drive down Dixie Highway. Then we walked past the old sergeant, nodding our thanks, Richie sniffling and blowing his nose.

"Got a cold?" the sarge asked.

"Virus," Richie told him.

CHAPTER 29

The Bait

Pamela Metcalf leaned on me and removed her shoes, sensible professional-lady blue pumps. I stood on one foot and hopped a step, taking off my battered Keds. High-tops. We rang the doorbell, said hello to my wacky secretary, and left our shoes on the front doorstep of her town house. Cindy's hair, once stained a rusty orange, was now dyed black and cut short with bangs. She wore a white silk kimono tied at the waist. She smiled placidly and waved us in. With mincing geisha steps, she led us past a collection of dried flowers in a green Oriental vase and into a small room set off with sliding paper walls. Silently, she motioned us toward pillows and a table barely eighteen inches off the floor. My right knee, the crosshatched one, groaned at the thought of it. My back, which hadn't gone into spasm in years, demanded an appointment at Hoshino Clinic in the Gables.

Cindy said, "I humbly offer my hospitality, lawyer-san."

"Still dating Morikawa," I observed.

"Tea?" she offered.

"No thanks, let's get to work."

"Care for a drink? Sake?"

"Cut it out, Cindy. Where's the computer?"

"Barbarian."

When Cindy had dated a bearded biker, her town house was furnished in Early Hell's Angels. When she took up with a weak-winged shortstop for the Miami Marlins, her place looked like Cooperstown. Now, her Tokyo-born beau had the Panasonic concession for the Caribbean and Central America, and Cindy was doing *Teahouse of the August Moon.*

"C'mon, Cindy. It's going to be a long night."

"If you're hungry, I can call a sushi place."

"Please! The computer."

She opened the paper doors and backed out of the room, bowing and shuffling. Oriental music tinkled from her CD player. We walked into the living room, a place hung with colorful silk paintings. The coffee table was covered with red lacquer boxes and bright ceramic pottery. Pam was admiring black-and-white ink prints of little fishes and big flowers.

"Ito Jakuchu," Cindy said.

"Gesundheit," I responded politely.

"The artist, silly. That one's called *Fish in a Lotus Pond.* Do you sense the mix of humility and grandeur?"

"Cindy, we need to get—"

"Don't you find the brushwork almost Zen-like?"

"Cindy!"

"All right, already. Over here."

In the corner of the living room, under a painting of more fishes in more ponds, sat her computer. Japanese, of course.

"I signed up as Lady Chattery," Pam Metcalf said, after Cindy turned on the juice. "Your friend Mrs. Blinderman was quite helpful."

"Uh-huh."

"Despite her apparent hostility the other day, I get the distinct impression she is attracted to you."

"Uh-huh."

"Jake?"

"Huh?"

"Why do you become uncommunicative when I mention her name?"

Cindy rescued me. "Say, Dr. M, you didn't have to sign up. You could have used my handle, Barely Legal."

My mouth dropped open. "Cindy, you?"

"Sure, boss. With Mori traveling so much, a girl gets lonely. I been on-line a couple months now."

"Cindy, don't you know there's a freak out there?"

"Don't I ever! I been single a long time."

"Jake, perhaps Cindy is right," Pamela said. "A new name may alert the killer. Perhaps using a familiar handle will be reassuring."

I thought about it. "Okay. We start with Barely Legal, maybe switch to Lady Chattery if we come up empty."

"Have fun, kids," Cindy said. "Gotta meet Dottie the Disco Queen and catch the last shuttle to Paradise Island. Twenty-four hours in the casino, hitting the slots, fending off Romeos. *Sayonara.*"

Pam sat, posture perfect, at the keyboard. I stretched out on the sofa, hefting my .38-caliber revolver, courtesy of Mr. Smith and Mr. Wesson. It's the air-weight bodyguard model with the checkered walnut stock and the blue steel cylinder, an ugly little five-shot gun with a two-inch barrel. At fourteen ounces, just about anybody can fire it, whether they ought to or not. Every assistant state attorney gets one, along with a laminated badge and an autographed, smiling photo of Nick Wolf. The gun shouldn't scare me. It has the requisite safety devices and fits snugly in the hand, a solid feel. It should be reassuring. But it scares me.

I hate a knife.

I hate a needle.

And I hate a gun.

A gun doesn't do you any good unless you're willing to shoot. You can't aim at somebody and not mean it. You can't pull the trigger and take it back. I put the gun down and picked up a four-foot gaff I keep on the skiff. A mean hook at the end, but the whole thing is lightweight aluminum. You could bend it over somebody's head, he'd need a couple of aspirin, but could still shoot you if he had a gun of his own. Our visitor, if any there be, wouldn't have a gun. He'd have a sport coat and cordovan loafers and a trendy car. And a closet full of goblins that scream in the dark.

I was sleepy from too much sun, and the muscles of my shoulders were bunching into angry little knots, telling the wise guy who used them that he hadn't read the owner's manual. There it was in boldface: after forty thousand miles, use an engine to push the boat.

Pam watched me handling the .38 and said, "We could ask the police to stop by."

"There aren't any secrets in the department. Rodriguez would find out. Besides, I can take care of you."

She regarded me skeptically.

I waggled my gaff and showed her my tough-guy face. Pam Metcalf shrugged and logged in. Barely Legal was on the air.

It must have been a slow night for the electronic buzz-and-whisper set. Clark Kent said he'd like to come over and change clothes; Katz Meow asked if being Barely Legal was kosher; Camera Man allowed as how he only wanted to watch. A couple of women made connections. Phyllis Ph.D. complained about the intelligence of the men you find on your monitors these days. Bi Di asked if maybe it wasn't time for a change in direction.

But no Biggus Dickus.

I had called the station; Alex Rodriguez wasn't on duty. He should be home, opening a six-pack, watching TV, growing bored. He should be warming up the beige box, rolling those microchip dice. Come on, Biggus, we're waiting.

I was tired and hungry. I checked the refrigerator. Typical bachelor-girl fare. Six cartons of yogurt, some old enough to earn interest at the CD rate. Two cans of diet Pepsi, one opened, two sips missing. A forlorn tomato with no other veggies for company. A can of tuna, a couple eggs. A take-out carton from Joe's Stone Crab that emitted an astonishing odor. No wonder, Joe's closed for the season in April. It was nearly Labor Day. The freezer was packed. Six pints of Ben & Jerry's, all different flavors. I tried Chunky Monkey.

Back in the living room, Barely Legal was logging out and Lady Chattery was logging in. Muff Diver popped up and asked if the new lady omitted a letter from her name.

NIGHT VISION

NO, IT'S A PUN, she responded.

A WHAT? he asked.

Pam pushed a few more buttons and joined Compu-Mate's party line. Rita Cane was verbally abusing Señor Slave, who seemed to like it. Another code and she was in the mating room, singles meeting new talent. Charlie Horse said hello and complained about his rheumatism. In the Dungeon, Bum Swatter was looking for passive women. I hoped he didn't run into Rita Cane; there'd be hell to pay.

I left Pam there, then lay down on the sofa, picked up the *Journal*, and got my daily dose of Miami madness. The usual collection of crime stories. Another policeman shot another drug suspect; another three women had their car windows smashed with bricks and their purses grabbed at downtown traffic lights; and another cache of automatic weapons was seized at the airport. Standard local fare.

Something else, too. A story about how dry we are, and are going to be. The Biscayne Aquifer keeps shrinking and we keep chugging the water in great wasteful portions. We are overpopulated and overpampered. We water our lawns while thunderstorms rage. In one plush suburb overflowing with hibiscus and impatiens, each household uses an astonishing six hundred gallons of water every day. So there is a push on to replace thirsty palms and St. Augustine grass with ferns and satin leaf trees, bougainvillea, and other shrubs that thrive without irrigation.

As the water table drops, the garbage piles up. Mount Trashmore overflows. Our old landfills leak poisonous crud into the porous sand-and-limestone aquifer. Instead of recycling, we use and discard. Disposable diapers take five hundred years to decompose, many times the rate of our greatest books. Our shorelines are clogged with plastics and Styrofoam. Our fish and turtles and birds become snared in six-pack rings or strangled in illegal nets. We dump thousands of old cars and used tires in places where sludge leaks into the groundwater. One gallon of oil contaminates a million gallons of water.

This very day, a freighter slammed into a coral reef off Key Largo not far from where Charlie and I chased bonefish. It takes six thousand years to build a reef, from the Pleistocene limestone and calcareous mud to the skeletal sand and the miraculous living coral, swaying brightly in the tidal flow. It takes seconds for the steel bow of a Panamanian rustbucket to destroy it.

241

We are a vain, greedy, and foolish people. We squander and spoil, befoul and defile. We take for granted the beauties and bounties of nature, but in the end nature will out. We will dry up or smoke out or choke on our own waste. In the end we will pay the ultimate price.

I put the paper down and closed my eyes. Cops say surveillance is the worst. They use the wartime cliché, hours of boredom followed by moments of terror. At this moment the sofa was rocking gently, just as the skiff had done. Lulling me to sleep with the soft tap, tap, tapping of fingers on electronic keys. Through faraway clouds I called to Pam but could not see her. I heard Nick Wolf's voice. What was he saying? Suddenly I was cold. And wet. I was wearing fatigues and my boots were squishing in the mud outside a village they call Dak Sut. My back was bent under the weight of my gear, my stomach knotted with dread. From somewhere I heard the echo of small weapons. I dived into the mud. I heard Nick Wolf again. "Evan," he called. "Evan, where are you?"

I awoke to Pam's voice. "Jake, you might want to look at this."

She was calm, but underneath the flat tones I heard the tension. I imagined a nurse calling the surgeon to the gurney to inspect an appalling wound.

I shook myself up and wobbled to her desk. The monitor was humming.

AND YOU, LADY CHATTERY, WHAT DO YOU SEEK?
A GARDENER, STRONG OF LIMB, PLAIN OF TALK,
  BRIMMING WITH PASSION. KNOW ANYONE WHO FITS
  THE BILL?
THE PRINCE OF PASSION, AT YOUR SERVICE.

Professor Gerald Prince or some impostor. I didn't know which. Pam wrinkled her forehead and started typing.

A PRINCE IS EVERY GIRL'S FANTASY.
AND YOU, MY LADY. IF YOU FOUND YOUR PRINCE,
  WOULD YOU KNOW IT, OR WOULD APPEARANCES PUT
  YOU OFF?

242

Pam paused and turned to me. "What's he saying?"
"Ask him if he's a prince or the phantom of the opera."

WHAT DO YOU LOOK LIKE, PRINCE?
NEVER MIND ME. WHO ARE YOU, LADY C? WHAT ARE
* YOU?*
WHAT DO YOU THINK?

The screen stayed blank. Where'd you go, Prince? A minute passed. Maybe he went to the john. But then it started and I tried to picture him, huddled in some room, tapping out the words. I didn't have a picture.

TILL BACK I FELL, AND FROM MINE ARMS SHE ROSE
GLOWING ALL OVER NOBLE SHAME; AND ALL
HER FALSER SELF SLIPT FROM HER LIKE A ROBE,
AND LEFT HER WOMAN . . .

Pam looked at me, but I just shrugged. Again she typed.

THAT'S LOVELY, PRINCE. WHAT'S IT FROM?

The answer flickered white against the black background.

DO YOU KNOW YOUR TENNYSON?

No, I thought, but I'm learning.
I skimmed back over the words. My mind was racing and nothing made sense. Of course, it could be coincidence. The Tennyson messages left at the Newcomb and Wolf murder scenes, and now this. Sure, Lassiter, sure. Most horny guys with computers quote Tennyson every chance they get. But this stuff, Victorian verse, might as well have been Greek to me. I started to ask Pam something, but she cut me off with a wave of her hand. She had once deciphered kidnappers' notes and was back in her element—dissecting the words of a psychopath.

PRINCE, WHAT'S IT MEAN, "HER FALSER SELF"?

Again, we waited, watching the little white cursor blipping hypnotically on the dark screen. Then:

FOR WOMAN IS NOT UNDEVELOPT MAN,
BUT DIVERSE: COULD WE MAKE HER AS THE MAN,
SWEET LOVE WERE SLAIN: HIS DEAREST BOND IS THIS,
NOT LIKE TO LIKE, BUT LIKE IN DIFFERENCE.
YET IN THE LONG YEARS LIKER MUST THEY GROW;
THE MAN BE MORE OF WOMAN, SHE OF MAN.

"What's he talking about?" I said,

"Hush, Jake. I have to think and type, and you're hovering over me like an Auntie Busybody."

"Well, ex-cuse me. I'm just trying to catch a murderer, here. If he asks for your phone number, give it to him. If he wants to come over, invite him in for a drink. Hey, don't you owe him a reply?"

PRINCE, YOUR POETRY PUZZLES ME.
WHY, PRINCESS?

"Holy shit!" I said. *"The Princess."*

Pam Metcalf shot me a look over her shoulder. I paced behind her. "On Priscilla Wolf's computer. 'Man is the hunter; woman is his game.' It's from *The Princess* by Tennyson. You're talking to the murderer."

"I'm quite aware of that," she said dispassionately.

Suddenly I wanted to call somebody.

Who? Gerald Prince.

Why? To know if he was on-line.

I picked up the phone. Dead. Of course, dead, dummy. The computer modem was using the line. Frugal Cindy. A fortune on Japanese doodads, but only one telephone line. I am not one of those lawyers who carries a cute little phone in my briefcase. At traffic lights I listen to Peter, Paul and Mary on an oldies station or the surf report on the weather band. I can't return all the urgent calls until the next day, by which time hopefully the urgency has passed. But now, damn it, I needed a phone.

"Be right back!" I shouted as I raced for the door.

A sidewalk connected Cindy's town house with four others on a cul-de-sac. I didn't bother with my sneakers, which were still on the doorstep. Instead, in my sweat socks, I padded my two hundred twenty-five pounds to the next door and rang the bell. If eyes can frown, a blue-shadowed one frowned at me through the peephole. I gave my name and mission and the eye disappeared. The door didn't open. Instead, a double bolt clicked into place. A woman's voice from behind the door: "I've got a shotgun and know how to use it."

Now why would anyone do that? I looked at myself. Clean blue jeans, a T-shirt from my favorite oyster bar with the logo "Eat it raw," and a four-foot gaff in my right hand. *Whoops.* I tucked the gaff behind my back and hotfooted it to the next town house. Nobody home. At the third door I flashed my laminated, temporary, specially appointed assistant-state-attorney badge at a beefy man with a Doberman at his side. He let me in and seemed to hope I'd try something. While the man and the dog watched I stood in the kitchen and dialed Prince's number.

Busy.

That could mean he was on-line with Pamela Metcalf at this very moment. Maybe he fooled me. But how did he fool the DNA test? Maybe someone else had sex with the women, and a crazed Prince waited for them to leave, then came to kill. It still didn't make sense.

I dialed again.

Still busy. The guy was getting bored watching me. The Doberman looked hungry, or do they always drool?

I dialed again.

It rang.

"'Even-ing," sang Prince's voice.

"Prince, it's Lassiter. What are you doing?"

"Doing? About world illiteracy or are you interested in more personal concerns?"

"Right now, what have you been doing the past half hour?"

"Ingesting the contents of a clear bottle with a brown liquid, why?"

"Have you been on-line with Compu-Mate?"

There was a pause. Then: "As a matter of fact, I was just on with Eager Beaver."

"Not Lady Chattery."

"Check D. H. Lawrence's line."

"Not Chatterly, Chattery."

"Never heard of her. Now see here, Biff, you have no right to interfere with—"

But I hung up the phone. I was running back to Cindy's place, having sidestepped the big black dog.

Something was wrong.

People tell you they feel things, something that's going to happen, and you laugh. But there is a chill behind the laugh.

I felt something that made me hurry.

My old car was still in the space in front of Cindy's town house. Next to it was a mud-splattered jeep that wasn't there ten minutes ago.

The front door was cracked slightly open. Had I left it that way or did someone else? Why had I left? Because, smart guy that I am, I figured if the murderer was typing away, he couldn't be here. Now I fought the urge to burst through the door, gaff swinging. I entered without a sound and stepped into the small foyer. The paper walls of the Japanese den were in front of me.

From the living room I heard a man's voice. It was familiar but I could not place it.

I crept around one corner, holding the gaff at my side. I heard Pam. "But *why* must you? It's so terribly cruel."

Calm, collected Dr. Metcalf. What a pro. Trying to talk her way out of it. Using her experience with rapists and killers. Buying time. Waiting to be rescued by the blockhead who left her alone.

The man's voice now clear: "Once I got used to the blood, there was nothing to it."

I turned the corner, and there he was, his back to me. He wore brown pants, black leather boots, and a buckskin shirt with fringes. The back of his neck was bronzed from the sun. In his right hand he held a knife with sawteeth that could chop down a redwood. The knife was pointed directly at Pamela Metcalf's sternum.

Two steps and I could lunge at him, take him down with a shoulder in the small of the back. But if he turned, I'd catch a foot-long blade in the belly. So I bent at the waist, put a hand on a

246

knee, carefully picked up my right leg, extra high, then gently placed my right foot down on the outside of the ball, rolled to the inside, and finally brought down the heel silent as a wish.

Then I did it again with the left foot. Why not? He's the one who taught me the Tom Cat Stalk.

CHAPTER 30

Yin from Yang

My second step was perfect. Even I didn't hear it.

Pam was facing him, the blade of the knife inches from her chest. "Surely you can't go on with your bloodletting, oblivious to the consequences."

Then she saw me. Her eyes widened.

No, Pam, no! Look away.

I hurried the next step. I didn't snap a twig or step on a squirrel's tail. But he heard me. It could have been his woodsman's ears. More likely it was the crash of ceramic bowl on tile. Moving too quickly, I had swung the gaff to one side where it clipped the bowl, sending it to the floor. So there I stood, one knee tucked under my chin, broken pottery covering my socks.

Tom Carruthers pivoted and glared at me. "You!"

"Me."

He smiled ruefully. "Of course. I should have recognized those foolish sneakers out front."

"Okay, Carruthers. It's all over. I'm going to take you in. Now either drop that knife, or I'm going to jam this—"

"Jake," Pam interrupted. "Perhaps—"

"Why not try it?" Carruthers offered, gesturing with the knife. In the light of a Japanese lantern, the blade shone red.

I circled to my right, keeping the knife in view. He circled to his right. He had the sharper weapon; I had the longer. I raised the gaff as if it were a foil. I got into the classic fencing position, feet at right angles, right foot and knee pointed at my enemy, and shouted, "On guard," as if I were Errol Flynn. Then I advanced, my feet skimming the floor in the two-count tempo.

"Jake, he's—"

"Not to worry," I called out.

Carruthers raised the knife in the saber grip, thumb on top, four fingers below. He stood with left foot forward, shoulders square, left hand extended to block any blows, right hand back, protecting the knife, out of my reach.

"I'll gut you, lawyer," he said through clenched teeth.

"No!" Pam shouted.

I skimmed forward some more, then lunged, aiming at his heart, the *prime quarte*. If he'd been a tarpon, I'd have nailed him. But Carruthers parried with his free arm, taking a glancing shot. He flexed his knees and came forward, going for the throat. I leaned to the right, lengthening the distance he had to go to reach me with his right hand. When his knife shot forward, I sidestepped, letting the blade go by my neck, and at the same time I swung the gaff up and bounced one off his right hip, *quinte septime*. Carruthers brushed it off and said something impolite, accusing me of intimate relations with a close family member.

He squared up again, and I resumed the fencing position, right foot forward. He slashed downward, going for my front leg. Unsporting. I skimmed backward, then, as he advanced, brought the gaff up hard, slapping the steel blade of the knife. The screech of metal on metal. He didn't lose his grip, but I did, the gaff skittering across the floor.

Oh shit.

He had a knife and I had two hands and a gimpy knee. There are ways to disable someone with a punch. A good shot to the ear can burst an eardrum, cause nerve shock or a concussion. A solid punch to the weak bone of the temple can cause unconsciousness and even death if a hemorrhage results. A blow to the throat can sever the windpipe. But you have to get close enough, and if the other guy has a survival knife with sawteeth, you have to avoid spilling your guts on the floor.

He shifted the knife to an icepick grip, took two steps forward, slashed left, slashed right, then went overhead and brought it down from the top. I could have tried a fancy move to either side, but there comes a time when you stand your ground. There is a concept in martial arts known as harmony. Don't oppose the force of your opponent. Harmonize with it. Where your opponent is strong, yield to him, and as he overextends or goes off balance use your strength against his weakness. It is the yin. Then, where your opponent is weak, overpower him with your strength. The yang.

In the gym you practice the harmony and study diagrams of stick figures using motion and misdirection and leverage to throw opponents around. Here, staring at the glinting blade coming down, I didn't know yin from yang. I just shot two hands up on either side of the descending arm and caught his wrist in a figure-four armlock. He was pushing down, using all his triceps, taking advantage of the angle, but I was bigger and stronger and had two hands against his one and was pushing the knife back toward his ear. Which meant his left hand was free. Just when I was wondering where it was, he plowed a short hook into my rib cage. I heard a crack and felt the pain, and the knife came two inches closer until I steadied myself and pushed right back. He was winding up for a bigger punch, so I just tucked my chin onto my chest and exploded straight up with a burst from the legs, my skull smashing him under the jaw. He yelped and staggered back, his mouth spurting blood where he had bitten cleanly through his lip. My head was ringing, Pam was screaming something at me, and little black flashes were lighting up my eyes. The knife was somewhere on the floor.

As he tumbled backward I came at him, shoulders square, legs pumping, head up, a decent linebacker making a tackle. My legs were a little shaky and I didn't have enough drive. I hit him too high, and he refused to fall, but I drove him backward until we both hit a wall, Japanese prints clattering to the floor. I had him wrapped up, and we danced that way a moment, his blood smearing my face. Then he brought a boot up high and crashed it down into my left instep where my hundred-percent-wool sweat sock did little to cushion the blow. I tottered backward, hopping on one foot, cursing, the pain closing my eyes. I lost my balance just before I hit the tearoom wall. If you're going to crash through a wall, ass over elbows, a paper wall is best. It didn't hurt a bit, my foot and head and ribs hogging all the headlines in the pain department.

I was lying on the low-slung tea table amid rice cakes and bamboo mats when Carruthers appeared, poking his head through the hole I had carved in the wall. I didn't know if I could stand up. He just looked at me.

"Milk or lemon?" I asked.

He growled like one of his large, furry forest friends and stepped through the wall toward me. I rolled off the table into a crouching position and told myself I was just getting warmed up. I wanted to hit him on the side of the neck just below and slightly to the front of the ear. If I could smash the jugular vein, the carotid artery, or the vagus nerve, I could put him into shock. But I couldn't put any weight on my left foot and didn't know how I'd get anything behind the punch.

He just stood there bleeding onto his buckskin, bent at the waist with hands on hips, sucking great gulps of air. "Hunters have rights," he said.

"What?"

"And trappers too."

I thought about it. "Man is the hunter. Right, Carruthers?"

"Right."

"You hunt them for the beauty of their skins."

"That, and for food."

"Food?"

"You animal-rights nuts have gone too far," he said, still huffing. "First furs, then what, beef and chicken?"

"What are you—"

A gunshot inside a small apartment makes a terrible racket. Especially when the bullet connects with a large Oriental vase. Carruthers hustled out of the tearoom. I limped to the opening. "If you two boys have finished your macho game, perhaps we could have a little talk," said Lady Chattery, her two hands gripping my blue steel revolver, a perfectly furious look on her beautiful face.

• • •

There was no use putting the sneakers back on. Galoshes wouldn't fit over my swollen left foot. My ribs were throbbing, my head was on fire, and my ego was under siege.

"Apologize? Apologize for what?" I asked.

"For attacking Mr. Carruthers. Just as you attacked poor Clive and Francis. I'm beginning to think your hostility has its basis in a true psychosis, Jake."

Carruthers sat on the sofa, smiling, if that's what it was, under a towel of ice cubes fastened to his mouth. I surveyed the damage. Shards of ceramic pottery covered the floor; ink prints dangled at crazy angles on the living-room wall; and the tearoom was a shambles of splintered wood and ripped walls. In about three minutes, we had transformed Cindy's town house from Oriental Moderne to post-Apocalypse.

"I was trying to save your life. I thought Davy Crockett here—"

"You thought! You might have killed him."

"Sorry, I'm not used to seeing strange men brandish knives at my lady friends."

"Humghfeeldauhdeer," came a sound from under the icy towel.

"What?"

"He was showing me how to field-dress a deer," Pam explained helpfully.

"Is that different than city-dressing one?" I asked.

Carruthers dropped the towel. His face was not a pretty sight. "I was advising against making the incision between the hind legs. Cut into the sternum and go back toward the pelvis. It's not a bad job if you don't mind being up to your ears in blood and offal." His voice was thickened by a swollen tongue.

Pam said, "And I told him how barbarous and cruel it was, hunting those fine animals. And then you came in and . . . and pounced."

I turned to Carruthers. "What the hell were you doing here?"

"I was in town and stopped over to see Cindy. The door was open, so I—"

"You know Cindy?"

"Sure. Barely Legal. We don't go out that often, what with her import-export friend and my living so far away. But she's the first down-to-earth woman I've met in Mia-muh town."

"Cindy? *My* Cindy?"

CHAPTER 31

Mercy

My foot was propped on the phone directory and swaddled in ice. Elevation and cold. Every team trainer worth his smelling salts knows that.

My ribs were swathed in Ace wrap. They only hurt when I breathed.

My head was bobbing on ocean swells. Two Darvons and a grapefruit juice with Finlandia, a linebacker's Sunday-night beddy-bye cocktail.

I was dreaming of sunny days and force-four winds, watching a nine-foot sliver of fiberglass jumping three-foot chop. I looked around inside the dream and couldn't find Pam Metcalf or anyone else. A lousy, no-bikini dream. I looked at the sailboard, but I wasn't there. It was a board without a sailor, skimming the waves, darting on a broad reach along a rocky coast. The board jibed, its inside rail digging hard, the tail shooting a plume of water. Then, like a riderless horse, it sped toward open sea.

Someone called my name.

It didn't sound like Pam.

I reached across the bed. Empty. The sheets cool.

"She ain't here, Jake."

Funny how dreams can seem so real. I smelled a cigarette and I don't smoke.

I opened my eyes. The paddle fan clocked its slow turns above my head. A toxic green glow filled the room, my neighbor's mercury-vapor, anticrime light, seeping through open shutters, mixing with the smoke. So I was in my bed in my house. All alone. Except for the voice.

"Got trouble keeping them in bed, do you, Jakie?"

I tried lifting my head. It weighed a ton. Someone was standing by the window, looking out, a cigarette dangling from his mouth. I saw him in silhouette, a strong, bulky shadow in the noxious haze.

"Nick?"

"Who'd you expect? Felix Frankfurter?"

I lifted myself to an elbow. "What'd you do to her, Nick?"

"Her?"

"Pam. She doesn't know anything. You didn't have to—"

"Easy, Jake. You've had a hard night." He exhaled a trail of smoke, iridescent and willowy in the gaseous light. "You know, I made a real mistake appointing you."

"Yeah. I saw right through you."

He inhaled and the red ash of cigarette flared. "No. You fucked everything up."

I tried to sit up straight, but the pain kept me stretched out. "What do you want?"

"To take back something of mine. Something you stole. Breaking and entering, Jake. Trespassing. Larceny. Maybe obstruction of justice, too. I got good neighbors, Jake. One of them spots a guy get out of an old convertible and go into my garage the hard way."

I kept quiet. He could be wired.

Nick continued. "When I get to the house, only thing missing is an old memory." He watched me, waiting for a response.

Despite my better judgment, I opened my mouth. "Why not cut the bullshit? You're not going to press charges. You can't stand the heat. If the papers got hold of what's in the log, you'd—"

"What *is* in the log?"

I knew the important stuff by heart:

1330—VC ambush on dike. Gallardi, Boyer, dogwood 6.
Rosen, Williams, Colgan, Miciak, dogwood 8.
1800—Dak Sut. Firefight. 3 VC greased. Zippo approx.
20 hooches. Phuong MIA. Lt. E. Ferguson. Rest in peace.
May the Lord have mercy.

"Evan Ferguson wasn't killed on the dike. He was killed in the village after the sniper attack. In your own words, Nick."

"So what? What's it prove?"

I didn't know so what, and he knew I didn't know so what.

He dropped the stub of his cigarette into the neck of a half-empty beer bottle on the dresser. "Do you want me to tell you what happened on a rainy, shit-eating, bloodsucking day in-country in 1968?"

Not if it's going to get me killed, I thought. "Sure, Nick, tell me all—"

"I was fighting for my country, Jakie. What were you doing that day—getting a hand job from some pom-pom girl under the bleachers?"

"Most likely a majorette," I said. "Great hands."

"My men were exhausted, wet, cold, hungry, and scared of being scared. Some of them were popping pills and smoking weed like there was no tomorrow. 'Cause maybe there wasn't. But most of all they were mean and angry. There were two ways to get to our objective, Dak Sut, where there was supposed to be VC activity. They didn't want to go either way. They didn't want to meet the enemy or do anything but go home. The long way was through forest. Some danger of snipers, but there was cover, too. Evan wanted to go that route with his platoon, but I talked him out of it."

WHO GAVE THE ORDERS TO WALK ALONG THE DIKE PRIOR TO ENTERING THE VILLAGE OF DAK SUT?

"We went across the paddies, the men sinking into the mud, cursing the war, cursing LBJ, cursing me. Some of them were sick, three later came down with malaria. We took the men onto the dikes that run through the paddies, Evan's platoon and ours, moving parallel. Evan didn't like it, out in the open like that. There was cover maybe three hundred meters away. Evan thought Charley could be laying low there, waiting for us to come up on the dikes."

"Was he right?"

"Yeah. But first, just like I told you, some naked kid comes up out of the mud with an AK-47 on Evan's dike. At the same time, an RPD opens up from the cover. I lose Gallardi and Boyer, plus four wounded. Evan's men kill the sniper. The machine-gun fire stops, probably a fifteen-year-old with a hundred rounds total, and we're lying there, facedown in the mud, pissing our pants."

"So Evan wasn't killed?"

He lit another cigarette, inhaled once, then dropped it in the beer bottle. "No. Never touched. We radio for a dust-off, evacuation of the dead and wounded by slick. By the time we gather and get to Dak Sut, it's just after dark, and the men are jumpy, mean, and trigger- happy."

AFTER THE MEDIC AND RADIOMAN WERE KILLED, WHAT WAS THE STATE OF DISCIPLINE OF YOUR MEN?

"Like I told you before, Charley owns the night. The place is deserted except for three old ladies, some babies, and a few water buffalo. There's no moon and it's the blackest night you've ever seen. It's raining and it's cold. People in the world didn't realize how cold it got there. The men, both Evan's and mine, are near mutiny. They get Phuong, our translator, to interrogate the old women. 'Yankees numbah one, VC numbah ten.' The usual bullshit. So one of my men hits the old lady with his rifle butt. Really bashed her. Opened a gash in her forehead that bled like a son of a bitch."

WERE THE VILLAGERS ARMED, AND IF SO, DID THEY THREATEN YOUR PLATOON?

"Phuong gets upset. Starts chattering in Vietnamese and the women start running. They didn't get twenty yards."

WERE ANY VILLAGERS WOUNDED OR KILLED BY YOUR MEN?

"Who shot them?"

"Who cares who? A farm kid from Indiana who a year before played high-school basketball, a street kid from the Bronx who enlisted for the GI benefits. Red-blooded American boys with M-16s who were tired and scared and a little crazy and would have shot

Westy and LBJ and me, too, if they had the chance. So instead they shot three old women."

"So your log is false. There was no firefight in the village. There was no enemy in Dak Sut."

He sat down on the bed and leaned his elbows on his knees. Somewhere in Coconut Grove, a police siren wailed, then grew softer. Inside the house, the only sound was the gentle whir of the paddle fan. "No enemy? Who was the enemy? The old women hated us, maybe fed breakfast to the poor son of a bitch who spent all day in the mud waiting for us."

"And your translator wasn't kidnapped?"

"Not by the enemy," Nick said softly.

I waited. He was staring at the wall. He lit another cigarette. "Haven't smoked since I was discharged." He inhaled, sucking it in, holding it, then emptied his lungs. "Phuong knew. The second she saw the women shot, she knew. She turned to me. Her eyes were pleading. A corporal who had twelve days left in-country called to the others, 'Let's get the gook cunt.'"

WHAT HAPPENED TO YOUR TRANSLATOR?

"Phuong started running. He chased her, tackled her, dragged her off. Four or five others followed him. When they were done with her, they each shot her. They'd made a pact. Then a few others started a Zippo raid, burning down every hooch. A few other women scrambled out, girls really. My men, Evan's men, went after them. Got them."

"You were in command. You could have stopped them."

He laughed. There was no pleasure in the sound. Outside, a neighborhood wren sang its early-morning song in a poinciana tree. "You think it's like a football team, Jake. The coach blows the whistle, everybody listens up, slaps each other's ass."

He turned and looked straight at me. "They would have killed me. My own men. Evan's men. I saw it in their eyes. A sergeant comes up to me and says, 'Stay out of this, sir.' He didn't do any of the killing, but he knew when to turn his head."

"And Evan?"

"He was outraged. You'd have to know him. Eagle Scout, Sunday School Evan. Straight as an arrow, tough as nails. I admired him. Hell, I *loved* him, and if you'd have been in combat instead of playing ball, you'd know what that means. It's the purest, deepest kinship, something you can't have with a woman."

THE LAST TIME YOU SAW LIEUTENANT FERGUSON ALIVE,
WAS HE

"Was he trying to stop the raping and the burning and the killing?"

"He ordered his men to drop their weapons. They laughed at him. One of my grunts raised his rifle. Evan drew his sidearm. He tried to arrest them. He looked to me for help."

Nick Wolf was silent again.

"But you turned away," I said. "You let them kill your best friend."

He dropped his head between his knees.

"Nick?"

His broad shoulders quaked and he stared at the floor.

"Nick? What happened to Evan Ferguson?"

When he finally lifted his head, the eyes were blank and his voice was choked. "I pulled my .45, and I told Evan to forget it, to look the other way, that we could file reports that would dovetail and no one would ever know. 'I'll know,' he said. I argued with him, begged him. We stood there in the dark with the rain coming down, and I was shivering and scared and crying, because I knew what I had to do."

He stopped, but now I knew, too. I knew the secret he carried for so long. I knew the darkest part of Nick Wolf's soul, the shining life built on a lie. Behind the medals, the hero was worse than a coward. He had committed the most unpardonable sin.

"You pulled the trigger," I said. "You joined the pact. Because you were afraid they'd frag you and say you stepped on a mine or got it in a firefight. You didn't even try to stop them."

"They were going to kill Evan, and they wouldn't trust me to keep quiet. I had to do it. It was the only way to get out of there. Evan was a dead man either way."

"Keep telling yourself that and maybe you can live with it."

"I shot him in the chest. It knocked him down. I stood over him, and he looked at me, just looked at me, this incredible hurt in his eyes. I shot him twice more, and there isn't a day that's gone by since that I haven't seen that face, that look. It's there when I sleep and when I wake. It's always there."

Lt. E. Ferguson. Rest in peace. May the Lord have mercy.

Now it all made sense. May the Lord have mercy, Nick Wolf prayed, on his own godforsaken soul.

CHAPTER 32

Shades of Gray

An orange glow from the east summoned a new day. During the night the wind had shifted. In the summer our weather comes from the southeast, light breezes carrying the heat and moisture from the Caribbean. But sometime during the night the wind clocked around— southwest, northwest, north, finally northeast—at a steady fifteen knots. An unusual front for this time of year, a breath of air nearly cool.

My kitchen window was open to the breeze. I wore canvas shorts and an old jersey, number fifty-eight. Nick Wolf wore his navy-blue suit. You never know when the TV boys will show up. I poured coffee, then sat at the table, my leg supported by a chair.

"I want something from you," I said.

"Yeah, what?" Suspicion knotted his forehead. Nick's mood had changed with the morning light. Blustery again.

"Your blood. Rodriguez's too."

"Go fuck yourself," Nick Wolf said.

"Sperm samples, if you want some fun."

"Up your ass, Lassiter."

"No, in a little glass bottle. If you want, you can jerk each other off."

He lit a cigarette, changed his mind, crushed it into a priceless saucer with an illustration of Larry Csonka's face. If I hadn't broken the Jim Kiick dish, I could've auctioned the set at Sotheby's for six figures.

"What's this bullshit about Rodriguez?" he asked.

I told him that Biggus Dickus was trying to diddle every woman in town with a working modem.

"I asked him to do it," Wolf said.

That didn't make any sense to me, and my blank look must have said so.

"I asked Rodriguez to join the damn club, to talk with Michelle and Prissy, scope them out."

"And his dating Priscilla . . . ?"

"Same thing, I asked him to."

"Why?"

He looked at me, took a sip of the coffee, and said, "You really don't know, do you? That's the problem with you. You see a slice of the moon and think you've got night vision. But you've got to spend time in the jungle, Jakie, before you can see in the dark."

He turned away and looked like he was deciding how much more to say. "Once you had the log, I knew you'd jump to the wrong conclusion."

I wanted to laugh but didn't. "No wrong conclusion could be worse than the truth."

"No? What about your deciding I had Rodriguez kill Michelle and Priscilla?"

Suddenly the room was stifling despite the breeze. "I figure you'll have an excuse for those, too. It was them or you, right?"

"Damn you! I knew you'd fuck it up. I've got an excuse, all right. I had nothing to do with it. I don't know who killed them, but I know where you've been and what you're trying to prove. I know you were at Compu-Mate and copied a bunch of records that Rodriguez already had. I know you played some scam in the property room, and I know your English girlfriend signed up at the horny women's club. I know

261

you got busted up by some cowboy who drives a Jeep, and I know who sneaked out of here about an hour before I showed up. Jakie, I know when you piss and when you shit, and when you step in it."

It made me smile, the irony of it. I was investigating him, and he had *me* under surveillance. "Look, Nick, what am I supposed to think? Especially now. You've just admitted the motive. I don't know how much Michelle knew, but it was enough to make you nervous."

"Everything. She knew everything. Priscilla told her."

"What? You told me you never talked about it."

"She was my *wife*. When I got back, I was a mess. They were pinning medals on me, and I was dying inside. She took care of me. I told her. She said it would go away, she would make it better, and she did."

"Until you left her."

He picked up the mug of coffee, then put it down again. "She set me up. She pretended she didn't care, that she'd get along without me, but she wanted me back. If she couldn't have me, she'd get even. She made friends with Michelle, up-and-coming TV personality, told her everything she knew. It wasn't enough for a story, no confirming sources, but Prissy figured a journalist could do some research, put it together. Prissy could ruin me, Michelle would get a promotion. They'd both be happy."

"So you planted Rodriguez in their little garden. Like I said, you're the guy with the motive."

He looked at me straight on. "Listen, you thick-skulled, lead-footed linebacker. Would I tell you this if I had anything to do with the killings?"

"Sure, 'cause you're so much smarter than me—"

"Cut the crap. I told you the truth to get you on track. We've got to work together. You, me, Rodriguez. These cases are making too many headlines."

"Right, may cost you some votes next time around."

He ignored the crack and drained the coffee, which had turned cold. He didn't seem to notice. "Yesterday, I ordered Rodriguez to start over. Go through the files. What did we miss? Re-interview everybody. Talk to that loony Blinderman babe, Doc Riggs, your English friend, anybody who knows anything. I want you to put some heat on Max Blinderman. He's got a record."

"Anything else?"

"Be creative. Do what you do best."

"You want me to hit somebody?" I asked.

I could never be a prosecutor.

A really good prosecutor must have no doubts. The prosecutor is the vengeful instrument of the state, a man or woman who sees the effect of depravity and must not care about the cause. The defendant is filth. No matter that as a child, he may have been abused, impoverished, and ignored. He is a blight on society, and the prosecutor is the street cleaner of our times.

I always have doubts. I see the glimmer of humanity underneath masks of evil. I see reasons and causes and justifications. And mitigating circumstances. I feel pity. Nick Wolf would say I misdirect my sorrow. He would say I am soft. But now my anguish was for *him*.

I had listened to his tale of horror and fear, to his admission of cowardice and betrayal. And I mourned for *him*, undeserving recipient of my grief. Evan Ferguson was dead. A few seconds of pain, nothing more. Nick Wolf was dead, a lifetime of nightmarish torment.

He was right. He never should have appointed me. I didn't belong here anymore. Keep Lassiter away from the cops and the crooks. Let him try his fancy-pants divorces. Let him argue which conglomerate breached which contract to sell a million widgets to which multinational corporation. Let him defend the rights of reporters to fib and to fumble. But he doesn't have the stomach for the place with steel doors and the men with hard eyes. He doesn't see in black and white. All he sees are shades of gray.

"How do you feel?" Pam Metcalf asked.

"Compared to what?" I answered.

I was sprawled on my sofa, left leg hoisted onto my sailboard cocktail table. Three donuts were spread on the fin.

"I went out," she said, sitting down on a wooden rocker Granny Lassiter had given me.

"I know."

"I couldn't sleep."

"That makes two of us."

"You were dead to the world when I left. You look better now."

I didn't ask better than what.

She walked over and sat down but didn't take a donut. "Did you have any breakfast?"

"Coffee and cyanide with Nick Wolf. He stopped by after you . . . left."

We were dancing around it. I consider myself a modern man. Maybe I never took a vote on it, but I like to think I am enlightened where relationships are concerned. I try to be sensitive to a woman's needs, her independence, her space. Still, I don't think it impertinent to ask where my bedmate has gone at three A.M. while I lie there, battered and drugged.

So why didn't I ask?

Because she would think me a Neanderthal, a clinging, possessive, antiquated jerk. Instead, I told her of my talk with Nick, and she listened quietly, asking only if I believed he was innocent in spite of the obvious motive.

I didn't know.

Then I mentioned the northeasterly breeze and how today might be a bit cooler, and she nodded in silent appreciation of my meteorological insights. Finally I grabbed a donut from the daggerlike fin, took a healthy bite, and blurted out, "So where the hell were you?"

She looked away and said, "Is it going to be that way?"

"Sorry, but I'm not used to falling asleep with company and waking up solo."

"And I'm sorry if I deflated your engorged male ego."

"Look, it's not as if I don't trust you, it's—"

She bolted from the rocker, which pitched forward and back even without her. "Trust me! What right do you have to even think about me in those terms? I don't seek your trust. I don't want your trust. If you have some romantic notions about us, let me disabuse you right now, Jake. You and I have gone bump in the night. You have great vigor in your performance, so you may paste a gold star on your report card. You try hard to please, and if you are a bit rough around the edges—you rub my breasts as if you're waxing your car—you are by no means unique in that regard. You are not an unpleasant fellow most of the time, although your penchant for unprovoked violence prompts me to suggest intensive therapy. As for our relationship, you are involved in a most interesting investigation that furthers my research. When it is completed, I seriously doubt that either of us will desire the other's company. So please, Jake, for your sake, face reality."

I sank into the sofa and brooded. *Reality.* The medication had worn off and my head throbbed. But not as much as my ego. So far I had been wrong about everyone and everything. I ran through the roster. Alex Rodriguez wooed computer ladies because Nick Wolf wanted him to. Nick killed his best friend but not the wife who set him up or the girlfriend who would have destroyed him. Tom Carruthers was a charming guy who dated my secretary and hadn't strangled her yet. Rosemary Newcomb didn't fit in anywhere. Gerald Prince was merely a drunk who wanted a comeback on the stage. And Pamela Metcalf? She was using me to further her research, and the first night I wasn't up to bedtime games under the paddle fan, she hotfooted it elsewhere.

Or did she? She hadn't said. It shouldn't make any difference, but it did. Okay, so I'm not that enlightened.

"Are you saying you weren't with someone else or that I have no right to ask whether you have been?"

"Jake, must you?"

"Yes."

"Very well. I have found a lover."

And what am I, chopped liver?

"I see," I said softly. A look of martyrdom.

"Really, Jake, you're acting very immature. It is not as if we pledged ourselves to each other."

"So I shouldn't have a sense of loss."

"You can't lose what you don't have."

It made sense to my brain, but the rest of me wasn't listening. My eyes were watery.

"Who is he?" I asked. "Do I know him?"

"Oh, Jake. Don't go looking to be hurt."

She was right. No need to look. The pain would find me soon enough.

CHAPTER 33

Metamorphoses

Professor Gerald Prince thrust his chin forward, and in his best upper-crust Rex Harrison voice intoned: "'The great secret, Eliza, is not having bad manners or good manners or any other particular sort of manners, but having the same manner for all human souls, in short, behaving as if you were in Heaven, where there are no third-class carriages, and one soul is as good as another.'"

I hobbled to my customary spot in the back row and wondered if I'd get in trouble for not doing the homework. On the stage a young woman read Eliza Doolittle's lines as they worked their way through the final act.

When Prince told the community-college Eliza that he'd grown accustomed to her face, I believed him. He was a damn fine actor.

They wrapped up the final scene and the class applauded politely. "What is Shaw telling us in the play?" Prince asked.

"It's about abolishing the difference between the classes," said an earnest young man up front.

266

"Perhaps that is the result, but the mechanics of the change?"

"Language, clarity of thought and speech," said the woman next to me.

The class mumbled its agreement. They had learned something since my last visit.

"Quite so," Prince said. "The play is unapologetically didactic. Shaw sincerely cared about the language. He—"

"I don't get something," interrupted a student near me. "In the movie the professor gets the girl. Here . . ."

"Here, she leaves to marry Freddy Eynsford Hill," Prince said. "And why? Because Higgins is a confirmed bachelor more attached to his work than to a pretty face, even one to which he has become accustomed."

"And his mother thing," the young woman said. "Higgins was a momma's boy."

"A mother thing, indeed," Prince said. "In his notes Shaw discusses the mother as rival. As intelligent and articulate as he was, Higgins was not fully developed emotionally."

Prince looked toward the clock on the wall, nodded his head, and the students obediently closed their notebooks. I gingerly worked my way to the front. Prince was stuffing some papers into an old briefcase.

He saw me and bowed formally. "Did you fancy my reading of Higgins?"

"First rate. Much lighter fare than Edmund Tyrone. Not all that in-love-with-death stuff."

He beamed. Like trial lawyers, actors never hear too many compliments. The professor wore a checked shirt under a blue blazer with a rakish yellow ascot. His eyes were clear. "You were worried about me, weren't you? I am moved by that, Biff. Have no fear. I am sane, stable, and as happy as can be expected. As for Edmund's speech, in drama, if one looks hard enough, there is the antidote to every expressed emotion:

'No life that breathes with human breath
Has ever truly longed for death.'"

"Good to see you so chipper. And I like the line. Shakespeare?"

"No, Alfred Tennyson."

Him again.

Prince smiled slyly. "Your policeman friend was here yesterday. He apologized for unfairly accusing me. Then he showed me printouts of someone calling himself Passion Prince chatting with Miss Newcomb and Mrs. Wolf. Some very good poetry, if you like that sort of thing, taken badly out of context. I thought I'd get a rise out of you with the reference to Tennyson."

"You did."

"The policeman said you always believed in my innocence. That means a lot to me, Biff. If there's anything I can do for you . . ."

Of course, there was.

I ordered an iced tea and Prince said make it two. I gave him a look.

"There's a repertory company auditioning in Lauderdale," he explained. *"Inherit the Wind.* The collision of blind faith with the inquisitive search for truth. It wouldn't hurt me to show up sober."

"Henry Drummond?"

"But of course. Would you care to hear his cross-examination of the self-appointed prophet, Matthew Brady?"

"Maybe later."

He looked great. The silvery hair was swept back and combed. The blazer was either new or freshly pressed, not a gravy stain in sight. Best of all, he was cold sober. He had acknowledged his problem. So few do. A doctor asks a patient how much he drinks and how often he has sex. To get the truth, multiply the former by two and divide the latter by three.

The waiter brought our broiled snapper and fried plantains. We were in a bayfront restaurant two weeks old that tried hard to achieve the dilapidated sea-shanty look. Unpainted, knotholed boards were bolted to walls of sturdy concrete block. Lobster traps and colorful buoys hung from the ceiling, and an old dinghy sat wedged on the roof, as if a hurricane deposited it there. None of that bothered me. I could even tolerate the plastic pelican on a Styrofoam piling. But the snapper had that too-late-frozen, too-early-thawed, four-day-old fishy taste.

A sad truth: it is hard to find good, fresh local fish in a city that sits on the sea. I used to visit the docks in Bayfront Park when the fishing boats came in. The fishermen would fillet yellowtail, grouper, or dolphin that had been caught an hour earlier, and an hour later, you could be home marinating the catch in pineapple juice and soy sauce while the charcoal turned white. Then the city fathers evicted the fishing boats and built a trendy plaza of shops and restaurants, where we now sat, eating last week's fish.

"What did Rodriguez want?" I asked.

"The poetry. What it might mean. I told him what it meant to Tennyson was quite different than what some warped soul might read into it."

"What did the poet mean when he wrote, 'Woman is the lesser man'?"

He smiled at me and finished the stanza:

> "'And all thy passions, matched with mine,
> Are as moonlight unto sunlight, and as water unto wine.'

What do you think it means, Biff?"

"I don't know. It contradicts most people's beliefs. Most would say that women's passions run deeper than men's, though my recent experiences would belie that."

Prince didn't seem interested in my personal life. Instead, he began the lecture. "The poem was written shortly after Tennyson's unhappy love affair with Rosa Baring. Her marriage to another man may have prompted the bittersweet imagery."

"So jealousy is the emotion."

"The poem is more complex," he continued, "and frankly, a bit whiny for my tastes. If you're looking for a theme, Tennyson's important later poetry was naturalistic and utopian. He saw mankind's struggle as an ascent to a nobler life. His poetry hinted of evolution even before Darwin's *Origin of the Species*."

"Henry Drummond would approve."

"Yes, and he also wrote of evolving to a new happiness. Man was still unfinished, still evolving. Tennyson was optimistic to the end. In his last poem, 'The Dreamer,' an old man speaks to a despairing Earth, which is wailing of its destiny, 'darkened with doubts of a faith that saves, and crimson with battles, and hollow with graves.' But the poet tells the Earth that 'less will be lost than won. Whirl, and follow the sun.'"

I wanted to know more. I showed Prince the printouts from Pam's conversation of the night before.

Prince frowned. "Someone's still using my handle. Perhaps I should sue. Know any honest lawyers, or is that an oxymoron?"

I ignored the insult. "What about the poetry?"

He read part of it aloud:

"'Till back I fell and from mine arms she rose,
Glowing all over noble shame; and all
Her falser self slipt from her like a robe.'"

He considered it a moment, then said, "It's from *The Princess*. It was written about ten years after the lesser-man diatribe of *Locksley Hall*. It's Tennyson's view of feminism, women's aspirations juxtaposed against the requirements of marriage. The poem raises numerous questions about sexual identity but the answers are left somewhat open."

"Sexual identity?"

"In the beginning, the gender of the prince and princess are confused, each taking on characteristics of the opposite sex, perhaps even hermaphroditical, at least figuratively. The prince has blue eyes and hair 'of yellow ringlet, like a girl.' The princess is a dark and masculine woman. She wants to live apart from men. Her identity needs to be adjusted. At the end—"

"'Her falser self slipt from her like a robe.'"

"Right. She became womanly, he manly, but only in an androgynous way idealized by the Victorians."

I read aloud from the printout:

"'Yet in the long years liker must they grow;
The man be more of woman, she of man.'"

"That's it," Prince said, "man into woman, woman into man."

"Would Professor Higgins agree?"

"Perhaps to the extent he believed in a relationship with a

woman at all. When Eliza threatened to leave, he told her to come back for his good fellowship."

"Not very romantic," I said.

"No, not like his progenitor."

"Shaw?"

"Pygmalion."

It took me a second. "But Pygmalion wasn't real," I protested. "He was a figure from myth."

"And what was Higgins or the princess or the old man speaking to the Earth, or even Biff? Mythical characters who represent universal thoughts, common experiences. Do you remember the *Metamorphoses*?"

"Something from high-school biology?"

Prince grimaced. "Ovid's Latin poems, written at the time of Christ. Surely you read of Echo's ill-fated love of the selfish Narcissus, Apollo's pursuit of Daphne, and of the sculptor Pygmalion."

"I missed it in Latin," I said, thinking of Charlie Riggs, "but caught it in Classic Comics. Pygmalion carved a woman from ivory and fell in love with her."

"Galatea by name. He prayed to Aphrodite to bring her to life, and she complied. He created his beauty and willed her to live."

Now there's a sexual-identity issue for you, Tennyson. Statue into woman. Hang some rhymin' on that, Al, baby.

CHAPTER 34

Pink Flamingos

Max Blinderman was right where he was supposed to be, next to the fountain with the statue of Citation.

"Hello, shyster," Max said, taking the last drag on a cigarette.

"Hello, shorty," I said.

Citation didn't say a word.

Max's shifty eyes flashed from me to Charlie Riggs and back to me again. The ex-jockey wore a baseball cap and a nylon jacket in the ninety-degree heat. "Whacha want? I gotta lay down fifty on the turf feature, so hurry the hell up."

"Blood, Max. Yours."

"Whaddaya mean?" He flipped his cigarette butt into Citation's fountain.

I cranked up the volume a notch. "I'm looking for an impostor, somebody logging in as Passion Prince. The women he talks to are ending up very dead. I'm giving you a chance to prove you're not the guy who bangs 'em and strangles 'em."

His sneer wrinkled his mustache. "I don't have to prove nuthin.' I know my rights."

"Sure, you do. They've been read to you a few times."

"Go piss in the wind."

I heard Charlie's disapproving tsk-tsk.

"I've seen your rap sheet," I said.

"Bad luck, a couple businesses went bad. Like a horse going lame, nothing you can do about it. An airline goes bankrupt, nobody gives a shit. A small businessman can't make it, he gets thrown in jail."

"Issuing worthless checks, mail fraud, buying, receiving, and concealing . . ."

"Big deal. Restitution on one, probation another, dismissed on the BRC. I've never done time, you can look it up."

I already had. A thief and a con man with no history of violence. But every killer has to start sometime.

From the other side of the bleachers a man in a red tunic and black boots was blowing a bugle. In the walking ring the jockeys mounted their horses and prepared to enter the track.

"C'mere," Max commanded, and we turned toward the ring. "Whaddaya think of number two, Radar Vector?"

"I think he's a big, brown horse," I said. "And he uses more tape on his ankles than I used to."

Nobody knows something about everything.

"Good blood," Charlie Riggs interjected. "By Diplomat Way out of Hawaiian Love Star. Florida-bred. But out of the money the last four races. He did finish strong the last two, however, and at a mile and a half, he should like this longer distance. He may be overlooked and go off at ten or twelve-to-one. So . . ."

Almost nobody knows something about everything.

"Yow," Max said, "but you left out something."

"Bellasario's up," Charlie continued, "in the money sixty-two percent of his mounts. Wouldn't mind laying two dollars across the board."

"The jockey," Max agreed. "Never overlook the jockey. The horse gotta have the blood and gotta have the heart, and the horse carries the jockey on its back, not vice versa, but a lousy jock can still ruin a great horse, and a great jockey can get the best out of a fair-to-middling horse."

Made sense to me. I nodded. So did Charlie. So did Radar Vector, who was prancing his way on the parade to the track.

Charlie started packing his pipe with tobacco and said, "Mr. Blinderman, I saw you ride Pax Americana in the Flamingo a number of years ago. To this day I believe your protest should have been upheld."

Max's dark eyes brightened. "Damn right! I moved left, Salazar moved left. I moved right, he moved right. When I took the inside, son of a bitch whipped my horse and nearly drove me over the rail."

"A shameful, dreadful decision, or should I say nondecision, by the stewards." Charlie clucked, pushing all the right buttons.

"Yow, you said it. C'mon. I'll introduce you to the fifty-dollar window. Forget that two-dollar stuff."

They took off for the stone staircases with the carved balustrades. Purple bougainvillea spun down the mezzanine, clinging to the green-and-white latticework. Hialeah Park was a place of old terrazzo floors and unpretentious lawn chairs, a graceful faded garden of pink flamingos, green shrubs, tropical flowers, and sweet-smelling earth.

I sat on the edge of the fountain next to Citation. He stayed on his pedestal. He was by Bull Lea out of Hydroplane II, bred at Calumet Farm. He won the Triple Crown. I was by a nomad shrimper out of Katy Lassiter, raised by my granny. I was a triple threat, just good enough in baseball, basketball, and football not to get good enough at anything else. By the time I learned that games were not forever, I had a lot of catching up to do.

Maybe I was just a step too slow to ever be good at this. I was starting to feel sorry for myself, which is not the most endearing of my qualities. But let's look at the facts. Nick Wolf was right. I'd been spinning webs for Rodriguez and Wolf, and they were clean. They said they'd humor me, take the blood tests. They did, and young Dr. Sanford Katzen, mathematician and geneticist, brought his autoradiograms and his scientific mumbo jumbo to my office. I told him to spare me the lecture about chopping up the DNA and he did. He held the X-rays up to the window and showed me, by golly, there wasn't one chance in a quintillion that either man's DNA matched that of the semen from Rosemary Newcomb or Priscilla Wolf. If that wasn't enough, Wolf said, they'd each take polygraph tests. It was enough.

So I asked Charlie Riggs to spend a buck and hop on Metrorail for the ride to Hialeah. He agreed, and we sat there, gliding above the treetops, past the marble-and-glass skyscrapers of Brickell Avenue, past the downtown government buildings, through the cheerless streets of Overtown, looking down at the tar-patched roofs and asphalt courts where skinny kids dropped a ball through netless rims. From a distance I peered into the Orange Bowl, my own house of pain. We shot by the civic center, Allapattah, Brownsville, and Northside and came to rest in the parking lot beside the old racetrack.

The winter and spring dates go to Gulfstream and Calder, leaving Hialeah with the stifling summer season, smaller crowds, slower horses. Like many aging institutions of charm and character, the Hialeah track was also going broke. The summer meet would be cut short, closed without ceremony, and already there were plans for plug-ugly condos around the flamingo pond. Inside the clubhouse, amid ragged, curling photos of Sunny Jim Fitzsimmons and the litter of discarded tickets, an elderly barber sat in the reclining chair of his empty shop beneath a stained-glass window of a pink flamingo. He studied the *Daily Racing Form.* Just memories now, hundred-dollar tips from grateful bettors in need of a shave.

And here I was, trying to bully a tough monkey who used to steer thousand-pound beasts with his knees, and he tells me to shove it where the sun don't shine. But old Charlie Riggs, master of the microscope and the anecdote, found common ground with the little weasel. When they came back from the window, I was sure, Max would be rolling up his sleeve and asking if we wanted a drop or a pint.

And how about my personal relationships, as long as we're engaging in self-flagellation? Ms. Pamela Metcalf, where is she now, O man of many charms? In a hotel room, ocean view. Do not disturb.

I'm sorry, Dr. Metcalf is not taking any calls. Would you care to leave a message?

Yeah, tell her she wasn't that great, either. No, never mind.

Okay, Lassiter, you've struck out before. You've had good relationships go bad and bad relationships get worse. There've been lady executives who cared more for their work than you, new-age types who declared you obsolete, touchy-feely artistic types who found you impenetrable, and a couple of cocktail waitresses who thought you had a cute tush.

So don't start romanticizing this one. This was weird from day one. First she stiff-arms and belittles you. Then drops you in the soup with a bunch of sicko killers and gets angry when you fight your way out. Next she shows up under the sheets, then *boom*, she's furious. She cuddles again, sharing bed and board until she finds someone else. Who was it? A psychiatrist at one of her speeches. Or a beachboy type, Mel Gibson with a deep tan.

Okay, grow up already. She left. Accept it for what it was. "Sweet love were slain," old Tennyson wrote. A meaningless joining of bodies, a sharing of mutual heat, a momentary exchange of breaths. Nothing more.

The ex-coroner and the ex-jockey hadn't come back, so I limped up the stairs to the mezzanine, the left foot still swollen and angry at me. There were cries of joy and anguish from the grandstand, and by the time I got to the bar, the TV monitor was showing the replay, number two, thundering down the stretch, five lengths ahead, Bellasario leaning forward, talking horse talk, I imagined, in Radar Vector's ears. He paid $25.80, $9.80, and $5.20.

I ordered a draft beer and was joined by two elderly men in polo shirts, golf slacks, and sneakers. A second TV was tuned to the Yankees–Red Sox game and it was clear these guys didn't come to drink. One had a hundred bucks on the Yankees at six-to-five.

Five minutes later, Charlie Riggs and Max Blinderman pulled up, laughing, slapping each other on the back, counting their money. Literally counting it, unfolding greenbacks as they walked.

"Jake, buy you a beer?" Charlie thundered.

I didn't say no.

"Never played a perfecta before," Charlie announced. He dropped two fifties on the bar and stuffed one in the pocket of the old geezer who was polishing glasses. "But couldn't resist pairing Radar Vector with Internal Medicine. How could I lose?"

How, indeed?

"Paid ninety-eight dollars on a two-dollar bet."

"Great, you can buy dinner," I said.

"He can buy more than that," Max said. "He bet a hundred bucks. Say, doc, you're not doing anything tomorrow, we'll have breakfast, study the charts."

"Tomorrow?" Charlie raised an eyebrow.

"Don't worry. I'll be at the lab by eleven, they can stick me, and we'll make the one o'clock post."

"Done," Charlie said.

The bartender drew a pitcher of beer for the coroner and the lawyer, then delivered a Preakness—rye and vermouth with a dash of Benedictine—for the jockey.

Max sipped his drink and looked at me, his smile gone. "Hey, shyster, that English-bred filly of yours came by the other day to sign up. What's the matter, she want to graze in other pastures?"

"Thanks for the news bulletin, Max," I said. "Give Bobbie my best."

He showed me a shit-eating grin. "Yow, I'll do better than that. I'll give her my best."

I laughed. Not at him. At us. A couple of immature punks in the school yard insulting each other's prowess with the opposite sex.

"Whaddaya laughing at, shyster?"

"Just wondering. When Bobbie comes sniffing around, should I tell her to skedaddle, go home to Max? Or should I give her a run around the track?"

I don't know why I said that. Stupid and vicious. That wasn't the man Granny Lassiter raised. There was no need to respond in kind to his ridicule. Charlie would tell me later how disappointed he was in me. Max told me something else. He came next to my bar stool and stood, maybe on tiptoes, pressing his face close to mine. His breath smelled of tobacco and whiskey.

"Look, shyster, you try anything with Bobbie, I make you a gelding quicker'n you can say Eddie Arcaro."

"Eddie Arcaro," I said.

Oh boy, aren't you big and tough, taunting someone who makes Michael J. Fox look like Rambo. Little guys always want to fight you, to prove something to themselves. If you take them up on it, throw them from here to second base, you're a bully. Get whupped, you're a wimp. Jockeys prove something to themselves squiring six-foot-tall models and driving block-long Lincolns. Don't ask me what or why. Maybe Pam Metcalf knows. I'll ask her. Maybe get the promised therapy at the same time.

"Nobody fucks with Bobbie," Max Blinderman snarled, turning on his heel and disappearing into the grandstand.

CHAPTER 35

Sublimations

I had the top down and the pedal to the metal climbing our Miami mountain, the great looping causeway from the mainland to Key Biscayne. The causeway soars skyward to let the sailboats pass underneath, and it gives you a copter's view of the city, sun-sparkled and gleaming. Cruise ships and condos, beaches and sports cars. It is the cinematographer's vision of the tropical paradise. Phony as a bar girl's smile.

The Olds roared over the crest, eastward toward the morning sun, and I eased off the gas, cruising past the marina and the Marine Stadium, past the entrance to Virginia Key, and on through Crandon Park into the small downtown of Key Biscayne. The Key is turned inside out. Surrounded by water, the condos and hotels on the east open onto the sea. The houses on the west open onto the bay. In northern climes, houses have front porches. You can walk the block and salute your neighbors. Here, we're all out back at the beach or pool. The fronts are deserted, out of the action.

I tried the house phone at the hotel. No answer in her room. At least the operator didn't give me the *non disturbate* message. I tried the lobby. No luck. The pool deck had its usual collection of buttocks in bikinis, the South American tonga, alongside heavyset men weighted with gold. But no English lady from the Cotswolds. I stepped onto the beach, my black wingtips sinking into the sand. I don't know what's worse, being underdressed for your surroundings or over-dressed. It is impossible to wear a shirt and tie on the beach and not feel both foolish about yourself and resentful of those properly unattired.

I checked the grill at the chickee hut, not thirty yards from the surf. Bare backs, the smell of coconut oil, icy red strawberry daiquiris, and the sizzle of burning burgers. But no Pam Metcalf.

I tried the front desk, where a slim young man with a slim young mustache smiled at me and chirped g'morning. For a moment I thought I was two hundred twenty miles up yonder in the land of the mouse. The plastic tag on his brown blazer said "Carlos." I allowed as how it was a fine morning indeed and asked him for Dr. Metcalf's room number. Still smiling under his whiskery lip, Carlos told me he couldn't do that but the operator would be oh-so-happy to dial the room, she might fall off her ergonomic, three-hundred-sixty-degree swivel chair. So I flashed him my laminated, semiofficial badge, which was starting to show wear around the edges, and Carlos punched some buttons on his computer and gave me a suite number, twelfth floor, ocean side. I headed for the elevator and he looked after me. Smiling.

There was silence after the first knock on the double doors. And the second.

After the third she asked who it was.

When I told her, she cracked the door, chain still affixed, and asked what I wanted.

Beaches without footprints, I told her. Eternal happiness, too. But I'd settle for fresh-squeezed juice, eggs over lightly, and a basket of toast with three or four of those little jelly jars.

She unchained and let me in. We faced each other awkwardly in a sitting room tastefully done in muted tropical colors. A sliding glass door led to a balcony with a floor-to-ceiling view of the Atlantic. She wore an ankle-length floral satin robe and no makeup. The sculpted cheekbones still showed their granite planes. Her green eyes were still spiked with flint. Her auburn hair was pulled straight back and tied in a ponytail.

I was too late for breakfast. The room-service cart was there, covered with a white tablecloth and decorated by a vase with fresh-cut lavender flowers. An empty cereal bowl sat on one side of the table and the remains of a western omelet on the other. Two chairs, two place settings, one big pot with two coffee cups. My inductive reasoning told me that Pamela Metcalf had not dined alone. I was getting so good at this I decided to ask Nick Wolf for a raise.

"Kiss me quick before I die," I said.

"What in heaven's—"

"The flowers on your table. I don't know the real name, but as kids, that's what we called them, kiss me quick—"

"Before I die." She picked up one of the flowers, a white eye in the center circled by a lush lavender. "How quaint."

"The color doesn't last. Even on the shrub, it'll fade to pale lilac and then a ghostly white in just a few days."

"Gather ye rosebuds," she said, twirling the stem in her hand.

"Something like that. Flowers, people, we're all a-dying, aren't we?"

She didn't answer. I thought I heard the water running in the bathroom, but it might have been the next suite down the hall.

"Coffee?" she asked.

I nodded and she poured into a used cup. The coffee was still hot.

"Business or social call?" she asked.

"I was wondering how you were doing."

"Fine."

"Think you'll stay here long?"

"No."

"You need anything?"

"No."

Reluctant witnesses either blather incessantly about irrelevancies or one-word you to death. I drank somebody else's coffee and stared through the glass door at a tanker three miles offshore, heading south. I wanted to put all the little fishes on the reefs on red alert.

"Pam . . ."

"Yes?"

"I thought we could talk about—"

A sound from inside the bedroom stopped me. Maybe a dresser drawer closing. I watched the door.

"Oh, Jake. Just come out and ask. There's no reason to be so sensitive about it. I'm surely not."

"All right. I'll ask. Why? Who? What's going on?"

The bedroom door opened and out walked Bobbie Blinderman.

She was dressed in a hot-orange, body-molding leather mini held up by two straps. The shoes were matching orange with stiletto heels. She puckered her orange glossy lips and blew me a kiss. "'Morning, Lassiter."

I wished it had been Mel Gibson.

"Jake, don't look so surprised. My goodness, you're actually turning pale, isn't he, Bobbie?"

"As a ghost," she said.

"Jake, I'm helping Bobbie with some of her problems. She's—"

"Great, who's helping with yours?"

"Oh Jake, don't."

"Is the little boy angry?" Bobbie jeered. "Somebody steal his candy bar?"

"Jake, bisexuality is quite normal, really. Some of the greatest figures in history were bisexual. Socrates, for example."

"Elton John," Bobbie added.

"Oscar Wilde," Pam said.

"David Bowie," Bobbie countered.

This went on for a while, like a vaudeville routine.

Pam said, "Henry III."

And Bobbie said, "Janis Joplin."

Pam said, "Colette."

And Bobbie said, "Bessie Smith."

"Okay," I said. "I get the point."

Pam said, "All of us are born bisexual and have those tendencies until puberty. The heterosexual merely sublimates his homosexual cravings in friendship and other social engagements with the same sex. Some don't sublimate it."

"I understand," I muttered.

"So why are you so . . . threatened?"

Bobbie sat down on the sofa and crossed her legs, hiking the leather dress toward her hips. What was it she told me that day in the courthouse? That I really didn't know her at all, and the less I knew the better.

"Hey, I don't care if people are homosexual, bisexual, or if they like inflatable dolls or rubber duckies," I said. "It just gets personal when somebody I'm involved with, somebody I thought I was involved with, turns out differently than I had supposed."

"Would you be as upset if I left for a man?"

"I don't know, maybe not."

"Why?"

I was getting tired of her analyzing me. "While we're talking about why, tell me why you're the way you are."

"Do you really want to know or do you need reinforcement that your manhood isn't diminished by my choices?"

"No. I want to know. I came here today because I missed you, couldn't understand why you left. So now I know part of it, the tip-of-the-iceberg part. . . . "

"I suppose I could tell you about the positive and negative Oedipus complex. For a girl it's very complex. To become heterosexual, she has to transfer her love from her mother to her father, then must repress that love and transfer it to other men while still identifying with the mother. If the girl has incomplete identification with her own sex, she combines characteristics of both sexes. If she cannot resolve the positive Oedipal complex, if she cannot transfer her love for her father to other men, she will become homosexual or bisexual." Pam studied me to see if I was following the lecture. I just looked out the window and watched the tanker steam south, black puffs belching from its smokestacks.

"You get an A-plus for clinical psychology," I said, "but I want to know about you. Your childhood, your parents. What made you what you are?"

"What I am!"

"Wow," Bobbie breathed. She squirmed on the sofa and turned toward Pam. "He thinks you're a thing, an it, a lesbianic creature from outer space."

"You two are having fun with this, aren't you? Baiting me."

Pam stood and walked toward the balcony. The tanker was gone.

"Jake, it doesn't greatly concern me what you think of me, though I should like to enlighten you. A hundred years ago, Dr. Krafft-Ebing declared that *heterosexual* cunnilingus was a perversion of fetishists."

"He probably didn't like oysters, either," I said.

"My point is that attitudes change. In ancient Greece—"

"I don't care about ancient Greece. I really don't. But I care about you, or I wouldn't have come here."

"Good. I care about Bobbie. And there is no reason we cannot all care about each other."

"Before we start caring too much," Bobbie said, hoisting herself up on long legs, "I gotta go to work."

"Me too," I said. "Too much enlightenment before breakfast gives me a headache."

"Your sarcasm is readily apparent," Pam said.

I shrugged. The two ladies said ta-ta and their lips brushed, Pam giving Bobbie a little squeeze on her burnt-orange behind.

I examined the tops of my shoes as Bobbie Blinderman and I shared an elevator. A middle-aged man with a fresh sunburn, an aloha shirt, and a conventioneer's tag identifying him as a risk-loss specialist from Omaha stopped talking to his wife and stared at my six-foot-tall orange lollipop. Bobbie showed her hundred-watt smile, and then turned to me. "I'm gonna be sore for a week, you big moose." My risk-loss friend snickered and slapped me on the back when the doors opened at the lobby.

It took the valet ten minutes to coax the Olds out of the stable. If you drive a Rolls or a Jag convertible or if you arrive by limo, they leave your machine out front in the shade of the palms. Impress the tourists, justify the room rates. If it's a convertible older than the valet, they often put it on a concrete deck in the broiling sun where the salt spray can speckle it.

A sleepy-eyed teenager in a red vest was opening Bobbie's door as I got in on the driver's side. I had my right foot inside and my left foot on the ground when I saw the blur.

The blur hit the side of the door and slammed it into my shin. The pain shot through me and I fell backward into the car, my leg still pinned by the door to the frame. The blur opened the door a few inches and slammed it back again, smashing me harder. It felt like a sledgehammer had crushed me.

Then my leg stopped hurting but only because my head ached. Something hit me above the eye. A fist.

A left fist that did it again. Not much of a punch, but I couldn't move. My leg was on fire, still pinned in the car. Red flashes streaked across my brain. Then a flurry of punches bounced off my forehead and chin. Quick combinations, pop, pop, popping off my skull. I felt two hands reach for my neck, and I heard Bobbie screaming. Somewhere on the edge of my peripheral vision I had the impression of people staring. Parking attendants, tourists, a crowd frozen by the sight.

I pivoted with the leg inside the car, got both hands on the door, and shoved. It tossed him backward into the driveway, and he stumbled but didn't fall. I struggled out of the car, one-legging it toward him.

He glared at me, dark eyes blazing with hate. "Nobody fucks with Bobbie," Max Blinderman declared.

CHAPTER 36

The Message

The Harman and Fox receptionist didn't bat an eye. She just wished me a pleasant afternoon and tapped a glowing button on the phone with the tip of her polished nail. A law clerk stopped in the corridor, started to ask, thought better of it, and ducked into the copying room. My partners were either at a late lunch or an early golf game, so I was unmolested all the way back to my two-window, bayfront office where Cindy sat in her cubicle, pretending to type.

"Holy shit! Did you get the license number?"

I lifted my standard-issue, rubber-tipped aluminum cane and said, "It's not as bad as it looks."

"It looks like you stuck your leg in a manhole and your head in a beehive."

True. I could barely walk, little welts were popping out of my forehead, and my right eye was swollen shut. Max's jabs had left more marks than pain. The leg wasn't broken, but not for lack of trying, and the foot still hurt from where Carruthers danced on it. I stretched out the leg and eased into my high-backed chair.

"Musta been a mean hombre," Cindy said, fishing.

I didn't bite.

"I mean, he musta been one big nut crusher."

"Right. Runs about a hundred twenty, including his saddle."

"C'mon. Probably a whole gang of thugs with chains and clubs."

"Cindy, it was a tough morning. Bring me the mail and the messages and any work you may have inadvertently done, then leave me alone."

"Okay, okay, I been working. The usual pleadings to sign. Motions to continue, motions to defer, motions to forget. Nothing in the mail to interest you except a trial lawyers' convention in Aruba."

"Great winds," I acknowledged, wondering when I would be able to put weight on my left leg. If I couldn't windsurf in the Aruba–Bonaire classic, maybe I could qualify for the wheelchair races.

"Bunch of calls piling up since you been out of touch. Charlie Riggs says the bass are biting. Granny Lassiter asks whether you're eating enough greens. Dr. Katzen wants to talk. Oh, your friend Rodriguez called."

I picked through the stack of pink forms.

"What the hell does this mean?" I asked her.

"Dunno. Figured you would . . ."

I read the Rodriguez message aloud: "'Got story for your friends at the paper, on the record this time.'"

"What else did he say?"

"That's it, word for word, or best I can do since shorthand isn't my strong suit. Said it was priority one, or category red, or some cop talk."

I dialed Rodriguez's number, but it rang busy. I signed some letters and some pleadings, barely pausing to note the typos.

Tried again. Still busy. I reviewed some memos from the managing partner about indiscriminate use of the firm's credit cards at a Surfside massage parlor.

Tried another time. Still busy. What did Rodriguez want? Last time he talked to the paper, he was a "source close to the investigation" and let everyone know about the Compu-Mate connection.

One more try, then I rang the operator. I told her my name and semiofficial part-time government position, and through infinite willpower, she concealed how impressed she was. She took a moment plugging into the line. Off the hook, she said.

Okay, maybe he was taking a nap. Could have been at a homicide scene half the night. I grabbed the cane and my cotton duck Tilley hat with the wide brim to hide my battle scars and hobbled toward the parking garage. Cindy advised me not to pop two Tylenols with codeine, but it was the only way to use the clutch without my left leg declaring mutiny. By the time I reached I-95, nothing hurt that much. I felt fine. Even the traffic seemed more tolerable than usual, though there was an inordinate amount of horn-honking headed west on the Don Shula Expressway just south of the airport. I looked at my speedometer and discovered I was doing thirty-five in the passing lane. A little too mellow, the pills woozing me into outer space.

I slapped my face a couple of times, stuck my head into the wind, and put the old buggy into fourth gear, giving it hell. Ten minutes later, I pulled into Alex Rodriguez's driveway, bouncing over the curb when I missed the cutaway.

It was a small concrete-block, stucco house with faded green shutters and a carport. The county-owned Chrysler was there, locked up tight, the hood cool in the shade. The house was old and the yard belonged to a guy who didn't know crabgrass from crawfish. There were no children, so when Maria left him, she really left, heading to Honduras with a man who said he owned twenty-seven percent of a coffee plantation.

I rang the doorbell and waited.

I tried the door. Unlocked.

I stepped inside. The air-conditioning was on, whimpering and groaning. The coils could use cleaning. I called his name. The compressor whimpered. I tried again, louder.

I eased my way, cane-first, through a small living room with lime shag carpeting. The dining room was a raised section to the rear. The kitchen was dark. I flipped on a light. Rodriguez would never win homemaker-of-the-year award. Beer cans, paper plates, and the fossilized remains of home-delivery pizza covered the sink and counters. The kitchen phone dangled down a wall by its cord. I put the receiver back on the hook and called his name again. Nothing.

Down a narrow hall were two rooms. The first was the master bedroom. The bed was unmade. A rumpled short-sleeve shirt was draped over a chair. Heavy black oxfords sat on the floor, a sock balled in each one.

I peeked back into the hall. One other door to try. It would be a spare bedroom used as a study. The Biggus Dickus sanctuary. Despite the air-conditioning, I started sweating.

The door was cracked an inch. I pushed it open with the tip of my cane. No one went in or came out. I raised the cane like a sword, figuring I could handle anybody armed with an umbrella, maybe even a crutch.

The room contained a chair, a desk, a phone, bookshelves, a computer.

And Alex Rodriguez.

He lay on his back. His bare feet stuck out from beneath the desk. The chair was overturned. He wore gray slacks and a white T-shirt. The T-shirt had a small, blackened hole just over the heart. The hole was surrounded by a spray of gunpowder. Somebody had gotten close. I felt for a pulse, didn't expect to find any, and wasn't surprised.

I was breathing hard and my mind was racing. I tried to think like Charlie Riggs. What would he do? Slow down. Talk to me, Charlie. *There are four manners of death. Accident, suicide, homicide, and natural.* Even I knew it wasn't a heart attack. I looked around for a gun. Suicide or accident, and it would be right there on the floor. No gun. Okay, Lassiter, it's a homicide. Very good. Step to the front of the class.

Now, try not to disturb anything and look around. What do you see? A fairly neat desk. Some bills, a day-old newspaper, some advertising fliers, and a police-department fingerprint kit. Something else that looked familiar, the logo of interlocking male and female symbols. I picked it up. It asked for name, address, handle, and password. It asked how often you used the service and if you had any suggestions. It asked, on a scale of one to ten, how you would rate the overall quality of the fantasy and the flesh produced by your pals at Compu-Mate.

Alex Rodriguez never answered the questions. Before he had a chance to fill in the blanks and stick on his stamp . . . wait. There was no return envelope. The questionnaire didn't come in the mail. It would have been brought by Bobbie Blinderman, who personally surveyed her customers.

Satisfaction guaranteed.

Somewhere in the back of my mind a buzzer was going off. The Compu-Mate connection. Of course.

Nick Wolf and Alex Rodriguez didn't kill anyone. The murders weren't to silence anyone. And they weren't the work of a motiveless serial killer. They were planned and carried out for the oldest and best of reasons. Jealousy and revenge.

Nobody fucks with Bobbie.

Bisexual and promiscuous, Bobbie Blinderman waltzed door-to-door with her cockamamie surveys. You never know who'll invite you in for a drink and a tickle. Maybe a TV Gal, a Flying Bird, a Forty Something. And you never know who'll be right behind. An enraged husband who borrows a dead guy's poetry and a drunk guy's handle. He finds the bedroom, too, gets his revenge. Uses a gun to force his way, then ends the rivalry with his powerful jockey's hands. Until the next one comes along.

Larynx snapped in two. Fractured hyoid, thyroid, and cricoid cartilage, the whole shebang.

I remembered his hands, clawing reflexively at my own throat. With the women, it was easy enough. But that's not how you kill a man. If you target a man, a cop, you bring a gun and use it.

I gingerly picked up the phone, trying not to leave prints. I called the state attorney's office and told Nick Wolf where I was and who lay on the floor.

"Oh Jesus," he said.

I told him about Bobbie and Max Blinderman, and he said it sounded crazy.

"Nick, the guy's flipped out. He assaulted me this morning because he thinks *I'm* diddling his wife."

"Are you?"

"No! What's that got to do with it?"

"You musta beat the shit out of the little punk."

He waited. "No, I took it easy on him."

"Okay, I'll send homicide out there. You stay put. Let's hope we get lucky, and somebody saw him going in or coming out of the house, or we come up with a gun."

"Lucky! We've got the printouts, and Max had the motive and the ability to sign on as Passion Prince. He raped the women and strangled them, and now he's shot Rodriguez. What more—"

"Jakie, simmer down. And start returning your calls, or don't they teach that downtown? Your pal Doc Katzen stopped by about twenty minutes ago. Blinderman's blood doesn't match up."

"What?"

"You heard me, Jakie. No match on the DNA. You got nice theories, tying everything up and all. And maybe you're right for once. But Max Blinderman didn't do the screwing, so you tell me how you're gonna prove he did the strangling. . . ."

I didn't know.

"And one other thing, Jakie."

"Yeah?"

"You're fired. I'm taking you off the investigation. Back to your divorces and whiplashes. I'll handle it from here. Turn in your badge and your gun. And give me some blood."

"Blood?"

"Yeah, Jakie. Bleed a little. You like to take it. Time to give. It's for a worthy cause. Just stop at the lab and see Dr. Katzen. And bring the gun into ballistics."

"The gun. Why?"

"Standard procedure. A man says he found a gunshot victim and the man doing the finding has a gun. Routine request, nothing more."

The gun.

The last time I saw the gun it was on a black enamel table in Cindy's apartment taking a breather after Pam fired it.

Oh brother. It's one thing to lose your new fountain pen, another to lose a county-owned gun. But what was I worried about? I hadn't done anything wrong. My blood would be red with just the right amount of calcium, phosphorus, and potassium and a tad too much cholesterol. The gun would be right there where I left it, oiled and shiny. Wouldn't it?

CHAPTER 37

The Saint

Max Blinderman. Ex-jockey, penny-ante con artist, a life told in a series of yellowed newspaper clips and scraps of microfilm.

Roberta Blinderman. Goes by Bobbie. Ex . . . Ex-what?

Just who the hell was Roberta Blinderman? No criminal record, at least not under that name. I had been watching her swiveling walk but not paying attention to anything else.

My thoughts were interrupted by someone pounding on my front door. They do that after pushing the button half a dozen times. The doorbell hasn't worked in years. I yelled that it was unlocked. I heard some feeble pushing, but the door didn't budge. In the humidity it swells up like a patrolman's feet.

"Hit it with your shoulder," I yelled.

A thud, a curse, and a moment later Bobbie Blinderman high-heeled it into my combination library, living room, conversation pit, and entertainment area. It's a library because the sports pages are usually spread across the floor. I spend most of my time here, hence the living room, and I entertain myself with one-sided conversations. At the moment I was lying on a sagging sofa, nursing a sixteen-ounce Grolsch, my gimpy leg propped up.

"I was just thinking about you," I said, telling the truth.

She wore a black scooped-back dress, molded to her body, with a sweeping skirt. It was the first time I couldn't see a mile or so of thigh.

"You look very nice," I said. "Almost ladylike."

"We need to talk."

"About Max."

"No. About Pam."

"Pam?"

The name sounded familiar, but I hadn't thought about her since she had hustled me into an elevator at the hotel. The emotional wounds must be healing, or were they only superficial? I hoisted myself to a sitting position, offered Bobbie a seat, and she gracefully bent at the knees and lowered herself into the cushion at the far end of the sofa. She had spent some time tending to herself. The blush emphasized the sanguine complexion, the black hair was in a cultivated shag that suggested wildness under control. Her dark, wide-set eyes were accented with liner, shadow, and mascara.

She took a breath and said, "I thought Pam and I might really have something special. And we do, or did. I gave her all my love, and believe me, Lassiter, it's a lot. You have no idea how hot I burn, the depth of my passion."

She looked at me with eyes both smoldering and vulnerable. It was a new look, as if she had been playing a role, tough and loose, and now something else had opened up, sensitive and giving. As for the depths of her passion, if I didn't know now, the look said I might soon learn.

"Now Pam wants to know all about you and me," she said.

"A short conversation."

"That's what I told her, the truth, that you arouse me and I flirted with you, but you never responded."

"I responded, but you're married, and even if you weren't, it would be a conflict of interest with the investigation going on."

I patted myself on the back, gave myself the discretion-is-the-better-part-of-ardor award. Then I realized I wasn't investigating anything anymore. I had been fired. I was supposed to give blood but said to hell with it. I was supposed to turn in my gun, but Cindy couldn't find it. Now, revising the equation, the only hang-up was that Bobbie Blinderman was married.

And promiscuous.

And bisexual.

And her husband may be a maniac who kills anyone who dallies with her.

Other than that, we were made for each other.

"Pam doesn't believe me," Bobbie said, her eyes on the paddle fan, seemingly hypnotized by the churning blades. "She's obsessed with the thought that you and I are lovers. . . ."

She let it hang there, and unspoken words passed between us. *And if she believes it's true, why not make it true?* Because, I reminded myself, she's married, promiscuous, and bisexual, and her husband . . . and so on and so forth.

And another reason, too, Lassiter, old buddy. The days of easy flesh are gone, my friend. Oh, a guy with an itch can still find an evening's diversion, just a bar stool or computer terminal away. There was a time when even a semi-tough linebacker knew every nightspot in the AFC East and most of the barmaids therein. But no more road trips, groupies fluttering in the lobby bar, then up the service elevator for curfew-busting pregame revelry. It's not the seventies anymore. The sexual revolution has been repealed by a vote of the electorate. And not just because of communicable rashes and deadly viruses. There's an old-fashioned word that makes us smart guys wince: morality. Or if that's too self-righteous for you, remember the flip side. Chilly awakenings in strange beds, the harsh light of morning, and not a word to say. *What was her name: Susie, Sandy, Mandy, Candy? A flight attendant or travel agent or cosmetics salesgirl who liked opera or Cancún or hockey.* Hey, it's hard enough when you're aglow with the buzz of someone special and it turns out to be a false alarm. No use sighing and sweating just for the exercise.

Jake Lassiter, number fifty-eight, placed on waivers, emotionally unable to perform. Refuses to hit and run. Welcome to the grown-up world, Lassiter. I'm almost proud of you, buddy.

"Look, I don't mean to be rude," I said, "but I've got other things on my mind besides your relationship with Pam."

"Such as?"

"Where's Max?"

She shrugged.

"I mean, if he's following you around, maybe I ought to find my Louisville Slugger, get ready—"

"I told him not to bother you again," Bobbie said.

"How considerate. Did you tell him not to bother Alex Rodriguez?"

She looked puzzled, so I told her. She kept shaking her head and biting her lower lip. "What time did it happen?"

"ME says between noon and three P.M. yesterday."

Bobbie let her face relax. "Max was in the office all afternoon. He drove me back from Key Biscayne after your . . . disagreement, and we worked all day."

"Who else was there?"

"Just the two of us."

"Uh-huh."

"You don't believe me."

"No. I think you're covering for him."

"Max would have no reason to kill the cop."

"Really? Who would he have reason to kill?"

She didn't answer. "Let's play a little name association game," I said. "Michelle Diamond."

"What about her?"

"You tell me, Bobbie."

"She belonged to Compu-Mate. You know that."

"Ever make love with her?"

"No!"

"Never shared her bed, had that something special you had with Pam?"

"No! We never met. I've already told you."

When a witness starts to open up, keep the questions coming, short and sweet. Process the information later. "Rosemary Newcomb."

The long, black lashes fluttered. "She was so lovely. Bisexual since her teens. We were together off and on. I was shocked when she was killed."

"Priscilla Wolf."

"She wanted to experiment, that's all. Very adventurous. A one-nighter. We laughed about it. She was so full of life. It's awful what happened."

"Alex Rodriguez."

"The flatfoot! Give me a break. Except for a vice cop when I was a kid, I never—"

"Where were you married and when?"

"Miami Beach, three years ago, August third."

"So why doesn't Dade County have a record of the marriage license?"

"I don't know. Max handled all that."

"What's your maiden name?"

"Why?"

"What is it?"

She stood and walked to the wall. She was staring at a poster of a Hawaiian kid doing a three-hundred-sixty-degree flip on a sailboard. Either she was fascinated with aerodynamics or she was thinking.

"St. Simeon," she said. "Roberta St. Simeon."

"Unusual name."

"I'm an unusual person."

"If I ran that name through the Metro computer, what little shocks would I get?"

She turned back to me. "How easily do you shock?"

I didn't answer. I just sat there studying her. For once, she wasn't trying to be provocative. No risqué jokes, no limericks. Something was bothering her. And me. If I could only draw the two bothers together.

"Was there really a Simeon who was a saint?" I asked.

"I'm told there was. A monk who lived on top of a pillar, just praying and praying, denying all flesh."

That almost made me laugh. Life is more pleasurable if you develop a sense of irony.

"Saint Simeon," I said, the name tickling my mind.

"Saint Simeon," she repeated.

"There's a name for it, isn't there, an ascetic monk who lives atop a column or pillar."

"I believe there is."

"What is it?"

"Can't remember," she shot back, too quickly to have tried.

Something was there, creeping around the shadows of my mind. I wanted to open a book, but what book?

"Well," she said, "if the interrogation is over, perhaps I should leave."

I didn't try to stop her.

She gathered herself in the way women do before making an exit. "You said you responded to me. Did you mean it?"

"You're a sultry enchantress and damn well know it."

"But you're still not interested."

"Lately, I've been trying to do my thinking north of the equator."

She smiled and looked at me straight on. "'Then I shall fly for my good, perhaps for thine, at any rate for thine if mine is thine.'"

It took me a moment to decipher. "That's very good. Original?"

"I wish."

"Who wrote it?"

"Tennyson. Ever heard of him?"

Bobbie Blinderman was telling me about Alfred Tennyson's emotional problems and his letter to Emily-somebody breaking off their engagement, flying for his own good, perhaps for thine, blah, blah, blah. But I wasn't listening. Not really listening. I was thinking, running it all through my head.

> *Woman is the lesser man,*
> *And all thy passions, matched with mine,*
> *Are as moonlight unto sunlight, And as water unto wine.*

Why belittle women that way? What does Bobbie Blinderman know of male passions, anyway?

"Who is the hunter, Bobbie?"

She spoke slowly, her voice heavy. "You know that, Jake. You've read it so many times. Man is the hunter."

And woman is the game. All I knew were the words. But now I remembered more of hers. *The less you know about me the better.* Flippant at the time, meaningful now? Come into focus. Come on, think. Two hyenas sniffing around, Charlie had said. What was it she had asked? *Would appearances put you off?*

Saint Simeon. She was trying to tell me something.

"You're the Passion Prince, aren't you?"

"I liked the name, borrowed it."

"You never met Michelle Diamond, but you computer-talked with her the night she died."

"Yes, but I was so new at it, I was . . . too crude. It was the beast in me."

"From then on, you took the poet's words."

"Yes."

She moved closer to the sofa. Tears formed in the corners of her dark eyes. Her eyebrows were scrunched. She was silent.

On the sailboard was a stack of books and old newspapers. I fished around and pulled out the worn volume Prince had given me. *The Poems of Tennyson.* I thumbed through it, found what I wanted, and said, "They're called stylites, aren't they, the monks on the pillars."

"Yes," she said.

"Saint Simeon isn't your name. You took it from a poem called *Saint Simeon Stylites.*"

She nodded. I read:

> "*I will not cease to grasp the hope I hold*
> *Of saintdom, and to clamor, mourn, and sob,*
> *Battering the gates of heaven with storms of prayer,*
> *Have mercy, Lord, and take away my sin!*'"

A tear ran down her face.

"Help me figure you out. What does it mean? What is your sin?"

"You don't care about me," she said.

"I want to help you. Tell me."

She stood two feet in front of me. I was still on the sofa, my head at the level of her waist. She faced me and slid one shoulder free of the black dress. Then she pushed the other side away, the dress sliding over her breasts until she was naked to the waist. It was a flat, smooth waist. The breasts were small and pointed. She placed a hand on each of her nipples and stroked them erect. Softly, she spoke the lines, "'Her falser self slipt from her like a robe, and left her woman. . . .'"

NIGHT VISION

She closed her eyes and moved closer to me, straddling my knees with her legs. She reached down and gently circled my hand with hers. "'Lovelier in her mood than in her mould that other, when she came from barren deeps to conquer all with love.'"

She placed my hand underneath the hem of her dress and moved it slowly up her leg, guiding me.

Then she chanted it, as if in a trance:

"'But woman is not undevelopt man,
But diverse: could we make her as the man,
Sweet love were slain: his dearest bond is this,
Not like to like, but like in difference.
Yet in the long years liker must they grow;
The man be more of woman, she of man.'"

My hand slid between her smooth thighs, higher and higher. When it would go no farther, she held it there.

And then I knew.

CHAPTER 38

The Thing They Dare Not Do

She had been born Robert Simon, she said.

She laughed. "Bob. Let's throw the ball, Bob. Do I seem like a Bob to you? I should have changed it to something more feminine. What do you think of Melissa?"

"Bobbie's just fine," I said.

"I always wore dresses and jewelry and my hair was long and beautiful," she said, running a hand through the layered shag. "My mother used to brush my hair."

"Your mother wanted you to be a girl."

"*I* wanted to be a girl. As long as I could remember. She didn't object when I used her cosmetics or learned to sew or dressed in her underthings."

"What's your earliest memory?"

"Sleeping with Mother. She would curl herself around me. I remember how warm she was, her bare breasts pressing into my back.

She would tuck her arms and legs around me, holding me tight. So womblike. Every night until my teens."

"And your father?"

She had pulled the shoulders of the dress back up and was leaning on my kitchen counter. I was displaying my culinary skills by boiling a pot of water, two tea bags cleverly dangling inside waiting mugs.

"You expect me to say he wasn't there," she said.

I shrugged.

"He was there but not there. He'd leave for work before I awoke and come home after I was asleep. On weekends he'd lock himself into his workshop and cut and hammer and saw, making all sorts of useless things. He had his hands on wood and sheet metal far more than on my mother."

"You wanted to be like your mother."

"So very much. But I'm not a fetishist, you know. I didn't just want to dress in women's clothing."

I thought of Stephanie, the man-killing transsexual, mocking transvestites. No weekend cross-dressing here.

"I wanted breasts like Mother's," Bobbie continued. "I wanted to dress like her. I wanted to be rid of my penis. Do you know I never, never peed standing up. Not once. Not then, not now."

The pot threatened to boil over. I poured the steaming water into the mugs. "You have the breasts."

"Hormones. Lovely breasts, don't you think, though not so large as I would like. And a beautifully pitched voice. But I still have the ugly thing."

She pointed to her crotch. "I didn't pass their tests, so they wouldn't cut me." She imitated a supercilious doctor: "'Mr. Simon, you don't unequivocally believe yourself to be a woman.'"

"Because you still have sex with women."

"Partly, I suppose, though is that any worse than hooking, selling yourself to men? Many TS's do that to pay for the operation, you know. You'd be surprised how excited men get when they're with a woman who possesses both breasts and a penis. They don't know what to grab first."

"Telling themselves it's not really a homosexual experience because she looks like a woman."

She shrugged and sipped the tea. "I could show you things, Jake, take you to heights—"

A little light bulb flashed. "That's how you met Max, wasn't it? You were raising money for the operation that never came."

"He loved me, took me out of a filthy room on South Beach. You don't know what I've been through."

I thought I did. "I'll bet if we ran the name Robert Simon, we'd come up with a few busts, wouldn't we? What you did for love. And money. Maybe rolling some johns who would never file charges. Maybe jail time for soliciting."

"Is it a crime to fulfill my destiny, to be what I was meant to be?"

"What are you, Bobbie?"

She shook her head. "Something. Nothing. Something stuck between here and there. I don't know anymore. I lust for you because I'm a woman. I lust for Pam and I hate myself for it."

Little bells were ringing. What was it Stephanie had said? *When I need a woman, it comes over me in waves. My passion inflamed a thousandfold.* Then she had whispered something else. *And hate her for it, for making me the male beast.*

"Who do you hate, Bobbie?"

"I told you. Myself, for my weakness, my own lack of total identity with my femininity."

"Maybe, but you also hate her. . . ."

"Don't start playing shrink with me. That's what she does."

"Do you hate Pam for that, too?"

"You're nuts!"

"Man is the hunter," I said.

"Sure, sure. And woman is his game."

"*You're* the hunter, Bobbie."

"No! The game."

"You *want* to be the game. Or part of you does. Part of you is shamed to be a woman and another part shamed to love a woman."

She closed her eyes. "'I am shamed through all my nature to have loved so slight a thing.'"

"Yes, that's it, isn't it?"

"'Weakness to be wroth with weakness! Woman's pleasure, woman's pain. Nature made them blinder motions bounded in a shallower brain.'"

"You believe it, don't you, Bobbie?"

"No. Just words. Just a man's words. It isn't me."

"You had sex with Rosemary Newcomb the night she was killed."

"Yes."

"And you were the male, weren't you? You had vaginal intercourse. It's *your* blood we've been after."

"Yes, but—"

"And the same with Priscilla Wolf. You had sex with both of them and left your borrowed poetry behind."

"Yes, yes."

"And then strangled them, the sleek and shining creatures of your chase."

"No. I'm a woman. I want to be loved by a man. I want to change."

"You hunt them for the beauty of their skins."

"No, no!"

"The rest of the stanza. Say it."

She turned away and hugged herself, hunching over, the fragile blades of her shoulders delicate as the wings of a bird.

"Or shall I do it?" I asked.

In a whimper, she recited the verse:

"'They love us for it, and we ride them down.
Wheedling and siding with them! Out! For shame!
Boy, there's no rose that's half so dear to them
As he that does the thing they dare not do,
Breathing and sounding beauteous battle, comes
With the air of the trumpet round him, and leaps in
Among the women, snares them by the score
Flattered and flustered, wins, though dashed with death. . . .'"

"Bobbie, you're not a woman. . . ."

Great sobs racked her body. "I am, I am."

"You're a man and you blame them for it, hate them for it."

She whirled and brought her hand toward my cheek. Her slim-fingered boy-girl fist wouldn't have hurt, but it held a Miami Dolphin mug half-filled with hot tea. The mug glanced off my forehead, and the tea splashed square across my face. I yelped and hopped backward on one good leg. My eyes were half-closed, but I sensed her bending over, and something black was in her hand. I tried to pivot, and if my left leg had held the weight, I would have dropped her with a straight left hand. But it couldn't and I didn't, and the leg collapsed, and as I fell without help from anyone she bashed me square on the skull. It felt like a hammer, and great gongs went off as I crumpled to the kitchen floor. I started up and she hit me again, this time at the base of the skull. The world lit up and I lay down.

I took a futile stab at a leg as she stepped over me, and as she stepped away I saw the blurry image of her shapely calves and stockinged feet. In each hand she held a stylish black shoe with a stiletto heel.

I was woozy but awake. I had not been out long.

The kitchen floor was cool and sticky against my face. I looked for my own blood, would maybe send some to Nick Wolf. But there was no blood. Last week's spilled beer, tacky on my skin.

I touched my face. Raw skin that would blister from the hot tea. I felt my head. Two bumps with round dents where the metal-tipped heel jolted me. I pulled myself up with my good leg and totaled the score. I figured I was the first guy to be KO'ed on consecutive days by Mr. and Mrs. Max Blinderman. Even if the missus was nearly a mister, it would not look good on my résumé.

The cobwebs were clearing and I picked up the phone. First I called Nick Wolf, who didn't believe me and wanted to know why the hell I hadn't delivered my blood and my gun. I yelled at him to shut up, then told him about the hermaphroditic nature of Robert Simon aka Bobbie Blinderman.

"You touched it?" he asked, incredulous. "You really touched it."

"Listen, Nick. She or he is the killer. Get somebody to the Sunset Beach Hotel right now. Pam Metcalf's suite."

He was still skeptical but said he would take all necessary precautions. I hate the way politicians talk.

I called the hotel, hoping Pam Metcalf was there.

Her laugh was filled with derision. "Are you trying to tell me you just learned of her sexual identity? I find that hard to believe, though it's not surprising she was at your house. Tell me, were you doing her or vice versa?"

"What are you talking about? Do you think I—"

"You and that promiscuous creature . . ."

"Pam, if you're jealous, let me assure—"

"Jealous! Of her, of you? Do you think either of you means anything to me?"

"Pam, listen to me. I'm trying to tell you she's a killer. She wants to kill you."

"Rubbish. She's had sadistic fantasies quite normal among transsexuals, and she's as slutty as the rest of them, but—"

"Pam, I'm telling you she's coming over there."

"I know that. She called from the lobby a minute ago. I would expect that's her at the door just now."

CHAPTER 39

A Freak Accident

The medical examiner's van was angled in front of the hotel, its front tires sinking into a bed of geraniums. The van bears little resemblance to the emergency vehicles favored by police and fire rescue. There is no oxygen, no plasma, no sophisticated electronics for monitoring hearts and brains.

There is no need.

The state attorney's car was pulled off the driveway under a sweet-gum tree. Nick Wolf hadn't spent four years as a patrolman without learning the first rule of survival in south Florida: never park in the sun.

A uniformed sergeant stood guard at the suite's double doors. He looked at my cane and at my face and let out a low whistle. Then he blocked the door and made me negotiate.

"Let 'em in!"

It was Nick Wolf. "Been expecting you, Jakie . . ." He did a double take. "Jesus H. Christ, you look like shit warmed over."

I looked around the room. No Pamela Metcalf. No Bobbie Blinderman. "You were too late," I said hoarsely.

"It happens that way sometimes."

"Where's the body?"

He jerked a thumb toward the balcony. The sliding glass doors were open, and a humid breeze from the Atlantic puckered the flimsy curtains. I hobbled out. A police photographer was crouching, taking a shot of something on the concrete slab of the balcony. He was blocking my view. I stepped around him.

A woman's shoe.

A black shoe with a stiletto heel cleanly broken off. The heel was jammed in the track of the sliding glass door. The rest of the shoe lay forlornly on its side near the edge of the balcony. I looked straight down over the railing, gripping it tight. One hundred twenty feet below, on the pool deck, lay a body in a black dress. The legs were splayed at an unnatural angle, and a pool of blood seeped from beneath her head and across the hard chattahoochee. Alongside, a man in a white coat was taking photos. Another man was on his hands and knees, whisking the deck with a brush.

"Dr. Metcalf's in the bedroom," Nick Wolf said, standing behind me.

My eyes must have had a desperate look. "She's okay, don't worry. Now, before you go in there, I gotta ask you a couple questions. The other night, you were at your secretary's place, and you had the .38, right?"

"Right."

"Did the gun discharge?"

"Yeah."

"Did Dr. Metcalf shoot the gun?"

"Yeah."

"Why did she shoot?"

"To get my attention."

"Maybe I should try that. How many shots?"

"One."

"You're sure, just one shot."

"Yeah. What the hell—"

"You ever shoot it?"

"Never."

"Okay, c'mon. Let's see your girlfriend."

Pam Metcalf sat on the bed. She wore a double-breasted coatdress in purple-and-black houndstooth. Epaulets and padded shoulders, not your typical daytime resort wear. A female detective sat next to her, scribbling notes on a pad. The detective wore a blue skirt, white blouse, and blue jacket, and her holster was visible on the left side. Clipped to the jacket was a plastic shield with her photo and name and large black letters spelling "Homicide." I moved closer. Her name was Sigorsky. She was short and bleached blond, but she hadn't made it to the beauty salon in a while. She was wide through the hips, and her dark eyes walked me up and down, taking their sweet time. Her report would probably record each welt, bruise, and blister. Two other cops in uniform stood around, admiring the wet bar, every liquor under the sun in miniature airline bottles. Cops always travel in packs.

"Jake, oh Jake, thank God you're here. It was so awful."

Pam Metcalf stood and rushed to me, throwing her arms around me. If she noticed that my face looked like steak tartare, she didn't mention it. I held her. It was impossible to do anything else. I felt her tears against my neck.

Detective Sigorsky said, "That will be all, Dr. Metcalf, unless you want to add anything."

Pam just shook her head.

I eased up on her padded shoulders. "What happened?"

She shook her head again, tears streaming from her green flinty eyes.

"A freak accident," Sigorsky said.

Behind me Nick Wolf chuckled. "A freak's accident is more like it."

The detective continued: "Dr. Metcalf was treating the subject for psychological disorders related to her . . . or rather, his sexual-identity confusion. Did I get that term right, doctor?"

"Gender-identity disorder. Possible schizophrenia."

"Maybe he wasn't used to walking in those high heels," Sigorsky said. "Lord knows, I have trouble with them; maybe he wasn't watching and he stepped in the door track, the heel broke, he fell forward and flipped over the railing." Sigorsky shrugged and smiled a rueful smile. "We've had some of those spring-break college kids go off balconies, but usually they're trying to climb from floor to floor when they're all liquored up. Now a shoe does it. I tell you, it gets weirder every day."

I heard Charlie Riggs's voice. *Accident, suicide, homicide, and natural.*

Pam gathered herself and sat down again. Nick Wolf came up and nudged me. "Hey, Jakie, know a good lawyer, maybe sue the shoe manufacturer, or the hotel, eh?"

I ignored him.

"Too bad the little jockey won't be around to collect the settlement," Nick continued.

"What's that mean?" I asked. "What happened to Max?"

"Nothing till the grand jury meets Monday. Then I'd say he'll be indicted for Murder One, just like you said."

"No. I was wrong. Bobbie did the killing."

"Jakie, shut up and take some praise. You ain't gonna hear it for long. You were right the first time. Old Max couldn't handle Bobbie's flings. He'd tail her, wait around, and just after she left, he'd go to the door, knock, and imitate her voice. He's pretty good at it, if you want to hear. Then he'd push his way in. With that jockey's quickness, he was on them in an instant. Manual strangulation. When he came over here and saw his so-called bride like that, he just broke down. Said he wanted to talk. Confessed to killing the Newcomb girl and Prissy. He's in a room down the hall giving a sworn statement right now. We Mirandized him ten ways from Sunday, but he refused a lawyer. Wish they were all like that."

"I don't believe it."

"Don't worry, Jake. You'll get the credit for breaking the case. It may help you."

"But Bobbie . . . her poetry. It cried out with her guilt."

Pam Metcalf was shaking her head. "Oh Jake, that's the problem with laymen thinking they're analysts. The poetry expressed her psyche's guilt, her confusion about her sexual identity, but had nothing to do with her actions. Fantasies, Jake, nothing more."

Now they both looked at me. Why was I so out of it? But something else was bothering me now. Sometimes, my brain rolls a thought around like a chrome pinball, bouncing off the bumpers before finding the hundred-point socket.

"What did you mean, Nick, it might help me?"

"With the judge, Jakie. One of the crime-scene boys found a Smith and Wesson bodyguard .38 in the bushes outside Rodriguez's house. Blue steel with the checkered walnut stock. Three bullets still in the cylinder, two fired. Serial number matches the gun assigned to you, my friend. The gun had two sets of latents. Want to know whose?"

I already had a pretty good idea, but Nick just kept going.

"One set matched Dr. Metcalf's, who was kind enough to lend us her pinkies."

She looked at me. "A dicey situation, Jake. They asked me not to tell you."

"One set matched yours," Wolf said, "which we took when you were sworn in. We dug a .38 caliber bullet out of Alex's bed. Ballistics fires the gun, and guess what, it's the murder weapon. Are you with me, Jake, or you want I should slow down?"

I just glared at him, and he continued: "Now we know that Dr. Metcalf fired only one shot. Who fired the other one, Jake?"

"You've got to be kidding."

"Where were you yesterday, Jake?"

"You can't be serious."

"Okay, I'll tell you. In the morning, you were in this very hotel suite, and at about eleven you caused a hell of a scene out front when you got your clock cleaned by a shrimp who used to ride the ponies at Hialeah and for the last few years pretended to be married to a broad with a dick. From there you went to Mercy Hospital for X-rays, but you were out of there by twelve-thirty. You didn't get to your office until two o'clock, spent maybe twenty minutes there, and got to Rodriguez's house at about three, when you called me upon allegedly finding the body. That about right?"

"Yeah, what of it?"

"ME says Rodriguez was shot between noon and three, most likely around one P.M. Where were you, Jake?"

"Home changing clothes. I try not to mix blood and plaid in the office."

"Great. Somebody corroborates that, you'll beat the rap."

"I live alone. Not even a parakeet. You know that. I've got no witnesses. Look, somebody must have stolen the gun from Cindy's place. Go pick up Tom Cat. C'mon, Nick. I didn't kill Rodriguez, and you know it. Why would I kill him?"

Wolf showed me his wise, political smile. "You and Rodriguez were rivals in the investigation. I'd seen you argue, myself. You both sought my approval, wanted to be my right-hand man in the new administration. . . ."

"What new administration?"

"Don't you read that daily fish wrapper? I announced yesterday for governor, Jakie."

"Sorry, I been busy killing detectives, fell behind on my current events."

Wolf gave the cops his sad, tolerant look. *See what I have to put up with.* "Still the wise-ass, aren't you? I should take you in right now, Jakie. Call a press conference. Your pals at the *Journal* have been mighty friendly ever since I leaked the story on Compu-Mate. But considering your clean record, if you'll agree not to leave town and to let me know at all times where you are, and I mean call my office every hour, I'll wait. Who knows, maybe the grand jury won't indict. Maybe they'll think some phantom stole your gun and killed the guy that stood between you and your career goal."

"Are you fucking insane? You're setting me up, you phony bullshit artist. My career goal? Shining your shoes in Tallahassee, reminding you to zip up when you come out of the john. What the fuck is going on here?"

I stepped toward him. The two deputies had some quickness for guys who had a liter of booze in their pants, all in three-ounce bottles. Each grabbed a wrist. But there was nothing wrong with my arms, and I shook one off the left and used it to hook the other one in the gut. He wheezed and fell back. I took two more steps toward Nick, who had drawn his weapon from a shoulder holster.

I stared down the barrel of his service revolver. It looked like a cannon. Then I saw his face. He was ready to squeeze. I was a problem for him, just like Lieutenant Evan Ferguson, and in a second I could be just as dead. I wondered if he would see my face in his sleep. I put my hands over my head.

"Now, we could tack on simple assault and resisting arrest with violence if we wanted to," Wolf said, "but I'm cutting you a break, Jakie. Stay out of trouble over the weekend, and I'll be in touch.

Remember, I'm your friend. Maybe I can even come up with a way to help you out. Maybe I can still teach you."

"Teach me what, you miserable fuck?"

He smiled. So wise, so kind. "To keep your ass down, Jakie. Before it gets shot off."

CHAPTER 40

The Source

Friday came and went. It was a day of oppressive heat, and I lay in the hammock strung between live oak and chinaberry trees in my backyard jungle of overgrown weeds and bushes. I wore canvas shorts and nothing else and let the sweat trickle down my chest as I thought it over.

And over.

They had it nailed down pretty good.

Item one: Max kills Rosemary Newcomb and Priscilla Wolf. No doubt there. In tortured mourning, Max spills his guts.

Item two: Bobbie trips over the raised track of the sliding door and cartwheels to the pool deck. Clumsy in those high heels, the lady detective said. But I had seen Bobbie gliding through life on four-inch sticks, and they suited her like fins on a fish.

Item three: An envious lawyer named Jacob Lassiter uses his government-issued .38 to kill a homicide detective, then conveniently drops the weapon in the bushes. Oh, come on, good and true citizens of the grand jury, you will see through that malarkey, won't you? No. Because a grand jury is the tool of the prosecutor, and if one of those eighteen faithful citizens asks the question, smiling Nick Wolf will be ready.

"It was not a carefully planned execution," Wolf will say. "Perhaps they argued, Lassiter becomes enraged. He is a former football player prone to sudden violence. You have heard the testimony of Dr. Metcalf and Mr. Carruthers as to his propensity for unprovoked aggression. Without warning, Lassiter shoots his rival for a high government position. Panicked, he flees, discarding the weapon. Ladies and gentlemen, murderers act irrationally. If they did not, we might never apprehend them."

Oh well, under that scenario, it's only second degree.

All buttoned up tight. Bodies get buried, files closed, Blinderman and Lassiter imprisoned, and Nick Wolf becomes the governor.

But how tight is it? *Somebody* killed Michelle Diamond. Did everybody forget about her? That was how I got into this. Investigate Diamond's murder and prosecute the bad guy. Only I didn't find the bad guy. Instead, I managed to get myself framed for somebody else's murder. And with that thought, I had a cold Grolsch and dozed off in the muggy shade of my infinitesimal slice of the planet Earth.

Saturday arrived, just as hot, just as sticky. My leg and foot were healing in the steaminess. My face looked better, though I hadn't shaved in three days and I needed a trim, shaggy hair covering the ears, flapping down the neck. Lying on the warm, crinkly grass I did fifty stomach crunches, twenty one-armed push-ups, first right then left, then used both arms for fifty more. I gave myself the rest of the day off and resumed my place of contemplation in the hammock, two cold beers to battle the elements.

I thought about Alex Rodriguez. I remembered the phone message. *Got story for your friends at the paper, on the record this time.*

This time.

Last time was Compu-Mate.

Or was it? What was it Nick Wolf said yesterday? The folks at the *Journal* were mighty friendly since *he* leaked the story on Compu-

Mate. I had always assumed Rodriguez was the source. If he wasn't, when did Nick talk to the paper and why?

I called Symington Foote at home, got him out of the pool where he was doing his laps. His phone was in his cabana on a waterfront pool deck. I pictured him dripping onto the turquoise tile.

"I never know the identity of confidential sources," he said formally. "House rules. The publisher doesn't interfere with the newsroom."

"Are any of your investigative reporters working on projects involving the sheriff's department?"

"I don't think so."

"What about the state attorney's office?"

In the background I heard a powerboat going too fast in the channel behind Foote's home. The speed-crazy weekenders are slaughtering our manatees, those big, slow, lumpy mammals of our waterways. After a moment Foote answered. "Henry Townsend's been looking into Nick Wolf for more than a year, but you know that."

"I thought that was over when we lost the libel suit."

"Townsend's still poking around, trying to turn up something we can go with, somebody on the record who knows the story behind the campaign financing."

"Who's his source?"

"Don't know."

"Can you have him at your house in an hour?"

"I can, but he won't tell—"

I had hung up. I stripped off yesterday's sweaty shorts and headed for the shower. I turned it up hot, lathered my old battered body, which didn't feel that bad after all. I smeared shaving cream on my face and chopped off the stubble. I washed my hair and combed it straight back and left it wet. Then I put on white jeans, white sneakers, white socks, and a white polo shirt. I looked in the mirror. A spanking-clean, overgrown, blue-eyed angel. Good. I could grow horns later.

The Olds purred on the way to Gables Estates, the ritzy waterfront enclave south of Coconut Grove. A canopy of banyan trees cooled Old Cutler Road and the breeze dried my hair. In the yards of Miami's privileged, the petals of red hibiscus flowers were opening for the day. Timed sprinklers watered sprawling lawns despite almost daily thunderstorms. On Symington Foote's handsome grounds, a gardener fertilized lush beds of impatiens as delicate hummingbirds flitted around the flowers of cape honeysuckle bushes. The flagstone path to the house was bordered by white gardenias, their rich fragrance filling the morning air.

It was a glorious Saturday, the day before a game, and I was getting ready. *Life is war,* Nick Wolf had told me. Now all I needed were the weapons.

They sat under a lime-green umbrella on an immense patio behind Foote's gleaming postmodern house. The house was a series of stark white boxes of different sizes connected at odd angles by concrete passageways painted highway-marker orange. It was the creation of a trendy Argentine architect who won several awards given by people who live in SoHo lofts. Foote once confided that he hated the place, especially the fact that you couldn't get to the downstairs bathroom without either going up one set of stairs and down another or walking outside and coming in another door. When he complained, the architect told him he was missing the point of our disjointed, fragmented lives. The point, Foote replied, was that he had to roam his property just to take a piss.

Henry Townsend was thirty-five and rangy, with a hawk's nose and a mortician's smile. His eyes were dark and knowing, his hair parted in the middle. He wore running shoes, khaki pants, and a T-shirt that said, "Reporters Do It with Any Type." He sat, drinking a margarita in the boss's polyurethane-lacquered deck chair, as if he owned the place.

Symington Foote wore gold boxer-style swim trunks and a matching terry-cloth jacket with pockets. His white hair was wet and his forehead speckled from too much sun.

We exchanged pleasantries and I asked Townsend whether he was looking into the activities of our esteemed state attorney.

"I don't talk about investigative pieces," he said, with journalistic self-righteousness.

Symington Foote cleared his throat. "Hank, treat Jake as you would your publisher."

"That's what I'm doing," Townsend replied, then sipped at his green drink.

Reporters are like that. Professional cynics who play pinochle in the courthouse press room and crack wise in the middle of rape trials and executions. A bunch of gunslingers who love spitting tobacco in the boss's eye. Get fired, just pack up the portable—computer, these days—and mosey on to the next town.

"Think of this as prepublication libel review," I told Townsend.

"Fine. When I've got a first draft, I'll call you."

"Maybe if you had last time, I could've swung a defense verdict."

His tongue was flicking the salt off the rim of the glass. "The editors chopped the story to shit."

Reporters are like that, too. Every fuck-up is blamed on the editors.

"As I recall the discovery," I said, "the editing took out the most serious allegations. The paper would have been hit harder if they'd printed your stuff. What was it, alleged ties between Wolf and major drug dealers?"

"Drug money financed his campaigns. We only published the details of technical campaign law violations, and we substantiated them. Plus there was one unattributed reference to a cash contribution that was drug-related. I couldn't get the source to come forward, so we got nailed."

"Who was the source?"

He dismissed me with the wave of a hand. "Forget it. I gave my pledge of confidentiality."

I was ready to give him my pledge of a broken face, but I decided to stick with the nice-guy routine. "What else did the source tell you?"

Townsend looked toward Foote, who nodded. "Lots that I couldn't use without backup documents or a second source. Dynamite stuff. I needed corroboration up the kazoo and didn't have anything. If I had, the headline would have said, 'State Attorney Tool of Medellín Drug Cartel.'"

"An attention grabber," I conceded. "What's behind it?"

Townsend must have felt he'd already made his point about keeping secrets. Now, he was practically squirming to tell what he knew. "It goes like this. A thousand years ago, Wolf was a low-level heroin courier in Vietnam. He comes home and makes some interesting connections as a street cop. By the time he runs for state attorney, he's an ass-kissing buddy of the first-team All-Pro Colombia cocaine kingpins. Lehder, Ochoa, Escobar—you name 'em, he played footsie with 'em. They finance his campaign, plus deliver cash to him on the side. We're talking a few million, walking-around money for them, but a fortune for a guy on the public payroll. He's a good soldier. He keeps the little house and plays the role of the hardworking civil servant. He bides his time. They give him inside information on rival drug dealers so he can make some cases, get his picture taken standing on a boatload of contraband."

"Phony hero," I said, stirring up memories.

"Yeah. It's part of a long-range plan. Build Wolf up. Along the way he has to return some favors. If someone close to the cartel gets busted, he'll give them something that can tank the case. Maybe the identity of an informant who then meets with an unfortunate accident, that sort of thing. Mostly, he trades in information. He keeps in touch with the feds. Anything he learns from Customs, Strike Force, or DEA, he delivers to the cartel. You can't buy information like that."

"Sure you can."

"Right, well, anyway, the long-range plan was to keep Wolf in the public eye, win some cases as the crusading, drug-busting prosecutor, get him elected governor. Then, who knows, president someday."

"*The Manchurian Candidate*," I said, remembering my earliest thoughts about Nick.

"Yeah, bizarre, isn't it? Create an image exactly opposite of reality."

"Truth and illusion. Distinguishing the two is your job, Townsend, and mine."

"Well, I was still working on my source, trying to get him to go on the record. He claimed to have documents, cables in code, bank accounts in the Caymans and Panama in Nick's name."

It was all starting to fit together. "When's the last time you talked to the source?"

"A week ago. Said he would think about it. Then . . ."

"Then what?"

"I can't say."

"I can. Then he got shot, right? Somebody took him out. Does your pledge of confidentiality survive his death?"

He looked a question at the publisher, didn't get an answer, and said, "Even if your supposition is correct, I could not confirm—"

While he was busy not confirming, I came out of my chair and grabbed him by his T-shirt. I yanked him to his feet and drew his face close to mine.

"Jake!" Symington Foote was profoundly unhappy with his legal representation. "I hardly think this is necessary. . . ."

I ignored him and tightened my grip on Townsend. "Tell me his name! Tell me, you sanctimonious son of a bitch or I'll give you a headline: 'Reporter Drowns in Publisher's Pool.'"

His eyes showed fear, but he shook his head. I dragged him across the patio toward the deep end of Foote's splendid twenty-five-meter pool. Foote let out a yelp. I hoisted Townsend over a shoulder, then dangled him by the ankles, dunking his head. He thrashed around and I hauled him up, sputtering, and he called me several names they don't print in a family newspaper. I lowered him again.

"Now see here, Jake," Foote was saying from behind me.

I saw very clearly. I saw my six-figure retainer slipping away and didn't care.

I let Townsend stay under long enough to consider a career change, then pulled him out, choking and gagging. I dropped him into a chaise lounge, where he burped up a couple of jiggers of chlorinated water, and then I asked again. "Who is he?"

He hawked and coughed and wheezed and finally said, "You know. You already know, you bastard."

I knew I knew. I had to hear the name. "Say it!"

"Alejandro Rodriguez."

"Why did he talk to you? What was his motive?"

He drank in some air. "I don't know. That's not my department."

"Then how do you know Rodriguez was telling the truth?"

The sound was half gag, half laugh. "We never know that. We just print what people tell us. It's not our job to tell the public what to believe. We just give them choices."

Sunday. A breeze from the east tickled the leaves of the live-oak trees. Just a breath of air, but it makes a difference. I called the weekend crew at the state attorney's office every hour like a guy on house arrest. I thought a lot about Nick Wolf. I needed to trip him up, to bait him and trap him. I couldn't call Metro because there was no telling who was loyal to him, and the feds would take too long. I thought of the logistics and came up with a plan. But it would take two of us, and one had to be somebody Wolf wouldn't recognize. That left out Charlie Riggs, the only person I trusted completely other than my granny. So where did that leave me?

I lay in the hammock again and thought about Michelle Diamond. TV Gal, I've let you down. Been too wrapped up in saving my own semiprecious hide. I walked into the house, pulled out three cardboard boxes, my copies of the Diamond file. I reread the printouts. Bobbie Blinderman had chatted with Michelle, pitching crude woo, but got shot down. A short time later, Michelle gets strangled. I read the rest of them—Oral Robert, Bush Whacker, and the other cheap-thrill hackers.

I found the photos Dr. Whitson had taken of the scene. There was Michelle, head jammed into the monitor. There were scenes of the room. There were the close-ups of the body, and the shots of Pam and me, Charlie demonstrating the fallacy of the crescentic fingernail abrasion. There were a variety of shots of the room itself, Nick Wolf pacing in the background.

I spread all the photos on the floor, moving some empty pizza cartons out of the way. I tried different arrangements. All body shots here, all room shots there. I arranged them by field of view. Long shots here, close-ups there.

Then here.

Then there.

And there it was. Where it had been all along.

CHAPTER 41

Kiss Me Quick Before I Die

The grand jury would convene at nine A.M. Monday, take up old business, and approve a report on the sorry state of the county's juvenile detention facilities. The jurors would break at noon and reconvene at 1:30 to hear new cases including *In re Alejandro Rodriguez.* Which would soon become *State of Florida* v. *Jacob Lassiter.*

At 7:30 P.M. Sunday, I called Wolf's office and left a new message with the weekend crew: *Leaving for Rio on nine o'clock flight.* Five minutes later, my phone rang.

I picked it up and said, "Hello, Nick, what took you so long?"

"I'm glad you're there, asshole. I want to talk to you. Maybe we can work something out."

"Wonderful. Great, Nick," I slavered, gratitude and humility coating my voice like honey.

"I'll be there in an hour."

"I won't be here," I said.

"What?"

"I'm going fishing."

"Are you nuts?"

"Snook are running, or at least swimming."

"Don't jerk me off, Lassiter. The grand jury's going to hear—"

"Nighttime bridge fishing, good for the soul. I'll be on the MacArthur Causeway just east of the tender's shack. I'll have an extra spinning rod."

Then I hung up and didn't answer the phone when it rang ten seconds later. Twenty minutes later, I was putting my gear in the trunk when it rang again. I went inside, lifted the receiver, and listened.

"Hello, Jake, is that you, darling?"

The crisp British accent that first sucked me in.

"It's me, darling," I said.

"Oh Jake, I wanted to say good-bye."

"Good-bye?"

"I just finished my last lecture and I'm booked on the red-eye to Heathrow."

Whoa. Too much was happening too fast. I couldn't deal with both of them at once.

"Can't you stay a little longer?"

"Would that I could. We could spend some time together, perhaps rekindle that spark." Her voice tinkled with promises. "But my work calls."

"Wait. Where are you?"

"On Miami Beach, at Mount Briar Hospital."

"Great. On your way to the airport you can stop and say a proper good-bye. I'll be on the causeway. Fishing."

"Fishing?"

Why didn't anyone believe me?

I told her where and said nine-thirty, and she'd still have time to catch the flight.

And then I went to find some bait.

The moon was three-quarters full and rising over the ocean. Silky moonbeams flashed across the surface of the bay and bounced off the steel and concrete of the bridge. I had watched the late summer sun set, dangling over the Everglades, the sky tinged vermilion from the foul breath of our two million cars, most of which seemed to be passing on the bridge just now. Carbon monoxide hung heavy and low, the air was soggy with heat and moisture, and I wondered why anyone would fish here. It was like jogging in the Lincoln Tunnel.

I wore jeans and a sleeveless vest. On the vest was a lamb's-wool patch festooned with flies. Streamers and poppers and super bugs and flipping shrimp, and my all-time favorite, the cockroach. I held a stout rod with a heavy butt and an open-face spinning reel, and if Nick Wolf wanted to fish, I had another one, too.

Four lanes of traffic rattled the bridge, cars heading from downtown Miami to South Beach and back again. I stood on the catwalk near the tender's shack, just off the steel grating of the drawbridge itself. The metal hummed and sang with each passing tire. Kids on bicycles rode along the catwalk, and a collection of old coots sat in lawn chairs, digging bait out of tin cans and dropping their lines into the water. Near the lower portions of the bridge, weekend shrimpers shone their flashlights toward the bottom and swung fine-meshed, long-handled nets into the water. Two swarthy men in T-shirts angled their casts near the shrimpers. Fish are attracted to shrimp, and fishermen aren't far behind. Ten feet from me, a guy who needed a shave and a bath dangled a pole over the side. He had already borrowed some pinfish for bait and was now asking if I had any mullet. When he came close, the smell of cheap wine overpowered the tang of the bait. Despite the heat he wore a heavy plaid work shirt and a cap with earflaps pulled down.

"T'ank you kindly, guv'nor," he said.

At five before nine Nick Wolf's impressive bulk appeared over the rise of the bridge. He was backlit by the powerful vapor lamps on the eastern tower. He wore a light gray suit and was alone. He arrived a moment later, sweating and furious.

"You're a first-class number-one asshole, Lassiter."

"Good evening to you, too," I said.

"I parked at the marina and walked a mile in this heat, a man could have a heart attack."

"Most men would take their suit coats off."

"There are voters who use this bridge," he said. "They expect me in a suit."

"Image," I said.

"Don't knock it. It may not get the job done, but it makes it possible to get the job done."

"What's the job, Nick? Besides getting elected?"

"Law and order. Sending away your basic shitheads. Making streets safe for little old ladies and children coming home from school. Locking up your burglars and your strong-arm robbers."

"And your drug barons," I said. "Let's not forget about them."

He studied me. "We didn't come here to talk about my work. What the fuck's going on?"

I baited my hook, raised the rod, flicked my wrist, and watched the twenty-pound test line drop toward the water in a poor imitation of a cast. "Told you. Wanted to fish. When the tide starts in, I think my luck's going to change."

He studied my outfit. "What the hell are those flies for? You can't use 'em up here, you'll give an earring to some asshole in a Benz convertible."

"Flies are just for decoration. Like your medals."

"I'm trying to help you out, Jakie. Don't fight me."

"Help me out! That's a hoot. You framed me for the Rodriguez murder."

He studied me. "I can get you out of it. I'm willing to compromise my position to help you."

"What are you talking about?"

Just then the distinctive aroma of rotgut breath invaded our space. "'Scuse me, gentlemen, could you spare a shrimp?"

"The fuck out of here!" Wolf ordered, and my wino friend shrank away.

"You killed Rod," Wolf said, "and I'm ready to cut a deal with you."

"No. You killed him, and I'm going to nail you."

"You are so fucking stupid, Lassiter. Why would I kill Rodriguez? He was my friend."

"So was Evan Ferguson."

He took a step toward me, thought better of it, and looked around.

"What's the matter, Nick, too many voters here?"

"Okay, asshole, you got something to say, say it."

I took a deep breath and loaded my ammo. I only had one round. "I know all about you and the Medellín cartel. I know about the prosecutions you tanked and the information you passed to Bogotá. I know about the bank accounts in the Caymans and Panama and just about everything else that could put you away. And in case you're thinking about using that howitzer under your coat, everything gets delivered to the *Journal* in case I miss my breakfast meeting tomorrow."

Nick Wolf didn't call me an asshole and he didn't pull his gun. His bluster was just for effect. I had tried enough cases to know that. Now it was all business, Wolf trying to figure if I had the proof to back up the allegations. What cards does the guy with the fishing rod hold?

A minute passed. He still hadn't said a word. A second minute that seemed like a year. The bridge rattled under our feet as the cars thundered past. Three hundred yards away in the channel, a fully rigged custom Swan, maybe fifty feet, tooted its horn three times. The bridge tender pushed a button, the yellow lights flashed, and a moment later, the traffic gates lowered and the bridge began its slow ascent.

Finally Nick Wolf said, "Rodriguez told you all this."

"Yep."

"Just words, and hearsay at that. Just a dead man's words."

Already he had considered the evidence and decided I had nothing admissible. So I bluffed. "Plus photocopies, microfilm, and a bunch of bank records he delivered to me for the paper."

That stopped him, but only for a second. "Bullshit. He never had access to the accounts."

Confirmation. Instead of denying it, just letting me know I couldn't prove anything.

"Never? You never sent him to pick up cash, make a deposit. While he's there, maybe a friendly banker gives him what he wants in exchange for a tip."

He chewed it over. It must have made sense. "That shithead Rodriguez! That simpleminded fuck."

And this is how he talks about his friends, I thought.

"Once Prissy was killed, Rodriguez cracked," Wolf said. "He

loved her, always loved her. When we broke up, I gave him the go-ahead. But she wasn't interested in him except as a friend. He was still hoping and groping until she was killed. I should have figured he'd do something like this. He never wanted a piece of the action. Wanted to live a simple life as a cop. I was gonna make him head of a statewide crime commission. Supervisory powers over all capital cases. The best investigators, the latest equipment. I needed to get elected, that's all, and I needed a middleman for the financing."

"To tote your bags, to haul your drug money. To aid and abet you in selling out your office. Maybe he got tired of it."

"Drugs are bullshit, Jakie. Read the papers. Federal judges, congressmen, your egghead professors are all calling for legalization. We can't stop the flow. We close down Colombia, they move to Peru and Ecuador. Christ, they're manufacturing in Europe now. We seal off the Bahamas for transit, they move to Mexico. We put on the heat in Miami as a port of entry, they come in through Texas and North Carolina. Forget drugs. It's like booze. You can't stop it if the people want it."

"You can rationalize anything, can't you, Nick? Killing your best friend, selling out your office, framing me."

There was a tug on my line, then a leap, and a silver fish with a black streak from gills to tail took off. The wrong way. It headed under the bridge. Snook. Maybe twelve pounds. I yanked on the rod and tried to drive it out. Too late. It had fouled the line on a piling. I jerked the rod this way and that and then the line broke free.

"Damn shame, guv'nor," said rotgut breath from a few feet away.

Wolf was thinking. I didn't know what, but I was hoping. He didn't disappoint me. "Okay, let's assume you have what you say you have. All the more reason we work this out. You have something I want. Two somethings, as it turns out. I hold your keys to the jailhouse. You give me the Vietnam log plus whatever documents Rodriguez gave you, and you've got a free pass."

The Swan had putted through, its mast towering above us. Inside the shack, the tender pulled a huge lever and the bridge lowered again.

"I've already got a free pass. I didn't do it. You did. You had me under surveillance at Cindy's apartment. When I limped home, you took the gun. Then you killed Rodriguez and planted it."

He gripped the handrail and stared toward the flickering lights downtown. "Jake, think about it. I didn't know the asshole talked to you. I never suspected. It was suicidal for him. He'd have to do time. Look, I've been straight with you. I told you I killed Evan Ferguson. I ran dope out of 'Nam, and I skimmed shipments here when I was a cop. As a prosecutor, I dumped some cases, and I took major-league bread from some very bad actors because I had other priorities. But I never killed Rodriguez. . . ."

Over the rise of the drawbridge appeared a figure shimmering in the artificial light. Pamela Metcalf.

Oh shit. Early. Just when I was getting ready to lower the boom. I couldn't deal with both of them at once.

Wolf saw her, too. "Hey, Jakie, isn't that your English squeeze?"

She wore a beige linen suit and matching shoes and pursed her lips walking across the steel grating of the catwalk. She called to me: "Jake, my cab is at the end of the bridge. Double-parked. I must say, this is a most unconventional meeting place. And I must catch—"

"A lady in our midst," proclaimed the old wino, bending from the waist and extending an arm.

"Dr. Metcalf," Nick acknowledged, nodding. "Perhaps I shouldn't say this, but you have the greatest legs I've ever seen, and I've seen them from here to Hong Kong."

Pam nodded politely but kept her eyes on me. "Well, Jake, you seem to have drawn us together in this hellhole. What is the purpose of it?"

"I wanted to tell you a story. Nick, you might as well listen, too."

Pam cocked a hip and pouted. "Jake, really. It's stifling and smelly"—she looked toward old fishbait nearby—"and I have to catch—"

"A short story about a beautiful woman. She grew up in the English countryside, a picture-postcard place. But she was unable to resolve what they call the positive Oedipal complex. She couldn't transfer her love for her father onto other men. At the same time she hated her mother's promiscuity, which had driven Father off. She once told me, 'Never underestimate the damage a mother can do.' So she had a horrible dilemma. She was attracted to other girls, yet hated them for it, especially their heterosexual promiscuity, which reminded her of Mother. She began experimenting with homosexuality while a teen, and when she learned that her lovers, also country girls, had taken up with boys, too . . ."

"You're no good at this, Jake," she said, an edge to her voice. "You're just as wrong about me as you were about Bobbie."

"We'll get to her in a minute. Let's cut to the chase. The heroine of our story killed two of the Cotswolds girls, strangled them in their barns or pastures or wherever they met to entangle limbs. The experience fascinated and repelled her at the same time."

"Jesus, Jake," Nick said, "what's going on?"

"Shut up for once and listen. This girl was different than most psychopaths. She wanted to stop, really wanted to be normal. And maybe she could. After all, we are all born psychopaths. Maybe she could find the emergency brake. And she was smart enough to learn everything there was about the subject. Study, become a doctor, a psychiatrist. Spend years interviewing serial killers, dissecting their psyches, staffing mental wards. And for a while it worked. She ran group therapy and no one knew she was one of the patients. Except maybe the *real* patients. What was it the Fireman said? That she wasn't my type, only I didn't know it yet.

"She'd take an occasional male lover and tried to convince herself that everything was in sync. But sometimes she drifted back to those early days in a hayloft in the Cotswolds. And the urges returned. To love and to kill. Finally she found radical psychiatry. She stopped delving into the reasons why. After all, the unconscious is a myth. There's no such thing as mental illness. Her choices were as rational as those of an officer who killed his best friend on a rainy day in a muddy village far from home."

Wolf's eyes hardened and he started to say something, but I kept going. "So now she finds occasional lovers, and when they stray, they die. But it's suspicious if your girlfriends keep dropping off. So she controls it, maybe confines the killing to her travels. If we studied her passport and air tickets, what correlations would we find? An unsolved murder of a young woman killed in Paris, Barcelona—who knows, Miami Beach? And the corpses, some evidence of sexual activity, but of course, never any semen."

"Jesus H. Christ," Nick Wolf breathed. "You got any proof of this?"

"At a homicide scene on Miami Beach a young assistant ME

shoots enough pictures to make a family album. It's good training. You never know what you'll find. He takes close-ups of Michelle Diamond's neck. He thinks he can tell if a strangler is right-handed or left-handed from the crescents. Charlie Riggs sets him straight. No big deal. Charlie notices that one of the crescents isn't a crescent at all. It's jagged because of a torn nail. But that's no big deal either, because it'll grow back in a few days. No use looking for a guy with a hangnail. It's not like DNA, where your genes are your genes for life. Then Whitson takes shots of all the spectators, including one of Pam Metcalf squeezing my forearm and a close-up of the marks. Nobody pays attention to anything but the reversal of the crescents. And that's all you can see until you blow it up to an eight-by-ten and compare it to the enlargements of Michelle's neck. They match, Nick, four crescents and one jagged edge."

I opened my tackle box and showed Nick Wolf the blowups. He held the photos in the light of the tower and studied them. Then he grimaced. "This shit won't hold up. There can be ten thousand people with a busted nail. This ain't fingerprints. Jake, you're off the deep end again."

"Nick," I said, "do me a favor and shut the fuck up."

Pam was forcing a condescending smile. I hadn't gotten through to her, and Nick wasn't helping.

"I should have seen it earlier, but I couldn't or didn't want to. But it was there all the time. She has a good grip, really dug her nails into me. Maybe her hands aren't as strong as a jockey's. No fractured larynx, but she was strong enough to cut off the air, squeeze Michelle into unconsciousness, and from there into death. Then there was the lipstick message on the bathroom mirror. 'Catch me if you can, Mr. Lusk.' Who's the expert on Jack the Ripper? The lady from England, that's who. And how about a motive? Insane jealousy. Infidelity infuriated her, and she found Michelle sweet-talking on her computer just after they made love. What was it Jack the Ripper wrote: 'I am down on whores and I shan't quit ripping them till I do get buckled.' They were all whores to Pam Metcalf, too. But one thing kept bothering me. Why did Michelle Diamond get out of bed with one lover—a lover who left no trace of semen—and start seeking another on the computer?"

Nick Wolf shrugged. Pam Metcalf looked away.

"Because Michelle knew this lover was just passing through, a one-night stand who was heading back across the Atlantic. I wasn't listening, Nick, but the clues were everywhere. Maybe she wanted us to know. Even the title of her book, *The Murderer Within Us*. It was there, within her, now and always."

"Mr. Wolf," Pam said, "surely you don't believe—"

"It's my fault, Nick. I couldn't see. I was dumb enough to think she came back to be with me. She came back to be part of the investigation, to relive the murder, just like the ambulance driver who killed and rushed to pick up the body. It's a thrill, isn't it, Pam? Tell me, did you really want to be caught?"

"Madness!" she spat. "Sheer madness."

"But you were right about one thing, Pam," I said. "I fouled it up with Bobbie Blinderman. She wasn't a killer. She was a pathetic lost soul in search of herself. She didn't come to the hotel to kill you. She came to love you, to tell you there was nothing between us. You didn't have to do it."

"She fell," Pam said, "that's all."

"She never would have hurt you, and you knew it."

Pam turned away and stared across the water. The cruise ships were lined up at the seaport on the south side of Government Cut, thousands of tourists prepared for their seven days, six nights of prepackaged Caribbean fun. When Pam turned back, she said, "Bobbie already had hurt me with her slutty ways. I could have treated her, arranged for her operation, everything. But she couldn't help being a trollop, could she?"

"And you hated her for it, just as you hate your mother and you hate yourself. But you would never kill Mum and you would never kill yourself."

"I would never kill anyone, not even a strumpet who deserves no respect whatsoever."

Nick Wolf's head was bouncing back and forth. Finally the enormity sank in.

He grabbed my arm and said, "She killed them both?"

"That's what I've been trying to tell you," I said.

"Christ, the two of you are something. The broad kills my girlfriend and some she-male. The guy I hire kills my friend."

That stopped me.

He *really* thought I did it. He was willing to cut a deal to save his own skin, but he really thought I murdered Alex Rodriguez. *Which meant, of course, that Nick Wolf didn't kill him.*

Pam said, "As you just indicated, Mr. Wolf, you can't prove a thing. You have no—what do you call it?—hard evidence. Just the pathetic ramblings of a man I assure you is quite unbalanced. Now, this has really gone too far, and I have a plane to catch." The breeze was blowing her auburn hair into her eyes, and she brushed it away.

"Wait," I said, the fog in my mind beginning to lift. "Of course. Nick, was Rodriguez keeping you informed of everything he did in the Diamond investigation?"

"Sure. You told him not to, but he worked for me."

"Rodriguez wanted to interview Pam again. He told the professor. What do you know about it?"

"Fingerprints. She was never considered a suspect, but she was one of the last people to see Michelle alive. Rodriguez thought it was just covering the bases to get them. Compare with latents from the apartment. Apparently, he never did."

"No, she must have kept putting him off. But she couldn't just refuse to give him the prints. How would it look? At the same time she figured he was the only one interested, and if he wasn't around anymore . . ."

"You're quite mad," Pam said.

"I must be, to have gotten involved with you." She shot a glance toward the end of the bridge where her cab waited. I couldn't keep her from leaving, but as long as I kept talking I figured she would stay put. "The story's not over yet, so humor me. The problem is, she can't strangle a cop. Then she gets lucky. A gun drops into her lap, a .38 registered to me. Better yet, my fingerprints all over it. So are hers after she fires it, but that's fine, too. After we go to my place, I'm knocked out with the large economy-size dose of vodka and Darvon. She leaves to meet Bobbie but stops at Cindy's and picks up the gun. Next day or so, she calls Rodriguez, says she'll stop by his house, save them both some trouble. He could have a fingerprint kit there. He's expecting a helpful witness, but he gets a slug in the chest. Then she dumps the gun where it's sure to be found. Her prints are easily explained. One shot in the apartment, two witnesses. Second shot?

Must have been fired by that hothead Lassiter. Now I see, Nick. You didn't frame me. She did."

Again, three toots from an air horn. A big Bertram with a tuna tower was idling near the bridge. The tender hit his buttons and the traffic gate came down next to us.

Nick Wolf thought about it. "It's just crazy enough to be true, and easy enough to find out. Dr. Metcalf, we're going to check your prints against the latents from the apartment. If they don't match, you'll be free to go. If they match, I'm going to hold you on suspicion of the murders of Michelle Diamond and Alex Rodriguez. As for the death of Mrs. Blinderman, Jake's got his own ideas, but there's no proof, so that's between you and your Maker."

Pam Metcalf didn't stop to plea-bargain. She ducked under the traffic gate, ignoring flashing lights and warning signs in three languages, and headed up the bridge. She moved quickly, but the bridge had already started its jerky ascent. She stumbled after three steps, the heels of her beige pumps wedging into the steel gridwork, each opening big enough to swallow a man's fist. She fell to her knees, then kicked off her shoes. Regaining her balance, she started again, on all fours now, slowly climbing hand over hand.

The bridge tender saw what was happening and hit the air horn, which bleated a frantic warning. Drivers poured out of their cars, pointing, laughing at the crazy woman scaling the drawbridge. Others began honking their horns, cheering her on, the same yahoos who holler "jump" at the guy on the ledge. One middle-aged man leaped from his custom van, videocamera already running.

I called after her. "Pam! No. There's nowhere to run."

Nick Wolf grabbed me by the arm. "Let her go, Jake." I shook him off and moved closer to the foot of the rising span. As she climbed uphill the increasing grade slowed her. In a moment I knew she would never make it. The opening at the mouth yawned wider. She couldn't reach the top, and if she did, she couldn't jump it. So she hung there, a hundred feet from the base of the bridge, clinging to the steel grating with both hands, digging her bare feet into the open grids, poised at a precarious angle as the bridge shuddered even higher. Then she looked back over her shoulder at me. In the eerie green haze of the vapor lamps I could not make out her face. She was calling to me, but the cacophony of horns drowned her out.

I wasn't doing any good where I was, so I sprinted to the tender's shack and pounded on the wall. "Stop it! Bring it down."

I looked through the window, covered with a metal screen. The tender was on the far side of sixty, a skinny guy in a Yankees T-shirt, propped on a dirty pillow in an old wooden swivel chair. He pointed to the Bertram about to chug through the opening and shook his head. I didn't care about a rich guy's tuna tower. I tried the door. Locked. But it was peeling plywood, and one good shoulder caved it in. I faced the control panel, a series of black and red buttons, four three-foot levers.

"Which one?" I demanded. "How do I stop it?"

He froze, eyes widening. "Unless you're from DOT, you're not allowed—"

"Which one!"

"It's against regulations to—"

I grabbed the front of his shirt and lifted him from his chair. "Tell me!"

He was frightened senseless. I dropped him onto his pillow, my eyes skimming the control panel. Under a button covered with red plastic was a hand-lettered sign: EMERGENCY HYDRAULIC STOP. I smashed it with my fist and grabbed for the lever where the sign said, DESCEND, EAST SPAN. I leaned back and pulled. It didn't give.

"No!" the tender yelled. "It's got—"

I bent my knees, grabbed the lever with two hands, and yanked it toward me, hard. It jerked away like an ornery gearshift when you've missed the clutch, gave a bit, then pulled loose, and I nearly fell over backward.

"—to stop before you bring it down."

A hydraulic whoosh from deep inside the bridge slowed the huge piston that was pushing the span upward. A second later, from somewhere inside the motor, there was a clangor of metal. The span was just reaching its peak, and it jolted and quaked. Below us, in the belly of the mechanical beast, sparks shot from the motor housing, orange bursts reflecting off the water below. The span lurched to a stop, first pitching, then yawing, the vibrations reverberating through the metal. Beneath my feet I felt the main bridge sway.

I looked out the window of the shack. Pam Metcalf had lost her grip. She slid down twenty feet, her face scraping the metal. She caught hold again, a death grip on the hot steel. There was a grinding of gears, and the bridge shuddered again and began its descent, and again she lost hold. The Bertram gunned it and just made it through, a bare-chested fat man at the wheel blasting his air horn and screaming obscenities.

Pam's slide slowed, but still she could not hold on. She slid another ten feet and was bleeding from the nose and mouth, a crimson trail across the steel. Then the span shook once more and stopped dead, electrical sparks crackling from the heavy cables strung along the railing. From beneath us, a puff of gray smoke drifted like a cloud from the motor housing.

"Shorted out," the tender said, shaking his head mournfully. "I'll hook up the emergency generator, but it'll take a bit."

I ran from the shack. The drivers had stopped their honking. As the main bridge continued to sway they held their steering wheels in white-knuckled grips. A ten-foot gap separated the main bridge and the tilting span. Nick Wolf saw what I had in mind, moved toward me, and started to tell me to forget it, then changed his mind. If I didn't make it, so much the better for him. I ducked underneath the traffic gate, took three giant steps, and leaped across the gap, landing on all fours on the span. I scrambled upward like an overgrown monkey. When I stopped, I latched onto the grating with one hand to steady myself and reached up, toward her, with the other. She was ten feet above me and three feet to the side. An instant later, she lost her grip again.

She clawed at the grating as her slide began, and she called my name. "Jake!"

"I'm here, Pam."

"Jake, I can't hold on."

Still clinging to the grating with my left hand, I reached out with my right and caught her by a wrist. I pulled her up next to me, her feet dangling helplessly. I inched my hand up her arm, then slid it around her back, gripping the back of her head, pulling her face next to mine. Blood seeped from two gashes in her forehead, smeared her hair, and ran down her face. The back of her neck was clammy with cold sweat.

"Help me, Jake," she whimpered. The color had drained from

her cheeks. Her face was a ghostly pallor streaked with red. "Kiss me quick . . ."

Stunned, I didn't move. Clinging to me, she hoisted herself up and kissed me, at first softly, with parted lips, and then harder, our teeth scraping. I tasted the warm sweetness of her blood.

". . . before I die."

"Hush, now. I've got you. You're not going to—"

"Take me away, Jake. Don't let them—"

"I'm going to get you help. The best doctors, the best hospital, the best—"

Suddenly the span shuddered again and, with a clatter of meshing gears, began a slow, balky descent. She pulled away, digging her feet into the grating. She climbed out of my grasp, dragging herself up again. "I've seen the *best*, Jake. It doesn't work. I am what I am."

I caught her by an ankle, but she jerked it away. She clambered up, hand over hand.

"Pam, there's nowhere to go."

Still, she climbed toward the sky, and I followed, overtaking her a few feet from the top of the span. Hanging on again with one hand, I grabbed a handful of her hair and pulled her to me. As Pam turned she clenched her right hand into a claw and raked my face with her nails, now ripped by the steel. She drew four tracks of blood from my forehead to beneath each eye. Instinctively, I let go of her hair, my hand shooting to my face. My forearm collided with her shoulder, knocking her off balance, and I heard her gasp. She had lost her grip. I reached for her as she skidded by me and our hands touched, but only for an instant. I grabbed for her, but my timing was off, and she slid past me, her head glancing off the grating. Farther she fell, trying vainly to hold on, slowing down, but only for a moment. An instant later, she disappeared into the blackness between the raised span and the bridge.

I waited for the splash, but there was none.

There was no scream, no plea.

There was just the heavy, deadweight *thumpety-thump* of body on metal. I pressed my forehead into the hot steel and looked through the grating. In the milky reflection of the moon off the water below, I looked into the guts of the motor. She was pinned in the gear housing, feet first. Her face was twisted into a grotesque mask of fear. She extended an arm upward, toward me or toward heaven, I couldn't tell which. Slowly, the span descended, the gears churning, and her body disappeared into a mammoth, oily black-toothed wheel that groaned and creaked as it dragged her into an unseen crevice.

I heard her scream.

A piercing wail of pain.

And then silence except for the sound of the bridge itself.

I waited an eternity for the wheel to emerge from its turn. When it did, the crusted blackness ran wet with crimson. The wheel chinked and chawed and then clunked to a stop, spitting out shards of linen, obscenely red. It came to a stop and, with a final jangle, expelled the bony stump of an arm and a clenched fist.

I closed my eyes, said a silent prayer, and wondered if one without a conscience could have a soul. When I opened my eyes, the bridge had lumbered into place, and the gates lifted. I scrambled to the catwalk, cars zooming by, one nearly clipping me.

The old bridge tender was jabbering frantically into his phone. Nick Wolf leaned on the railing, mouth agape. "Jesus H. Christ," he said. "As bad as anything I saw in 'Nam." He took off his suit coat and ran a hand through his hair. "You're a little pale. You okay, Jake?"

I was not okay.

CHAPTER 42

Night
Vision

Charlie Riggs inserted the serrated knife at the base of the tail and sliced forward with a steady hand. He took care to avoid the razor-sharp bone at the outer edge of the gills. He cut off the gill plate and removed the stomach cavity. Then he slid what was left of the snook into the chicken-wire drawer of his homemade smoker, a six-foot-tall contraption with a brick floor, tarpaper roof, and cypress sides covered with wooden shim shingles. Charlie wore his hiking boots, old gray socks, a canvas hat, and khaki shorts with six pockets. He looked like a sixty-five-year-old Boy Scout.

I was wearing gray sweat pants, sneakers without socks, an old practice jersey, and an AFC Champions ball cap. I looked like an over-the-hill ex-jock. My job was to gather the wood and stay the hell out of the way. Get buttonwood or mangrove, Charlie commanded. Not hickory. If I had known this would be so much trouble, I would have chosen the veal porcini at Cafe Baci in the Gables. But Charlie wasn't

3 3 7

much for cream sauces with mushrooms and wine, and besides, he knew that making me work for my dinner was a form of therapy.

The trick with the fire is to keep it burning, but not too hot. The idea is to smoke the fish, not dry it out. When the fire was going just right, we sat there in Charlie's battered lawn chairs, watching the tangy smoke seep out of the roof. He was waiting for me to start, but I couldn't find the words. So finally he asked me, and I told him of a sweltering Sunday night on the bridge.

"I killed her," I told him finally. "She was reaching to me for help, and I tried to save her, but I killed her."

He thought it over before speaking. A great blue heron circled low overhead in the drifting smoke, its long legs swept back. "She didn't want to be saved, Jake. She probably didn't even want to live, given the choices available to her. As Pliny wrote, *Natura vero nihil hominibus brevitate vitae praestitit melius.*"

"Something about the brevity of life," I said, taking a stab at it.

"'Nature has granted mankind no better gift than the shortness of life.' Pamela Metcalf knew there was no cure for her. She knew better than anyone else what her remaining years would be like. Stop blaming yourself. You tried to save her."

The heron dropped its legs like the landing gear on a jumbo jet and drifted to the ground near the smoker. The big bird would settle for some fish innards in the scrap pile.

"No, Charlie, you don't understand. I really *killed* her. I've replayed the moment a thousand times. Trying to read my mind. It's harder than reading someone else's, but this is what I've come up with. I wanted her dead. In my mind I tried her and convicted her and sentenced her. And then I executed her. I just didn't know it at the time."

Storm clouds gathered in the west, and the wind was picking up. The temperature was falling in advance of a squall line. "The mind plays tricks on us all," Charlie said. "You don't know what you intended, Jake, trust me."

In the distance a thunderclap. "So much has happened," I said. "So much blood."

He let it hang there, and I rattled them off in my mind. Rosemary Newcomb and Priscilla Wolf dead at the hands of the insanely jealous ex-jockey. Michelle Diamond, Bobbie Blinderman, and Alejandro

Rodriguez dead, too, killed by Pamela Metcalf. And what about Pam, psychotic lady psychiatrist, a woman who moved me to—to what? I didn't know what. She was smart and beautiful . . . and homicidal. *Deceptio visus*, Charlie would say, and he was right. A deceptive vision, and I had only seen the illusion, not the truth.

"What about Nick Wolf?" Charlie asked. "What will happen to him?"

Two laughing gulls circled overhead, guffawing at us, and I told him all about Nick Wolf.

Police sirens were wailing from both sides of the causeway, Miami cops from the east, Beach cops from the west.

"Hey, we just have a minute, Jake," Nick Wolf had said. "Let's close. Shit, neither of us needs any trouble. Come on. Name your price. Special counsel to the governor. Beachfront estate on Grand Cayman. Ten percent of my take."

"Too late, Nick."

"Twenty percent. You name it."

"Nick, I can see now."

"What . . . ?"

"Night vision."

"What the fuck are you talking—"

"You were right about me. I couldn't see in the dark. The creepy crawlies come out at night, the beasties, too, and just like you said, they don't play by the rules. I don't like them, so I looked away. But now I see, and it's too late to close my eyes."

"Don't be an asshole. You've got nothing on me."

"Nothing but your own words. Say hello to the wire, Nick."

I pulled the hand-tied cockroach fly off my lamb's-wool patch. Underneath, where the hook should have been, was a tiny microphone. I said, "How'd we do, professor?"

Ten feet away Gerald Prince took off his earflapped hat and lifted his plaid work shirt. A pair of earphones were on his head. A miniature tape recorder was taped to his belly. "Despite the atrocious acoustics, the audio is quite acceptable, guv'nor," Prince said. Then he did a perfect impression of Nick Wolf: "'I told you I killed Evan Ferguson. I ran dope out of 'Nam, and I skimmed shipments here. I dumped some cases, and I took major-league bread from some very bad actors.'"

Wolf reached for his gun, just as I knew he would. Just as he did with Evan Ferguson. He didn't want to do it, but he had no choice. The hand was halfway out of the shoulder holster when I hit him with a straight left that made him blink. The gun clattered to the pavement. I followed with a right hand over the top that caught him on the point of the chin and sat him down. I rubbed my knuckles. Hitting hurts the hitter, but it's still better than being the hittee.

Two police cars pulled to a stop in front of the shack. The tender leaned out the door and stabbed a shaking finger toward us.

Nick felt his jaw and started to say something. Somehow he looked smaller. "I'm going be all right," he said. "I'll be okay."

There was bile in my throat and I told myself that my eyes stung from the wind.

"Who gives a shit?" I said.

Two big uniformed Miami cops took their sweet time getting out of their cars and walked toward us. They blocked traffic in both directions.

"I can cut a deal with the feds," Nick said. "I know all the major dealers in the southeast and who supplies them. I know staging areas and which ships haul which shit. I'll be in the witness protection program in two weeks."

"Great, Nick. You'll have every drug thug in two hemispheres looking for you."

"I'll be okay."

"Sure you will. Just keep your ass down. Maybe it won't get shot off."

Charlie Riggs was opening the drawer to the smoker, painting the snook with some butter and sprinkling it with salt. Heavy gray thunderheads moved over Shark Valley, heading toward the city. Farther west, above Onion Bay and Big Lostman's Key, the squall had already begun. Overhead, the first bolt of lightning creased the sky, followed a five-count later by a boom of thunder. Fat drops of cool rain pelted us, but we didn't move. Charlie shot a sheepish glance at me.

An unusual sorrowful look, maybe thinking it was his job to bring me out of my despair, and he didn't know how.

But it wasn't his job. All of us live with our own demons, do penance in our private ways. We need our friends for support and advice, but we draw our strength from within. In the end we are alone.

Charlie's eyes were wishing me better times. Now I was depressing him, and Charlie has always been irrepressibly chipper.

Okay, Lassiter, stop wallowing in it. Stop telling yourself you really must be a great guy to be broken up over your loss. Wait. What loss? Pam Metcalf had said it: *You can't lose what you don't have.* And while you're at it, obliterate the guilt. Self-flagellation is an insufferable ego trip all its own; undeserved guilt is just another form of indulgent self-pity.

A flash of lightning backlit the low, dark clouds that scudded overhead, and a burst of thunder filled the sky. A couple of scrub lizards, brown with blue patches, scurried into the bushes. Cold water dripped down my neck. "Charlie, have I ever told you how much you mean to me?"

He looked up skeptically from under his soggy canvas hat. "Gracious no, and don't start now."

"Okay, it's up to you. I was just going to tell you that you'd have made somebody a fine father. Now, let's get out of the rain. Do you still keep cold Dutch beer in that cabin of yours?"

He nodded a yes.

"You have any stories to tell I haven't heard for a while?"

He smiled. "Have I told you about the carnival dummy that turned out to be the mummified body of a homicide victim?"

"Don't remember that one," I said.

We started up the muddy path to his cabin. A bright green tree frog with white pinstripes studied me a moment, concluded I wasn't a spider, and hopped away.

"Well, it's quite a story. The dummy was in the haunted house, hanging by the neck from a rope, covered with phosphorescent paint. In the dark it would glow purple when an ultraviolet light was switched on. Of course, the idea was to give the customers an old-fashioned funhouse scare. One day this college boy wants to show off for his girlfriend, so as they're going by he yanks on the dummy's shoe, tearing its leg off, and lo and behold, he's left holding the stub of a real tibia."

"Got his money's worth," I said, scraping my muddy shoes on Charlie's steps and holding the screen door for him. Inside, it was dark but dry.

Charlie was getting into it now, tales of murder and mayhem lifting his spirits. "Well, the authorities were intrigued, as you can well imagine. So many unanswered questions. How did the man die? Who was he? How did the body get into a carnival?" He paused to tamp some tobacco into his pipe. The matches were soggy and it took three tries to light up. He looked at me apologetically. "Jake, I'm afraid this story will take a while. It involves an Oklahoma train robber, a shoot-out with the police, embalming with arsenic, and it all starts back in—"

"Take your time," I told my old friend. "I got nowhere to go."